ORDNANCE

BY: ANDREW VAILLENCOURT

Ordering Information:

Special discounts are available on quantity purchases by corporations, associations, and others. For details, contact the publisher at the address above.

Orders by U.S. trade bookstores and wholesalers. Please visit:

www.AndrewVaillencourt.com

Chapter One

The inconveniences started, as they so often do, with a woman. Not in a sappy, romantic adventure sort of way; but in that specific manner that always seems to follow the introduction of two people who, for better or worse, were going to be stuck with each other for a good long while. That the person in question was a woman, it could be posited, was entirely irrelevant. But it was a woman nonetheless, and no one could deny the inconveniences started with her.

She stood exactly five foot seven, with short, dark hair worn in a fashionable pixie cut with a single magenta stripe in the front, obviously done by a professional. She was just on the lean side of curvy, but with taut thighs and a hint of definition in the muscles of her shoulders and arms. The shape and tone reminded Roland of a dancer's body. It was the body of someone who took care of her health and fitness without getting obsessed with it. He decided it was a good body.

Roland approved of the look, in the style of banal acknowledgement that the males of the species were inclined to bestow upon the females, entirely unencumbered by the females' complete and utter disinterest in such. Roland had grown accustomed to the disinterest of women, so his approval went unvocalized and subsequently unacknowledged. This was probably for the best since Roland was not the kind of man women wanted any kind of acknowledgement from. Most people were happier if Roland did not acknowledge them at all. So was Roland. It was a system that worked for everyone.

Other than her general good looks, there were other reasons to keep an eye on the girl… no… woman as she entered the room. Roland adjusted his estimation of her age to mid-thirties as her face caught the dim light near the bar. Pretty face, too, he acknowledged. Not that it mattered.

No, she commanded the eye for reasons other than attractiveness. First among the interesting phenomena was her presence here at all. This was a spacer's bar; located one long block from Farragut Shipping's main platform. Arguably cleaner than most Dockside watering holes to be sure, but the furniture and décor were showing their age. As were many of the patrons, for that matter. The lights burned dim and yellow, and both music and clientele leaned towards the 'loud' and 'old' ends of the spectrum for either. The bar, a long hardwood affair at the back of the room, had more gouges than grain left in it. Coincidentally, this is how an astute observer might have described the bartender as well.

It was an old-school watering hole, with old school sensibilities. It did not have a stage for bands to play, nor did it have a wine list. Beer they had though, in wonderful variety and quality, which elevated 'The Smoking Wreck' above most gin mills this side of the Sprawl. The suds ran cold and flowed cheaply. This pleased the clientele; who were decent enough folk (for Dockside, at least).

The uniqueness of the surroundings and the patrons meant no one came here except longshoremen, spacers, pimps, thieves, and whores. She did not belong to any of those groups, Roland was sure. Her clothes appeared nice and fashionable, but also practical. She wore tight blue pants with black leather boots that rose to just below the knee, with a wide belt trimmed to match the leather of her footwear. A black shirt made of some style of shimmery material that looked comfortable and durable covered her upper body. It had no sleeves and had been tailored snug against her body. Not sleazy-snug… more like… fitted. It was a garment for practical purposes, and it looked well made. She carried a small bag over one shoulder. Black, and about eight square inches in size, it sported a simple silver button at the flap. Everything about her screamed "Upper-class socialite." Which made her a very strange addition to the current cohort of Dockside lowlifes and ambitious street scum who liked this bar. "The Smoking Wreck" wasn't just a wry turn of phrase; it was truth in advertising.

Second, she moved funny. She was twitchy as if hopped up on chemical speed or perhaps neurologically augmented. This might make her presence more à propos, but her eyes were clear and there was no sign of ataxia or shuffling. When she spoke to the bartender, her voice was a sure, unshaken alto that neither stammered nor slurred. To

Roland's practiced eye, she didn't look like she was on anything. But every move she made had the aspect of an old film reel run at a speed just a little faster than it should have been. The woman walked too fast. She talked too fast. Her hands darted like striking cobras with even the most basic movements. The effect appeared subtle, but consistent. Roland doubted anyone but he had even noticed it.

The last thing keeping Roland's attention on the girl was what she said to the bartender. It started innocuous enough, and Roland could hear it quite well despite the noisy bar.

"I'm trying to find someone. I was told he would be here."

The animated mass of tanned leather and scars that served as bartender was an old war veteran named Marty Mudd. He had been slinging watered-down gin in this dive for twenty years, and he knew better than to give a straight answer, "Lots of people come here, doll. Don't really know every one of 'em. Lot of 'em come here hoping to not be found, if you know what I mean." He looked left and right in an exaggerated caricature of clandestine chicanery, "Not sure it'd be good business if I started acting contrary to their wishes." He winked an overly conspiratorial wink at her. His bushy eyebrows and shock of unruly white hair made it a very comical gesture, indeed.

Roland smiled in quiet approval. Marty was good people. He had done his tours during the Venusian secession without complaint and came home to a planet that didn't need him anymore. He didn't take it personally. It just wasn't his style.

No, Marty had stepped off the dock still in his uniform, walked into this bar and took a job sweeping the floor. Sixteen years later he bought the place. Smart, friendly, and tough as tungsten, he proved to be a man Roland liked very much. This made Marty special in a world full of people Roland didn't like at all. The feeling was mutual. Marty liked Roland as much as Marty could like anyone. Roland wasn't big on 'friends' in the classical sense; but he and Marty had history.

The two old soldiers enjoyed a professional arrangement as well: Roland took care of Marty when Marty needed his particular kind of help, and Marty did not charge Roland for every single drink he consumed. Marty also helped ensure that Roland's privacy remained sacrosanct and unmolested by too much unvetted scrutiny. Truthfully, a lot of the people in Dockside helped with Roland's desire for privacy. Docksiders liked having Roland around because Roland kept problems away, and in exchange the folks respected his privacy. Which of course, is another reason the woman at the bar needed watching. Unfortunately for all of them, the next words she uttered were a big 'ol heap of problem.

"I'm supposed to say the word 'breach' to you. Does that mean anything?" A hint of desperation tinged the edge of her question. Marty flinched in surprise, and he could not help but blink and cast a glance back over the high-top tables and across the dimly lit booths. It carried all the way to a dark corner of the room deep in the back. She caught the look and whipped her head to the left, and Roland knew she could not help but see him seated in the corner booth.

He stared vehemently down at the table and his empty beer glass. His mind swam in a frenetic crossfire of desperate thoughts, all of them pushing the same agenda.

He furiously willed her not to have said the damned word. But she had said it.

He sat silently and tried to will the woman to walk out at that instant. She stayed put.

With a sinking heart he willed his beer glass to be full. But the glass remained stubbornly empty.

He did not want to look up and meet her eyes.

But he had to look. And he did look. She saw him, and he saw her.

Marty held up his hands in mock surrender and gave Roland a look of abject apology. Roland heaved a mighty sigh and waved the woman over. The packed bar was loud with drunken conversations and bad rock-and-roll coming from the ancient music machine in the corner. A few of the locals stopped to stare at the attractive woman in the nice clothes supremely out-of-place in their happy little slice of hell. But as she passed through the dive bar and got to Roland's table, they made it a conspicuous point to look at something else. Another reason Roland liked this bar: People knew to mind their damn business here. The woman sat down in her nervous, twitchy way. She snapped her head left and right to check her surroundings, and Roland started in before she could get a word off.

"Who told you to use that word here?" Though phrased as a question, Roland took for granted most people understood that he did not simply 'ask questions.' What he had meant was, "Tell me who told you to use that word here. Now." Clever people rapidly figured out that his veneer of politeness was merely a courtesy. He was a brusque guy, and he liked it that way.

She responded, "My father. He said to come find you and to call you 'Breach' if you didn't trust me."

"Yeah well, I don't trust you, and using that word doesn't necessarily mean you are trustworthy. Who is your father?"

"My name is Lucia Ribiero. My father is Donald Ribiero."

Roland could only think of one thing to say, "Well. Shit." This information changed everything.

She went on, "My father said he knew you from the Army, and if I ever got into trouble to find you here and say that word."

"And you're in trouble?"

"Yes." There was grim finality in that lonely syllable.

"The kind of trouble your father thinks I can help you with?"

"I hope so," she shrugged weakly.

"Did your father say I'd help you?"

"He said if you didn't help me, it was because you really were a soulless bastard and the only part of you worth a shit leaked out of you onto some off-world battlefield decades ago. He said you owed him, and even though you were going to act like a complete asshole you actually were a very nice man and just didn't want anyone to know." She looked sheepish.

Roland cocked an eyebrow, "He said all that, huh?"

"I'm paraphrasing. There were more swear words and some yelling I couldn't make out," she shrugged. Roland had to admit that sounded a lot like the Don Ribiero he remembered.

"He talked about you a lot when I was growing up. Mostly when he drank too much. He said you were solid." She spoke more quietly now. She sounded sad and scared at the same time.

Roland sighed, "You don't know the half of it, lady. You need to know every bad thing he ever said about me is true, and the good things are likely exaggerated."

"He only ever said good things about you."

"Then he lied. But yes, I knew Don Ribiero, and yes, I owe him." Roland rubbed his eyes wearily, "And the best part of me absolutely has leaked out onto some off-world battlefield, for the record. But I'll listen to your story, anyway. No guarantees on what I can do for you though."

Lucia never got the chance to tell her story though. The doors to the bar chose that moment to open with a melodramatic bang; and four men strode in. These did not look like spacers or longshoremen either.

This group was a study in clichés: Four big goons each wearing tailored gray suits having all they could do to contain musculature one could only describe as 'excessive.' They sported identical crew cuts with suspicious bulges under their arms, and they scanned the room's occupants with curt, professional efficiency. Their practiced and tactical positioning upon entering pegged them as high-quality hired muscle of some sort or another the moment Roland saw them.

The whole aesthetic appeared deliberate, and it made their intentions transparent to anyone with a three-digit IQ. Five newcomers from the right side of town in this dive on a Friday night was not a coincidence. Roland did not believe in coincidences under the best of circumstances and he did not believe one out-of-place rich girl and a squad of armed goons would all come to this Dockside bar at the same time for the beer selection.

The men were pros, it was obvious. They could not be local talent, either. Roland was familiar with all the local talent personally. But he would have bet a month's pay they were here for a certain now-terrified woman sitting across from him. That much was obvious. Roland weighed his options as the four newcomers moved quickly and professionally through the bar. It did not take a tactical genius to ascertain that he really had none. There was no way to get out the back without being noticed, and there was no viable way to slip by them. Roland was not great at slipping by people under the best of conditions, so it was hopeless in this case.

But, true to their irascible nature, the patrons of The Smoking Wreck made all tactical considerations moot when, with their customary pugnacity, they rebuffed the inquiries of the men in gray suits.

One of the regulars, John Rikker, worked as a professional sled driver for Farragut for forty hours a week, and liked to moonlight as an amateur tough guy the rest of the time. He took pride in being a big strong man from a hard part of town. He had so many rough edges, referring to him as a 'troublemaker' could only cover the most superficial aspects of his personality. John Rikker, Roland conceded, was an asshole on a very fundamental level. More importantly, he was not a man who suffered the rudeness of outsiders gladly or with grace.

He clearly took exception to the demeanor of the pushy, well-dressed invaders. So, in true Dockside fashion, he invited them to engage in an anatomically improbable and certainly uncomfortable sex act with several different inanimate objects. It was too impressive a bit of vulgar eloquence to have been extemporaneous. Roland assumed that John had practiced the insult ahead of time in preparation for the joyful day he could unleash it upon some unsuspecting joker. This was John's big moment, and he got his jaw busted for the trouble.

The quickness with which the lead goon blasted poor John in the head with a right hook was beyond impressive. This set Roland's jaw a little. It was beyond human. Superhuman speed meant one of two things: Either he had his neural and physical capabilities boosted through drugs, or he was physically augmented. Both were bad, the second one very bad. Knowing Don Ribiero was mixed up in whatever this mess was meant it very likely leaned strongly toward the 'very bad.' Roland realized he needed answers, and he only knew one way to get them. He spared a longing look for his empty beer glass and sighed. So much for a relaxing Friday night.

"Stay down," he ordered Lucia, curtly. Then he got moving.

Chapter Two

The well-dressed man searching for Lucia Ribiero was not having a good time. Paying gigs were nice, and nice-paying gigs were even nicer, so Roger Dawkins didn't like to bitch too much about it. Complaining was for hourly chumps, and he was a goddamn professional. But he very much resented having to leave his nice, clean, uptown apartment and schlep all the way to Dockside chasing some skirt whose Dad didn't know well enough to play ball. When that stinking, grubby, Dockside asshat had mouthed off, Roger indulged himself with a little well-earned justice to make up for having to come here at all. It wasn't the most professional way to have handled that, but busting that rube's jaw would also likely loosen up the other tongues in this craphole. He considered it an investment in getting the job done in a timely manner.

Maybe, just maybe, he could get out of here before the smell of working-class trash and shitty beer bonded permanently to his nice 4,000-cred suit. That would be nice.

When the man in the corner booth stood up from his chair, Roger's day went rapidly from bad to worse. Roger did not know how to process what he saw when the big shadow stepped into the dim light of the main bar. It was six inches shy of eight feet tall, and impossibly wide. He had what appeared to be normal human anatomy, but the physique was hyper-muscled in a manner akin to caricature. His chest was beyond thick, with a wide, powerful waist. The thighs were like oak trunks. His shoulders looked like over-inflated basketballs, and what passed for the neck was just endless cords of sinew and muscle connected to trapezius that looked like ship cables.

The big man was in simple black military-style pants, slightly baggy, and a tight black shirt that had long sleeves and a high crew neck collar. He wore gloves, which Roger thought was strange. But then again, everything about this guy was strange. The huge man was completely bald and had a pug nose and wide jaw. Small black eyes were set deep under heavy brows, and the face sat locked in a scowl of grim purpose. His skin had a flat, almost waxy tone to it that nagged at Roger's subconscious, but that could have just been the bad light.

Roger was not necessarily afraid of this new development. To be honest, he was never really afraid of anyone. The man had invested wisely in his professional development and had the best advantages money could buy. Much of his early earnings had gone towards several dozen highly illegal augmentations that made Roger unshakably confident no matter what situation his employers dropped him into. He took great comfort in the fact that he was quite literally built for danger.

His bones were as dense as granite and his musculature could handle picking up a small car. If that wasn't enough, he could flat out run forty-five miles per hour if he had to. His reflexes were five times as fast as any regular person's and his equilibrium, proprioception, kinesthetics, and other neural processes were far above what normal people could achieve.

As extra help, he had brought along three of the latest model security androids for extra speed and muscle. These were utterly illegal as well, since they were not painted the mandatory bright yellow of registered security 'bots. Androids not dressed and colored according to their designations seriously violated municipal code. Taking them along had been a calculated risk, but their tracking modules were essential to hunting down the girl in a city this size. No, as big as this bastard was, Roger felt great about his chances. It was still slightly unnerving to look at though. That was one seriously big bastard. Roger reckoned he was probably boosted in some manner as well, which could make this very interesting.

"Can I help you gentlemen find your way out?" the big man asked politely. If one were to translate that from 'what was said' to 'what was meant,' the result would have been, "Get the fuck out. Now." Roger was not intimidated. Nor was he inclined to leave. Granted, he hated this place, and hated being there, but he hated not getting the job done even more. The boss could be a real prick when the job didn't get done.

Roger was not interested in that scenario. So, Roger responded in kind:

"I can't leave without my friend." Translation: "I'm looking for someone and I ain't going anywhere until I find 'em."

Roland picked up on the tone, but he was not playing ball, "Your friend is not here. Go look somewhere else."

Roger was getting aggravated, "Well Mungo, I'm just gonna hafta poke around until I'm sure. You understand, right?" He smiled an oily, toothy smile, "Unless you want to direct me right to her and then I'll be outta here just as quick as you please." Roger didn't want it to go that easy. He did not like the big man, and he did not like The Smoking Wreck, or Dockside, or anything to do with today at all, really. The whole mess was conspiring to make him unreasonable, and he was in the mood to be difficult.

But, Roger reminded himself, he was a professional; and this conflicted with his professional pride. Pros don't bust up bars and make extra noise if such could be avoided. Pros did the job with minimal fuss and extreme discretion. Roger intended to avoid being unprofessional because he had been paid to be discreet. Besides, it all seemed quite moot. Something about this big fucker told Roger he would get his wish under any circumstances.

Roland was also seriously trying to restrain himself. He had to get the girl out of the bar, and he knew with a high degree of confidence he could accomplish this at any time. He was aware of the fact he was dealing with at least one augmented human, and likely three more to boot. This did not really bother him much. His confidence may not have appeared sane to anyone else, but Roland was definitely not 'anyone else.'

Roland Tankowicz was not illegally augmented. He was not an illegal security android, either. Roland was half-a-ton of something else entirely. Roland's origins and aptitudes were his own business, and thus not common knowledge in Dockside. Great care had been taken to secure that information, and Roland wanted it to stay that way. If everyone at the Wreck saw what he was capable of, his mysteries would not remain his own for very long. This reticence was a strictly practical consideration and it would not prevent him from doing what he had to do to get out of there alive, though. So, in the interests of preserving his own secrets, Roland continued with his attempt to be as reasonable as he knew how to be.

"Listen, pal. I get it. You're on the clock, and you can't go back empty handed. But we can't help you. I'm sure Marty's called the cops by now, and even with their shitty response time in Dockside, you still don't have time for this." Roland's voice changed to an exaggerated whisper, "I don't think an enhanced guy like you wants to deal with cops, do you? I hear there is a special prison for you guys on Titan. Do you want to go to Titan? I've been there. It sucks." Roland was bluffing, but it was a calculated bluff. Nothing short of explosions or plasma fire would bring the cops to this part of Dockside, but dealing with the police when you are illegally augmented was a legendarily grim process. He hoped that this would shake the newcomer.

Roger wasn't biting. He smiled that big, oily, fake smile, "Maybe I go to Titan someday, maybe I don't. But I promise no cops are coming, Mungo. I promise that." Money had changed hands to ensure that this little operation was unencumbered by law enforcement. Roger was far too experienced not to have handled that potential complication already.

He made a show of adjusting his cufflinks and straightening the sleeves of his obviously expensive suit, "Now I know the bitch is here, and I'm not leaving without her. Me and the boys here can take this place apart, and all of you lowbrow scum with it, or you can make nice and hand her over." Roger, too, was doing his best to be reasonable.

It was a sad irony, oft spoken of after that day, that neither man was actually being reasonable. It was all just preamble to one inevitable conclusion. As Marty later told it, "We all wished they'd just get on with the stupid fight at that point. It was like the only people who didn't know they were going to brawl was them two idiots!"

Roger's 'bots moved to his flanks and quartered off the bar from the doors. Everyone knew it would come down to

Roland and the jerk in the suit. Some things are just obvious like that. Roger held his hands out the sides, palms up and implored with as much fake courtesy as he could, "Just hand her over Mungo, and we'll leave."

Roland responded with his characteristic eloquence. "No."

Roger Dawkins did not hesitate for one second. Technically, due to his accelerated reflexes, he hesitated one eleventh of one second before he pressed on the floorboards with his right foot hard enough to launch himself in near-horizontal flight at Roland.

Roland did nothing.

When Roger's right fist connected with Roland's jaw, it had enough kinetic energy to crack the skull of a rhinoceros. Roland's head whipped to the side and blood sprayed from Roger's fist and Roland's cheek. Dawkins hit the floor and rolled to his feet, already pivoting for a savage low kick to Roland's right knee. The kick was less than a half second behind the punch and executed with a fluid and practiced ease. About one fifth of a second before his foot made contact, however, Roger noted that something was wrong with his hand. Just as his foot connected with the outside of Roland's knee, he realized what it was: the bones had shattered. His foot was now broken as well, since his enhanced leg muscles had just driven his tiny metatarsals into what felt like a column of pure steel.

Roger was confused. Confused and angry. His bones were not supposed to break. At least not from punching and kicking people, anyway. Even when he fought other augmented people, his bones held up just fine. Roger did not get any time to ponder this development as Roland's ham-sized fist closed around his broken foot and hoisted him upside down and into the air. As he was being hefted aloft, Roger had to acknowledge that his own 290-pound mass did not seem to be much of a strain on his opponent's muscles. Neither were the enhanced structures in his skeleton it turned out. Pain exploded from his foot and radiated to his tibia as Roland squeezed until an audible cracking sound sent lightning bolts of agony to Roger's panicked brain.

Roger's world was collapsing around him. Everything he knew and counted on to be true and absolute was being challenged in a most unsatisfactory manner. Roger Dawkins beat people up, professionally. It's what he did, and he was good at it. But now someone was beating him up and he was most perturbed by this development. As it was with musical theater and modern art, Roger did not appreciate irony.

All this was rendered moot when the flick of a thickly muscled arm sent Roger flying across the room in a most ungainly style. His enhanced proprioception allowed him to categorize each injury with infallible precision. So when he collided with the far wall of the bar, he knew with certainty he had broken his collarbone, his right ulna, and two of his lumbar vertebrae.

His impact also buckled the heavy masonry blocks and sent radiating cracks shooting across most of the ferroconcrete structure. The whole building shook in an alarming manner and his impression made a sound like a bag of wet dirt falling from a truck. Pain from his foot and leg stopped at least, as his semi-conscious form slid down the wall in a sodden heap to rest in the corner.

From his vantage point as a bleeding broken mess of a man slumped against the dirty wall of a seedy Dockside bar, Roger got to watch Roland Tankowicz tear three expensive security 'bots to pieces with his bare hands. The security 'bots were tough, fast, and strong as hell. They were specifically designed for hard combat in the urban environment, yet the fight was a brief and violent affair as the three machines attempted to surround their quarry and pick him apart.

It wasn't working though. To Roger, the huge man looked like a grizzly bear going through a pack of coyotes in the melee. The giant had adopted a strategy of buttoning up into a defensive posture like a boxer and waiting for the androids to attack. When the androids would score a hit (with little effect), they would receive a catastrophic injury from the resulting counterattack.

Roland's footwork was tight and mathematical, and his hands snaked out like darting sledgehammers with pinpoint accuracy and blinding speed. Roger, through the rapidly dimming haze of his own fading consciousness, could not help but admire the big man's work (If he was even a man at all... Roger had his doubts). It wasn't just smashing the androids, it was outfighting them; taking them apart meticulously in a manner designed to spare the building from extra damage in the process.

Roger watched him snap a stiff jab into the face of one android, return to a high guard in time to catch the blow from another, and then counter-punch the third with a right hook. There was a pivot on his rear foot, a head slip to make the first android miss its next attack, and then a brutal hook to the body that broke something inside the expensive 'bot and sent it crashing to the floor in a spastic, heaving, heap. The big right hand then immediately caught the head of the third android, and casually raised the four-hundred-pound thing in the air long enough to punch its body away with the left hand. The body-less head was then tossed over the big man's shoulder contemptuously.

The second 'droid was still functional, but only for a moment. A few deft movements from Roland, and it was armless. Then Roland smashed it to pieces with its own arms. He finished by stomping the twitching android, still squeaking and sparking on the floor, until it stopped moving entirely. A faint wisp of smoke rose from the twisted scrap that had once been a very expensive piece of paramilitary hardware.

This big sonofabitch was something different from the usual industrial cyborgs and back-alley augmentations that Roger saw from time-to-time. Roger did not know what he was looking at, but he now knew why the girl had come here, and he suspected that his job (if he lived) had just gotten a whole lot more interesting. On that wry note, Roger Dawkins slipped into blissful unconsciousness.

Chapter Three

Lucia Ribiero was panicking again, and she hated herself for it. Watching some terrifying giant smash and kill a bunch of robots in a bar was more than she was ready to deal with, which was an entirely understandable limitation to her worldview, she felt. That her father had been kidnapped and whoever did it had sent a bunch of cyborgs and robots to get her added a new dimension to her terror. That was a level of distress she was categorically unprepared to deal with. She worked in advertising for crying out loud, this was not how her days usually went.

Lucia tried to give herself credit where it was due. She was as tough as anyone, and smarter than most, but this was all too much. The day really hadn't started out that bad to be honest, so the rate and scale of its deterioration into the current state of affairs was quite significant and disheartening.

It had all started with a quick stop at the corner coffee bar for a latte, which was nice. Lots of normal days started with lattes and lattes were a perfectly nice way to start a day. After that, she went into the office where she was the VP of Customer Engagement for a large beverage distributer. It was a meaningless title for a meaningless job at a meaningless company, but the pay was fantastic and the people were nice. With the unemployment rate over 14%, it was just nice to have a job at all right now; so she didn't complain. Work had been fine, and all she had to do before getting home and soaking in a nice warm bath with a good cabernet, was to stop in to see her father for a bit. That's just a lovely damned day in general, and Lucia had no reason to doubt that this is exactly how it would go.

Lucia had been visiting her father a lot, due to a sudden increase in migraines and anxiety attacks lately. Her feeling of overall jumpiness had gotten rather pervasive, and she wondered if it wasn't time to see her psychiatrist about a prescription. Donald Ribiero was an excellent neurologist and biotechnologist and had been supervising her treatment himself for the present. The headaches were much better under his care, but she could not shake the feeling that the whole world was moving slower than she remembered. She should probably lay off the lattes, but Lucia loved coffee more than sanity, so that was not likely to happen.

When she dropped in to see her father earlier, she had been unprepared to find the place in complete disarray and her father gone. His beautiful top-floor apartment was always in perfect order; so, finding it a mess was a very clear indicator that something was terribly wrong. A meticulous man, Donald Ribiero was not the type to tolerate that kind of untidiness under any circumstances, and certainly not if he was going out. Don was the type of old coot who would occasionally bring a lady back for a nightcap, and he liked his place to be tidy for just such a case.

A girl would have to be into some weird stuff to want to hang out in the apartment as she had found it. Every stitch of her father's clothing was pulled out of his closets and drawers and strewn about the place. His antique hardwood desk had been torn apart, and the carpet peeled back from the wall in places. The kitchen cabinets were open and the contents pulled onto the floor where they sat in messy piles of cookware and utensils. His mattress was off the bedframe and left askew as if whoever had tossed the place simply dropped it when it became obvious that it was not hiding anything. Every piece of furniture was shifted or thrown over. Lucia did not need a tin star on her chest to work out that the place had been professionally ransacked. That was the first time today she had panicked.

Ninety seconds after getting to her father's apartment, her comm had buzzed to tell her she had a message. She was not ready for what it had said.

"Breach," was the one word message. Automated and electronic, she knew the coded signal was part of a triggered alarm response from her father. It was a word with a lot of meanings, but in this case, it referred to a very specific bug-out plan that she had rehearsed with the old man since she was fourteen. She never really thought she'd have to execute on it, but now she was doing exactly that, apparently.

It felt surreal. Her father's obsession with security had always seemed an idiosyncrasy driven by guilt over the loss of her mother. Lucia had never really taken it seriously, but the fight training and gun stuff had been a lot a fun. She simply enjoyed the private lessons and treated it as little more than her father's personal guilt causing him to act in a hyper-protective manner. Now she wasn't so sure.

She remembered that the 'Breach' protocol meant immediately going to a place in Dockside to find one of Dad's old army buddies. She couldn't use any electronic devices or payment methods. Hard creds only, and no personal vehicles, either. 'Breach' was one of the worst-case-scenario plans. It meant something terrible was going on.

Lucia felt her pulse racing when she left the apartment to go find "The Smoking Wreck." When she stepped out onto the moist black streets of New Boston, it was to the tune of a thousand tiny alarms ringing in her head. Every possible bad thing she could think of competed for primacy in her rapidly boggling brain. She gritted her teeth and made a conscious effort to focus on the job in front of her with sufficient vehemence to shove the buzzing to the back of her mind. The frantic woman couldn't make it go away, but she didn't have time to deal with it right now.

New Boston was the home of the largest collection of spaceports and docking platforms in the northern hemisphere and boasted a population of thirty-one million souls. A few short centuries ago it had been a dirty mill town filled with red brick manufacturing facilities and the choking black soot of a Dickensian dystopia. She could still be a loud, dirty, cantankerous old lady of a city if you went to the right places, but for now, New Boston was a shining, towering metropolis. The whole planet envied her city as a global center for trade and culture.

Right now, to her mounting unease, all that shining grandeur was lost on Lucia. The city now seemed a tepid jungle full of millions of potential evils waiting to entrap her. She put it out of her mind as best she could. It wasn't much help to think about it.

Lucia understood her city and her place in it all. She knew that Dockside wasn't where she was supposed to be, but it was where she had to go. So, it was with very real trepidation and no small discomfort that she hailed a cab and hopped in to take the long ride over the container tram lines into the seediest and most dangerous area in the whole sprawling megalopolis. The cabbie knew it too, but was too polite to say anything.

Lucia had her second bout of panic when the cab driver stopped the car four blocks away from "The Smoking Wreck" and told her that he could go no further. Only cabs that were paid up with the local crime syndicates were allowed to operate in the Dockside district, and her guy was behind on his dues. She would have to walk the last mile, and hope that the local criminal element was not interested in well-dressed urbanite ladies walking down dark alleys at night in the bad part of town.

It turns out that this was a silly thing to hope for. When she felt the two men settle in behind her as she walked, she knew deep down in her lizard brain that they intended to rob her… or worse. It just wasn't fair! She was scared, worried about her father, confused, and she could feel a migraine coming on. Now two assholes were going to jump her for the seventy-one creds left in her purse. She quickened her pace to try to put some distance between herself and the two men behind her, but that only hastened the outcome.

Those two men behind her, affectionately known among the folks in Dockside as "Mooch" and "Poco" were professional-level losers. They had never met a get-rich-quick scheme they didn't like, and they were prone to bouts of intense physical violence whenever the mood (or the drugs) came upon them. They were street-level opportunists with a moral compass that never pointed north. The sight of an uptown girl with expensive boots and a purse that just had to be stuffed with creds was just too appealing to the two young men. Especially since the word was already trickling down about a certain short-haired rich bitch that might be worth some serious creds to the right people. They had no clue at all if this was the right girl, but either way, they were going to have some fun tonight.

They fell in behind her to see if she would turn onto a less-used side street or even an alleyway so they could make their move in private. When she sped up, they knew they were caught. All thoughts of strategy went out the window at that point, which did not change the results by as much as one might think. The duo were not high-level strategic thinkers on their best days; and today wasn't even close to their best. They simply ran and clutched at the fleeing woman.

Lucia, now fully panicking, experienced the strangest sensation when Mooch and Poco started to grab her: Everything slowed down. A lot, really, when she thought about it. The closer their hands got, the slower they seemed to move. The headlong charge looked more like an underwater ballet as the two men hurtled toward her, arms outstretched and fingers reaching. All the terrified woman saw was the languid loping of a pair of drunkards.

Her own reaction was slower than she expected as well, but it was light-years ahead of the two thugs. Her right hand, clutched tight in a balled fist, came under the first one's arm and arced cleanly up to the chin and made solid contact. Poco's jaw clicked shut hard enough to break teeth. His head snapped up and back in an abrupt u-turn and a stream of blood and tooth fragments began a torpid parabola from his broken mouth.

Mooch registered none of this as his own clumsy fingers closed on the empty air where his erstwhile quarry had just been. He saw Poco's misfortune in passing, but he could not alter his own trajectory in time to do anything about it.

As soon as he had control of his momentum, Mooch spun to take another swipe at the small-yet-slippery girl. He got his bearings on her just in time to catch a savage kick to the groin. It was the first time in two years a woman had touched him there, and sadly, the previous contact had also been a soccer-kick to his tender bits. His knees buckled immediately as fireworks of pain danced on his retinas.

Lucia was already turning back to Poco, who was still holding his leaking face. His eyes grew wide for a moment as they caught the image of a small, well-dressed woman streaking towards him. He never even saw the ferocious whipping trajectory of her tiny, bony elbow as it traced a horizontal path to, into, and through his left cheekbone. Poco checked out of reality at that moment and took a nap on the street, blood and dignity oozing pathetically from his ruined face.

Mooch decided at that moment to try to extricate himself from the rapidly deteriorating situation. His crushed testicles limited his mobility, and the bottled lightning he and his unconscious partner had tried to abduct got to him before he ever found his feet. She punched him four times in one second, with alternating hooks fired with machine-gun-quick patter. Each impact whipped his head in the opposite direction, turning his cranium into a spastic oscillating speed bag. He was unconscious before he hit the ground. Which was a blessing, really.

So, it was less than twenty minutes after winning her first fistfight ever, that Lucia found herself hiding under the table at a bar, watching a man she knew only from her father's stories fight a battle against superhuman enemies to protect her. She felt, as the incessant pressure of a mounting panic attack began to fray the edges of her sanity, that it would be entirely justifiable if she lost her mind completely and fainted from all the pressure.

And that's precisely what she did.

Chapter Four

"So what, exactly, are you?" was Lucia's understandable, if not entirely polite, question. For reasons purely practical, Roland had brought her unconscious form back to his apartment in Dockside. Since she was obviously being pursued vigorously, he needed to get her out of sight quickly; and he lived in highly convenient proximity to The Smoking Wreck. He liked to consider that a coincidence, but he knew deep down that living close to his favorite bar was more than a little intentional. Lucia sat in one of the two normal sized chairs in his otherwise blandly furnished apartment. Roland did not entertain often, and his domicile reflected both his girth and his military background in its spartan décor.

A generous Army pension and numerous paying gigs as a Dockside 'fixer' meant a comfortable existence, if not an extravagant one. His apartment was bigger than most, and in a section of Dockside that was at least two standard deviations above the mean for squalor and crime level. Roland didn't have to sweat petty crime that much. Every mugger, bruiser, drug-dealer and pimp in Dockside knew to give Roland's apartment a wide berth. Roland appreciated peace and quiet. Those that disturbed the peace became examples for the rest, and it had been a long time since he had needed to reinforce the lesson.

The apartment had three largish rooms. A kitchen, a bedroom, and a living room; as well as a bathroom. His furniture was sized and built for his stature out of necessity and represented the only really expensive items in the place. It was kept to military standards for orderliness, and while tidy, exuded no real warmth. Lucia acknowledged, in an archaic fashion, that it certainly lacked a 'woman's touch.'

Roland had not been expecting company, but he was lucky enough to have a few beers in the fridge. He offered the lady a lager while she pulled herself together. Of course, Roland always had beer handy, so luck may not have been much of a factor. When you weigh a thousand pounds, and have things inside you that make getting drunk very difficult, you are going to go through a lot of beer.

"What am I?" Roland feigned offense, "I'm a decorated veteran. What are you?"

Lucia at least had the decency to appear sheepish, "I'm sorry! I just..." she gestured at him, "I mean... uh... what are... uh... you? Like a cyborg or something?"

He tried to smile in a disarming manner. He was bad at it, and he hoped she accepted the gesture in the spirit he was trying to deliver it. She relaxed visibly at his feeble attempt, and he took that as a good sign. Roland was not what most would call a 'people person.' But neither was he a stupid man. He had muddled through a few years of engineering school and had been a proficient combat engineer during his traditional military service. He understood physics and chemistry better than most, and further schooling during the process of making him into what he ultimately ended up becoming had made him fairly conversant in his own systems. His imperfect understanding of the harder science coupled with his natural inclination to brusqueness made explaining it all somewhat tricky.

"Technically, it's classified. I can go to jail for telling you and you could go to jail for knowing. But," he paused for a moment, choosing his words carefully, "... since the answer probably has a lot to do with your father's trouble, I'll clue you in." He gestured to the fridge, "It's a fairly long story, so grab a fresh beer if you need one."

Lucia took his advice and cracked open another can of beer. She settled into the chair and assumed an exaggerated listening pose, "I've got nowhere to be, buddy."

"I'm not what most people think of when they think 'cyborg', per se..." he began in a wholly inadequate introduction. "I mean, I have inorganic components, but it's different from a regular prosthesis," he continued, as if that cleared everything up.

Lucia's scrunched brow only reinforced the sinking feeling in Roland's guts that he was making no damn sense.

He sighed, "Cyborgs get body parts replaced with artificial versions of stuff. If a guy gets his regular arm blown off, the army puts a metal arm back on. That arm is just a mechanical replacement for the organic thing that got lost."

Lucia looked at him; took in all seven and a half feet and nine-hundred-and-forty pounds of him, and politely asked, "So none of… that…" she gestured in his direction, "… constitutes 'mechanical versions of stuff?' "

"Well… sort of…" Roland backtracked. This was not going well, "It's not so much 'mechanical' in the traditional sense. It's…" Unable to find a better way to explain, he simply told her what he had been told, "It's mostly techno-organic myofibrillar and osteoplastic analogs." He shrugged, "my body is not strictly organic, but it's close enough that my brain thinks it is, and my nervous system treats it like it is."

Lucia did not look convinced, "I'm not going to lie. I have no idea what any of that even means."

"My body parts were not built in a shop and then attached to me like other 'borgs," he sighed. "The body was grown, molecule by molecule, from polymers that mimic human muscle and bone. My own DNA was used as blueprint, so my nervous system would treat it just like my own bones and muscles."

She gasped, "Oh my god! Is your real body underneath all that…" she gesticulated wildly, "… stuff?"

Roland shrugged, "Some of it. We call the techno-organic stuff the 'chassis' or sometimes the 'frame.' It helps differentiate the systems." He went on, "The chassis was grown separately, but most of my organic mass was removed long before my nervous system was transferred." Roland wasn't sure that was the right way to phrase it. His arms, legs, and several of his internal organs had conveniently been removed by separatist explosives prior to his conversion, but that was a much longer and grislier story. One he'd prefer not to get into at this exact moment, to be honest.

"My liver, pancreas, heart and other organs were replaced with better synthetic versions grown from my own DNA by the program." That wasn't the whole story. He didn't mention that he didn't have lungs or that his heart was an actual mechanical pump. It seemed like unnecessary detail. His spine and skull had been reinforced to an absurd degree with liberal quantities of bleeding-edge polymers. The skin of his face and head were laced with a fast-repairing mesh of artificial skin lattice. It gave his face a flat, dull, sheen; and the greatest scientists of Earth's mightiest military hadn't been able to figure out how to get hair to grow on it, either.

The program had regrown or rebuilt the balance of his limbs and organs, peeled the skin from his torso, and mounted the depleted, raw, and bleeding meat that was Roland Tankowicz into a home-grown cybernetic body built right to the specs of his own DNA.

"I was a big boy before I got all cyberized, so my chassis ended up looking like this," he flexed playfully, straining the seams of his 4XL shirt. "I don't think this is the look they were going for, but it's what they got," he added, trying to lighten the mood. She chuckled politely.

Roland had been a large, powerful man when he joined the United Earth Defense Force. What had been six-foot-six and nearly three hundred pounds of idealism and enthusiasm got pulled right from the front lines of a Venusian border dispute and plopped into the most ambitious warfighter enhancement project in human history. This had been for the best, really. The injuries he sustained on Venus were not going to be survivable, and everyone knew it. He mentioned this without going into too much morbid detail.

"Thankfully, it seemed, the Army had plans for me, and it was all going to be OK. They would just build me a new body!" He snorted derisively, "You know, as long as I agreed to a few terms and signed some waivers. Shoulda read the fine print, first."

Since his options had consisted of "sign here or die a horrible slow death," he had gone ahead and volunteered for the program. The Army delivered as promised: the new body grown for him matched all his genetic potential and enhanced it. Impressive musculature became extreme, and what had once been a big, strong man was now a towering technological juggernaut.

"Most of me is just high-tech synthetic versions of regular human tissue. I have a synthetic immune system and even synthetic blood."

That was a rather gross oversimplification. A veritable swarm of nanomachines took the place of blood and other cells in the techno-organic hulk, and billions of microscopic robots moved resources around and suppled energy and fuel to the various systems. Roland's remaining organics (such as they were) still had and employed human blood, but thanks to those little 'bots, most of the resources he needed could be gleaned from any environment. Minerals and chemicals could be consumed as raw materials, or synthesized from available properties in the environment. Oxygen was scrubbed from virtually any combination of atmospheric gasses, or simply used in a miserly fashion from the onboard stores.

A testimony to his builder's commitment to durability, approximately 150 pounds of Roland's total mass was allocated just for spare resource materials. His faithful nanobots could rebuild an entire limb from these stores, provided Roland had the time and energy to accomplish such a task.

Which was a bit of an issue, actually. Energy was not a big deal when he was still with the army. Roland was equipped with the same military-grade ShipCel that powered the Avenger-class strike drone, and the Army had lots of those lying around. If Roland limited himself to basic locomotion and everyday tasks, then the power source was good for close to a decade before the core needed recharging. At standard combat-theater output, he might get nine months out of a full charge. Full Power? He'd be lucky to get thirty days. It was something he had to stay on top of though, because when Roland ran out of ShipCel power, his body stopped moving. That can be a very big deal when one is built from a half-ton of exotic metal and plastic. In an emergency, he was capable of absorbing most frequencies of electromagnetic radiation and converting them to power, but it was brutally slow and exposure to direct sunlight on Earth would net barely enough juice to walk very, very, slowly. It was an ugly proposition.

Adding another layer of complexity to his power issues, Roland's body was not strictly his own. It remained officially classified as "defunct military ordnance" and as such he could not easily acquire new ShipCels for it. The Army had scores of them, but Roland was not in a position to requisition any from his former employer. Purchasing one would cost more than a nice house in the suburbs, and he was nowhere near having that kind of money. Basically, Roland had to get creative when it came to managing his power needs.

ShipCels could be recharged, but that meant plugging in and sitting for a very long time; and ShipCels had a limited number of recharges in them before they required new cores. He had been out of the military for twenty-five years, and Roland was on his third ShipCel. The last one he had to 'acquire' from a black-market gun-runner who had a crashed Avenger stashed on one of Saturn's moons. Roland was not slavishly loyal to the government, nor was he overly fastidious about operating in strict legality, but dealing with that gun-runner had left a bad taste in his mouth. He had set himself more than one mental reminder to murder that particular bastard at some point. He just hadn't gotten around to it yet.

His current 'Cel was in good shape, and he did his best to keep it topped off by plugging in at night. The power bills were brutal, but he didn't know what else to do. If he stayed out of pitched battles and charged obsessively, he might get twenty years out of this one. That was the plan anyway.

Keeping his power consumption low wasn't all that hard. At 100% output, Roland could press close to twenty tons over his head, or sprint sixty miles per hour on a straightaway. Hilariously, he had virtually no ability to turn corners at that speed, but technically he could go that fast if he needed to. Since that sort of silliness was rarely necessary, getting through the typical day used only the tiniest fraction of juice. If he avoided strenuous activities, then eight hours on the charger was usually enough to offset a typical sixteen-hour day of working and drinking. The power bill was a little painful, but he could afford it. Roland felt it was worth it if it helped put off sourcing another 'Cel.

The eighty-six pounds of organic material that lay cocooned inside all this high-tech wonderment was easier to handle; as the needs of the flesh were comparatively tiny compared to those of the machine. Why he retained eighty-six pounds of organic material was an altogether different story. Organic components served very little purpose in the interstellar combat theater, and were technically a weak link in the system due to their inherent squishy-ness and incessant need for fuel, air, and water. Lucia wondered aloud if it would have behooved the project to eliminate them, "Why didn't they make all of you... uhm... synthetic?"

Roland paused. It was a good question, but the answer was difficult to explain. The technology for full prosthesis certainly existed. But his human components remained part of him all the same, for reasons that Roland didn't really want to get into. But, he was forced to admit, the answer to that question was likely linked to why Lucia's father had sent her to him.

It seemed he would get into it, anyway.

"If the military had wanted another robot, they could have just built a robot," he shrugged. "As a matter of fact, the military builds robots all the time." The battlefield of the twenty-fifth century was almost entirely unmanned; namely because most of the places humans fought over were extremely hostile to mankind. It was just good strategy to send robots and drones to those places, instead. "Robots don't satisfy the need for ethical command and control on the battlefield, though," he said, "Somebody on-site needs to decide when to pull the trigger and when not to. Somebody has to handle communications with locals and any person-to-person interactions that pop up."

The problem was that a robot could not make the sort of life-or-death decisions in real time that a person could. Remote drones at least had a human operator somewhere to make the call, but deep in the field there was still a demand for a thinking, feeling, decision-making person. "We've got Anson Gates pushing us out to entirely new solar systems, now. We're going to all sorts of weird planets, dealing with new lifeforms and landing in all sorts of screwed-up situations. We needed human boots on the ground. Space suits are just too damn flimsy and power armor is too clunky and expensive. Sure, the Army runs a few cyborg armatures at any given time, but most men are unwilling to be mounted to one since the army is already required to pay for prosthetics for veterans."

"The first attempts were almost entirely cybernetic. The only human element they left was the brain and a portion of the spinal column; which they transplanted into a big, heavy mobile chassis." They were essentially human nervous systems contained in armed and armored delivery systems. The result was a super-durable, highly self-sufficient variable threat response system with robotic speed and modularity, with a human being at the controls in real time and space. Or, "Tanks with brains," as Roland explained it to Lucia, "Ugly, but tough as hell."

"But the robot bodies with human brains tended to… uh… go nuts under the pressure," was Roland's truncated version of the problem with the first generation of cyborg soldiers. While the actual surgeries to produce these units were fairly successful, the minds of the soldiers themselves became very unstable very quickly. With no humanity to cling to, they simply went insane. Most committed suicide, several had to be decommissioned manually. Roland thought (almost wistfully), "'Decommissioned manually' is just a nice way of saying 'blown to pieces because they went on murderous rampages.' "

"They tried putting human brains in android bodies, too, but that was only a little better." This was a grievous understatement.

He went on to explain that the next attempts tried to minimize this effect producing a more analogous chassis. The theory was that if the chassis felt more human, more normal, to the brain driving it, then it would be less likely to disassociate in a manner that led to sociopathy. Those versions were supremely unwieldy and combat effectiveness was poor. Human brains in android bodies were awkward and a little dangerous; the control systems were just too incompatible. Also, these units went just as insane as the previous ones. The human psyche just could not tolerate a total prosthesis.

The researchers eventually realized that psychological stability was linked to the mental and physical needs and desires that people had to navigate as fickle and emotional creatures. Removing a human brain from all its needs, desires, and physical feedback; and then dumping it to a hardened weapons platform did not deliver the desired results. Roland said it succinctly, "Turned out to be a terrible idea."

Human sanity, and the decision-making ability the program needed from its participants, required humanity. Roland continued, "A soldier in the field fought for something. They fought for greed. They fought for patriotism. They fought for sunsets out at the lake on a summer evening. Even a man permanently mounted to an armature still felt like a man. Total prosthesis took that all away from a guy, and it drove them insane."

Good soldiers are supposed to fight for all the things that make life worth living and turning them into machines made life not worth living anymore. At least not as a human, anyway, and therein lived the problem. When life had no value, these former soldiers very quickly deteriorated into nihilistic AI's.

Nobody wants a nihilistic AI piloting a hyper-tough weapons platform, it turns out. Suicides and catastrophic psychological failures plagued the second generation. Two notable members of that cohort found their way into action, but the rest either died or were 'decommissioned.'

"Success rate was .01% for that generation," he explained.

Roland tried to gloss over the grimmer aspects of these failures, but Lucia wasn't stupid enough to misunderstand what he meant. Roland pushed onward to the important parts. "For Project: Golem, they decided to take a completely different track: They built a better human, but still let it be human."

Essentially, Project: Golem scientists grew a synthetic body based upon each volunteer's DNA. The new tissues and structures were grown to the exact specifications dictated by the donor's own genetics, making the new synthetic body move and feel like it should to the nervous system controlling it. It was important to the project that the body feel exactly like a flesh and blood version to the brain driving it. This resulted in some loss of performance compared to more mechanical models. Roland explained, "Big 'ol linear actuators and high-torque motors would have produced a more powerful machine, but human muscle fiber was mimicked, anyway. They could have replaced my nerves with computerized electronic control signals, and that may have made me faster and more efficient, but the point was that the whole body would work off of the soldier's existing nervous system and motor control." He shrugged, "We were weaker and slower than the other generations. But more successful in the field because of it."

"So, the short version is that to keep the guys from going nuts, they built an android chassis that was EXACTLY like the original body, just better. They basically grew new bodies out of better materials for us. Which was great. Except for when it wasn't great."

Lucia frowned, "When was that?"

"I'm gonna need another beer for this part."

Chapter Five

Roland pulled his gloves off, revealing jet black hands the size of bear paws, "Yeah, well for all the trouble they went to keep us human, they sure as hell didn't treat us like people." He rolled up his sleeves, revealing massive forearms corded with black synthetic muscle fibers that rolled and flexed exactly like human muscle should. Lucia's eyes widened at the sight. She hadn't realized it, but only Roland's face and head had any normal skin tone. The rest of him was kept a flat matte black, because that was the base color of the surface chromataphors that allowed him to assume various camouflage patterns. He could certainly shift the color to something almost human, but keeping his body any specific hue took up power that was better conserved. Roland simply wore long sleeves and gloves most of the time, because life was kind of tricky for a guy who walked around looking like an onyx statue.

Roland did not want to explain this part. He knew that it would likely have a deleterious impact on what Lucia saw when she looked at him. Right now, he was just a big military cyborg; just one of many ex-military veterans walking around with government-issued body parts. But there was real, inescapable ugliness involved in his creation, and nobody wanted to hear about that part. But, it all had a lot to do with Donald Ribiero, so out it came.

"So. You now know that they deliberately left over some of the more… human attributes to keep us psychologically grounded." Roland wiggled all his fingers in an intricate wave pattern to demonstrate his dexterity, "As far as my nervous system can tell, these are really my fingers." He picked up an empty beer can, balanced on his index finger for a moment, then let it fall to his palm where he crushed it into a lump the size of a ping pong ball. "I can feel through my skin, even though it's heavily armored, and I use my own nerves to do it. They get help from force-feedback sensors, but the actual signal still gets carried by my own nerves to my own brain, not a computer. There is no disconnect between what my brain tells my body to do, and what my body tells my brain is happening. I can hold a baby while punching a tank to death with no problem; the same way you can pick up an egg in one hand and swing a hammer with the other."

The entire design was geared towards making the body feel as human as possible to the brain that would have to live in it. "This is why many of my basic organic functions ended up intact, even if they didn't have much combat value. Preserving non-essential functions meant preserving the will to live and the empathy required to make the appropriate decisions in the field." Roland grinned, "I still need sleep. That could have easily been engineered out of the new body," but the languid, lazy, decadent joy of sleeping in until noon on a Sunday is worth fighting for. He summed it up, "but sleeping is part of being human. Good for the brain."

Roland smiled, "I still need food." Which left him connected to eating, and to the simple human joys of mealtimes. Sourcing organic fuel off-world was a logistical nightmare, but, he chuckled, "Steak dinners are worth fighting for, y'know? After your third week fighting aliens in an ammonia atmosphere, the thought of a juicy T-Bone keeps you going." Roland could still have sex. That sort of thing was not entirely necessary when you are fighting a corrupted AI at a mining station on Enceladus, but getting laid was definitely worth fighting for. He didn't mention that, though; it felt a little uncouth going there with a girl fifteen years his junior.

All of these things made life meaningful, and keeping those connections allowed Roland's unit to not lose their minds. They still loved life, and so they wanted to preserve it. They understood what they were taking away when they took it. They weren't machines, they were men. The small reduction in combat effectiveness was completely acceptable since they did not devolve into amoral murder-bots like their predecessors. Nobody likes an amoral murder-bot.

Lucia cocked her head and sniffed, "Makes sense, when you think about it. They wanted human soldiers, not organic robots."

It really had been much more complicated than that. Rejection of the newly-grown techno-organic bodies was still an issue. Of thirty-six participants who made it to the final stage of integration, thirty-one suffered partial or complete rejection. Only five participants out of an original 230 applicants had made it into the field. This ended up being a blessing in disguise, because it was out there in the cold expanse of space a hundred light-years from Earth that they found out about the fail-safe: or the actual reason they called the project "Golem."

He found the next part difficult to explain to her, but she needed to know. He did his best not to sound like an asshole while telling her that he was used to murdering hundreds of innocent people.

"My whole body is driven by my regular old organic brain, with no help from any cybernetic enhancements." He gestured to his body, "Yeah, there's a ton of nanomachines and computers managing oxygen levels, repairs, and stuff like force feedback so I don't smash everything I try to touch, but that stuff is all hard-wired and hard-coded."

There was no way to externally program (or reprogram) these devices, and this was intentional. "It makes me completely unhackable." This was why there was no direct connection between the chassis and an external network. All of the enhanced imaging, tactical feeds and data acquisition that a cybernetic super-killer might need came from a helmet, and not through any sort of optical or neural bionics, either. "The Army wanted to make sure that these new soldiers could not be taken away by a clever bit of software or a hijacked net connection." He explained, "There is no way to connect to the computers in me without a special plug, military software, and the ability to convince an irritable super-soldier that you are trustworthy." He scowled, "Very trustworthy."

But then there was the Golem. Each member of Project: Golem carried a secondary control module. According to the program leads, its purpose was to allow for retrieval of the unit if the organics failed. It was presented to the team as a pre-programmed retrieval AI that would animate and return the chassis to a predetermined location if the organic components failed in combat.

At the time, it seemed a reasonable precaution. Roland was tough, but he could still get knocked out or decapitated under the right circumstances. The Golem was in place to walk his body back home under those conditions. At least, that's what they had been told.

Roland grimaced, "We were supposed to be real humans. The whole goddamn point was that we were self-aware and capable of making our own decisions." He snorted, "but the powers-that-be in the military just couldn't help themselves." The threat of one of these expensive soldiers executing free will at an inopportune moment had been just too much for them to bear.

He had been the first of the squad to see it happen. A few years after the first stable Anson Gate had come online, Roland's unit had been part of a force dispatched to quell a small rebellion on one of the first of the new worlds to be colonized. It was an ethical quagmire, and it was not long before the squad's objectives had run afoul of what even the most morally flexible soldier could allow. It was exactly the sort of issue that had led to the development of the squad in the first place, so it came as a horrible shock when Roland's commanding officer and friend turned into a mindless robot and executed an unarmed village of colonists. "They used a hidden piece of software to knock us out, and then drove our bodies around like kids playing video games to get the really dirty shit done," was how Roland explained it. Saying more than that was just too difficult for the big man.

What had followed was a nightmare that Roland was never likely to overcome. At any time, their chain of command could turn their organic brains off and control their near-unstoppable techno-organic frames from afar. Any time they refused to follow an order they felt was unjust or illegal, they would be blacked out and forced to do it anyway. "Golem" wasn't just a catchy project code name, anymore. It was their reality. Roland and his unit were completely and categorically betrayed by the planet they had sacrificed their humanity to serve, and made slaves to the will of their superiors.

"Sneak and Scout committed suicide within a week of finding out." They were all very tough, but any decent military expedition had sufficient firepower to take them down if it had to. Standing in front of the dropship's main cannons was all it took. Naval-class weapons had been more than powerful enough to vaporize their cyborg bodies, technological marvels or not. Their ends were quick and painless. Roland envied them, but he was not one for suicide.

"Both Lead and Comms died when they tried to have the Golem protocol burned out of their operating systems by underworld hackers." He didn't explain that the resulting shutdown bricked the cyborgs' OS completely, and his two friends died in slow terror when their nanobots stopped bringing energy to their organs and oxygen to their brains. Roland watched them die, helpless to do anything.

Roland alone survived. He did so by following orders when he could, and getting shut down when he couldn't. He still knew little about what his puppet masters had made him do when they blacked him out, but he usually saw the aftermath. Great smoking craters or stacks of burning bodies were the most common. They were kind enough to wipe his memories every time, but he was a clever man and he could guess what had gone on. He consoled himself with the fact that it wasn't actually him doing these things; but someone still had to wash the blood and ash off of his chassis afterwards, and he was always awake for that part. While he relived this time, he spared Lucia many of the terrible details; she didn't need them and there was no reason for her to have the nightmares, too. He told her enough, though. She held her composure with stoic politeness, but he could see the edges of terror and disgust encroaching on her otherwise impassive face.

"When I returned to Earth, they sat me down in a cell miles below a mountain and told me that if I played ball I'd get a shiny medal and a fat bonus." He snorted, "And if I made a fuss about the situation, they would shut me down permanently and leave me there to rot." Roland had agreed at the time, as there was no real choice for him. He cursed his own weakness and cursed the people who created him. But he lived, and he played ball, and he waited.

"It was only the stupidest of luck that got me out of that shit with the Army. It took some time, but the incident with the Golems had gotten back to some of the civilian contractors who had helped create the team. Create us." More than one of them took great offence at the shear Machiavellian horror of what had been done, and threats and blackmail began to erode the secrecy of what Project Golem had really been about.

"It was pretty tense. No one knew who was going to go to prison or get black-bagged to some other planet for knowing too much. Eventually, a ballsy young scientist, the guy who had built most of our neural networks, decided he would nuke the rogue AI that I was carrying around in my brain on his own." Roland smiled, "Next thing I know, the same crazy bastard who built my nervous system is sneaking into my cell with a computer, telling me to shut up and let him work."

It was a long story that Roland broke down to its most salient points:

One late night.

One very brave man.

One very risky operation.

"Boom. Just like that, I was free of it." He smirked an evil smirk, "And without their little fail-safe, I was real fucking hard to contain. I'm not a man you can easily keep locked in a cell."

Lucia's smile returned slowly, "I'll bet you had a lot to say to your Army superiors about the whole thing. How'd that conversation go?"

Roland loomed to his full height and bared his teeth in a predator's grin, "Superiors? Hah. Once the Golem was out of me, it was pretty damn easy to illustrate to the program directors that as of that moment... I had no superiors."

He was embellishing a little; but not much. What had actually transpired was that the scientists who had developed Roland's technology threatened to go public with what had happened, Roland threatened to kill everyone and everything associated with pulling his strings in the field, and the various elected officials who were just realizing what had happened threatened to cut military spending. Recognizing a complete cluster-fuck when they saw it, the Army dumped Roland like the political hot-potato he was, and fired everybody involved with the project. The planetary government then swore them all to secrecy under penalty of prison; including Roland.

It took six months of lengthy government hearings, several murders, and a government-wide cover-up to get an honorable discharge for Lance Corporal Roland M. Tankowicz.

"They still refer to my body as 'defunct military ordnance' in my file. But I'm otherwise off the hook with a nice pension as long as I don't tell anybody what they did to me."

When he finished, she stared at him, eyes huge with a mixture of horror, awe, and sadness.

"The man who risked his life to save me was Donald Ribiero, Lucia. Your father freed me from a life of slavery. So why don't you tell me exactly what's happened to him and I'll see what I can do."

Chapter Six

With Roland's story complete, Lucia thought hard about everything she had just heard. She tried to reconcile all the staggering truths that had been laid on her with what she knew of her father. She knew her father was a successful biotechnologist and did most of his work with cybernetics and prosthetics. What she had not known was that he was part of a top-secret super-soldier program that made cyborg killing machines for a corrupt cabal of high-ranking military leaders. This was new information.

He had never talked about anything like that, but he had raised Lucia with an obsessive attention toward security and safety. She remembered all the 'bug-out' plans and secret code words she had been made to memorize as a child. She had been given martial arts and weapons training from the most prestigious instructors available; no expense was spared where her safety had been concerned. Her whereabouts, friends, and habits were all carefully monitored, straining her relationship with her father through her teenage years. But Donald Ribiero was a doting father, and Lucia never really rebelled all that hard.

Lucia had always attributed this behavior to her father just being an obsessive and paranoid wealthy man with a daughter he wanted to protect. Kidnap and ransom schemes were not unheard of in New Boston. There were enough desperate poor folk and ambitious criminals around to make any well-to-do single parent nervous.

Now all of that took on a different timbre. Now her father's disappearance was, if possible, even more ominous. Had he been abducted by black-bag government operatives? Industry rivals trying to re-build this 'Project Golem' thing? What other crazy top-secret things had her father done that she didn't know about?

The list of suspects had just gone from 'fairly specific class of criminals,' to 'endless unspecified groups, corporations, and politicians.' She didn't even know where to start.

She quickly relayed the conditions of her father's apartment and the incident on her way to The Smoking Wreck. Roland took particular interest in her attackers and her reaction to the mugging.

"You getting mugged in Dockside isn't all that hard to believe. You look like you have money and you definitely don't belong here. But something isn't right. They were too desperate, too eager. They took too many risks just for the contents of your purse." He scowled, "Someone must have the word out to look for you, specifically. Judging by the fact that you got hit twice in two hours, and by the quality of those goons in the bar, there's serious cash behind it, too. We've got everything from high-end augmented criminal thugs to lowlife street scum, so I'm guessing everybody will want to take a crack at you."

"But why me?" She almost yelled, "They already have my father, and all I'm good at it is advertising and marketing!"

"I have a theory about that. Have you ever beaten the crap out of two grown men at the same time before?" Roland asked with a raised brow.

Lucia was pensive, "I've never beaten the crap out of anyone before. I've had all the classes and training, but I've never used it on anyone."

"Need another?" He gestured to the fridge.

"Sure," she replied. "It's been a hell of a day."

Roland opened the fridge, grabbed a fresh beer, and without warning threw it directly at her face. It was not a gentle toss, either, he put some speed and force on it. Lucia didn't even blink but caught it easily and cracked it open.

She took a pull from the can and continued, "The whole thing felt so weird. Is that what real combat is like: all slow-mo and surreal?"

"Not for most people." Roland walked over and pretended to stumble, dropping his own beer can in the process. Lucia casually reached out with her off hand and caught the can easily without spilling a drop and handed it back to him. She looked at him with concern, "You feeling all right?"

Roland kicked the chair out from underneath her and it skittered across the floor with a clatter. Lucia didn't fall or even appear to be off balance, she simply stood up smoothly as the chair flew away, beer in hand and entirely undaunted by the violent upheaval. She glared at him scowling furiously, "What the fuck are you doing!"

Roland sighed and put his face in hand, "You really aren't getting it are you?"

"What?!?!?" was her frustrated reply. Roland shrugged and threw a punch directly at her face. It never got within a mile of her. She slipped it easily, with inhuman speed, and spun with dancer's grace behind him. He turned, and she rolled backward, cleanly clearing the counter backwards and landed effortlessly on the balls of her feet, eyes flashing.

"What the fuck!" It was the only thing she could think to say. Lucia didn't know if she was more scared or angry. Roland held up his hands in surrender.

"You don't even know you are doing it, do you?" He chuckled.

"Doing what?" Lucia looked like she wanted to cry.

"I just beat the shit out of three androids and an augmented super-douche, but I can't put a hand on you?" He continued, "You just back flipped over my counter holding two beers and haven't lost a drop from either one of them."

She looked down. She hadn't even realized that she had snatched the beer back from Roland in the exchange. Understanding crossed Lucia's face, "Oh! Oh… Shit." She breathed limply, "Oh no."

"Yeah," the big man said, "Looks like your Daddy's been tinkering with your nervous system. Speed, reflexes, proprioception all look to be waaaay above normal." He took his beer back and clunked it against hers, "Congratulations, kid. You're augmented. Welcome to the club."

Lucia slid to the floor with a thud, "I'm augmented!" She began to breathe heavily, "That's illegal! I'm illegal! Oh shit."

Roland sat heavily on an oversized chair, "Relax, kid. Don's not stupid. Smart money says there's no way he put anything in his little girl that would get you in trouble. I'm betting whatever mojo you got from your old man, he damn sure made it undetectable; and since it all appears to be neuro stuff, there's no real way to scan for it." Roland waved his hand at her body, "Doesn't look like he altered anything fundamental or added any technical stuff. Your strength and density are all normal, I'm guessing. Enhanced muscles, bones, organs: that's the kind of stuff that can be easily found out with a scan."

Roland continued reassuringly, "But it looks like he figured out how to juice up your nervous system without adding any hardware or tweaking you out. That's some seriously high-grade shit." He explained, "Most neuro augmentations need to come with additional tech to handle the loads. Just speeding up the brain isn't so hard, but without something to help with the all that extra stimuli, it turns the guys into twitchy, tweaky, messes."

He waved to the window, "Hell, half a dozen guys on this block alone will sell you junk to pep you up, if you don't mind frying your brains like bacon. Too much feedback delivered too quickly taxes the brain over time." He looked into her eyes for signs of brain trauma, and found nothing but clear, focused baby blues looking back. Actually, they were brown eyes, but that was immaterial. She had nice eyes. "Doesn't seem to have been bothering you at all, except for your poor perception of how fast things are happening around you."

"How do you know so much about what he did to me all of a sudden?" It was a legitimate question, so he answered honestly.

He smiled. "Time dilation is a bitch for me when I crank my reflexes up for combat, too. That's normal. You've been so worked up all day that you've been dilating without knowing it." He took a pull from his beer, "Your dad invented the system for interfacing augmentations to existing neural pathways. All that stuff's in my head already. Hell, I'm the prototype."

The big man scowled, "Of course, my body was built for that sort of thing. I seriously wonder if he didn't figure out how to enhance your nervous system without all the… uh…"

"Hardware?" she offered, helpfully.

"Yeah," he nodded. "If he pumped up your neural activity without frying your synapses, and then piggybacked it to your regular adrenal response, that would be pretty amazing. There's about a zillion problems that have kept that sort of thing impossible, though."

"He wouldn't have done anything to me that would hurt me," she sounded emphatic, but there may have been some trepidation in there, too.

"I think it's safe to assume that's true. Everyone seems to be going to great lengths to take you in alive, anyway. Probably as leverage to make your old man do something he doesn't want to do." Roland smirked, "I know from experience that Don is a tough nut to crack. I'd put good money on you being leverage." He paused, "Expensive leverage, to boot. I trashed about half a million credits in illegal android back there, and that guy's augmentations cost well into the millions, I'm sure."

Lucia's face betrayed fear and sadness in equal proportions, "They must want whatever he has very badly."

Roland was grim, "If he can really produce augmented people like you; ones who can't be detected and don't suffer crippling side effects? That'd be worth billions to the right people. Even more to the wrong ones."

"But I didn't even know about me. Do you really think somebody else out there does?"

Roland thought for a moment, "I guess we can't know for sure, but that's a good point. You may have just been a side project he kept secret. Something special he did just for his daughter." He rubbed his bald dome of a head. The gesture struck Lucia as oddly comical from someone so large. "But yeah, Don is a genius and a master of bleeding-edge biotech. There's a million reasons someone might want him… and you."

"The way I see it," Roland opined, suddenly very businesslike, "There are two ways to go about this." He ticked points off on black fingers the size of bratwurst; "We can figure out exactly what they want, and use that to narrow down our lists of suspects." - one finger down - "Or we can figure out who has been paying to grab you and start there." He scowled, "I'm not sure which will be easier. I can start cracking heads and running down the usual sort of scum who would take this job without too much trouble, but I will have to claw my way up the underworld ladder to get to any usable intel. It will take time, and it will attract attention."

He began to pace, "Or, we can go through all of Don's stuff, and look for clues as to who he has been working with, or signs that any of the old players have been sniffing around lately."

Lucia offered, "We could split up. You run down the criminals and I can go through Dad's things."

Roland shook his head emphatically, "No way. I'm not letting you out of my sight, pretty lady. You are one seriously hot commodity right now. If it's as bad as I think, the only reason we aren't dealing with more assholes at this exact moment is that people in Dockside are more afraid of me than they are greedy."

The big man shook his head, "That won't hold for long, trust me. Once word gets out of Dockside that you are here… and it will… my gut says we will be dealing with uptown and off-world muscle." Roland punched his palm, "You can't handle that without me, and if we lose you, we lose the game."

He shook his head again, "Nope, no splitting up. That's B-movie bullshit."

"Fine, herr kommandant," she sighed. "What's first?"

"More beer," the giant cyborg replied. "We're dry."

Chapter Seven

Roland was, in fact out of beer. This was rightly and fairly considered a catastrophe in Roland's opinion, as he loved beer. Beer made Roland happy in ways many other things could not. First of all, he could not drink beer fast enough to get drunk. This was a blessing as 'drunk Roland' was a very bad thing. His liver was organic, but augmented to the point that he could likely drink rocket fuel without injury; and his kidneys were so suped up they could turn it into tap water.

Once, on a dare posited by his idiot cohorts in the squad, he had tried to get drunk. It had subsequently been discovered that if he power-chugged straight ethanol, he could get there in about two hours. Of course, the unit then had a drunk super-soldier with armored skin and a multi-ton bench-press on their hands. The good news was that Roland's ultra-liver had him sobered up within an hour or so. The bad news was that Roland could do a positively fantastic quantity of property damage in an hour.

His CO had to stage an industrial accident to fabricate a believable cover story for the destruction that had resulted. Roland avoided hard liquor after that.

À propos to the current situation, there was another reason for the sudden need for a beer run besides his obsession with dark ale and Belgian pilsners. Roland needed to talk to the Dwarf.

So, after some preparation, they left the apartment and started walking. It was cool, but not cold. It wasn't even ten o'clock yet, and the night-time crowds were just starting to trickle onto the dirty streets. Dozens of scruffy Docksiders emerging from squat grey apartment buildings looked like insects scuttling from under rocks and leaves to bicker over the day's leavings.

Blue-white street lights sprayed garish iridescence over streets that Roland knew to be dull slate-grey thoroughfares under the light of day. But when it blended with the flashing signage of the hundred petty diversions that peppered the main drag, the resulting photonic cacophony was almost poetic to

Roland. It reeked of humanity. It thrilled with the energy of teeming swarming masses of people.

Ninety percent of Roland Tankowicz had been built in a laboratory. He needed this place to be alive. Needed it like fish needed water to breathe.

Every so often, a car would streak overhead, likely carrying some fat Uptown bastard to whatever whorehouse, drug den, or seedy dive he'd be slumming in that night. Roland knew he lived in the sordid underbelly of the great shining beast that was New Boston. Dockside was a densely packed forty squalid square block area reviled by the respectable folks who worked uptown. Located far enough from the Old Fen Way that the big docking towers for the cargo shuttles that moved goods from the giant freighters in orbit didn't spoil the views of the harbor, Dockside was the heart of the commercial empire that sprang up from the discovery of Anson gates and the fantastic worlds beyond them. Naturally, the folks in Uptown did not want to see that heart beating. It was enough for them to know it was there.

But when night fell, and the shadows were deep, the luminaries would come down from the well-lit towers to partake of those delights that could not be found in the shining towers of the Old Fen Way.

And there was no shortage of delights in Roland's little corner of the city. A person could indulge any fetish, addiction, or depraved proclivity in the warrens of Dockside. Law enforcement was an afterthought at best, and a purchasable commodity at worst, once you crossed over from the Sprawl. Not entirely missing, but certainly not 'present.' For the right price, the police would make sure that you had no issues at all with the local color. For the right price, you could make sure the police were entirely blind to your activities as well. If you were very rich, you could get both services at the same time.

There was a refreshing moral flexibility to that section of the city. It was an open secret; one that kept the seedier members of the New Boston populace from seeping upward, like gangrene, to the heights of Uptown and the anointed Cambridge royalty. To Roland, it was home.

Roland was wearing his blocky wool overcoat and a flat cap in Donegal wool to mask his bald head and bulk. Both were black, and together they did a decent job of keeping his asinine proportions from being too obvious. His height and size were an oddity, but there were enough mutants, cyborgs, steroid-freaks and other weirdos out there in Dockside that he rarely rated more than a clandestine gawk from the people he passed if he made the effort to cover up. People just assumed he was some sort of 'mad science gone awry' and minded their own business. There was plenty of that going around these days.

They weren't exactly wrong either, and the irony of that was not lost on Roland. But thankfully, the people in Dockside didn't ask those kinds of questions, and Roland was uninterested in risking the wrath of the planetary government by answering them. The arrangement worked just fine for everyone, so Roland left them to their assumptions.

Roland was a Dockside fixture, having lived there the better part of two decades, now. The players, movers, and shakers of their little community were well aware of him, and while his origins and abilities were still mysterious, his reputation was not. Roland had worked for, with, and against everyone in Dockside at various points in his career, and he was respected as a neutral party and the sort of guy that it was (to put it delicately) best not to fuck with. If you had a problem in Dockside, Roland could fix it. For a price, of course: he wasn't a savage after all.

Roland stayed out of the drugs and crime for the most part, but he was no do-gooder busybody either. If you wanted to get high on blaze and fry your brains for fun, Roland didn't care. But if you wanted to sell blaze in front of Roland's apartment, you would be directed to a new location.

If you decided to get high on blaze and start shooting up the street? Well, if you were lucky, one of the locals would talk you down before Roland made it downstairs to address you personally. If Roland addressed you personally, you were going to the hospital or the morgue. Those were the rules. Everybody knew the rules.

This was the only reason that Lucia was fairly safe for the moment. After the dust-up at The Smoking Wreck, crime lords across Dockside were almost certainly scrambling to figure out who had sent high-dollar goons onto their turf, and pissed off the one guy who they all knew to leave the hell alone. They would be furious at whoever made such a bold move, and they would be falling all over themselves to make sure Roland knew they had nothing to do with it. At first, anyway: For enough money, none of that would matter.

Lucia, not being privy to all of this pertinent information, was apprehensive. "Is it OK for me to be out in the open?" She was moving in that twitchy, hyperactive manner again, just like at the bar. Roland now understood that her nervous system was dilating her sense of time, a sure sign that she was agitated.

"For at least a few more hours, yes. Probably."

"Probably?" she replied, just a touch shrill.

"Yeah. Probably." The big man shrugged, "Right now, a bunch of local bosses are probably calling their regional bosses who are going to call the big bosses to see who ran a high-profile job in Dockside without clearing it. Criminals are very territorial. This is a serious breach of protocol."

"What if the people after me aren't crime bosses?" she asked, displaying a very astute understanding of bureaucracies.

"They probably aren't, but even if it is god himself after you, the major crime syndicates will have a lot of influence over whoever did this, and they'll be pissed. Whoever tried to grab you tonight is going to be having a very difficult meeting about it, with some very scary people."

"But money will change hands and apologies will get offered." He continued, "And the next attempt will go through the correct channels, with the correct fees getting paid along the way. People here know to leave me alone, but there will be too much money on the line for that to hold once the word comes down from the big bosses."

"How do we know it didn't already go through channels?" she asked.

"I'd have heard about it by now, or someone would have hit my apartment." He shook his head, "No, people are holding back right now while everyone figures out who broke the rules and why. Once they sort it out, we will have to get gone, and fast."

"That's why we are going to see this 'Dwarf' guy?" she asked.

"Yup. I need to see him before the word comes down that you are fair game even if I am in the way. Once that happens, he won't be able to help much."

She looked confused, "But he'll help now?"

"Yup."

"Why?"

"Because if he doesn't I'll kill him."

Lucia's face went a new shade of pale at that grim proclamation, "You'll just… kill him?"

Roland nodded, "Yup. He's a professional criminal and a certified asshole. The world won't miss him. If he won't help me, I kill him and go ask the next one. The next one will help because he knows I killed the last one who didn't. That's how it works."

Lucia's heartbeat quickened, and her breathing went shallow. She looked sick, "I… don't know if I can do this." It wasn't an admission of defeat, just a bare assertion of a fact, "I'm in advertising and marketing, Roland… I'm not the kind of person…who can…" She was hyperventilating now.

Roland stopped walking and put his hands on her shoulders. He looked her in the eyes, saw fear. Not just fear for her father, or fear for herself, but fear of him.

He looked at her again. She was pretty; no, more than pretty. She was beautiful, and while he liked to think that he was past the point where that sort of thing mattered, he knew she was. He had joined the army decades ago so people like her wouldn't have to see this world, yet here she was. He had failed again. She shouldn't be here. *I don't know how to do this Beauty and the Beast shit,* he thought to himself, *this sure as hell is no fairy tale, and I am no kind of prince.*

Roland found it easy, living in Dockside, to forget what he was sometimes. Forgetting what he was and what he had done was a critical part of his day-to-day existence. If he thought about it too much, the guilt and despair would become overwhelming. But it was OK for him to be here. In Dockside he was just another bit of refuse from the shining towers of uptown, not even good enough to live in the Sprawl. Here he was just another enigmatic freak; someone to be feared and avoided. Fear and respect were the same thing here, and that made him a big deal in this little slice of hell. No one here knew, and no one here could judge him for the crimes of his past. He could still judge himself, and he often did. But at least here in Dockside he was neither special nor unique for carrying all his sins.

Now a piece of that other world had fallen from the lofty heights and landed in his little puddle; and she was terrified of him. He looked at the woman. Really looked. There was no evil in her. No guile or malice. She was so bright and clean that he feared the grime of his world might stain her forever.

The same hands holding her slim, terrified shoulders had murdered hundreds of unarmed civilians. They had wrought more death and pain than she would ever realize. They would do more before they were done; he knew that with the absolute certainty of a man who made his bed on the battlefield. He knew that. But he didn't know how to make her understand it. She was too clean, too nice. She didn't know evil, she didn't know what it was to be at war, even though a war had been brought to her, anyway.

Roland was war. From the bottom of his armored feet to the top of his reinforced head, he was built for this in the most literal way. He lived for this, and at this moment he hated himself for loving it. It made Roland feel like an ugly twisted thing; a lumbering mechanical monster, little more than a weapon forged to serve his betters.

He broke the spell and simply told her the only truth he could, "I'm sorry. I'm sorry you're here, and I'm sorry I'm the guy who can help you. Christ, you should be sipping cocktails with the girls from the office or going on a date with some lawyer or doctor or whatever."

She was crying now, big wet tears sliding down her cheeks to hang from her jaw. Quiet sobs were shaking her shoulders, tiny in the massive paws of the big cyborg.

"I'm sorry for all the stuff you're gonna see me do. I'm sorry that I'm gonna have to do it, too; if that makes you feel better. Every part of what's coming is going to be terrible, no way around it. I will be dealing with terrible people, and that means doing terrible things." He sighed. A big, heavy sigh. The sigh of a man who knows exactly what is coming.

"These are monsters, Lucia, and that's why your old man sent you to me. I can do this because I am a bigger monster than they are, that's all. I'm sorry about that, I really am."

Her eyes widened as the perceptive woman saw a pain and loathing in his features that went much deeper than the armor, "No! No. It's not that. It's not you. You are what you are, and I don't have anything to say about it." For a fleeting moment, she saw a small terrified thing at the heart of the towering mechanical killer. It was strange and sad, and she wondered if he even knew it was there. Her father's stories had always described Roland as a knight in shining armor, a war hero who bravely vanquished the enemies of peace. This didn't look like the paladin from Dad's stories to her. For a split second, she could only see a tired old soldier.

She shook her head, "I just wanted to be so strong." She gasped, "I want to find my father. I want it all to be okay." She looked back up at him, "Yesterday my life was perfect. Normal! But now I'm… augmented, and you are talking about killing people, and I just can't…" She threw her hands up in disgust, and let them fall to her sides, defeated, "I don't know how to do this. I just want my dad back!"

He tried to smile, "Then just let me do it. Close your eyes, hum your favorite song, or just pretend it's not you. I would do this for your father just for the asking, and I'd leave you out of it if I could." He shrugged noncommittally, "But I will see you through this and we will figure it all out." She was getting control of her crying, thankfully. He let go of her shoulders and squared his, "I'll do the hard parts. You just stay alive. Deal?"

She nodded, "Deal." She straightened and wiped her eyes, "I kinda feel ridiculous now."

"Are you laughing?" Roland's face betrayed abject confusion.

The woman chuckled, "It's all just so fucked up, y'know?"

"Better than anyone, Lady. Let's go talk to the Dwarf."

"Or kill him, right?" She sounded less horrified with the prospect. Apparently she had just needed a moment to come to grips with it.

"The night is still young, kid. We all may see the morning, yet. Even the Dwarf."

"Meh. Fuck him."

He laughed, "That's better."

"Roland?" She said quietly and hooked her small arm around his. She did not know why she did it, or why she felt like she needed to say anything. But she trusted her gut.

"Yeah?" The big man grumbled.

"I don't believe in monsters."

Roland appreciated the sentiment, he really did. But he knew it for what it was.

"You will."

Chapter Eight

The Dwarf would be at Hideaway this time of night. It was an apt and descriptive name for the bar, as the door was an unadorned piece of brown metal sculpted with panels to give it the appearance of an old-time wooden door. The only indication that there was anything behind this passage was a painted sign directly above the door that said in simple block letters, "Hideaway." Facing the grey street was a facade of gray windowless expanse, and the pair had to go down three steps below street level to stand at the door. It was without a doubt, the least-interesting-looking night-time destination Lucia could ever remember going to.

The door thrummed with the regular rhythm of music, an indecipherable tuneless thumping, muffled and low. For whatever reason, Lucia imagined it was going to be all kinds of loud in there when that door finally opened. She braced herself. Roland rapped sharply on the door.

A rectangular viewing panel opened and a pair of beady black eyes blinked out at them, "Private party tonight, guys. Go somewhere else."

The panel started to close but was stopped by two gloved fingers that darted through the opening and latched onto the frame like a vice.

Roland's voice, at an octave low enough to rattle Lucia's molars barked, "I am the private party, Barney. Open the door or buy a new one. Your call."

Beady-eyes grew wide with recognition, "Shit, Tank! I didn't realize it was you! The Boss said you might show up. Hold on."

Lucia heard the latches and bolts clang and clunk as 'Barney' set about getting the door open. She arched an eyebrow at Roland, "Tank?"

He grinned, "My last name is Tankowicz. Barney struggles with any word that has more than one syllable."

The door swung open, and it surprised Lucia to find it had hinges, and was not automatic. This must be an old building, she thought.

Music, smoke, and dingy red light spilled out into the street and washed over the pair. Some no-name industrial punk rock band was playing on a low stage at the far end of the large, open room. The atonal thumping of badly tuned guitars and heavy-handed drum riffs was mercifully drowning out the inscrutable shrieking of the band's "singer."

Roland stepped through the doorway, ducking slightly and angling his shoulders so as not to scrape through the narrow opening. Lucia followed. Roland could just barely straighten to his full height inside, with barely six inches of clearance between his head and the ceiling. He would need to take great care moving around if he didn't want to smash any of the long red tube lights running along the ceiling.

The assault upon Lucia's senses by the sheer volume of stimulus inside the Hideaway made her wince. Her eyes struggled with the garish, crimson lighting that made the room and everyone in it look like clownish caricatures of Faustian demons. Her ears were pummeled by the music's volume and lack of structure; none of it alleviated by the mediocre-at-best talents of the musicians.

And the smells, dear god, the smells. Smoke from a dozen different pipes, hookahs, vaporizers, and bongs slammed her nostrils in acrid waves of stinging olfactory assaults. The effluvia of several different inhaled intoxicants were recognizable, and Lucia wondered if she was going to end up high as a kite from just this second-hand exposure. The smoke was at least a mask for the sticky sweet stink of human sweat, stale beer, and cheap perfume that wafted from the sea of half-dressed human bodies writhing and bouncing in a glassy-eyed trance with the music from the end of the room.

It was no less than a Roman bacchanal in that bar, and Lucia, who had never been anywhere more exciting than a college house party found herself disgusted and terrified by the shear unrestrained energy of it all.

She looked to Roland, for lack of anywhere else to focus, and saw only grim purpose and irritated boredom on his face. That was sort of his normal look, and she found it reassuring.

Roland for his part, hated Hideaway. He hated the noise. He hated the drugs. He hated the people who went there. He hated that they only served shit beer and most of all, he hated the Dwarf.

The towering man moved through the crowd with practiced purpose. He didn't have to push, because bumping in to him was like hitting a wall. Drugged up ravers bounced off of him like ping-pong balls as he stepped through the crowd toward the bar. Lucia followed in his wake, enjoying the protection of the large opening he created. It was nice to not have to touch the lurching bodies all around her.

At the bar, Roland placed both hands on the scarred and stained synthetic wood surface and leaned in very close to speak with the bartender. She was a pretty blonde girl, with spiky hair dressed in improbably short iridescent pink shorts and a tank top that would have been tight if it was two sizes bigger. As it was, the only thing holding the beleaguered garment together was a dizzying assortment of pins, bangles, chains and ornaments employed to supplement the structural integrity of the too-tiny garment.

The bartender made a cursory attempt to flirt with the big man. Lucia couldn't tell if it was something she did out of reflex to get better tips or if she had a sincere thing for Roland. Lucia had a hard time imagining Roland frequenting a place like this, but she was forced to concede that she had only known the man for about four and a half hours at this point.

If Roland's face was any indicator, her instincts were right. With an irritated pout, the pretty bartender turned away and hit a button by the register terminal. A screen flashed, and she waved him over to the end of the bar where another door awaited.

A light blinked green on the panel next to the door, and Roland guided Lucia through the dim passage. It led to a hallway, about ten feet long and to another door. The door behind them closed, and Roland stood in front of the next one and waited. A panel to the right of the door lit up, and a voice crackled through a speaker, "Tank! Roland, ya' old fooker! How are ya?"

Roland's head cocked slightly to the side. He looked at the speaker and said in a low, enunciated growl, "Open. The. Door."

"Roland," the voice crackled, "ye need ta know I had nothing to do with tha' bullshite at the Wreck. I need ta know yer nae gonna get all bent out of shape and make a fuss in here before I let ye through, is all."

"Let me through?" Roland's voice was incredulous, "LET!?" Roland, Lucia realized for the second time that day, was fucking terrifying sometimes. The tone of his voice alone triggered her augmentation and her perception of the next eighth of a second seemed to stretch out to four or five.

A right hand like wrecking ball hit the door and crumpled the steel like so much aluminum foil. The door, frame, and part of the ceiling blew inward with a noise like thunder that left her ears ringing. Sparks flew and rubble fell like bulky rain for two full seconds after the door stopped vibrating on the floor. To Lucia's accelerated perceptions, it felt much longer.

In eerie slow-motion, Lucia saw the shadowy figure in the dim room beyond raise some sort of weapon. She tried to shout a warning to Roland, but he seemed not to hear because the only move he made was to take one step forward to block the door completely. There was a loud pop followed by a bright flash that silhouetted Roland in stark relief. Lucia screamed in spite of herself.

She heard Roland's growl and a wet thud, followed by a yelp and a string of profanity so long and verbose that Lucia was forced to acknowledge the rhetorical virtuosity of the speaker despite her abject terror.

She made herself creep forward and peek around the towering cyborg into the room beyond. On the floor was a man. Well... she assumed it was a man. He was short. Very short. Five feet tall at most, with an enormous shock of unkempt white hair wreathing his head in a ridiculous mane. He had a beard, an enormous thing that obscured his lips and cascaded down over a barrel chest. Completing the laughable picture, he was wearing a pinstriped purple three-piece suit that had the right sleeve removed. *That*, she thought, *must be the Dwarf.*

The right sleeve was unnecessary, for one obvious reason. His right arm was entirely mechanical, and obviously so. No attempt had been made to make the arm look remotely human. It was an oversized mass of steel and actuators, terminating in a three-digit claw that was snapping and clamping in futile rage.

Roland had one foot on the Dwarf's chest, and he was holding the industrial claw thing in his left hand while the Dwarf kicked, spat and, swore profusely.

Roland kneeled and shoved the bionic claw in his left hand into the floor with enough force to crack the floor plates. The Dwarf howled and Roland clamped a giant hand over his face to silence the torrent of invective that was forthcoming.

"I hate this fucking place, Rodney. I hate coming here." Roland's growl was a subterranean base that Lucia could feel in her guts. "You know where I do like to go?" He shifted and yanked the Dwarf up and held him aloft by his head and that bionic arm. Lucia realized that the Dwarf's arm must have been very strong, because Roland never loosened his grip on it for an instant.

Roland smiled a slow, terrifying smile, "I like to go to the Wreck, Rodney. I'm happy there. They don't let druggies and assholes and shit bands in there."

Roland's tone lightened, "Now, when I decide to put on my walking shoes and take a stroll to this shit-hole, it's because I have a damn good reason to do it, Rodney. When I take the walk down here, and I am polite enough to knock first, I do so under the assumption you will open the fucking door." Roland extended his left arm, stretching the Dwarf's bionic limb out to the side.

"When you don't respect my attempt at polite discourse, Rodney, when you don't show me the courtesy that I tried to show you? Well, then I start to think you don't respect me anymore."

Roland's next question was a whisper, "Don't you respect me anymore, Rodney?" The muscles in Roland's left forearm flexed, and there was the barest hint of clenched teeth, as the cords of Roland's neck muscles bulged. With a crunch, the wrist area of the metal claw clutched in Roland's left hand collapsed like a tin can in his fist. Sparks erupted in a hissing fountain from the elbow and the claw clenched spastically one more time before going limp.

The Dwarf tried to scream, but the platter-sized hand over his mouth made a mockery of the attempt.

"Oh, shut up," Roland drawled. "That thing doesn't feel pain." He removed his hand and dropped the little man to the floor.

"Yea', but it's muthafookin' expensive to fix, yah fookin' shite-brained baldie bastard." The Dwarf stood up and stalked over to an overturned chair. His right arm hung loosely and belched random sparks into the air with muffled pops. There was a loud snap and a hiss of coolant evaporated in a cloud of noxious steam, "ahhhh fookin' hell!" The Dwarf shouted as the sound startled him and he sat heavily in the chair.

"I fookin' told yer over-sized half-a-tard arse that I had nae ta do wit' that row!" He tried to make an adjustment to the arm but it was stubbornly unresponsive, "Why the fook are ye' here fookin, wi' my shite?"

Roland shrugged, "Should have opened the door, then."

The Dwarf waved with his good arm at the destruction around him and pointed to his wrecked arm, "You doin' shite like this is exactly why I dinnae open it, ye fookin' dip-shite! Fook!"

He threw his good hand in the air, "Ye don' think we are all up shite's creek as is, what with some cork-sookin' fookwad sending arse-buggerin' androids ta Dockside, already?"

Roland barked, "Who?"

"How tha' fook should I know?" was the grumpy retort from the hairy little man.

Roland took a menacing step forward, "Goddamnit, Rodney, I came here because I need to know who is sending uptown muscle onto your turf. I dare you to sit there and tell me you have no idea at all who might have that sort of cash and be willing to risk pissing off your boss."

The Dwarf looked torn, and Roland pressed his advantage, "Please tell me you don't know anything, Rodney. Because you just ruined my shirt, and I'd love an excuse to kill you right now."

"Don't start comin' over all hasty and assertive, ye big shite-stain." The Dwarf said calmly as he shifted in his chair to rest the broken appendage on an armrest, "I'm already workin' on that, and killin' me just means ye'll have ta start over."

Roland leaned forward, "What do you know right now?"

"Well, it ain't anyone from any of our little Dockside family crews, ye kin bet yer oversized chrome arse on that much. Them uptown slags, the Combine, have been makin' noise about encroachin' here, and dem shites have the money and brass ta' take a swing without clearin' it. But my first pass at 'em says they're fooked if they know shite about this, either."

He looked past Roland, "Besides, ye know damn well this ain't about local politics, anyway, don't ye?"

"I suspect things. Educate me." This was Roland's version of being coy. It was terrible and any effect it might have had was lost on the Dwarf. Fortunately, the tiny criminal was still sufficiently intimidated from having his arm crushed to be forthcoming.

"Word is, there's a VIP on our dirty streets worth seven fookin' zeroes to a certain party or parties what's lookin' for her." He looked at Lucia with unvarnished avarice. It made her skin crawl.

Roland suppressed a wince. Seven zeroes? This was beyond bad. This was a catastrophe.

"Who are these parties?" Roland asked evenly, betraying nothing.

The Dwarf smiled, "No fookin' clue, boyo." Roland took a step forward, and the Dwarf held out his good hand in a conciliatory gesture, "But I sure as shite know who put that word out, now, don't I just?"

Roland stopped and crossed his arms over the gaping burnt hole in his shirt. He cocked his head, and the Dwarf smiled, "It was that ball-garglin' fook-stain piece-o-shite shyster from Big Woo. Ye know… Marko."

Roland raised an eyebrow, and the Dwarf grinned even more, "Ye're a right fookin' arsehole, Tank me boy, and I happily await the day somebody nukes ye' from orbit like ye' rightly deserve. But the thought of ol' Marko getting a visit from ye' when ye're in such a right fookin ' dandy of a mood just warms tha' cockles of me wee heart."

Roland growled, "If you're fucking with me on this, Rodney…"

"Yeah yea, ye'll kill me. I've heard it before. Get on wit' ya, now. I need to get someone in here to clean up this mess, now."

He looked over at Lucia and waggled his bushy eyebrows, "Good luck there, lass. Ye'll need it. All of the fookin' universe is about to shite right on ye', I'll tell ye' that for free."

He gave her an appraising gaze, "Tell ye' what girly; if ye ever get tired of that great big arsehole yer walkin' about wit', just come back here. I'm sure I've got a few positions you ken fill, if ye know what I mean!"

He never got to laugh at his own joke because Lucia's heel connected with his front teeth at a speed no human could hope to match. She might have damaged her foot if not for the sturdy shoes she was wearing and technique honed flawless by expensive private lessons throughout her childhood. The Dwarf shrieked and sprayed blood and teeth all over the wall as he toppled off his chair and crashed to the floor.

"You wouldn't survive the experience, dickhead, "she spat at the crumpled mess sobbing at her feet.

Roland gave her an approving look, but then scowled, "I don't think your father would approve of the type of influence I appear to be having on you, kid."

Lucia gave him a sharp look, "Who do you think paid for the goddamn lessons? And don't call me 'kid.' "

Roland laughed, "Yes ma'am." He saluted sharply, and then smiled again, "But you best save some of that mustard for the crowd."

"Crowd?" she asked.

"Yup. Crowd. Thanks to your temper and daddy's muay thai lessons, we get to fight our way out of here, now."

Lucia's face was a mask of petulant irritation, "But you smashed his arm first!"

"That's different. It was business," He chuckled at the drooling prostrate form of the Dwarf. "We might have walked out unmolested before you defenestrated ol' Rodney, there. But now?" He shrugged, "Rodney's crew won't let a girl thump him like that without a response. Too much damage to his rep. I get a pass because I'm... well..." he gestured to his mass, "... me."

Lucia winced, "Oh. Sorry. Got caught up in the moment, I guess."

Roland stretched to his full height and grinned, "Don't sweat it, ki—er—ma'am. I've been meaning to do this for a while now and I am very much in the mood tonight."

"What should I do?" she asked.

"If they have guns, stay behind me. If they don't have guns, get your money's worth out of all those expensive lessons you got and kick as many asses as you can."

Lucia swallowed hard, "Ok."

Roland gave the Dwarf's crumpled form a savage kick and headed for the exit. This was going to be fun.

Chapter Nine

They had guns.

The first door was still closed and, apparently, locked from the other side. Why anyone thought this would make a difference, Roland didn't know. But he figured that on the other side of the door would be half a dozen or so of the Dwarf's goons waiting to extract punishment for the insult he had just received.

He suppressed a chuckle, thinking about how an Uptown girl had just reorganized the face of a serious Dockside crime boss. He was starting to like this chick despite his better judgment. He could not suppress a smirk, *Dockside could use the kind of shake-up she could bring. Things have been getting boring around here.*

His attention returned to the matter at hand. Respect was important in Dockside, and whether the Dwarf's crew had a prayer of winning this fight or not, tradition demanded that they try. The Dwarf would lose too much valuable respect otherwise.

Roland knew they'd be waiting because the awful music had stopped and he could hear the voices of several men murmuring and muttering on the other side of the door. The fact that the crew was there already told Roland that the Dwarf had figured ahead of time that something would probably go wrong and had sent for the crew as soon as Roland showed up. Roland was forced to concede that while the Dwarf was scum, he wasn't stupid.

He considered going back to the other room and using the Dwarf as a hostage to walk out of there, but rejected that idea. Doing that would imply that Rodney's goons could take Roland in a fight, and that would never do. Roland had a reputation to maintain. It had been a while since Roland had flexed his muscles in public, and Dockside was due for a refresher on why Roland was to be left alone. This would be as good an opportunity as any to reinforce that point.

Roland searched his memory for the Dwarf's roster of heavies, checking for anyone who might pose a challenge or require special attention.

There was Mook, a big dumb mutant who was strong as an ox or three, but he had a misshapen spine and couldn't move very well. Roland didn't anticipate he'd be much trouble. There were the Garibaldi brothers, but they were mostly triggermen. Roland wasn't worried about guns; anything light enough for those guys to carry wouldn't be heavy enough to hurt him. Of course, he had to keep Lucia alive too, so he made a mental note to take out the Garibaldis first, if he saw them. Roland seemed to remember an augmented ex-cop who had been running with this crew, but he couldn't remember the guy's name or how tough he was, so he put it out of his mind.

He looked at Lucia. "When I go through this door, things are going to go very slowly for you, you know?" He tapped the side of his head with a finger, referring to her augmentation.

She nodded, pale with fear. It was easy to forget she was an Uptown girl. While it was just another Friday night in this part of town for him, this was probably the most tense moment of her life.

"Well, use that. You are going to have lots of time to react to what's going on, but don't panic and try to move as fast as you can. Your brain is quick as hell, but your body is still just your body. If you try to turn too quickly or move too fast, you are going to break an ankle or pull a muscle. Move deliberately. You are already the fastest one in the room, so don't rush, OK? Got it?"

Her nervous system was already cranking, he could tell.

She nodded again, "Got it. Move slow. Don't rush. Don't panic. I'm fast. Got it." She was speaking like a hopped-up chipmunk and her hands were twitching.

"Hey!" he barked, grabbing her attention. "Stay. Behind. Me." He pointed to the charred hole in his shirt and the pristine, unmarked onyx muscles underneath, "Indestructible cyborg tank-man." He pointed at her, "Squishy flesh-critter. Got it?"

"Got it. Stay behind. Don't Panic. Move slow. I'm fast."

Roland shrugged. She was very inexperienced with her enhancements, and this was as good as he would get from her right now. Time to go to work.

For the second time in twenty minutes, a metal door flew from its moorings and crashed to the floor in a shower of debris. Lucia wondered why anyone in Dockside even bothered with doors at all when dealing with Roland. It was like the giant man was possessed of an unreasoning hatred for doors. Or of opening them, at least.

Roland had half a second to register the room full of thugs when the two men in black coveralls near the exit pulled two pistols each and opened fire.

They were using SpyderCo HVB-92 pistols that fired 5mm ceramic beads at twenty-five times the speed of sound, which made a terrific racket. The Garibaldis were firing in semi-automatic and making every bead hit dead center on Roland's chest. The friction they created set the air on fire as the beads flew, and on impact the beads carried huge amounts of both thermal and kinetic energy. These were serious weapons for serious men. Roland allowed himself to acknowledge the quality of both the technology and the marksmanship. Sparks showered and cascaded from every impact, turning the surrounding room into a holiday pyrotechnics display complete with orange blossoms of fire and burning acrid smoke.

Which was entirely irrelevant because Roland was wholly impervious to small arms fire. At the time of his creation, there was a very small, very discrete set of man-portable weapon systems on earth that could do more than minor damage to his skin. Small, concealable pistols were not on that list.

In the space of eight seconds the Garibaldis had dumped fifty rounds apiece. The barrage had drained their weapons dry, and one hundred rounds of potent ammunition had done precisely zero damage to Roland. It had, however, done an excellent job of wounding half of their own men with ricochets. Various goons lay sprawled about with neat 5mm holes in their clothes and faces, oozing blood and wafting smoke.

There was a very pregnant, silent pause for a moment while everyone assessed what had just happened. Aside from the groans of the wounded, there was very little to listen to as the gunmen stared open-mouthed at the tableau. Their target had just taken a hundred direct hits from four very nice guns. They had finished the job their boss had started in ruining his shirt, but that seemed to be about the extent of their effectiveness. They blinked at each other, faces frozen in stark incredulity. This was not a situation the famous Garibaldi brothers had come prepared to deal with.

Somewhat panicked, the two identical dark-haired and dark-eyed men dropped their magazines and fumbled for reloads, while the rest of their motley crew attacked.

This included Mook, a seven-foot gray-skinned mutant with a grossly asymmetrical face and very stooped posture. Flanked on either side, Mook advanced with four other local enforcers for back-up. Roland didn't recognize them and dispatched the first one to reach him with a casual backhanded slap. He was pretty sure the guy didn't die from the love tap. Probably not, anyway. Roland couldn't check because he had more pressing concerns.

Mook took one lumbering step forward and swung his club-like fist in a looping overhand right, aiming for Roland's head. Mook was nearly as big as Roland, but his knotted arms were longer, almost gorilla-like, which gave him a distinct reach advantage. Roland considered letting the punch land for a moment, betting his skull was tougher than that fist, but then thought better of it. He had seen Mook in action once or twice, and he didn't feel good enough about that bet to roll the dice right now.

Roland ducked the ponderous blow and thundered a right hook to Mook's ribs. He only used a fraction of his available power, not wanting to punch a hole right through his opponent. The solidity and implacability of the gray-skinned behemoth surprised Roland. Mook's body was far more dense than he had originally thought. The black fist drove against Mook with enough force to shift a car, but the towering mutant only exhaled a heavy puff of breath and swung at Roland with his left.

Roland had returned to a high boxer's guard and took the blow on his right forearm. It felt like a tree had fallen on him. Roland grinned, enjoying a real workout for the first time in a good long while, and countered with a straight left aimed for Mook's square, oversized chin. Like two pieces of industrial machinery, Roland's wrecking-ball mitt made solid contact on the lumbering giant's cinder-block jaw. This time the cyborg put some real power into the blow and felt the teeth click shut and the heavy head snap back. Mook staggered a step, glassy eyed and wobbling.

Roland pressed this advantage by landing two more straights, sending Mook flailing backwards into the scrambling Garibaldis, scattering the brothers. Despite the repeated blows, Mook refused to go down. He tried to catch his footing and square up with Roland again, but Roland was not having it. A big right boot collided with the mutant's sternum carrying enough force to hurl the poor thug into and through the exterior wall.

Mook smashed a ten-foot hole through the Hideaway and landed in a boneless heap across the sidewalk, six feet to the right of the door. His limbs were all bent at unnatural angles and his breathing came in ragged gasps. Anyone who cared to make the observation would concur there were many broken things inside of Mook, and Roland instantly regretted his kick.

Too hard. Roland thought to himself. *Dial it down*.

Mook was just a poor dumb guy that only had one way to make a living. He wasn't a killer or anything awful; just a better-than-average street heavy good for scaring deadbeats and junkies into paying their bills on time. Roland didn't feel good about hurting him, but a fight's a fight, and Roland couldn't afford to dance all night.

He whirled to check on Lucia. He could not decide if he was pleased or horrified to see her dealing with three of the Dwarf's thugs without much noticeable difficulty.

She was moving with fluid grace in and out of the way of their clumsy blows and attempts to grapple. Periodically, an elbow or a foot would snake out to break a nose or smash a groin. What made her task problematic was not her skill, but her mass. All three of the men had at least a hundred pounds on her, so despite outclassing her opposition in technical proficiency, she could not inflict much damage. She was fast and well trained, but just too small to put them down with anything close to efficiency. The agile woman was grinding them down one small injury at a time though, and would finish them off eventually. It was the only viable tactical option for the 130-lb woman: a version of hyper-velocity 'death by a thousand cuts.'

Realizing that she did not need immediate assistance, Roland had time to deal with the Garibaldis. Mook's unceremonious exit had scattered them like cockroaches, but they were professionals and they were already regaining their feet and weapons.

Nico Garibaldi was the first to get up and with practiced ease he sent three beads into Roland's left knee before Roland was on top of him. He probably assumed that Roland was wearing body armor and hoped that the knee would be an unarmored spot to shoot. It was as good an assumption as any, just dead wrong.

Roland clamped his hand over the top of Nico's head, engulfing it in a black fist and pulling the screaming man into the air. Nico slapped and punched at the massive forearm with one hand and emptied the HVB into Roland's chest with the other.

He felt the hits from Chico Garibaldi's HVB bouncing off his back while he held Nico's thrashing body off the ground. He felt a freezing, detached rage building inside him, and he knew exactly where it came from.

To say that Roland did not like the Garibaldis would be a catastrophic understatement. The twin assassins were not like poor Mook. They were professional murderers. But even that wasn't all that reprehensible in Dockside. Killing was as viable a trade as any other in this part of town. But the Garibaldis were a special case. They took pride in their work and in their lack of discretion. They did not care who the target was, where the target was, or how old the target was. Once the money changed hands, they did the job without question. Roland had seen what happened when the Garibaldis did a job, and the aftermath always reminded him of when he'd wake up after being blacked out by the Golem. When Roland saw the Garibaldis, he saw what his former masters had wanted him to be. What they MADE him be.

He turned, a savage snarl on his lips, and with more strength than was strictly necessary hurled Nico at Chico.

Roland suspected that his own neurological augmentations were inferior to Lucia's, but his dilated sense of time was sufficient to see the flash of flame and gas from Chico's last shot exit from Nico's back while he was still mid-flight. Blood and bone arced from the exit wound as the bead tore through the body with terrible ease, trailing smoke.

Chico's face went from grim determination to stark horror in slow motion as he registered what was happening. Nico's lifeless corpse struck his brother with enough force to pitch him over backwards and drive him into the ground. Roland spared them a quick glance and then remembered to check on Lucia. She had put one of her antagonists down somehow, and the two remaining heavies were very much the worse for wear. She looked tired though, and Roland left the surviving Garibaldi for a moment dispatch the thugs with stiff-yet-merciful blows.

Lucia's eyes were wide and her pulse was chattering in her veins. Her breathing was deep and rapid, and Roland recognized the signs of impending neurological overload.

"Lucia." He pitched his voice in a slow, soft baritone It the most soothing tone he could muster, "You need to relax. Remember? Go slow. Slow down Lucia."

Her eyes met his, panicky. He continued, "Slow down. Relax. Breathe." She relaxed, tension visibly leaving the muscles of her jaw and neck. Her pupils returned to a more acceptable diameter, and her breathing slowed.

"There you go. Perfect. Just go slow. Breathe in for a count of four, then breathe out for a four-count. That's right." It was called 'combat breathing' and it had been helping soldiers with panic since the twentieth century. She was calming down, and Roland was just assessing the room when her eyes went wide again and she dived into his arms.

Romantic implications were abandoned when Roland felt the searing heat and thunderclap impact characteristic of every time he got shot in the head. Goddamn Chico Garibaldi had recovered and was emptying a twenty-five-round bead magazine directly into the back of the big cyborg. Where the burning projectiles struck his back, there was a staccato tattoo of mild stings. His head, on the other hand, had much less armor. Every so often there would be a flash of white-hot agony as a bead would crease the skin of his scalp and rattle off his reinforced skull. It would leave a nasty rend in the skin for several hours before his nanobots could repair the mesh. Thankfully, his skull held up.

There was nothing Roland could do with that much gunfire coming his way but wrap his arms around Lucia and cover as much of her body with his. Fortunately for her, she was easy to envelop.

Roland waited until he heard the click of an empty magazine and then stood. His coat, entirely shredded by the barrage, fell from his body in smoking tatters. He shrugged out of the hanging rags and tore the undignified remains of his shirt away. He turned slowly and faced Chico.

Chico got his first good look at the most feared fixer in Dockside, and he did not know what to make of what he saw. Bare-chested, Roland was a seven-and-a-half foot black mass of writhing muscles and simian proportions. He stared down at the assassin from his full height. The scowling bald head was still smoking from a dozen direct hits, and the looming giant glowered at the stupefied killer with heavy brow furrowed and teeth showing. It was a face that told Chico that he was a dead man. The mouth tightened into a grim flat line and the eyes neither flared nor blazed, as the stories so often alluded to in these moments. They were flat black hollows, betraying no hint of emotion.

Roland had no emotions when it came to Chico Garibaldi. Roland was not emotionless: He had felt real terror when he thought Lucia might get shot, for instance. But then again, Lucia was a person, and Chico was just a monster who killed for fun and profit. He was just meat for the grinder as far as Roland was concerned, because Roland liked killing monsters. Every time he ended someone like Chico, he felt like it erased one innocent that had died because of him. It was all he felt he could do to even the score.

Roland had killed hundreds of people in his career, and the worst of them had been better men than Chico Garibaldi. Roland knew he could tear the tiny man apart and still sleep like a baby that night. For his part, Chico realized for the first time since the fight began that Roland was going to kill him, and there was nothing that could be done about it.

Chico sprinted for the door, his dead twin all but forgotten, and made it about two steps before a black vice clamped on the back of his neck and threw him across that room. His brief flight was terminated in abrupt fashion by the bar that had previously been serving drunk revelers. He struck with his right shoulder and his humerus snapped like a dry twig. His head bounced off the fake wood paneling with a dull thud and spots danced across his vision.

The concussion disconnected him from the pain of his broken arm, and with rubber legs he tried to stand, more from reflex than any real sense of purpose. He didn't see the blow that collapsed his ribs, but the stabbing fire of a punctured lung brought his situation into stark focus as his legs turned back to formless jelly. He slumped against the bar, hacking agonized coughs that sprayed foamy blood onto his coveralls.

"Roland, stop!" he heard the woman say, "Please!"

The gigantic black blur that took up Chico's field of vision paused. He heard the monster rumble calmly, firmly, "He's a killer, you know. He's killed women, children, innocents. He tried to kill us tonight. He'll try again, Lucia. This is just how it goes, here."

"Well, I'm not from here." Chico was losing consciousness, and the voices sounded like they were coming from inside a tunnel. "Just leave him. Let's just go. Please." She was pleading. Chico, having grown up in the slums and alleys of New Boston's underworld, was confused on a very primal level.

A woman he was supposed to kidnap was pleading with a man he tried to kill, so that he could live. Chico was briefly cognizant enough to appreciate the irony of his situation. Then he fell asleep.

Chapter Ten

Roland and Lucia exited Hideaway and moved onto the main street, colloquially called 'the Drag.' Their first concern was getting off the street and getting under cover. It was a nine-block walk back to his apartment, and they must have cut a bizarre figure to anyone who saw them. Roland was shirtless, but the contrast between his nominally Caucasian face and matte black skin below the neckline, coupled with the dim and oddly colored lights of the Drag, made it look like he was some sort of pro wrestler in a tight black shirt walking with his latest girlfriend. Or at least that's what they hoped it looked like as they quickly covered the distance between Hideaway and Roland's apartment.

Lucia was tight-lipped and frazzled, and Roland was a grim, brooding scowl with legs. A twinge of guilt had led Roland to call an ambulance for Mook, and he was irritated that Chico would also get medical attention as a result. Roland had refrained from finishing Chico off for Lucia's sake, but leaving a live enemy behind was not his style. It chaffed at him, and he wasn't sure if he was bothered by the strategic blunder of having a pissed off Garibaldi to deal with at a later date, or if it was how easy it would have been to make the kill.

The failures of the previous generations of military cyborgs were not lost on him. Currently, he just wasn't entirely sure if he wasn't eventually going to become an amoral murder-bot as well. The look in Lucia's eyes and the tone of her voice had been shocking. It felt weird. Bad weird. He didn't want to be an amoral murder-bot, but some people needed to be murdered, right? The Garibaldi brothers positively begged to be disposed of. Killing people like Chico made the world a better place, didn't it?

He didn't typically move in the rarified social circles that exposed him to the type of scrutiny Lucia had viewed him with. He had been playing by Dockside rules for so long, he had forgotten there were other ways to do things. He wasn't sure he was going to like 'other ways to do things.' But it was obvious that Lucia needed him to play by some different rules. He figured he could try, for Don's sake. He owed it to the old bastard to get his daughter through this without her thinking her old man had built a monster.

Lucia, for her own sake, was still trying to come to terms with her own issues. Roland's moral crisis was a distant second on her list of concerns because she had just been in a downtown bar brawl complete with gunmen, mutants, and a bionic midget. Literally twenty-four hours ago, she was avoiding going to a happy hour networking event because that dipshit Kyle Birdman was going to be there and she couldn't take his clumsy, patronizing advances anymore. Now she was fleeing a crime scene with giant cyborg, leaving at least one corpse behind her. All because she was an accomplice, and an illegally augmented combatant. She was going to need a minute to get a hold of all of that. Considering the three androids and the superhuman kidnapper she had escaped earlier that same goddamn evening, as well as her kidnapped father, this was shaping up to be the worst day of her life. It was just barely eleven-thirty when she checked her watch. There was still a whole half-hour for things to get worse.

The scrap in Hideaway had been yet another bit of craziness that she just wasn't ready for. She had hurt one of the men she fought seriously, and she knew she should feel badly about that, but she found that she just couldn't bring herself to give a shit. Crouching under Roland during Chico's final barrage had been terrifying, though. She had never been shot at before, and just knowing that someone nine feet away was making a deliberate and concerted effort to kill Roland and get at her had shattered a lot of naïve rich-girl illusions. She felt every round hit the big man's back and watched the beads stripe his scalp with yellow fire. She had never felt so small and helpless, and she hated it. She grimly resolved herself to never feel that way again. She was sketchy on exactly how this would be accomplished, but the resolve was there. That would have to do for now.

She looked over at her companion. She was simultaneously fascinated and horrified by him. He was quite literally, her father's greatest creation. A blend of man and machine so perfect, his very existence was a contradiction. He was obviously a weapon. It felt wrong to dehumanize him like that, but ninety percent of him was built specifically for war. She thought of an old saying her Dad often used to express disbelief: "… and if my grandmother had wheels, she'd be a wagon." *Well, big guy*, she thought, *if ninety percent of you was made to be a wagon… you are pretty much a wagon.* Her father had taken a man and put him inside a weapon so perfectly that neither realized that one was the other. *Roland is a hell of a wagon,* she thought irreverently.

As a teenager, she had 'borrowed' her father's AeroClast TDI and taken it out for a flight over Lake Winnipesaukee. She took it with every intention of going slowly and avoiding any dramatic bursts of exuberance. It was just supposed to be a dawn jaunt over the lake in an expensive toy.

She remembered that flight. Just touching the throttle on that thing was like hopping on Satan's back and slapping him in the testicles. She had wanted to be good, but the car just plain refused to go slow. It was impossible to fly that machine in a restrained manner because it wasn't designed for that. It was designed to operate at the ragged edge of sanity. That day was the first and only time she had ever been arrested.

That's what she imagined it felt like to be Roland all the time. A man in a hot rod trying like hell to drive it slowly. It had to be maddening.

Still, she hadn't been ready to watch him beat that guy in the bar to death. She was no fool. She was aware that she wasn't back in Cambridge anymore. She understood that this was his world, and that he was the one who knew how things worked here. She was merely a guest in Dockside, a tourist. It would be difficult, but she committed herself to not judging his warlike manner too harshly. She could learn a lot about her own augmentations by watching how he handled all of his, which she had to admit were far more extreme.

She wasn't sure she was ever going to be able to kill though. Roland made it look easy. She didn't want that sort of thing to ever become easy. Pretending that his casual reference to killing didn't make her uneasy was just lying to herself. She walked in studied quiet while she tried to sort it all out in her head.

Roland broke the silence first, "How are you holding up? Your turbo-drive kicked in pretty hard back there. Any side effects?"

She started to shake her head, then nodded instead. There was no sense in lying. "Yeah. I'm having a hard time calming my heartbeat. My head hurts too." She smiled weakly, "Not sure if that's a normal reaction to a gunfight in an underground nightclub or if it's the stuff dad put in my head, though."

"Fair question," the big man conceded. "Vision OK? No tingling in the fingers or toes?" Roland tried to think of all the symptoms of nerve damage that typical neurological acceleration augmentations might cause. She shook her head at all of them.

"Just a little light headed and tired. Slight headache."

He grunted, "Good. I know how to fix that."

They arrived at his door and stomped up the stairs. In his apartment, Roland sat her down at the kitchen table and went to the fridge. He pulled out a loaf of bread, and a jar of peanut butter.

"You like peanut butter?" he asked bluntly.

"Sure." She responded, just a little perplexed.

Roland began to make peanut butter sandwiches. He made them quickly and with a practiced economy of motion. The man obviously made a lot of peanut butter sandwiches, she observed. Lucia wrinkled her brow and asked, "Is this really the best time to have a sandwich?"

"Your head hurts and you are woozy because you just burned 2,000 calories in less than an hour. Your blood-sugar levels are shit right now," he explained. "I've only got eighty-seven pounds of flesh on me and I can go through 5500 a day when I'm operating."

"Really?"

"Yeah. The brain burns more calories than any other organ in the body, and yours is cranked waaaaaaay the hell up. Peanut butter is my go-to after a fight. Lots of calories. Eat."

"Thanks, Doc," she quipped. She hated to admit it, but she was in fact hungry as hell. She began to tear into the sandwiches with unladylike vigor, "at least I know I'll keep my girlish figure now. No more diets for me!"

"You've never been on a diet in your life."

"That is a fact," she mumbled, mouth full of peanut butter.

They sat there in silence for a few minutes. Two adults munching on peanut butter sandwiches like ten-year-olds. Lucia's headache began to subside almost instantly, and Roland grunted in satisfaction when she paused in her feasting after a third sandwich.

She locked eyes with Roland and spoke, "I'm sorry about back there. I know you were right, but I just couldn't let you kill that guy. I don't know why... I mean..."

He waved her off, "Don't worry about it. I sometimes forget that things are different in other places. Life is cheap here, y'know. Always has been. But that doesn't mean it's supposed to be that way, right?"

He looked down at his hands, "It's been that way down here so long, I wonder if it stays that way because we like it that way, right? Maybe the problem with Dockside is the Docksiders."

Lucia replied, "I think there's a bit of that everywhere. Uptown is full of erudite pricks because they like being erudite pricks. It's almost a contest to see who can be the most awful person." She laughed, and it was good guffaw, full of life, "We know that the money comes from the backs of spacers who spend their lives living in metal boxes on freighters. We know that people down here sweat and bleed and die in the dirt so we can sip Champagne and eat exotic fruits from across the galaxy." Her laugh faded to a chuckle, "We know and we don't care."

"A man died tonight." She was thoughtful now, all traces of humor gone, "He was a piece of trash, but he's still dead. Tomorrow morning, they'll clean up the mess, get on with life, and no one will care at all that he died. No one Uptown. No one here. He'll just be... gone... forgotten."

She faded off, and Roland didn't know what to say. Lucia's eyes came up, brimmed with tears she was trying very hard not to shed, "... because of me. Because of my dad."

Roland knew where this was going, and he put his hand down on the counter, hard, "Nope. Nuh uh. Stop." He jabbed a finger her way to emphasize his point, "Nico Garibaldi took money from Rodney the Dwarf to kill me. Period. He'd have turned you in for the bounty either way, and whether or not he and his brother raped you first would have depended on if that factored into the payday."

He crossed his arms over his chest and looked down on her, "Nico made his choices. He was there because he chose to be. He died because he was a dumbass who chose poorly."

"Now you? You chose nothing. None of this. Other people have put this on you. Don't take responsibility for anyone's choices but your own. It's a bad road. Trust me."

Realization dawned on Lucia, and her eyes grew wide, "Oh my god… I'm so sorry! I must sound like such a silly twit right now!"

The big man shrugged, "I have a different perspective than you. That happens when evil military assholes shut your brain off and use your body to murder a few hundred innocent people." He tried to make it sound light, but failed abominably.

"Just don't get caught up in what these pricks have put you into. It's not your fault… any of it. If I took responsibility for what other people did to me, I'd have stood in front of those cannons myself, two and a half decades ago."

"I'm sorry," Lucia said, "I must sound pathetic to you."

"Not even a little," he responded with no hesitation at all. "You have never been in this situation before, you have a lot of stuff to process right now, and you are doing a lot better than most people would."

He snickered wryly, "I've seen professional soldiers shit their pants the first time they saw real combat. Trust me, you smell just fine."

Lucia finally laughed again, "Yeah, well, it was touch-and-go for minute there, bud."

Roland laughed too. It felt good. But all too quickly reality came back, and he asked, "When did you sleep last?"

She thought for a second, "I woke up at five-thirty this morning."

"OK. We have maybe a few more hours of relative safety here. You should try to get some sleep. We'll move out of here around dawn and get set up to go visit Marko."

"I don't have any clothes your size," he went on, "but there is big shower in the bathroom and towels you could probably use as a quilt. You can take the bed, I don't have to sleep that much, so I'll take the watch tonight."

"I thought you still needed sleep?" she asked. "I don't want my cyborg bodyguard to be too groggy to bodyguard."

He shrugged, "I'll need to sleep. Eventually. My operational efficacy doesn't start to suffer until about sixty hours awake though."

She nodded in appreciation, "I guess my Dad does do good work, then!" She thought for a moment, "does that mean I'll be able to go a long time without sleep, too?"

Roland smiled, "Not unless your body and organs were built to operate nominally at ten gravities."

"Guess I'm off to bed then!" She saluted and headed into the bathroom, "good night!"

Chapter Eleven

Roland woke Lucia just before dawn the next day. It was a bright summer morning, and the sun rose early. Lucia was still groggy and struggled to wake.

"Come on, Lady." He tried his best drill instructor voice, "Breakfast is ready and we've got a full day ahead of us."

Lucia's brain was a hazy fog of scattered memories and fragmented terror. The smell of bacon gathered the frayed strands of cognition and began to draw them all in the direction of the kitchen. *Bacon*, Lucia thought, *has magical properties.*

She meandered into the dim kitchen and found a plate piled high with a mountain of scrambled eggs and a fortress of bacon stacked like cordwood next to it.

Roland was seated already, drinking an enormous frothy coffee drink that smelled of mocha and digging into what looked like a twelve-egg omelet with cheese and at least three kinds of dead animal.

He gestured to the plate across from him with the ridiculous portion of breakfast on it and said, "Dig in."

The woman gave Roland a look he had seen before. It was a look that told Roland that he was a particular type of simple, yet harmless idiot. She shook her head, "Roland, I couldn't eat that much food in a week, let alone for breakfast."

Roland looked up from his plate and smirked, "Lucia, you ate 1700 calories worth of peanut butter sandwiches in one sitting six hours ago." He gestured to her belly, "Are you still feeling full?"

Lucia saw where he was going with this, "Yeah... I could eat."

"Then eat. Today will be just as tense as yesterday... maybe worse." He shoveled omelet into his mouth, "So eat now. If your turbo-drive kicks in, you're gonna torch through a lot of calories today, and meals may be few and far between." He turned back to his plate, "Trust an old soldier on this: when you have the time and the supplies, eat big. You never know how long till the next meal."

She shrugged and sat down. Her hunger surprised her, and she tore into the food with gusto. In a few short minutes she was most of the way through her eggs and bacon and pouring a third cup of café mocha.

"Don't you have any real coffee?" she asked.

"Nope," the big cyborg shrugged. "Don't like coffee."

She couldn't suppress a chuckle, "Nine hundred pounds of muscles and he can't even drink real coffee! To think I actually respected you!"

"Eat 'em or wear 'em smartass. We'll see if you've still got jokes when we go see Marko."

"Please tell me that we don't have to walk. I feel like I'm going to pop."

"We'll walk to the storage unit and then get you some new clothes. Your outfit might look fine at the office, but where we're going?" He shook his head, "You'll get no respect at all in that."

She swallowed the last bit of mocha, "What's in the storage unit?" Realizing as soon as she asked that she sounded very naïve.

Roland smiled, "It sure as hell ain't boxes of old books, Lady."

She sighed, "Of course not. I don't even know why I asked."

———

The storage unit was full of exactly what Lucia assumed it would be full of: the kind of arsenal that could get a person imprisoned for life in a work camp in the Galapagos system 275 light-years from earth.

It was a regular, unassuming storage unit, about fifteen feet square and eight feet high. It was in the middle of huge storage facility on the outer rim of Dockside, with the Sprawl just to the north, Dockside to the east, and Big Woo to the south and west.

Roland stood in front of the opened storage bay and just looked at it all for a moment. Save for a wide aisle down the middle, the unit was positively crammed with racks of weapons stored in tight but neat bins and on well-ordered shelves. There didn't seem to be two of any given thing, and some of the items were completely foreign to Lucia. While she was not an ex-top-secret-military-cyborg-super-soldier, Lucia had spent plenty of time on the weapons range growing up. Her father's obsession with security had not been limited to martial arts training. She could handle most commercially available firearms and had even spent time with a few beam weapons, despite their egregious illegality.

The stuff in this storage unit, on the other hand, was straight out of a war holo. Some of it, she realized, was of a size to indicate that it had been made specifically for Roland. A few of the rifles had grips and trigger guards meant for his enormous hands. Several of the weapons looked like they weighed a hundred pounds or more, making them crew-served at best... unless you were the kind of guy who could pick up a house, of course. Most of the rest of it just looked like normal, everyday tools of mayhem; in staggering quantity and array.

Lucia had been operating in a cognitive fog since finding her father missing. It felt like part of her brain had been feeding her bits and pieces of reality, in measured doses, so she wouldn't choke on the crushing magnitude of it. But she had noticed that it could also all come crashing in at once in a flood of perceptions and dark ruminations. She could imagine a thousand horrible outcomes in one second, and it terrified her.

Standing with a government-built cyborg staring at a personal arsenal worth a million credits, on her way to meet some underworld capo and uncover who or whatever had kidnapped her father was just about the last bit of it.

Roland had killed Nico Garibaldi, he had probably killed the guy in The Smoking Wreck, and he had almost killed Mook. She was standing next to a killer, and this was his vault of death. She shuddered down to the bottom of her very soul. A wave of fear and despair washed over her as she wondered if she would ever see her father again, or if she'd ever be able to go back to the woman she had been just twenty-four hours before. She might yet see her father, but she already knew the old Lucia was gone forever.

"Let's suit up." The big man said.

Roland opened a cabinet and pulled out a big black army jacket. It was exactly like any other army jacket, made of sturdy materials and with a slew of pockets and pouches in strategic locations. He also grabbed a harness of some kind and slung his arms through the loops.

It settled across his wide shoulders and Lucia realized it was a shoulder holster. For what, she couldn't say, but whatever it was meant to secure, she could tell it was going to be big.

He grabbed a flat black hat with a short brim as well. Settling it on his head and shrugging onto the jacket, he turned to her and said, "Now for you."

"We're heading into Big Woo, so you are going to need a little protection," he said, "here, take this." He tossed her an armored grey under shirt and a set of arm guards.

"You any good with a gun?" he asked absently.

"I'm a good shot, but I've never shot anywhere but the range." She paused, feeling foolish, "I don't know if I could shoot someone, though…" She could feel a thousand little alarms going off in her head as her augmentation processed all the potential scenarios faster than she could control it.

Roland handed her a medium-sized flechette pistol. It was old Czech military model, and Lucia knew it well. It rested comfortably in her palm and she could probably hit a mosquito in the eye at fifteen yards with it.

Roland smiled, "So don't shoot anyone, then. But take this just in case someone starts shooting at you. At least then you will be in a position to reconsider."

She smiled, "Sound policy."

He rummaged through a bin, he took a few minutes, but he finally found what he was looking for and tossed a bundle the size of a basketball to her.

She caught it with fluid grace and opened the black canvas bag. Inside were a pair of black armored gloves with small metal lugs. They were long enough to go to her elbow and protected her entire forearm.

"Put 'em on, "suggested Roland with a shooing gesture, "Straps to fit them are along the inside of the forearm part."

She put them on and adjusted the straps to fit the gauntlets snugly, then she looked at Roland with a quizzical expression. "I know these must be some type of weapon, but other than making my knuckles pointy"— she pointed to the silver knobs over her knuckles—"I'm kind of at a loss here." More alarms were going off in her head. She really wished they would stop.

Roland walked over and took her right hand in his, with his other hand he twisted the first lug on the right glove. There was the audible whine of capacitors charging, but other than that, nothing happened.

Lucia raised her eyebrow at Roland, "Well… that changes everything, I guess."

Roland grunted, and held out his palm, "hit me," he instructed calmly.

"Uh, sure. OK." She cocked her arm and drove a textbook right cross into his palm, just like back in the gym with Rodrigo, her boxing coach growing up. Her fist landed flat and flush, with her elbow in line to drive all of her weight through her first two knuckles in a blow that would have rattled anyone's jaw.

There was a 'pop!' and a hiss when the knuckle lugs contacted Roland's palm and he stated in bland deadpan, "Ow." Smoke wafted in lazy wisps from the big black hand, and the capacitors whined again.

Lucia appraised the gloves closely, then gingerly touched one lug. Nothing happened, and she looked back up at Roland.

"They only discharge when there is a substantial impact. The harder you hit, the harder they zap."

"Taser gloves?" she said, sounding excited, "these are taser gloves?"

"PC-10 series, less-lethal pacification gauntlets," he intoned with forced formality. "The 'PC' stands for 'pain compliance.'"

She nodded, "Taser gloves."

He continued, ignoring her, "A light tap will be painful, a stiff punch will temporarily incapacitate, and your best shot could potentially be fatal. The whole point of these is so you can handle fighting a lot of people without having to swing your hardest."

"Am I going to be fighting a lot of people?" She was a little concerned about how unconcerned he seemed to be with that scenario. The alarms were getting louder and faster. She was having a hard time focusing.

"If you want to help get your Dad back, yeah, probably." He wanted to be reassuring, but honesty was going to be the best policy right now, "you are worth millions on the street to anyone who can bring you in. We know that. What we don't know is exactly who wants to bring you in." He went on, "Even though Dockside is my turf, that's just too much damn money for my reputation to be much of a deterrent." He smirked, "For that kind of cash? Almost anyone would roll the dice on pissing me off for that much. Which means I can't stash you anywhere in Dockside and go handle this on my own."

"So, you have to come with me. This isn't as bad as I thought it would be because you are apparently not some helpless Uptown waif." He tipped his hat to her, "Which is a nice thing because you can actually be useful."

She smiled back, her voice straining through gritted teeth, "I'll do my best not to be a burden. Even if it means fighting people... but until last night, I'd never fought anyone before!"

"Well, you did great considering your disadvantages."

"Wait, disadvantages? Is this a 'man' thing?" She looked annoyed, "I don't feel 'disadvantaged,' pal!" Now she was irritable. The million anxieties in her head were making it hard to think, and he just kept giving her more things to worry about. She wanted to hide from it all; just wanted it all to stop for a second so she could calm down and think.

He sighed, "Yeah. I said 'disadvantages.' There is a reason they built me this big. It's so I can hit and get hit very hard. You? You just aren't heavy or strong enough to bang it out with most of the guys we'll be dealing with." He waved off her objections, "Don't get me wrong, your augmentation means you'll be way ahead of all of them; and your skills are really goddamn impressive, but you still only weigh what, 125 pounds?"

She gave him a stern look, and tried to hide her terror with levity, "A gentleman would never ask."

"Go hang out with one of those, then. I've never been gentle and only 10% of me is man."

"Fair point," she conceded regally, "continue." Might as well get it over with, she figured.

"Yeah, so even though you aren't going to have a lot of trouble getting your hands on the other guy, you are going to have a hard time hurting him without some help." He shrugged in feigned sheepishness, "Sorry. Small people don't hit as hard as big people. Physics is sexist like that."

The big man smiled down at her, and pointed to the gauntlets, "Now, instead of wearing yourself out hitting 'em a hundred times"—he snapped a mock jab that stopped at her nose—"you'll be dropping 'em in one or two shots each." He continued in a more serious tone, "It will allow you to take advantage of your enhanced reflexes and kinesthetics, without having to break your knuckles or wailing on a guy for half an hour to put him down."

He scowled, "Or you can choose not to use them and ruin your hands so you can feel like you beat me in an argument."

"No, no. Gloves are good. I'm convinced," she blurted, then practiced some sharp, snappy combinations in the air. "Now I can hit like you!" she crowed.

"Nobody hits like me," Roland droned, and gestured to the vest and arm guards. "Moving on."

It was a subconscious choice, but he affected the tone he used when lecturing green troops in a hot LZ, "Put that armor on and never take it off. I survive stuff because I have armor. You will survive stuff because you will also have armor. The armor will be hot. The armor will be stiff, the armor will not be attractive or comfortable. None of that fucking matters. You love your armor and your armor loves you. That armor is the only thing you love. Get me?"

Lucia was feeling real terror take over. She often used levity to mask fear, and she had been keeping up gamely with the chirpy dialogue, but the edges of her control were beginning to fray. She started to pull the vest on and immediately felt like it was crushing her. The terrified woman wanted out of it as soon as she felt the weight settle on her shoulders.

All of this armor and weaponry represented a big shift in the tone of her interactions with Roland as well, and she was pretty sure she knew why.

"You aren't feeling great about going to see Marko, are you, Roland?" she asked, tension making her voice quiver.

"I never feel good about going into the Woo," was his terse reply as he deftly adjusted her armor so it sat comfortably and fit in all the correct places. She could tell he had done this many times. The vest was black and made of a stiff-yet-pliable material reinforced with heavier sections of plate at strategic locations. The sleeves were separate pieces, made of more supple substance with more reinforced areas. All of it had to be adjusted to fit, and this took a few minutes. Roland worked silently while Lucia steadily grew more anxious.

"Big Woo is nasty territory. They don't like me there. In Dockside, my reputation and contacts mean I can manipulate the scenario in a lot of different ways. In the Woo? I'm just another big mark, until I prove otherwise. I can do that, and I likely will, but that can get... noisy."

He sniffed, which was an oddly human gesture, "I've avoided trouble with the Army by not being noisy. But in the Woo, with the price on you? I'd be lying if I said I wasn't nervous."

Lucia did not like that. She liked 'confident, hard-ass' Roland, best. In a pinch, 'tactical soldier' Roland would do. But 'nervous' Roland was not a good thing. She began to understand just how precarious her situation was. Just like the previous night on the way to the Hideaway, she thought about all the things that could go wrong and all the potential consequences. Her heart fluttered in her chest, and her throat tightened.

"Roland," she said, and her voice was sounding more agitated, "I don't know... I don't... I feel strange," was all she could articulate.

He looked up from the armor and saw tears streaming down her face, she was breathing fast and shallow, and she looked very pale. "Are you OK? What's wrong?"

"I don't know! I'm just… my heart is racing and I can't breathe!" She was looking very panicked.

"Shit!" the big man spat and guided her to a stool. She sat, her breath ragged and wracked with sobs.

"Lucia! Breathe. Deep breaths. Look at me!" Her eyes, wide with fear locked on him. "You are going to be OK, Lucia." He held her by the shoulders, "It's your neurological upgrades, your brain is getting more stimulus than it's used to, and getting it too fast."

He kept eye contact, "It's OK. There is a way to fix it. It's a little weird, but do you trust me?"

She nodded and sobbed at the same time.

"OK," without warning he stuck his fingers into her armpits and gave her a serious tickle.

Lucia shrieked and squealed in horror, then surprise, and finally laughter. She nearly fell of the stool as he continued the assault, and he caught her and continued to tickle her until her howls of laughter degenerated into gasps and pleading.

"What the… what… aghh… you… stop it! Stop! Stopstopstopstopstop! Ahhhh!"

He stopped and sat her back on the stool, "Feel better?" he asked.

"What the hell are you doing?" She gasped.

"You were having a panic attack because you got stressed and your brain was working too fast."

She slapped him on the arm, hard, "So you violated my armpits?" Lucia was attempting to sound indignant but the act was unconvincing.

Roland wore a crooked smirk, "Laughter dumps endorphins. Endorphins get rid of stress hormones."

"NEXT TIME TELL A JOKE OR SOMETHING!" She yelled, but there was no actual anger. The whole scenario was just too ridiculous.

He grabbed her a bottle of water from a crate. It was warm and tasted slightly of dust, but she swigged from it in grateful relief, anyway. "Sometimes that happens with neuro augmentations. You end up processing information and stimulus so quickly your frontal cortex gets overwhelmed. When that occurs your amygdala can dump you into panic mode. Troops call it 'Condition Black.'"

He turned away and went back to the crates, "The trick," he said, "is to recognize it when it's happening and try to stay ahead of it."

"And when you can't get ahead of it?"

"Have someone tickle you."

"What if I wasn't ticklish?" she asked, "What was your plan then?"

"Strip tease." He said with no trace of emotion whatsoever.

Lucia howled with laughter again, "I don't think I could have handled that!" The thought of the big serious cyborg doing something so preposterous was just about the funniest thing she could have imagined. She laughed some more. It felt great.

"Yeah, well, that's sort of the reaction I was hoping for. I'm just really glad you're ticklish." He smiled, "My dignity can only handle so much, y'know."

Chapter Twelve

After a quick stop at a military surplus store to get Lucia equipped with some more appropriate clothing, the mismatched pair were off on their way to the Big Woo.

Lucia was sporting a much more tactical-practical look. Her fashionable business attire was replaced with sturdy grey fatigues with barely concealed leg armor underneath. Her armored vest was mostly concealed under a plain black long-sleeved shirt. It stretched a little too tight across the vest and was not likely to fool anyone who looked very closely. But the casual observer was probably not going to think there was anything underneath her shirt other than a well-endowed woman.

Roland had insisted that the armor was the best that could be obtained without going for a full 'set of plates,' and knowing she was now resistant to most forms of small arms fire did much to alleviate her anxiety. It made the discomfort of the extra layers more bearable.

She had to laugh at the sight of herself when she saw her reflection in the mirror though. The black boots, too-tight armored shirt and reinforced black fatigues, when equipped with her flechette pistol in a thigh holster, all made for a very interesting fashion statement. When she added the high-tech gauntlets, her outfit was downright cartoonish in its aggressiveness. Lucia kind of liked the look. *I look like a total bad-ass*, she smiled to herself, *just needs a cape...*

She had made the mistake of asking why they would bother with concealing the armor, and his tactless answer of, "Because we want the bad guys to aim for your chest, where the armor is. If they see it, they'll aim for your head," nearly triggered another panic attack. Fortunately, no tickling ended up being necessary.

Lucia had found that understanding what was going on in her head helped her to deal with it. With her mind processing and evaluating stimuli at many times the normal rate, a thousand niggling anxieties could gnaw at her all at once. It took very little to get that particular process started, and if she wasn't careful, it would cascade into a full-blown panic attack.

Knowing this, she could at least force herself to calm down when she felt it starting. It wasn't easy, and she knew she was going to need a lot of practice, but she felt confident she could beat this problem. Lucia was not a fan of the tickling.

Roland on the other hand, looked like Roland always looked: big and blocky. He wore the same black fatigues with the same black boots he always did. He wore the same black shirt he always wore. His hat was the same hat. Lucia mused that he must have bought out the store when he found things in his size. She pictured endless storage boxes filled with boring black army surplus clothing in size XXXXL in his closet. She made a mental note to take him shopping if any of them managed to survive this.

His old army coat covered his shoulder holster, which was now home to the largest handgun Lucia had ever seen. Lucia knew her way around guns better than most, and the monstrosity under his left armpit was like nothing she had ever seen.

Roland had built his own gun because that was the kind of guy he was. He wasn't so big that he couldn't use standard weapons, but they never fit his hand right. Why should he settle for a mundane weapon when he was built for so much more?

Roland, being an unapologetic gun-nut and a fair hand in the machine shop, decided to correct this misalignment of factors himself. Thus, 'Durendal' had been born. Roland had to explain to the illiterate philistines in his squad that Durendal was the name of the magic sword carried by Charlemagne's greatest warrior, also named Roland. Tankowicz thought it was very clever, but the squad had thought he was just a giant armored nerd.

The name stuck, and this Roland now had his own version of Durendal. Of course, this iteration was not a sword at all, but an eleven-pound, fifty-caliber electronically-triggered machine pistol. It sported a forty-round, fully indexed and modular magazine. The box mag contained four slots, with ten rounds allocated to each one. The individual slots could each hold a different ammunition type, and the weapon's selector switch was programmed to load from the corresponding index.

Roland chose his usual loadout, which was ten rounds of high-velocity armor-piercing flechette, ten rounds of anti-materiel high-explosive, and twenty rounds of hyper-velocity anti-personnel bead. The main difference between his beads and a regular load being that his beads were in .50 caliber, not 5mm. They were only good for about half the speed, but the mass and diameter made them devastating to both flesh and machinery alike.

The magazine itself was detachable, but individual slots could be reloaded from the bottom without dropping the whole mag. So instead of extra magazines, he carried four stripper-clips for each of the payloads in his various pouches and pockets. This allowed him to recharge individual indexes without having to swap in new magazines. Now, if he ran out of anti-personnel bead first, he didn't have to abandon all the other payloads when it came time to reload.

That was a lot of ammunition for a stroll through the Woo, even with Roland's overly pessimistic outlook on life. But Roland found that carrying two hundred rounds of ammunition was pretty easy when you were his size, and his personal philosophy was 'you can never have too much ammo.'

They pinged for an Aero Car and waited for one to respond that looked like it could handle Roland's thousand or so pounds. The fourth one to respond was an older cargo model, and Roland estimated that it wasn't likely to crash under his weight. Fuel surcharges were going to be painful though. This was the sort of thing Roland had become accustomed to, and he boarded with a sigh.

The car lifted off with a strained wobble and quickly entered the traffic pattern that exited Dockside and arced westward towards Big Woo.

Big Woo, or as it was more commonly known, "the Woo," was a dilapidated old section of post-industrial slums about forty miles outside of uptown. It wasn't officially part of the New Boston megalopolis, and as such had its own rules and regulations. The sanctioned town government was ostensibly a group of selectmen that each borough elected, but multiple successive generations of graft and corruption had twisted the lofty democratic ideals of the town charter beyond recognition.

What remained was a confederation of greedy middle managers in the indirect employ of various oligarchs and criminal masterminds. These were elected and re-elected based upon the machinations of these clandestine players, and the city languished in destitution as a result.

This could continue, election cycle after election cycle, for one simple reason: No one else wanted the Woo. It was so poor it made Dockside look like Uptown. The place was one thin, insubstantial degree above a refugee camp, and nobody with a whit of sense wanted to be responsible for it. It was a haven for drug-labs, sex-slavers, mercenaries and tin-pot dictators. There was no law in the Woo, and no one who lived there wanted any. Roland found it entirely distasteful. Dockside he understood. It was a working-class area for the rougher class; not very clean or very nice, but people stayed out of each other's way and there was a sense of respect and community. In the Woo, the rules were different: intimidate or be intimidated, take or be taken, kill or be killed. It was a bad place filled with bad people and civilized folk stayed well clear of it.

Roland meditated on this while the car entered the landing pattern over Front Street, by what had once been the town green. After the second global hegemony collapsed, the fighting in this area had levelled what had once been a promising pre-industrial hub of burgeoning enterprises. Two hundred years later, and the area had never really recovered. Towering steel buildings had been replaced with squat, brown commercial spaces devoid of character. These, in turn, were overrun by the various gangs and militias that had made the Woo their home. But they all served their purposes, he supposed. Being abandoned by subsequent governments for successive generations had led to the current state of Big Woo, and no one was interested in correcting that, anymore. What law there was in the Woo was theirs, and it was only marginally better than no law at all. It was a very insubstantial margin though, even under the most optimistic analysis.

His musings were interrupted by the arrival chime, and they landed at what was still called "the Green" by locals, and disembarked. As predicted, the fuel surcharge was asinine, but Roland paid it with little thought. Being in the Woo meant being alert at all times. He could gripe about the bill later.

The Green was just a wide-open series of rust-brown landing platforms adjacent to a mass-travel station with commuter trams and local ride-sharing facilities. Vendors of various goods and services lined the edges of the square, which was a quarter-mile per side and filled with Aero Cars, ground transport, and hundreds of the disheveled denizens of the Woo milling about in a perpetual daze of narcotics and depression. The air reeked of burning fossil fuels, a thousand varieties of food, and the unfiltered stink of the unwashed masses. Roland's stature, and Lucia's obvious good breeding were an oddity, and they attracted some unwanted scrutiny as they attempted to find their bearings.

Lucia was trying to stay ahead of the anxieties her hyperactive brain was downloading to her amygdala. Namely because she suspected this would be a supremely bad place to have a panic attack. *I really can't afford to lose my shit right now,* she thought to herself, *Go slow. Breathe in for four, breathe out for four....*

She looked to Roland for some reassurance and saw his face set in a grim mask of stoic irritation. That was less encouraging than she wanted, but she took solace in his indestructibility and to a lesser extent, her own body armor. *I will be fine,* she thought, *I will be fine and Dad will be fine.* She wasn't sure if she really believed that, but she intended to repeat it as often as necessary.

Roland was busy attempting to orient on all possible threats, while simultaneously figuring out the best way to approach Marko. He had to assume that all the nastier elements of the Big Woo crime networks as well as all the other groups of opportunistic criminals in this side of the planet would be after Lucia by now. It would be no secret that she was travelling with him, either. The best thing to do under these circumstances was to keep moving. That may have seemed counterintuitive, but the kind of firepower that could take down Roland would not be easy to move around. Taking Roland on the move meant using weapons that could be smuggled around town easily, and that meant weapons that were unlikely to be a threat to him. If they holed up in any given spot for too long that would give their opposition time to move more people and heavier weapons into position.

Roland intended to play on the general ignorance of potential pursuers as to his specific capabilities. Amateur thugs and professional bagmen alike would be operating under the impression that Roland was just a hired bodyguard; another professional goon no different from thousands of other hired goons used by rich people the galaxy over. He would perpetuate that myth for as long as he could get away with it. He figured he had thirty-six more hours of that misconception. Roland was too old and too experienced to pretend that he wouldn't have to flex his muscles to the extent that the 'hired goon' cover would stop working. Sooner or later word would get out that he was different. Then things would get much harder. The trick was to cover as much ground, and pick up as much intel as he could before it became general knowledge he was a super-cyborg and that the regular methods of all-purpose downtown thuggery would not be effective. Once that word got out, the exotic weapons and serious professionals would start to show up and make his job that much harder.

The Woo was a good place to be right now, the big cyborg conceded to himself. Even though it was a wretched hive of scum and villainy, it did not boast the highest-paid nor the most professional criminal class in the New Boston Megalopolis. Roland was confident that no one in the Woo besides perhaps Marko himself had enough horsepower to give him trouble in a straight fight.

On the other hand, Roland was forced to concede that what the Woo lacked in quality, it made up for in quantity. Furthermore, Lucia was not as invulnerable as he was. He made a mental note to adjust his thinking on that front and focus more on getting Lucia in and out of there in one piece, and less on his own invulnerability.

At the edge of the Green, Roland pulled Lucia into an alcove between two street vendors. Both were selling some vague meat-on-a-stick item, and despite her growing hunger, the smell of it was enough to put her off her feed for a while yet.

"We need to get ground transportation. The streets are too crowded right now," He fiddled with his comm.

Lucia looked around, "Isn't that a good thing? Don't we want to be around lots of witnesses?"

Roland shook his head, "There are no witnesses in the Woo"— he resumed pushing buttons—"and the crowd hides possible tails and hunters." He put the comm away, "We'll wait here for a ground transport. You hungry?"

She wrinkled her nose in disgust, "I think I'll pass."

"Suit yourself." Roland sidled over to the bedraggled vendor and ordered four skewers of indecipherable street-meat. When he returned to the alcove, the ground transport was just pulling up. It was an older model, but it looked big enough to handle his weight in the large, boxlike cargo area it sported. The heavy, solid tires looked to be a good sign as well. He made a quick scan of the street before he signaled to Lucia, and that's when he saw the two men in the darkened doorway of an old brown office building across the street. The sun was still high, so the shadow from the alcove hid most of their features, but Roland glimpsed the smooth curves of pistol butts and the blocky silhouettes of cheap armor under ratty long coats.

These might have been regular, uninteresting street muscle. It was common enough for local gangs to patrol prime territory like the Green, but this didn't feel right. They never took their eyes off of Roland, and as soon as Lucia came out from between the stalls, they moved from the doorway with strides designed to appear nonchalant, but transparently purposeful. Roland tensed; he knew he had less than ten seconds to decide about what to do.

He quickly scanned the rest of the street to assess the situation. It was a wide thoroughfare coming off the Green and heading out toward the bustling north side of the Woo. Both sides of the street were lined with old brown office buildings built to the same bland specifications. Graffiti and gang identifiers covered the first-story walls, and various vendors occupied dirty ramshackle booths that encroached onto the muddy street. People were everywhere. Hundreds of dusty, stooped residents of Big Woo meandered up and down the road. In that thronged mass, spotting potential trouble turned out to be remarkably easy. Roland picked out two more men stalking their way, distinguished by the mismatched bulk of their poorly concealed armor and their intense, focused attention.

Roland quickly shoved Lucia into the cargo bay of the transport and hopped inside after her.

"GO!" He yelled to the driver, and banged his oversized fist on the roof for emphasis, "Go Go GO!"

The driver, took one look at his passengers, then immediately opened the door and dived out of the truck. He hit the ground in an ungainly heap of malnourished limbs and scrambled to his feet. Once upright, the terrified man tore off down the street at his top speed and never looked back.

"Shit." Roland's voice rumbled, and he guided Lucia out of the truck with one hand on the back of her neck, "Keep your head down!" he instructed as he quickly ushered her down the street from the vehicle.

Chapter Thirteen

"What's going on?" Lucia asked, terror in her voice.

"Someone's onto us. We gotta move," was his curt response. He cast a glance over his shoulder as he muscled his way through the crowd. The four men had converged on the truck and were now moving with determined yet unhurried strides towards the fleeing pair as a group. Roland noted they were not moving in any discernably tactical manner, and nothing about them seemed to indicate formal training or military experience. They were moving like professional criminals, and not like professional soldiers. Roland breathed a sigh of relief. These were not high-level mercs at least. It was a small a comfort at best, but it was a comfort. Teams of Big Woo enforcers were their own special kind of trouble, and not a thing to be taken lightly, but they were nothing like the things Roland had seen off-world.

Roland took a moment to curse the capricious nature of the universe, and its apparent vendetta against him. The lengthy string of invective accomplished nothing material, but it made him feel better, at least.

He turned his attention back to the problem at hand. Roland very much wanted to escape the pursuers, but not because he feared them. There was just a real tactical advantage to *not* killing a bunch of gang muscle in the heart of unfamiliar territory. Doing so could end up pissing off any number of nefarious criminal organizations. If he did not handle this with care, he would add the unwelcome drama of a mob vendetta to the top of his current stack of issues. Petty criminals they may be, but respect was as big a deal in the Woo as it was in Dockside. Guys who may be otherwise inclined to leave him alone would die trying to avenge the insult to their bosses if Roland blithely chose to start stomping heads on a busy street.

Roland was trying very hard to avoid that exposure. The part of his mind that understood the nature of his scenario knew he was probably being naïve, but he would have to make the attempt. Minimizing potential carnage was not his style, but considering how Marko was likely to receive him under even the friendliest circumstances, discretion would be warranted. Though he suspected it was a forlorn hope, he intended to at least try to avoid having a running gun battle all the way to Marko's door.

He kept his body between their pursuers and Lucia as he hustled her through the crowds and down the street. The big cyborg was acutely aware of the fact that there was simply no feasible way to lose the tail in this crowd. He was a foot and a half taller than any of them, and Lucia was far too pretty and healthy to blend in with the disheveled mess of the rest of the population, even if she wasn't dressed like she was a spec-ops contractor. As they maneuvered down the crowded street, their pursuers stayed with them for the first two blocks, neither closing the distance nor falling behind. Worse, Roland noticed, they had picked up another two hunters along the way.

Roland really wished that he knew the lay of the land better, both physically and politically. If these were transient opportunists out for the bounty on Lucia, he could probably drop them without repercussions. That would be the best-possible scenario, but the only luck Roland trusted was bad luck, so he couldn't count on that. They were all dressed alike, which indicated a group affiliation. But he didn't know if it was a local gang or an out-of-town group. They weren't off-world mercs, the armor was too cheap and their behavior was that of experienced criminals, not trained paramilitary. That meant they were probably local boys of one stripe or another.

He picked a side street at random and ducked down it with Lucia in tow. It was less crowded, and much narrower. The street ran between two of the ubiquitous brown commercial buildings and dumped them into an open parking lot where assorted riffraff was congregating in hunched clumps around ground vehicles with open cargo containers. Roland swore vehemently.

Roland, in his supreme strategic wisdom, had stumbled into an impromptu narcotics market. These cropped up all over the Woo regularly. Mobility was a key element for long-term survival in the Big Woo drug game. Setting up a permanent shop stocked with money and product in the Woo invited far too much opportunistic raiding, so the gangs rolled in armed convoys and used multiple locations to peddle their wares.

Roland couldn't be sure if this development was a good thing or a bad thing. If the group tracking them was not part of the gang running this operation, they may not want to risk showing up here in force. That would be a good thing. If the money offered for Lucia was a known quantity, they may not care. That would be a bad thing. A quick scan of the lot set Roland's jaw in a grim line. There were no real exits to the lot other than a couple of very narrow alleyways and doorways into the buildings that framed the asphalt square.

Every eye in the square was on them as they strode from the between the buildings, and Roland made the spur-of-the-moment decision to just keep walking through as if he knew exactly what he was doing and where he was going. No one bought it.

A head wearing an explosively unkempt mane of red hair and a scraggly beard popped up above the roof of an old electric ground vehicle. The head had squinty black eyes and a thin long nose perched above narrow, pale lips. The skin was tan and leathery, and the jaw worked in a tight, wordless chewing rhythm. Roland pegged this guy for the gang leader right away. There was an easy confidence to his demeanor that only the top dog in this particular yard could have. The head turned and spat a stream of sticky green plant juice in a languid rope that struck the ground with an audible splat. He wiped his mouth on the sleeve of his shabby grey jacket before looking back and drawling laconically, "You folks lost?"

Roland's voice took on the subterranean bass he liked to use when dealing with potential hostiles, "Just walking though, man. Be gone in a couple seconds."

At that moment, their six pursuers turned into the lot and paused. Avarice and indecision waged open war in their minds as they sized up the new strategic landscape. Roland felt a twinge of hope as he watched their faces twist in soundless indecision. A local group would know the protocol for approaching this situation without causing a severe problem. It was becoming increasingly obvious that this posse of hunters was rather indecisive on how to proceed. They wanted their bounty, but they were outnumbered five-to-one in that lot. Dead men spend no creds, it was the first rule of The Woo and everyone respected it.

To Roland's supreme relief, this indecision pegged the hunters as non-local interlopers. It was the first bit of good luck he had enjoyed in weeks. This pleased Roland as it meant that just killing them all was not likely to piss off a local gang at all. It might even endear the local factions to him. This new intelligence opened a whole world of tactical options; mainly because it allowed for engaging in precisely the style of violent problem-solving Roland was built to do.

Red Head glanced over at the new arrivals. He took in their long brown coats and the undisguised weapons strapped to their hips and thighs. He looked at the seven-and-half foot monster in front of him, and then took in the armored girl as well. Nothing in his many years navigating the Big Woo gang scene had really prepared him for the situation he now found himself in. Red Head knew, deep inside his soul, that despite an otherwise unremarkable start, today was going to end up being a positively shitty day unless he turned it around.

"Well, well, well." His eyes narrowed, "Party crashers." He had been born and raised in the Woo, and while this scene was certainly very strange, he had seen more than one bounty hunt come through in his day. He looked at Roland, "Runner or running?"

"Running," Roland responded, watching as the hunters paused to engage in furtive to conference amongst themselves.

"How much you worth?" Red Head asked.

"Does it matter?" The big man evaded the question.

"Always, big boy. Always." Red Head was not stupid. A good leader made decisions based on having the correct facts and knowing all the facets of a conflict. Red Head was a good leader, thanks to almost four decades of Big Woo survival. The school of hard knocks was as good a teacher as any military academy if you could survive the curriculum.

Roland, for his part, was about done playing Big Woo gang games. He decided that the drug gang would be more reasonable than the bounty hunters, so he made a bold play, "It's not enough to die over."

As fast as he could (which was mighty quick, indeed) Roland whipped his army jacket back and snapped Durendal from its holster. He let the muzzle linger over Red Head's nose for a split second, watched the man's eyes just start to widen, then whirled and stroked the trigger twice, putting two flechettes through the lead hunter's chest.

Armor-piercing tungsten shafts burned through the coat, chest plate, torso, and finally the back plate of the unfortunate man. Both projectiles exited the body and buried themselves deep into the hunter standing behind the now-expiring recipient. The man in front collapsed, leaking blood and smoke from the two neat half-inch diameter tunnels that now occupied his thoracic region. Behind him, the other hunter sat down hard and coughed frothy blood down the front of his shirt.

In an instant, the four remaining pursuers scattered and drew weapons. The junkies looking for their next fix scurried to the edges of the lot and disappeared like cockroaches into the exits and shadows to avoid the impending firestorm. There was a depressing facility to how they accomplished this. It was obviously a technique oft-practiced for them. It also was an effective survival tactic as the parking lot then erupted in gunfire.

A dozen different weapons spat various forms of mayhem in as many directions. Roland grabbed Lucia and covered her head as he ran to the far side of the lot. The drug dealers were pouring fire into the hunters, confirming Roland's suspicion that the turf incursion was a more pressing concern to them than the potential windfall of a bounty. The hunters, having body armor and better weapons, had weathered the return fire with little difficulty and hunkered down in the alley, sending sporadic gunfire back at the gang.

Roland frowned and flung Lucia into an alcove by a doorway. Something wasn't right, "Stay here!" he growled, and headed back into the fray. He found Red Head behind a car, laying down suppressing fire with an ancient sub-machine gun. It barked fire and smoke while spewing spent casings onto the dirty asphalt like brass raindrops. Down by the alley, his bullets sprayed concrete chunks and ricochets into the hunched hunters. Red Head was a decent shot, Roland admitted to himself, but the armor under those coats was laughing at the assault.

He dropped an enormous hand on Red Head's shoulder, and the man turned in startled terror, bringing the subgun to bear on Roland only to find it swatted away like a toy.

"Why are they still here?" Roland asked over the din, "Why are they staying?" They should have left. No amount of money was worth getting gunned down in a parking lot. While the bounty hunters held the equipment advantage, they would soon get overrun on numbers alone. There had to be thirty drug dealers hammering them right now. It made no sense.

Red head slapped a fresh magazine into his weapon and snarled, "You tell me, Big Man! They either want you bad enough to die for it, or they are expecting... Oh shit!"

Roland figured it out at the same time he did: reinforcements. Gang skirmishes in the Woo were often brief affairs, consisting of sporadic exchanges of gunfire between two groups. With both courage and ammunition in short supply, both sides were often quick to retreat. As rare as a prolonged shootout in Big Woo was, thugs getting reinforced in the middle of one was unheard of.

"You in some serious shit, Big Man!" Red Head spat, and put more fire into the alley as another dozen hunters pushed into the alleyway. The return fire increased in intensity, and Red Head had to dive below the car as something big and fully automatic hammered their position. Screaming metal and a shower of sparks pinged off of a nonplussed Roland.

Roland looked back at Red Head, "I'll get their heads down. Have your men pull back to that corner and conserve ammunition. I'll arrange for cover." He grabbed Red Head by the shirt and spoke very clearly, "Keep your fire on that alley, but don't spray. Conserve ammo! Move in twos and cover that alcove!" He indicated where Lucia was hiding.

Red head gave him a sideways look, "You better not be fucking with us!"

Roland did not bother to acknowledge this, but turned and yelled, "GO!" Red Head tore off and began shouting commands to his men.

Roland switched to explosive rounds and worked gunfire into the building walls marking the edges of the entrance to the parking lot. He had no good angle for direct hits, but great gouts of flame, smoke and concrete shrapnel tore into the hunters as the mini-grenades tore massive holes in the masonry. They scattered like crows and scrambled back towards the main street as Roland squeezed off his last two HE rounds and switched back to flechette. No viable targets presented themselves, but two more hunters lay unmoving in the alley; Roland smiled. High-explosive ammo was a perennial favorite of his when dealing with massed opposition.

He used the resulting twenty-second reprieve to shove the cars over to the corner where the drug gang was regrouping. Moving a forty-one-hundred-pound car presented very little challenge for Roland, and it was short work to heave them over into position. He felt the first hostile rounds hit his back just as he settled the fourth car on its side, blocking the protected alcove and making a defensive bulwark for the gang to shoot from.

Judging by the dull, bruising thump he felt in his spine, he figured that the hits were standard anti-personnel rounds, and they did little more than punch holes into his jacket. He had a dozen more of these jackets in storage, so this was not particularly catastrophic. He fell back to check on Lucia and the drug dealers. Lucia was still in her alcove, doing yeoman's work controlling her mounting anxiety. Her face looked drawn and tight, and her hand clutched the butt of her gun, still in its holster, with a fevered intensity.

Roland had worked with green recruits on many occasions, and they didn't all have the stomach for combat. That was just the nature of the beast, and he held it against no one. But at the very least, those guys had volunteered for it. Lucia was not a soldier, she was a victim, and all of this had to be incredibly overwhelming.

It bothered Roland on a fundamental level that she was even here at all. Combat was Roland's profession, and he had chosen it. This was where he belonged. She did not belong here, and that angered him.

In spite of her fear, the woman was stubbornly refusing to crumple. He admired that gravel in her guts. He had seen enough panicking troops to know when someone was swallowing their fear with willpower alone, and Lucia was nothing if not willful. Roland smiled to himself, *she'd have made a good soldier*, he thought.

Turning back to the battle, he found to his pleasure the drug dealers were holding up well. A few were panicking and useless, a few more were wasting ammo by spraying careless fire at the opening where the hunters were regrouping. At least half had posted up in good shooting posture and were sending controlled bursts downrange though. Roland attributed this to Red Head's incessant berating and constant barking of instructions. There was little danger of being overrun at this juncture, so Roland could finally shift his focus to offense.

He slapped a strip of HE into the empty section of his magazine and flipped the selector over to anti-personnel beads. Smiling ever-so-slightly, he then slid it forward into the 'full-auto' setting. It was time to wake the neighbors.

Chapter Fourteen

Roger Dawkins woke up.

Which was a surprise, even for him. A quick inventory of his recent memories revealed no indications that waking up had been a foregone conclusion. He clearly remembered getting pancaked by a big-ass cyborg in a shitty bar, and he remembered how annoying that had been. He remembered being severely injured, and he remembered that in his line of work, losing a fight often meant dying. Roger had lost that fight and yet he was not dead. Today was looking up.

As consciousness returned, he became aware of a few more things. First, he was in a staggering quantity of pain. When he considered the severity of his injuries from the fight, he determined that this was appropriate. While he was not overly thrilled with the level of discomfort and the apparent lack of pain medication he had been given, it was at least a good indicator that that he would remain not-dead for a while yet.

Roger thought he might be in a hospital, or at least a place that looked, sounded and smelled like one. The walls were the same antiseptic white that hospitals liked to use; the ceiling was faceless, featureless white as well.

The air stank of isopropyl alcohol and sodium hypochlorite, like it would in a hospital, so the evidence continued to support that conclusion. Several things were beeping and hissing next to his bed, which was equipped with the standard-issue lumpy mattress and thin, scratchy blankets. He decided that he was definitely probably in a hospital.

He was certain his spine had been shattered in the fight, which meant he had not walked out of that bar on his own. That was curious. Roger was very heavy, and the guy who had nearly beaten him to death had spared none of the androids. When this sort of thing happened, it was usually his androids that got him to the body shop after a job went to this level of bad. But the 'bots had not been in any shape to do this, last he saw them.

Roger made a mental note to figure out what the hell was up with that big sonofabitch. There was a debt owed on that score, and Roger expected to settle it in due course. First, he needed to figure out how to not get his bones shattered in the process though. Roger did not consider himself a stupid man. He did not waste time or energy denying that the huge bastard in that bar outclassed him by several orders of magnitude. That situation was rare enough for Roger that he had forgotten it was even possible. Now his body radiated painful testimony to that very fact.

It had been a timely reminder that no matter how bad you thought you were, there was always somebody badder. Roger liked it when he was the baddest guy in the room, and the current situation hurt both his professional and personal pride. He intended to correct that.

Ruminations on vengeance notwithstanding, Roger decided it was time to try moving. His not residing in a body shop, coupled with the fact that he was not strapped down with vanadium manacles meant that whoever had brought him to this place either did not know about his augmentations, or did not care. The former scenario meant that he needed to get out before that changed and he got shipped off to the penal colony on Titan. The latter meant that whoever had absconded with him was seriously bad news. Both scenarios were cause for some concern, and Roger would rather deal with either from a more advantageous position than flat on his back.

Then Roger's body reiterated the nature of his predicament: namely that he was in a metric fuck-ton of pain and his legs didn't work. His attempt to rise accomplished little more than tearing a gasp of agony from his own lungs and a pathetic wiggle of the bed.

It seemed there may be a third reason he wasn't strapped down. Roger was a goddamned cripple and cripples need not be restrained. His irritation increased with exponential vigor as other factors began to align in his beleaguered mind. Cripples did not make a whole lot of money in the planetary muscle game. He had clients who paid top dollar for a high-tech superhuman problem-solver. His current situation precluded him from receiving said top dollars.

The injured man knew that he needed to get a message to one of his regular body shops soon if he wanted to keep those contracts. He was certain his guy in Africa could regrow the spine, but it would probably take a year. Roger did some mental arithmetic and was relieved to realize that his savings could handle a year off if they had to. That was irrelevant if he got shipped to Titan though.

A voice, wafting in from the doorway to his right, admonished him, "Try to hold still, Mr. Dawkins. Your injuries are quite severe and you will only hurt yourself further if you try to move." It was the dry, toneless baritone of a doctor who had repeated the same instructions to patients too stupid to know better a thousand times. Roger looked over. The man stood back-lit by bright lights from the hallway, and Roger could see that he was a small, stoop-shouldered balding man in a white coat. He held a DataPad in his left hand and was making assorted notes on it.

"Your spinal cord has severed and you have multiple fractures in your hand and foot. You have also sustained a rather severe concussion," the doctor droned. It was an unnecessary monologue. Roger needed no help to determine the extent of his injuries. His proprioception was enhanced to the extent he could count the hairs on his arms just by feeling them move in a breeze. Just trying to move had provided him with enough sensory feedback to tell exactly how many pieces his lumbar vertebrae had broken into - seventeen.

"Where am I?" he said with an internal wince at the cliché.

"You are dead, Mr. Dawkins," the doctor said, without looking up from the DataPad. "And this is where you get reincarnated, if you so choose."

If the doctor expected him to be shocked or impressed by the melodramatic proclamation, Roger did not oblige. The doctor was obviously not accustomed to working with an element like Roger Dawkins, who had been high-paid hired muscle for the better part of twenty years at this point.

This situation was not particularly uncommon in his line of work. Roger's 'death' had been faked twice before, and likely would be again. It was just good policy: Roger had skills and talent, so when he sustained severe injuries (it happened from time to time) his employers would often let him 'die' to avoid any of the legal hassles augmented employees could cause.

Roger had arrangements with several underground body shops set up to put him back together when this happened. Someone would pick up his body from the scene or perhaps the hospital, and swap it with another. He would 'die' taking all his criminal history with him and then get rebuilt as someone new. He would typically get a new face, and maybe just a few more enhancements than the last time if he could afford them. After a brief vacation and recovery period, he'd get simply back out there and get back to work.

So, Roger did not react with shock or disbelief, as the doctor was obviously more accustomed to seeing. He simply asked, "Which outfit are you with?" Roger was acutely aware of several potentially lethal conflicts of interest. If he was in the wrong guy's facility, it could cause a real cluster-fuck with some of his clients. It bothered Roger that he did not recognize this place or this doctor; a doctor who obviously did not work with men of Roger's profession on a regular basis.

As he looked around, Roger found his irritation being replaced with concern. This was different. He was not in a typical underworld body shop. His room was too clean, the equipment too nice. The doctor was not up to speed on men in Roger's line of work. Something was different here, and not necessarily in a good way.

The disparity with his normal procedures became all the more apparent when the doctor replied with, "Outfit? This is a Corpus Mundi research facility. Are you still feeling disoriented?" His pudgy face tilted downward to peer over the bridge of a lumpy nose, concern marring the otherwise paternal gaze.

Roger couldn't decide if this answer was terrifying or hilarious.

"Corpus Mundi, huh?" He chuckled, "Well, I guess that answers my question!"

At that moment, there was a commotion in the hallway behind the doctor, and a portly man with thick silver hair wearing an expensive black silk suit pushed into the room.

The man, whose florid skin reflected consternation with the situation, turned to the doctor and spoke in a tone that indicated a person accustomed to being obeyed.

"Johnson! You were to notify me immediately once he woke up!"

The doctor, nonplussed, responded with dry economy, "He is my patient, Mr. Fox, and I will treat him as I see fit. You would have been notified as soon as I determined he was sufficiently recovered to have a conversation with you. That has always been our protocol, here."

"You know damn well that this case is special, Johnson. And you don't get to play high-and-mighty doctor with me." Mr. Fox grabbed the DataPad from the doctor and roughly shoved him toward the door, "You can go now, *doctor*." He sneered the last word, and it oozed with sarcasm. Johnson left the room with his face wound in a tight snarl and his gait stiff with irritation.

Mr. Fox turned to the now-grinning Roger Dawkins, and spoke with the enthusiasm of an accomplished salesman, "Mr. Dawkins! Terribly sorry you had to witness that! Sometimes our various departments rub each other the wrong way. You know how it goes. All one big family, here, I assure you!"

Roger was beaming, "Corpus Mundi, huh? To what do I owe the pleasure?"

Fox scowled, "Well, yes. Doctor Johnson there may have dropped that bit of information just the tiniest bit prematurely." He sighed, "But yes, I would like to welcome you to the Corpus Mundi family, Mr. Dawkins. If you are amenable, of course. I am Mr. Fox."

Corpus Mundi, with the not-ominous-at-all motto of "One World, One Body" was an enormous corporation. From humble beginnings as a pharmaceutical and medical supply company, it had branched off into virtually every aspect of human development and technology. Their holdings rivaled in size the economies of several medium-sized countries. As a single body, the Corpus Mundi board of directors wielded more personal and political power than any other group save Gateways, Inc. and the Planetary Council itself.

Roger had experience here; he had worked for the company in the past. He supposed it would be more accurate to say he had worked for any number of smaller corporations owned and operated as subsidiaries by Corpus Mundi. But if one was to be completely honest, Roger had worked for criminal organizations backed and sponsored by these Corpus Mundi proxy companies.

Roger felt like that still counted as experience since he had been on a Corpus Mundi job when he wandered into The Smoking Wreck. Like any meandering galactic business interest, Corpus Mundi had operatives and operations that wandered all over the spectrum of legality and morality. Roger had no illusions about corporate ethics; it was all just business to the Board, and it was all just business to Roger Dawkins. That was just good business.

It was a quick and easy leap of logic to draw the obvious conclusion about this meeting. Finding himself at an actual, legitimate Corpus Mundi research facility could mean only one thing: Roger had just been promoted to the major leagues. All his hard work and attention to detail were finally paying off. This was his access to the kind of money and prestige that turned talented pros (like himself) into real bosses. This was turning into a truly great day.

With a herculean effort, he curbed his excitement. Roger knew his business, and this business was the careful choreography of competing self-interests and common enemies. It would be a complicated dance, and there was no mistaking who his partner in the ensuing waltz would be.

He remembered the words of his father, a minor capo in a medium-sized crime family from the Sprawl, "You can dance with the devil if you want to, kid. Make sure you enjoy the money and the fun while it lasts though. Sooner or later, the bastard is going to want to lead."

Roger was not sure what a corporate giant like Corpus Mundi would want from him, but his individual skill set was quite specific. He figured that he was not here because they felt sorry for him. If he wanted to dance with this devil, he had better be prepared to follow when the time came.

He turned his attention back to Mr. Fox, "I am a businessman, first, Mr. Fox. Corpus Mundi business seems like good business to me, and I am always amenable to working with good business partners."

Fox smirked at the exaggerated politeness, "We have always valued your contributions to our subsidiaries, and we find that you may be the right candidate for a special new initiative." Fox sat down on a plastic chair next to Roger's bed, "We would like to hire you, full-time."

Roger indicated his broken body, "Can I assume your health care plan is first-rate?"

"Oh, Mr. Dawkins." Fox's eyes sparkled, "It's so much better than that!"

Roger smiled back, "I bet it is." He chose his next words with practiced care, "What is the, uh…" he fumbled, "… position?"

Fox's smile never wavered, "What if I told you we wanted you to finish the job you were doing when we found you?"

"I'd tell you that there is a very big obstacle to concluding that piece of business."

"Yes," Fox agreed. "Bigger than we had been led to believe, ourselves." Fox leaned in, using a conspirator's whisper to ask his next question, "but what if we could help you to become… bigger… than the problem?"

Roger was already augmented. More to the point, he currently sported about as much augmentation as was feasible for a human being to support. He could lift five tons and see the wings of a fly at twenty yards, for Christ's sake! The big fucker at the bar had slapped him down like he was a child though. That was a different level altogether, and that was a level Roger would not mind moving to. The broken man in the bed was more than a little curious about what Mr. Fox may or may not have been referring to.

"What do you have in mind, Mr. Fox?"

Fox straightened in the chair, smiling broadly, "We here at Corpus Mundi's 'Better Man' division have been pushing the limits of cybernetic enhancements for some time now. I think you will find that our latest designs will help you become the kind of person who can complete this most important task for us."

Roger knew his next question was the important one.

"Why me? I know outfits like yours. You must have an entire crop of professional paramilitary types you could use. Why pick me?"

Fox's sales-pitch face fell into a more serious configuration, "Because our records show that you are the most augmented human alive, Mr. Dawkins." Roger was not in the least surprised by this fact. He had spent a lot of money on augmentations over the years. Roger searched for signs of deception in the other man's body language. He needn't have bothered, as Fox answered without subterfuge, "therefore you are the most likely to survive the process."

Roger's eyebrows rose, "Most likely, huh?" He considered for a moment, "'Most likely' is not the same as 'likely' though, is it? What are the actual odds?"

Fox smiled again, "Oh, we think your chances are quite good, in fact..."

Roger cut him off before the prevarication could continue, "Probability has a numerical value, Mr. Fox. Any answer other than a number is a lie. Please answer with a number."

Fox's face went blank, and his response was flat and expressionless, "Thirty-five percent, plus or minus two." Apprehension tightened Fox's jaw and drew his mouth into a taut line.

Roger decided to end his suffering, "One in three, huh? For the right pay? I'll take those odds."

"Your compensation will be very impressive, I assure you," the tension evaporated from Fox's neck and jaw and the oily smirk returned.

But Dawkins couldn't let him all the way off the hook, "My compensation was already 'very impressive,' Mr. Fox. We don't have a deal unless my compensation becomes..." he paused for effect, "... 'ludicrous'..."

Fox frowned ever so slightly before the smile came back. "That can be arranged."

Chapter Fifteen

Roland's code name in the Golem program had been "Breach." All his squad's call signs corresponded to their roles within the team. The group had consisted of "Lead," "Comms," "Scout," "Sneak," and "Breach."

So, the designation was descriptive: When they had to breach a bunker or building, the squad would send in Roland first. Breaching was dangerous work. Doorways and other access points were referred to as 'fatal funnels' in the military world, because they were choke points where a small number of hostiles could hold off a large number of assaulters by pouring gunfire into the smaller target area of the funnel. This meant that for most of his service with the squad, Roland's job, quite simply, was to absorb incoming fire.

Roland had gotten this dubious honor for a specific technical reason. A massive man before getting injured on Venus, Roland's nervous system had no problem assimilating to endless layers of armored muscles and reinforced skin. His body and nervous system could handle more protective mass than any other candidate, and his designers used this as an excuse to push the envelope for how much techno-organic armor they could stack onto a single humanoid frame.

Being enormous was Roland's natural state, so this turned out to be a staggering quantity of armor. The extra mass and bizarre proportions did not cause any insurmountable dyskinesia when his new body came on line. It's why his chassis had more reinforcement than any of his squad mates, and how his proportions ended up far more exaggerated.

While his armoring-up had been a success, there were a few cons to balance out all the pros. From the squad-level tactical perspective, Roland was practically invulnerable. He was by far the toughest and strongest member of a squad composed entirely of superhuman cyborgs, which was no small thing to be. He was also slower, heavier, and much more conspicuous than the other team members; and he burned through energy at twice the rate of his squad mates. In that parking lot, on this day, he had no issues with these trade-offs whatsoever.

What he had, was a fatal funnel in need of breaching. That was a problem with a solution he understood. It felt good to be back in comfortable territory again.

The bounty hunters remained twelve in number, and were again pressing forward from the alley. At least one of them had an electro-magnetic automatic rifle, and it would periodically spew bursts of steel-shredding aluminum and tungsten projectiles at them. The sheer volume of incoming metal rain would chew the barrier of cars to pieces if it wasn't handled in short order.

Roland wasn't sanguine about the thought of tanking incoming fire from a weapon designed to carve up vehicles. On the one hand, he was at least 95% certain it couldn't do much more than cosmetic damage to his body. On the other hand, his head was not quite so durable. He would have rather not had to take the chance under any circumstances.

I should have brought the damn helmet, was his silent rebuke. Not bringing the helmet along was an unforgivable lack of foresight. He just hadn't thought it would be necessary for a thing as simple as a quick trip to see Marko. The level of this conflict was escalating far faster than he would have thought possible. His strategic analysis of Lucia's situation appeared be inaccurate on multiple levels. He would need to adjust his tactics moving forward.

But there was good news, all strategic blunders aside. That alley was nothing more than a choke point, and he was built specifically to breach choke points. *Time to go to work*, he thought with a mental shrug. With a practiced psychological trigger sequence, he kicked his reflexes up as fast as his neural enhancements would go. He doubted he was as fast as Lucia, but unlike Lucia, his body wouldn't tear itself apart if he moved at top speed. His fifty-mile-per-hour charge at the alley was in no danger of harming him.

With time dilated as much as his brain could handle, his approach still felt like slow plodding. His feet pushed on the ground with enough force to drive his toes through the asphalt and leave divots where the soles of his reinforced combat boots struck. He was two strides into his charge before the first incoming rounds hit him, and he watched in absent disinterest as the ricochets spawled off his chest in showers of slow-moving sparks. By the fourth stride, every bounty hunter in the alley was pouring fire into him as fast as they could work their triggers. It sounded to Roland's warped perceptions like popcorn or a burgeoning rain shower, which meant it had to be an indecipherable roar to anyone not operating at five times human response speed.

The pistol and sub-machine gun projectiles flowed off of him like water droplets, and the only things Roland could feel were the heavier and sharper impacts of the big automatic rifle. By his sixth stride he was at the alleyway and into the first row of bounty hunters.

He hit the group without slowing or missing a step. His nine-hundred-and-forty pounds hurled gunmen back and into the air like straw in a hurricane. Human bodies thwacked into the concrete walls with dull claps and dropped to the ground while bones snapped like kindling under the booted feet of the hurtling cyborg. Roland stopped his forward motion by driving his heel into and through the asphalt deck and skidding to a stop twenty-five feet past the knot of gurgling and gasping hunters. His foot tore a furrow in the ground the whole distance and trenched a full twelve inches down before spending all his momentum.

Dust and debris was still settling when he spun a brisk turn on his heel to bring Durendal to bear on the alleyway. With the walls containing his prey, and the group still scattered and disoriented from being battered by his charge, there was no need for precision aiming. Roland smirked in anticipation and squeezed the trigger.

Durendal roared in a full-auto blast of noise and fire that Roland worked back and forth in a brisk arc traversing the breadth of the alleyway. A horizontal rain of steel beads tore through his enemies at ten times the speed of sound, slapping them back down to the ground and tearing fresh gasps and screams from the churning mass. The beads moved so fast they ignited from air friction, leaving white-hot tracks across their flight paths and trailing smoke from their impacts.

For most of the doomed hunters, their armor only slowed the large projectiles. Even when it blunted the impacts, the ceramic plates couldn't cover everything. The glowing beads hurt and maimed no matter where they struck and any hunter still standing went down under the storm of pellets. Hunters caught scrambling to recover from the charge were driven back down by the barrage of gunfire and the flailing of their teammates. The narrowness of the alley turned the affair into a thrashing, twisted nightmare of bloody limbs and broken bones. But Roland wasn't finished yet.

The bolt locked back on the empty HV-bead section of the magazine, and a small red light indicated that the weapon was no longer in battery. He thumbed the selector to flechette and waited the quarter second it took for the carriage to index the next section of the magazine. The light flashed green as the bolt slid back into battery, and the weapon was hot again. Then the grim giant revisited the sprawled mass of hostiles with his eight remaining rounds of armor-piercing needles.

These he took a little more care with, trying to get each round center mass on each hunter. He had forgotten that he was still on full-auto, though, and he ended up wasting three rounds sawing a single hunter in half with an unintended burst that did all but bisect the unfortunate target at the waist. Most flechettes would pass through its victim and often wounded a second before its energy was depleted and it lodged in some poor hunter's anatomy.

The red light came on again and Roland indexed the last loadout: High-Explosive. He paused at the blinking green light and thought about conserving these powerful rounds for possible later use. The rumination lasted an interminable one sixteenth of a second. Then he was stroking the trigger as fast as he could identify targets.

Every single hunter had an injury of some sort or another, many grievous. At least half their number was dead already. To his accelerated perceptions, the mass of bodies writhed and pulsed like a colony of bleeding snakes rolling over each other trying to escape the assault of some implacable predator.

When Roland dropped the HE on them, the alleyway erupted into a cyclone of fire, shrapnel, blood, human body parts, and death. As the bolt clicked out of battery for the last time, Roland did not even bother to reload. He holstered Durendal in a smooth motion and surveyed the destruction he had wrought. He examined the results with a skilled workman's satisfaction.

The alleyway was destroyed. It was an unrecognizable wasteland complete with meter-wide craters in the ground and man-sized holes in the walls where the explosive rounds had struck. Jagged rubble and lengths of bent rebar edged the ragged gaps where brick and mortar had been destroyed. It left them looking like horrible oblong mouths with crooked metal teeth. Body parts and charred pieces of cracked body armor littered the ground where sobbing lumps moved under the tattered remains of dusty leather coats. Smoke billowed from several small fires and the smell of ozone and burning bodies threatened to choke anyone who came near.

The coughing, moaning, and gurgling of the of the surviving bounty hunters were the only sounds one could hear, until Roland stomped back through the alley with footfalls like distant thunder. He stopped in the middle of the mess of charred flesh and body parts to cast his appraising gaze over the grisly tableau. None of the bounty hunters would walk out of here, and many would never be identifiable even in death. After a moment's searching, he spied what he was looking for and took one step over to the wall where he reached down into a mass of wounded men.

His hand came up clutching a wheezing, broken bounty hunter by the neck. The tall, gaunt man was bleeding from a dozen wounds, and his left arm was limp dead weight at his side. His face was a shredded mass of burns and scrapes, and his breath came in a wheezing cadence that did not bode well for his longevity. Roland propped the mess of a man against the wall of the alley and glared at him.

The bounty hunter slid boneless down the wall into a seated position where a paroxysm of coughing sprayed blood and foam on Roland's pant leg. Roland growled, "Who?" in a voice rumbling with menace.

The wounded bounty hunter gasped a clipped response, almost inaudible even to the man standing directly over him, "Chill, man. I'll play ball. It ain't nothing personal to me. Just tryin' to get paid!"

Roland understood. Honor had always a moving target in the Woo. In this part of town, loyalty to the boss was always proportional to the survivability of the job you were asked to do. The survivability of this caper had just gone to near-zero and thus went the loyalty. It was a pragmatic consideration and justifiable: As much as this guy wanted to make money, he sure as hell did not want to die in an alley doing it.

"Word came down from Marko…"

Roland cut him off with a growl, "I know already. Who wants her?"

The bleeding man smiled weakly, "As if I'd know. Or care…" He coughed, "… Marko knows who. He knows you're comin', Tank-man."

Roland was surprised and more than a little concerned that the man knew who he was. He supposed that if Marko had brought this guy in, then Marko may have read him in on Roland before sending him out. It would explain the reinforcements. Marko only knew Roland by reputation and professional services, not about his past or capabilities, which also explained the woeful inadequacy of said reinforcements.

A niggling question asked itself over and over again at the back of his mind. It had been bothering him from the start, and the answer was still elusive. Why had Marko been so certain that Roland would be part of this? Did Marko know about the connection between Donald Ribiero and Roland? That was impossible. If Marko had that kind of intel, he'd have sent tougher people.

The man tried to laugh again, but it degenerated into more tortured hacking, "… Marko is all kinds of fired up about this shit. Something real big is going down. Marko wants that girl and you out of here, and he sure as shit don't care how it gets done."

The man's eyes sparkled a little, "There's so much goddamn money in this, Marko's got pressure from everywhere."

"How many more are hunting right now?" Roland pressed.

More hacking laughter, "Fuckin' all of them, Tank. Everyone. Every crew, every freelancer, everybody planetside and some fucking frontier muscle, too. New guys from Thorgrimm Station and Galapagos coming in from the Enterprise gate tomorrow morning, man. Hardcore mercs." He spat more blood. It was frothy and bright. *Punctured lung*, thought Roland, *he's in bad shape.*

The wounded hunter continued, his face contorting into a wry grimace, "That's why we hit you so fast, man. Once those psychotic fucks get in on the action, we were never gonna see that bounty. Fuckers just kill every one and don't give a shit how much mess they make."

Roland could not help but concur with that assessment. He was very familiar with a variety of individuals who ended up as frontier mercenaries, and they all fell into a very specific category of sociopath. Things just kept getting worse. It was not possible that off-world muscle could be here by tomorrow, unless they had been summoned before Roland had ever encountered Lucia. *Two days, minimum*, Roland figured, *and goddamn Galapagos mercs, to boot.*

The Thorgrimm group was at least professional paramilitary. They were ruthless, but they were as ethical as anyone in that business could be. They followed the rules of engagement at a minimum. The Galapagos guys however, were just well-armed animals. Roland had dealt with them before, and it had not gone well for either side.

How had Marko gotten this far ahead of Roland? How was it that everyone knew Roland would be in this mess before he did? Pieces of the puzzle clicked together in Roland's mind: Bounty jobs in Dockside and the Woo almost never called for off-world professionals. *Somebody* had known serious heavies would be needed for this job. Worse, they had known it before Roland ever knew there was a job going on. Which meant that whoever put the bounty on Lucia had arranged for high-level muscle to be available before the word about it ever hit the street.

The pieces were coming together, but the big picture was still blurry. Somebody had laid a trap for Donald Ribiero and planned well in advance for dealing with Roland

Tankowicz. What didn't add up, was that the teams sent so far had been woefully inadequate for that job. If someone from Project Golem was behind this, they'd have known to send heavier weapons and better teams. One look around the alleyway at the more than a dozen dead bounty hunters was all it took to eliminate Marko and the Combine from the list of potential suspects. They had a stake in this game, no question about that, but they weren't the ones behind it.

There was also the unexplained presence of a high-dollar hit squad at a dive bar in Dockside last night to consider. Marko's boys were low-rent compared to that crew, which further reinforced that Marko didn't know what Roland was, and the real antagonist did. That is what Roland assumed had led to the issue of the inbound mercenaries.

That left some very uncomfortable realties on the table. Somebody had kidnapped Project Golem's top biotechnologist and put a multi-million cred bounty on his daughter. This party had also shipped three teams of high-end hitters from all over the galaxy to get her. That alone told him that there was an excellent chance this person or persons knew all about Roland and his past.

This someone was also making moves on Combine turf, unsanctioned. The androids and augmented goons at The Smoking Wreck were proof of that. Ergo, whoever was behind this didn't care about pissing off the Combine.

There were only a few possibilities left to consider when one measured all these factors as a whole. None of those boded well for Lucia Ribiero. His list of suspects now consisted of Military contractors, Giant biotech Companies, The Army, or 'Unknown.'

Every new bit of intel widened the scope of the operation in ways that were not good for Roland and Lucia's hopes of success, and the only real conclusion that Roland could draw was that it all added up to more evidence that he still knew very little about the emerging situation. He needed to get in front of what was going on if they expected to survive this. He needed to get to Marko without getting Lucia killed.

Roland shook his head in frustration. The sheer level of 'bad' encompassed by these realizations was a staggering concept. This situation had gone from 'kidnapping' to 'galactic-scale incident' in less than 24 hours.

The hunter's eyes closed for a moment, and Roland worried he might have passed out. Then they fluttered open again, "I just wanted to get paid, man. I played ball. That's what I know. Call me a medivac now or fuck off."

Roland briefly considered killing him, then decided against it. Lucia wouldn't approve of it, and he had promised himself he would try not to act like an amoral murder-bot for her sake. This guy would not be in any shape to bother anyone for several weeks by the looks of it anyway, and perhaps he could be useful. Roland made a strategic decision.

"Listen asshole, you are alive for one reason, and one reason only. Get this message to Marko, and anyone else you think needs to hear it."

Roland growled, "You fuckers broke the rules, so consider this 'fair warning' to everyone. Call off the hunt. From here on out it's total war for anybody who takes this bounty, all the way up to the bosses. You get that part? This includes the bosses. Once you go off-world, street rules are no longer in play. This is war."

The wounded hunter looked perplexed, "You ain't gonna warn off Marko, Tank. I think he knows all about war, man..."

"No," Roland interjected. "He only thinks he knows war." Roland straightened and pulled out his comm, "if he doesn't cut the shit I will educate him, though. Tell him that. Tell him I'm on my way to see him and I don't expect to be fucked with." His growl had become a roar, "Tell them all! Tell them that I will fucking kill every single shit bird they know and burn this entire fucking city to the ground if one more of you assholes so much as makes eye-contact with me before I settle this shit!"

He tossed the comm to the hunter, "Tell Marko that if he tests me on this, that I will make an example of him to the rest of the bosses."

He grabbed a magazine from his belt and reloaded Durendal, "Let 'em all know: The Tank is in town and he hates repeating himself."

Chapter Sixteen

Red Head, whose real name was Billy McGinty, was in a bad mood. He surveyed the wreckage of his marketplace with grim, unmitigated gloom.

They could recover most of their product from the carnage, but the cars were a total loss. That was a financial blow that would be difficult to bounce back from. The cars kept them mobile, and mobility kept them from getting hit by rival gangs. He could source more cars, but that would mean burning through cash or barter, and that thought was killing his mood.

After the big cyborg had exterminated all of those Regulators, Billy had flown on Roland in a rage. He even went so far as to shoot Roland in the face with his sub-machine gun. Roland responded to this assault with his characteristic poise. After regaining consciousness, Billy resolved himself to keeping a cooler head. It was a testament to Roland's better nature that he woke up at all, and this was explained to Billy in no uncertain terms.

Billy McGinty was a shrewd man and wanted to know if this strange pair of newcomers represented an opportunity he could exploit. Curiosity was one of his curses, and he endeavored to pry.

"What's the story, Big Boy?" He gestured to the smoking battlefield, "I don't get to know why you barged in here and cost me a shit-ton of money? I got four dead men and no fucking vehicles now. Who's gonna make me whole on this shit?"

Roland wanted to be sympathetic. He really did. Roland just wasn't that kind of guy though, "Do I look like I sell insurance?" His lopsided smirk was merciless, "Call your agent."

Billy had no shortage of personality flaws, one of which was a complete and utter lack of fear. Roland's mastery of intimidation was entirely wasted on the gang leader, who ignored Roland's jab to press on, "What's the story, man? I gotta lot of losses to cover here, and I smell money on you two." He held up his hands before Roland's glower could transform into violent action, "Easy! I ain't no thief, man. I'm just sayin' I've got turf and manpower that might help you out - that's all."

Roland weighed that for a moment, then chose honesty, "There's a lot more money in turning us over than there will be in helping us. Smart guy like you has likely figured that out already. Why would I trust you?"

"How many come after you so far?" Billy's voice intoned with sardonic confidence.

Roland shrugged, "this makes twenty or so, I think."

"How many dead?" Billy continued.

"Most."

"And the rest? Are they doin' just fine?"

"Badly maimed," Roland conceded.

"How much bounty money can a corpse spend?" Billy smirked, "I figure for a small fry like me? Hah. Getting you where you're going and the fuck out of my hair is worth more than getting killed over some invisible bounty that like as not gonna get me ganked in a fucking parking lot."

This was not Roland's first rodeo, "For a price, I assume, you'll get us out of here?"

Billy was having a thought. It was a big thought, the type of big ambitious thought that got people like him killed every day. But it was it a good thought, too. Billy wasn't always a big thinker, but he had achieved leader status in one of the largest gangs in town by seizing opportunities when they presented themselves, and by attempting big things from time to time.

It went a little deeper than naked ambition, too. Billy was tired of the Big Woo street wars and being driven down by rich out-of-town assholes like Marko. Living under the tyranny of white-gloved plutocrats who wanted to hide the drugs and slaves from prying eyes had made Billy McGinty an angry and desperate man. He had been harboring a secret dream for years now. A dream where the people of Big Woo stopped squabbling over Uptown scraps and built their own economy. It was a dream that was shared by many of the Big Woo gang leaders. It was an oft-whispered and frequently schemed dream, but they were all too scared to do anything about it. The bosses had enough money and muscle to crush any gang in the Woo any time they wanted to, and that fear kept everybody's head down. Billy had the strong impression he might be looking at a chance to alter that dynamic.

Marko was the lynchpin. He was the only one of the bosses willing to live down here and manage the gangs of Big Woo. If a giant machinegun-toting cyborg killer wanted to go after Marko? Billy nurtured that thought in his mind for a split second and made his call.

"I figure you're heading up to see Marko, right?" Billy shifted gears, "And Marko, he don't want to see you very much, does he?"

"That's about the size of it," Roland responded evenly. "If you can get me there without having to fight a running gun battle for the next twenty blocks, then we can do business."

Yes, Billy McGinty realized he was having one of those moments people talked about, where opportunity and preparation intersected to change everything. He liked the feeling and rolled his dice.

He tossed the big black machine a lopsided grin, "Well pal, Mama McGinty's favorite son would be delighted to assist."

"Here's the deal, Big Boy." Billy briskly rubbed his palms together, "You got twenty blocks of territory to cover before you get to Umas, where Marko's compound is. On that route, you got at least four different gangs' turf to cover, plus however many bounty-hunters are on your tail. I can convince the gangs to not only let you pass, but to run interference on all them bounty hunters, too."

Roland's eyes widened, "and how the fuck are you going to accomplish that?"

"We are gonna offer them something worth more than money, Big Boy." Billy's eyes sparkled, "Something we've all wanted for a long time now."

"And that would be…?"

"Fuckin' freedom, man! We all hate that these fat fucks from Uptown run everything here. The guys like me, who run the streets, are the real community leaders in the

Woo, and we can't do shit for nobody because of assholes like Marko."

He pointed at Roland, "So here's the plan, man. I'll get the gangs to cover you while you get to the Umas compound, but you gotta do one thing for us."

Roland tilted his head, "And that would be?"

Billy's face was grim, "Fuckin' kill Marko. No matter what your business with him is, you kill him. No deals, no bullshit. Dead. And make sure everyone knows you did it."

Roland caught on, "So while the bosses retaliate against me, you and your gangs prepare to take the Woo for yourselves."

Billy nodded assent. "Yup. If they go after us right away, we'll break. But if they think YOU are the problem, we can get settled in before a new boss sets up." His red head twitched over to the assortment of broken bodies in the alley, "It sounds like you're fucked no matter what you do, so it shouldn't make a difference to you, either way, right?"

Roland had never fought on this side of an insurgency before. He would be lying if he said it wouldn't feel weird, but the thought of breaking the stranglehold on the Woo was oddly thrilling. Also, he really wanted to kill Marko. "Are you sure the gangs will go along? It will only take one traitor to fuck this up."

"They'll go along. We've been talking about it for years now." He nodded again, as much to himself as anyone else, "Yeah. They'll do it."

Roland stuck out his bear paw of a hand, "Then we have a deal."

"Fuckin' A, man!" Billy grinned and grasped the gloved mitt. Roland clamped down with just enough force to make Billy squeak.

The big man leaned his head close to the gangster's, "Just make sure you do right by me, and do right by this place." He gave an additional squeeze, "or I'll be back."

"Message received," the red head replied.

It took Billy's gang, the "Center Street Teamsters" the better part of an hour to make the arrangements. In that time, Roland reloaded all his weapons and got Lucia calm and collected. She was holding up well and almost seemed to be acclimating to the accelerated sensory input. She wasn't quite sanguine about the furious street battle that had just transpired, but she hadn't suffered a panic attack or passed out from the stress or excessive stimulus. That felt like progress, at least.

They had moved to the basement of an old multi-story office building just off The Green. It had been a Teamster operating base for a couple of years now and was simultaneously defensible and centrally located. There was a level of hustle and bustle inside that base that belied the pedestrian conception of how a street gang operated. Roland could not help but compare to the camps of various resistance fighters he had witnessed in his time with the Army. The comparison seemed appropriate.

Lucia had listened to the new plan with keen interest. She liked the thought of getting to where they were going without having to shoot the whole way there. But what would happen when they got to Marko was still very nebulous. Roland did not believe in lying about this, so he told her about the deal he struck with McGinty and the Big Woo gangs.

"So we are hitmen now?" She thought she was making a joke, but her own sharp tone surprised even her, "we kill on contract?"

Roland sighed, "*We* don't kill anyone, remember? I do."

Lucia fired back, "We certainly do. Everyone you killed in the last day has been over me and my father. I am dressed like a fucking commando and following a giant cyborg around while people shoot at us both. We are definitely a 'we' at this point, buster. So please, convince me that we are not just contract killers in another crime war if we do this?"

Roland's irritation came out in his voice, "One: this is way bigger than a stupid crime war. The bounty on your head alone is worth more than ten gangs in the Woo could gross in a year. This is big-boy, no-shit, planet-scale conflict. I've been in those before. I know how it goes."

"Two: Marko is a drug-peddling, slave-trading, murdering, thieving, asshole who likes to run this town like a third-world dictator. You can take my word for it or I can show you things in his little palace across town that will curl your high-bred toes, lady."

"Three: I don't kill for money. Never have. Marko was on the target list the minute the Dwarf said his stupid name. Not because it was convenient or profitable, but because he is a major general in what is shaping up to be a big-ass war. Taking him off the board is just good strategy."

He calmed, "Lucia, I know you don't like any of this. You shouldn't be here at all. But I am playing to win, here, and I cannot afford moral absolutism right now. Neither can your father." He gestured to the tired, dirty faces of the gang members surrounding them. "The people of Big Woo have never been able to afford it. It's just one more luxury item people uptown get to enjoy that the rest of us don't."

Roland's tone surprised her, and left her more than a little insulted. "You can be such an asshole, Roland!" She let the hurt come out in her voice, "I'm not stupid. I know how the world works. But that doesn't mean I have to like it, or be part of what I think is wrong with it. Excuse me for giving a shit about human life!"

She softened a little, but not much, "I believe you about this Marko character, really I do."

She took a determined step closer to him, "But I am…"

She poked him in the chest, hard, "… always…"

Poke, "… going…"

Poke, "… to ask…"

She ended with a final poke, brutal and sharp, "… 'why' when you suddenly decide it's time to kill someone."

She folded her arms, "Get used to that, Tin Man, because it won't change. If I promise not to act like a high-strung rich-bitch about it, can you at least promise to always have a good answer? Because while I may in fact be that rich Uptown bitch, I still worry about watching you do on your own exactly what the Army tried really fucking hard to trick you into doing twenty years ago."

Roland now felt like a prince among assholes. She was absolutely, unquestionably right. Why did he feel it was unreasonable to ask for a good reason to kill someone? It was a question any free-thinking, well-adjusted human should ask before taking a life. It was exactly the scope of moral self-determination that his handlers in the Army had taken away from him. That irony stung a little: all Lucia wanted was for him to use the thing that the Army stole from him.

This is how you become an amoral murder-bot, he thought to himself. It was so easy to be smug when you ignored all other viewpoints.

He sighed, "Of course. I'm sorry. You are right." He rubbed his forehead, "I thought you were judging me and I got crabby. Maybe I needed to be judged. I dunno."

Lucia shook her head, "Stop being such a baby. I get it. You are a soldier, Roland. Soldiers have to kill sometimes. But when you stop asking why...?"

She let the last part trail off, and Roland finished it for her: "Amoral murder-bot?"

"Amoral murder-bot," she agreed.

"I guess cutting my strings was only the first part, huh, Jiminy Cricket?" Humor was ever the last bastion of the defeated male human.

Lucia laughed, and her face brightened. She stepped in and gave the massive cyborg a hug. It was the first time in decades anyone had hugged him. Her head barely reached the bottom of his pectorals. They looked ridiculous, but it felt nice.

"Keep it up, Pinocchio, and someday you may just get to be a real boy," she sniffled into his shirt.

Chapter Seventeen

Roland's threat to the bounty hunter either never went out or just plain didn't work. The various gangs were already reporting back with intel about teams of bounty hunters roving the streets. McGinty had his informants executing an aggressive disinformation plan in an active attempt to stymie the hunters. It was all a race against time now.

Billy McGinty was in his glory. It was obvious to even the most casual observer he had been planning this in his mind for some time. He snapped choreographed orders and missives to his crew with the practiced ease born of endless repetition. Billy had a three-layer contingency plan for everything. His contingencies had contingencies, which in turn had back-up plans. Roland approved and told him so.

"We won't get another chance like this," Billy responded. "When Marko goes down, the shit is going to hit the fan." He swept his arms in a wide circle, encompassing the whole area, "All the criminal infrastructure is here in the Woo, so once we cut Marko's ties loose, we will have all the major supply chains into New Boston locked down before they realize that it was us behind it." He paused, "You know, as long as you are occupying everyone's attention, that is."

Lucia chuckled, "He can manage that."

Billy looked down at an old paper notebook in his hands. He had never trusted this dream to a Data Pad, so it was all either on old-fashioned cellulose pulp or in his head. "That's the key, you know," he explained. "Getting the supply chain under our control means they will have to negotiate with us if there is going to be any narcotics or tail for sale for three hundred miles."

"Things will get really ugly when we cut the slavers loose," he added thoughtfully. "We're gonna get hit hard for that, but it's part of the new deal, now."

Roland scowled, he knew some of the bosses, and he wasn't so sure, "You think they will let it go without a fight? The supply chain and the human traffic?"

Billy shook his head, "Hell no. But there will be no drugs and no ass until they do. We can hold out longer than they can… we're already poor. When the junkies start coming to us anyway, the revenues become ours no matter what. As long as they don't wipe us all out in the first two weeks, they lose."

"Two weeks?" Roland smiled, "Can you hold out that long against the Combine? They can bring some serious heat." Roland thought of the elite paramilitary units he had seen doing contractor work off-world. These teams ran with equipment and support comparable to real armies.

"We can make it worse by slashing prices and dumping the inventory at a loss. The junkies are gonna need product, and junkies don't care how they get it. Once they are buying from us, the whole market shifts."

Lucia, being far more business-acute than Roland, explained to him why that might work, "The return on investment gets very unattractive if the product loses value like that. It will make any money spent on reacquiring the market share painful." She looked back at Billy, "But won't that hurt you as well?"

Billy shrugged, "What price, freedom? Life already sucks here, at least we will be poor without a group of sadistic pricks running our lives."

"Join the Army, sometime," Roland quipped, then shifted back to the subject at hand. "What about the other rackets?"

"The slavers are out, too many of us have been through that meat-grinder or know someone who has. They're done. Yeah, they'll run to the Combine for help as soon as we start slitting their throats." He shrugged, making his red mane bounce, "Then they'll learn the hard truth about their masters. Uptown suits can't afford to get caught anywhere near the slave trade. The whole reason the skin business stays here is so rich Combine fuckers can have a nice safe distance from that nasty shit. Combine won't go to war to protect them if the other rackets are already losing money. It's bad business. The little shits will get left to twist. I guess those pricks will end up going back off-world."

Billy had really thought this out. The level of planning he had done impressed both the soldier and the businesswoman.

"Numbers have always been an Uptown game, so fuck the gambling, right? Lost cause."

Most of the profitable gambling was electronic and legal, anyway. It wasn't the cash cow it had been in past times. "Loans and laundering will stay with us. Those are Dockside rackets and those boys never go uptown if they can avoid it. That shit needs lots of cash-business and shadows to work, and Dockside is all about cash. Not to mention, the lights will always be a little too bright in Uptown. It'll piss the Combine off to lose 'em. That will be the worst battle because that shit is profitable as hell. People are gonna die over those two gigs."

He looked up at Roland, "Word is you might be the guy to talk to about Dockside, actually. Some of my little birds tell me the best fixer for that is an eight-foot asshole who knocks building over when he's in a bad mood. Know anyone like that?"

Lucia waved her arms in cartoonish enthusiasm, "Ooh, ooh, I do! I know a guy like that! Ask me!"

"Must be someone else." Everybody gave the big man a scowl of disbelief, "I'm barely seven-and-a-half feet tall, and I only knock buildings over when I'm in a good mood," was his offered explanation. Nobody thought he was funny, so Roland nodded assent, "I can definitely make some calls and smooth out any rough spots on that front."

McGinty smirked, "For a price?"

Roland nodded again, "Naturally. I'm not a savage. Bills to pay, and all. I have a lifestyle and reputation to maintain."

Billy flipped a page in his pad, referencing his written notes, moving onto the next item, "As for the prostitution, tail is tail, man. Uptown pimps will always work for Combine 'cuz they always have. Big Woo pimps are on our side already. Dockside and the Sprawl will have to choose sides when the time comes, but Big Woo will want a much smaller cut than Uptown, so they'll go our way soon enough."

"Dockside pimps won't be an issue. They all work for Madame Madeleine in one capacity or another, and she'll be more than happy to be done with Marko and Uptown." Roland had done a brisk business for the Madame, ensuring that the Uptown class of johns understood that just because a girl's time was for rent, it did not follow that she could be treated like a rental car. Super-wealthy oligarchs struggled with the distinction, sometimes.

"I don't know her personally, but that has always been the consensus down here. Can I count on you to bring her in?" McGinty looked hopeful.

Roland couched his next words with as much polite honesty as he could, "The Madame will want to bring all your pimps under her umbrella to go along with this. She will not take 'no' for an answer."

McGinty winced, "The boys won't like that. Just get her to the table, and we will negotiate as best we can."

"She runs a tight, profitable ship up in Dockside," Roland offered, "there are worse ways it could go."

"Yeah, well, us Woo crews can be territorial. We'll sort it out though. Any ideas on the Sprawl?"

"Not my territory," Roland mused, "but I think they are mostly Combine out there. Combine always takes a huge percentage, and that's your best angle." Roland was a professional fixer, and he was in his element now, "If that's the case you may try wooing them over by offering better coverage for a smaller percentage. Combine have been fat and lazy for a while now. It's why they stay out of Dockside... they'd have to earn their percentage there, and they aren't interested."

Billy looked thoughtful, "We could arrange for some incidents to occur, and when Combine drops the ball, we swoop in and handle it at a discount..."

"Exactly," Roland said. "Expose them where they are weak, then offer to do a better job for cheaper. They'll come over."

"That's a lot of moving parts. Can you hold out for long enough to make all of this happen?" Lucia brought the conversation back to the critical issue.

Billy smiled, "Maybe yes, maybe no. Like I said, life here already sucks, might as well cross the Rubicon, ya know?"

The reference surprised Roland and it must have showed on his face. Billy laughed at him, "I may not have gone to college, Big Man, but I can read a book when I want to."

Roland nodded his approval and changed the subject, "Speaking of crossing Rubicons, what's the plan for getting us to Umas?"

McGinty smiled, "That part is fairly easy. We will stick you into a truck and drive you there."

"Really?" Roland managed a truly epic raised eyebrow. "He won't have security on high alert? I may have just threatened his entire operation and everyone he knows."

"Brilliant bit of strategy, there, Pal." Billy rolled his eyes, "Of course he will be on high alert, but he still needs his usual supply of drugs and alcohol, though. If his boys don't get booze they don't fight, and if his girls don't get their drugs, they start having independent thoughts." Billy shook his head, "Marko can't afford either right now."

Roland gave a tight-lipped nod, "And today is delivery day?"

"It is." McGinty confirmed.

"That gets us to the gate, what happens when they search the truck?"

The gangster gave a non-committal shrug, "Either they find you, and the shooting and smashing begins, or they don't find you and we get you right up to his office. Either way you're there."

"I liked this plan until that part," Lucia piped up.

Billy looked askance, "You going along, girl? We can stash you if you want. Let the Tank here handle it, maybe?"

Lucia flashed a coy smile at him, "With what I'm worth? Do you really trust ALL of your men not to turn me in for the millions of creds on the table? With my big ugly babysitter gone, someone just might get tempted."

Roland had to agree with her assessment. Not the 'ugly' part. His mother had assured him throughout his childhood he was a handsome boy, and he had no reason to doubt her. But the budding relationship with the Teamsters did not have enough history for that level of trust yet. Billy also didn't know about Lucia's enhancements. She may not be fast enough to dodge bullets, but Roland had seen enough to trust that she would not be a liability in a firefight.

The redhead nodded in wry understanding, "Probably prudent. But I figured I'd offer."

"Appreciated." Lucia's response was sincere, "But I'll stick with the big metal asshole for now."

Billy nodded, "He grows on you, huh? Like a big shaggy dog that no one else will love?"

Lucia shook her head, "More like a thousand-pound monkey with terrible manners and an alcohol problem."

Roland snorted, "I can metabolize gasoline, lady. It's biomechanically impossible for me to have an alcohol problem."

McGinty laughed, "What do you call it when you are out of booze then?"

"I suppose that would technically be an 'alcohol problem.' " Roland found the man's logic unassailable. Then he moved on, "Let's suit up and get rolling. I'd like to get to Marko around sunset."

"Gonna fight at night? Figured we'd wait until dawn, at least," Billy asked, looking concerned.

Roland smiled a wolf grin, all teeth and malice, "I can see in the dark. They can't."

Billy shook his head, "Of course you can see in the fucking dark. I don't know why I didn't just assume that. Anything else you want to tell me?"

"Your fly is down."

"Fucking hell!" McGinty fixed his pants with fumbling alacrity and looked to Lucia, "he really is an asshole, isn't he?"

She looked up at the big cyborg, standing with his arms folded and a smug grin on his face and scowled, "yeah, but I guess he's my asshole, now."

Both men gave her a look of confused amusement, and realization dawned on her. "Crap, that sounded different from how I wanted it to!"

Her mirth came with unexpected ease. The facility and speed with which she was managing everything was a welcome surprise. Even though the firefight in the parking lot had been terrifying, she had avoided any major panic issues during the ordeal. She hadn't told Roland, but her heart rate had settled back to normal within an hour, and she knew she was stifling her anxiety with pure willpower. It really felt like she was under control for the moment, and Lucia was oddly comfortable with their current situation. Almost too comfortable when she considered it. She wasn't sure why, but it felt like the buzzing alarms and overwhelming fears were moving to the background more. They were all still there, still real, still terrifying; but they weren't overwhelming the part of her brain that made decisions as much. She couldn't be sure if she was just acclimating to mental noise, or if it was getting better on its own.

With the planning more or less complete for getting them to Umas and Marko, her attention turned to more immediate concerns. She looked to the two men and asked, "I don't suppose there is time to eat anything before we embark on our little mission, is there?" Roland wasn't kidding about how hungry she would get. She regretted not trying the mystery street meat earlier, which was one of the strangest thoughts she had ever had.

Billy grunted assent, "Yeah. We got food. It sucks, but it's technically food, all the same. Sorry, but we don't get too many Uptown ladies down here. With any luck, you'll be able to digest it."

"'Technically food' is good enough for me right now." She was too hungry to be picky, and she resolved to acquit herself well in consuming whatever offerings the Teamsters could make. If only for the sake of her Uptown neighbors and the squashing of stereotypes.

Someone once said, "hunger makes the best sauce." Lucia had to agree, because in short order she found herself committing what could only be considered a hate-crime on some kind of burrito-thing stuffed with muddy brown meat-ish filling, and what the people in Big Woo colloquially referred to as "cheese." Lucia was fairly certain that it was not cheese, and may not have been an actual food item, but it was melty and salty and she ate it with gusto. Then she asked for another.

McGinty eyed her with a mixture of respect and fear, "Uhhh... Nobody's ever eaten two of those before, you know."

Lucia looked at the red-headed gangster askance, "What the hell does that mean?"

"Those are like, 3,000 calories each. No disrespect intended, but can your... uh... system handle that much synthetic protein?"

Lucia's face became a little more pensive, "Am I going to shit my pants later? Is that what you are asking?"

Billy laughed, "Something like that, yeah."

She shrugged, "I guess we'll find out, because I'm still starving!"

"As the lady wishes," said Billy, with mock severity.

Roland's voice was tremulous, "I don't want to ride in the back of the truck with her anymore."

Chapter Eighteen

Mark Anthony Johnstone slammed the comm down on his desk, destroying his third expensive handheld in two days. Breaking comms was cliché with Marko, but it wasn't really his fault. He was a large man, with large hands, and modern comms were just not built to handle the explosive nature of his personality. His personality was in a very explosive place at the moment and thus many of the less robust devices in his office were likely destined for a premature doom. Once, when a day was going particularly poorly, he had shoved his whole desk through the large window that made up an entire wall of his fifth-floor office.

His new desk, however, was far heavier and sturdier than the previous one, and Marko was not so young as he once was. The big antique desk, it seemed, was safe. For now.

Marko sighed and rested his head in his hands. Wayward strands of silver-grey hair peaked out from between thick fingers, and he heaved another exasperated sigh. Once a thick-muscled specimen of human genetic potential, Marko ran a little on the fat side these days. His bulk still held many external indicators of a man with prodigious strength, but age and appetite had blunted the sword-sharp look of the much-feared Big Woo enforcer he had started his career as.

As his weight approached four-hundred pounds, he was more likely to heft a pint of beer than a barbell. He massaged the bridge of a wide, pug nose and rubbed his face with brisk strokes. He had the heavy brow of a troglodyte, and thick eyebrows shaded striking blue eyes streaked with angry red veins. A jaw like a slab of concrete worked in wordless frustration for a few seconds. With painful slowness a confluence of guttural sounds assembled themselves into words, which he directed at the nervous man trembling in front of him.

"That piece of shit, two-bit, tall-ass mutant motherfucker from Dockside just declared war on all the bosses," Marko snorted. It was an explosive sound, replete with rage and frustration, "That big fucker thinks he can scare me off. ME! The goddamn motherfucking boss of Big Woo."

He looked for something else to break and settled on the decorative lamp sitting atop his antique hardwood desk. The lamp smashed against the far wall in a disappointing shower of glass and plastic. He had hoped for something rather more dramatic.

The thin man across from the seething boss adjusted the lapels of his dark grey suit, and offered such comfort as he could, "Have any of the crews found him yet?" His voice wavered, "I've heard reports that they were spotted just off the green."

Marko stood up and fixed the minion with a glare. He spoke with calculated deliberation, injecting each word with as much menace as he could muster, "Trey and Jimbo just tried to take them in the Teamster's quarter." He paused to make sure the shivering man across from him was listening very carefully, "Tank killed both fucking teams. Left one guy alive to spread the word that he was coming for me." He shook his head, "A fucking no-name fixer, from Dockside! Calling me out?!? Shit!" His voice escalated to a roar. Mark Anthony Johnstone had not fought and killed his way up from the streets to the level of Boss to have some punk-ass street-shit call him out. It was an almost unfathomable breach of protocol. It was an act of such irredeemable disrespect that Marko almost couldn't comprehend it.

There could be only one response, he knew. The rest of the Combine bosses already thought he was beneath them; as if his humble origins made him less of a Boss than they were. They let him have the Woo because it was too dirty, too dangerous for their white-gloved hands, and Marko was fine with that. He liked the Woo plenty and knew that he had control of the most important piece of the supply chain. But that didn't make their sneers easier to take.

Letting someone like Tank call him out could cost him dearly in the universal currency of respect if he did not handle it in spectacular fashion. It was a foregone conclusion that the other Bosses would use this insult against him if he didn't send the correct message and make a statement. He felt their merciless eyes on him, and he did not like it.

He liked nothing about the last few days. None of it was making sense. First, the bounty for that Uptown broad had hit the boards, and it was huge. Having a big-ass bounty to collect was exciting, but bounties happened all the time. The size made it obvious that this would be an interesting hunt, but no other red flags went up at that time.

Then somebody hit Dockside without clearing it, and they used some heavy shit to do it. Dockside could be a real no-man's-land, not having a Boss, but nobody should run that kind of op without checking with the Combine first. No matter where things went down in New Boston, the proper conventions should be observed; otherwise it would be constant gang warfare and anarchy. Even the criminals knew that much. That's when the calls came in from other Bosses. It seemed nobody knew who ran that hit.

Next, there had been the hit on the Dwarf's operation, where Tank had cleared out the runt's best boys. Marko knew Roland professionally and by reputation, and he was unsurprised that the Dwarf's crew couldn't handle the big man. Marko hated to lose a Garibaldi; good help was rare planetside, but at least the other one would live. The Bosses agreed to let that hit slide, as Roland's reputation in Dockside made him too valuable to antagonize, and the more pressing concern was locking down whoever was running jobs in New Boston outside the lines.

Then another call came in later that night, and that particular question found its infuriating answer. Some Corpus Mundi big shot copped to the hit, and told them that more 'contractors' would be on site in thirty-six hours. That didn't set everyone off until the company man explained that they would use off-world hitters.

The Bosses had lost their minds over this, Marko included. He remembered it very clearly. There was plenty of profanity and more than one disparaging epithet slung at the pudgy little man in the expensive suit on the screen. The company shill didn't realize that using off-world talent was a serious breach of the rules. Pops had made it clear in no uncertain terms that the Combine would handle this bounty, and that off-worlders were out of the question.

At that, the company bigwig had laughed. He laughed at Pops Winter! Nobody did that. Ever. That was how you wound up as assorted pieces in a recycling container on your way to the Moon. But what could they do? Corpus Mundi had unlimited money and just as much political swing as the Combine did. Not to mention, the relationship between Corpus Mundi and the Combine had been very profitable for the criminals. So, Pops acquiesced, and that brought the rest of them in line. They just couldn't afford, financially or politically, a war with Corpus Mundi.

After the call, it was decided that the proper way to retaliate was to declare the price for all Corpus Mundi work would now be triple the normal rate. Sometimes you must send a message, and the only way to hurt a corporation like that was in the wallet. The Combine could afford to push the company on that front. Corpus Mundi did plenty of outside-the-lines work, and all of it went through the Combine. Thanks to the temerity of that Fox character, every one of those jobs just got a lot more expensive. It was a plan that would send the correct message without a costly conflict and preserve the reputations and respect of the Bosses. As an addendum, the council of Bosses also resolved to bring the bounty in before the mercenaries arrived, thus preserving the rules and maintaining an orderly business environment.

The Board then dumped this unenviable job on Marko, and in turn he had sent it down the channels. It was a big enough bounty that word hit the streets in minutes, and every thug and punk from Big Woo to the Old Fen Way was combing the street hoping to hit that once-in-a-lifetime score within the span of fifteen minutes. New Boston was big, but there were eyes and ears everywhere, and every single one of them would be fixed on a single target.

Which should have been the end of the story, except that he had just lost fourteen guys to a single fixer and a spoiled Uptown bitch in the heart of his own turf. It was maddening beyond all belief. On the bright side, he didn't have to go hunting for them anymore. The big asshole said he was coming here, so that eliminated one whole aspect of the job, at least.

There was just one teensy little issue with that: Marko did not want that big mook anywhere near his person. Despite his fearsome past and unforgiving reputation, Marko was not the kind of man who enjoyed dealing with scary problems personally. One thing he had learned scrapping his way up from the street-level thug he had been, was that macho crap like that is how you got maimed and killed. No, this is precisely what moderately paid flunkies were for. Case in point, the sweating trembling mess of middle management in front of him right now.

"Who do we got in-house right now?" he asked his lieutenant, a man with the unfortunate name of 'Fatir.' When you work for a crime lord, having your name rhyme with 'fodder' came with certain connotations. While the irony was not lost on Fatir, it wasn't appreciated, either.

Fatir straightened his tie, "The Garibaldis are out of commission, obviously, but you had Tom Miner brought in for this already. There are three crews of enforcers in-house as well right now." He paused, and consulted a worn Data Pad, "Plus our normal Compound crews."

Marko grunted approval. He wasn't sure how Tank had dropped two crews of regulators on his own, but there was a serious compliment of hard-hitting bad-asses stationed here, and Miner was a goddamn monster. That made him feel better.

"How many regulators are out searching?"

Fatir tapped the Pad a few times, "Six crews remain in the city, maintaining the search. We appear to be getting interference from several of the street-level gangs, though."

Marko's chuckle was dry and bitter, "Fucking McGinty being a dick again, I guess? Why haven't we killed him yet? Remind me."

Fatir answered with robotic precision. This was a conversation that got repeated often, "McGinty's Teamsters run almost three quarters of the pharmaceuticals through Big Woo, and his labs produce the highest-quality product at the lowest costs. Nearly forty percent of our total revenues are directly related to his administration of the Teamsters. Our best-case projections have our financial losses upon his removal to be at least half that amount. Worst-case projections don't bear enumeration."

Fatir tucked the Pad under his arm, "McGinty currently controls, either directly or indirectly, approximately thirty percent of the street-level manpower in Big Woo. The other gang leaders respect him, and pacifying him keeps operations smooth and profitable at levels currently unmatched anywhere else."

Fatir paused and tilted a tired head towards his volatile boss, "I am certain that he is deliberately interfering with the bounty hunt, but I cannot figure out why. Tactical considerations indicate we should kill him immediately. But strategically, if we remove him now, we will lose a lot of money in the long term."

Marko frowned and grunted a belligerent approval, "I wonder if the little shit is just pissing me off for the fun of it... or is he finally making a move?" He thought about it for a moment, "Logistically speaking, Fatir, how much trouble can he make for us directly?"

Fatir turned his attention back to the Data Pad. He made some deft keystrokes and frowned at the screen before responding in slow measured tones, "In a direct confrontation, he would suffer a complete loss. He doesn't possess the manpower to do much more than annoy us, due to our overwhelming materiel and expertise advantage." More keystrokes and frowning, "Yes, he would absolutely suffer total loss in a short time." The lieutenant's scowl deepened, "His behavior makes no sense. The man must know how big this is, so why risk your ire now, of all times?"

"Fucker thinks he has an edge. He thinks this Tank guy can take me down and he wants to move in, the ballsy prick." Marko had always considered himself a shrewd judge of character, and this was a thing he suspected McGinty had always been waiting to attempt. Marko smirked, "Little shit is overplaying his hand, though. It sounds like all I have to do to slap him back in line is bring down Tank and collect on the girl." The big gangster sat back down, and his chair squealed in brisk protest, "Regulators ain't gonna find 'em if the gangs aren't helping, though. Fuck. That means he'll get here soon enough. I want security tighter than a nun's asshole up here. Nothing in or out."

Fatir cleared his throat, "There is a scheduled delivery today. From the Teamsters, sir. The usual revenues and supplies. Shall I cancel?"

Marko swore, "Shit. If I don't get the deliveries out to the Sprawl and Uptown, the other Bosses will think I've lost my nerve." He gave it a good long think. That delivery was not to be trusted, but he also needed to keep the product moving. An interruption of goods and services would make him look bad. Like he wasn't in control.

"Make them unload at building nine and hump that shit over to shipping by hoversled. I don't want that truck anywhere near the center of this compound. If there is any sneaky shit going on with that delivery I want it far away." He had a thought, "And put the Miner on it as security."

"Would you rather have the him here, sir? For protection?" Fatir offered.

"No. If something goes down, I'll have enough time to move as long as that monster can handle one fixer for a little while. I'd rather have him close to the threat, either way. Leave two teams of enforcers on me though."

Fatir made some notes in the Pad, and sent out the missives, "I have relayed your instructions, sir, and put the compound on condition red."

Marko leaned back in his chair and exhaled in anticipation. He set his jaw and cracked his knuckles loudly, "Ok. Let's see how this shit plays out."

Chapter Nineteen

The truck was old, with a fossil-fuel engine and solid rubber tires. It was loud, it smelled terrible, and it bounced and jostled with unnerving violence on ancient suspension that had been rebuilt and repaired a dozen times.

In the back of the ancient transport, stacked with crates of hard creds and a dizzying array of consumable intoxicants, was a tall crate marked in stenciled block letters, 'Ordnance.'

Roland wondered if McGinty had any idea how ironic that label was. He wasn't even lying about the contents, officially speaking. Unless you considered the smallish woman in body armor in the crate with him. It was a very tight fit, and Lucia's back pressed against him tightly. She was small and warm and he could feel her pulse pounding through her armor. She felt fragile and tiny, but Roland now understood the lie of that impression. Her eyes were clear and her movements controlled. Her jaw was set and her hands were as rock steady as any contract mercenary he had ever seen. He had seen less from career soldiers.

If he cocked his head to the correct angle, he could see the effort lines in the corners of her eyes as she controlled her breathing with will alone, forcing her senses to relay only important information to her overworked brain. She was a fast learner, and her determination was incredible. He was witnessing her mastering her augmentations in real time, a feat that took most people months or years. He didn't think she realized just how impressive she was.

Roland was proud of her, in a silly way. He had to remind himself that he hardly knew her, but her ability to adapt to this new reality was impressive as hell. Don Ribiero had a spine of steel, and it seemed his daughter was made of the same stuff.

Don would be proud, too, the cyborg thought. Then another, more urgent thought followed it, *I have to make all of this right. Every shitty thing I've ever done won't matter anymore if I can fix this.*

He felt a shudder of fear move through her body, but she suppressed it the instant it manifested. She moved and squirmed in the bouncing darkness until her hand fell to the butt of her pistol.

Please, he thought, *let me get her through this without making her a killer like me. She doesn't have to be like me.* A wave of sadness came over him, *Why did you do it, Don? Why her?* Roland had to believe that Ribiero had a good reason to augment his own daughter, since he knew better than most what that often meant for the person augmented. *Don wouldn't curse his own child to a fugitive's life without a good reason, right?* Roland shifted so he could rest a hand on Lucia's shoulder. It was awkward, but he wanted her to feel something akin to reassurance. His only experience was with green troops in warzones, so that is what he relied on now.

"Feel all right?" He asked, "How are you holding up?"

Her voice was quiet, but it did not waiver, "I won't let you down."

Roland couldn't stifle a chuckle. She was about to infiltrate an armed compound where they would fight their way to a fortified stronghold. Once there, they would then interrogate and assassinate a major crime lord. But the thing this untrained noob worried about was disappointing him?

"What?" she said, irritated by his amusement.

"I know damn well you won't let me down. I was checking to make sure you were doing OK. This could get hairier than the parking lot, and I want you to be ready."

"Oh." She smiled weakly, "Actually, I'm pretty goddamn terrified…but kind of excited too, y'know?" She looked down, "I want to find my father, and this is the closest we have gotten. I just kinda want to get to it to get through it, know what I mean?"

"But you feel weird about wanting to fight and hurt people?" Roland was familiar with this conversation. He had been new to combat once, too.

She nodded in the pitch black of the container, "Yeah. I don't know if I can kill anyone, but I'm not so sure that I can't, either. Like, I'll do it if it means getting Dad back. Does that make me bad?"

"Only if you think I'm bad, or every cop who kills a perp, or any soldier on any battlefield is bad."

He shook his head, "Don't lose sleep over it: These will be full-on criminal shitheads in there. They trap young boys and girls with drugs to sell them as sex slaves. They extort people for money they haven't earned. They steal, and lie, and kill for pleasure and profit." He took a long pause, "It's funny, but I never really gave too much of a shit about that stuff for a long time. It was just the way the world worked, and I had my own problems to deal with. I kept my stupid head down and I kept my corner of Dockside clean. It was enough to do that, I figured." The big cyborg gave her shoulder a gentle squeeze, "Don Ribiero would do more than that. He'd have helped more people. Your father risked his life to save me, even though there was nothing but trouble in it for him. He acted like a good man is supposed to act." Roland felt a lump in his throat, "He was a better person than me. Probably still is." A self-deprecating head shake followed, "His daughter sure is." He felt, rather than heard her flush at that, and it was adorable. That is, if you were prone to notice that sort of thing. Roland was sure he was not.

"Now these bastards have kidnapped your father, probably because they want to steal something amazing he built, and they don't care how many people die in the process."

Roland was getting mad now, "You think you're bad?" His head shook in the dark, "Hah! I know that I'm supposed to be better than this, but I would kill everyone in that compound and burn the whole damn place to the ground, just to see those pricks gone from this universe." He let the growl he felt in his chest be heard in his voice, "I'll sleep like a baby when I'm done."

The big man's voice dropped to a solemn hush, "I've done it before."

"No, wanting your Dad back and being willing to fight for it against the people who took him isn't bad, Lucia. It's the most honorable thing I can think of, really. This is every soldier's dilemma. Relax, Lucia. You'd make a good soldier."

In the dark, his enhanced eyes could see the beginnings of tears forming in hers, but her voice was strong, "Would you really kill them all, for my Dad?"

"For him. And for you. You don't deserve this. It's wrong. And I'm getting tired of people ignoring when something is wrong."

She wrestled and wriggled until she could reach up and put her tiny gloved hand on his, resting on her shoulder. It was a novel and uncomfortable feeling for Roland. The closeness of the moment, and contact of her body was bizarrely intimate. It just didn't seem right, to feel things in a storage crate on the way to a battle. But the woman pressed against him with claustrophobic intensity seemed quite at ease with the situation, despite the inexplicable madness of it all. He felt her body relax a little more, and heard her say, "Dad was right about you, you know."

"Really? How's that?"

"You actually are a nice man who just acts like a complete asshole." He heard her chuckle in the pitch black of the storage crate, "Thank you for doing this."

"Don't thank me until after you see the bill," he offered with mock severity. She responded in kind.

"There's that 'asshole' act, again," was her sardonic riposte, but there was no real venom in it. "It's OK to just be a person sometimes, you know. I won't tell anyone that you said anything nice or that you aren't really an amoral murder-bot. Your secret is safe with me."

His view of her face was imperfect, but he heard the smile in her words. It was probably the nicest thing anyone had said to him in two decades, and it moved him as much as anything could. He was quiet for a long moment. He stood in mute frustration with just how bad he was at these kinds of conversations. Being squished into a crate with a pretty girl who was saying nice things to him represented a new set of variables for him to process, and his processors were definitely on the fritz. Though awkward and brusque, Roland was not obtuse. He understood that this was the point in the conversation where he was supposed to compliment the pretty girl back, but he couldn't find anything to say. There was a moment where part of him was inclined to simply say what he was thinking, but experience had taught him that this was almost never the best idea. He was confident that this was not the correct time for her to hear something like, "For reasons I don't understand, my brain won't make words when you are this close to me."

He tried to imagine her as a new soldier who needed his guidance, but that just made it worse. Corporal Tankowicz had never been stuffed into a crate with a new soldier who needed guidance. Complicating his dilemma, some of the eighty-seven pounds of Roland that was still organic would not stop reminding him that none of the green troops under his command had ever looked or felt like Lucia Ribiero, either.

The silence was dragging on, and Roland knew he had to say something, because this may be the last chance he had before they were both thrust into combat. So, he simply said what needed to be said.

"Thank you. I appreciate that more than you know."

"You're welcome." She squeezed his hand and let her head rest against his torso, "Promise me we'll get my Dad back?"

Roland's throat caught, "If it can be done, I'll do it. Count on it." He did not like thinking about what that meant, but he had to be practical. War was no place for sentiment or wishful thinking.

She nodded, recognizing what his equivocation implied, "I understand. If he can't be rescued, what then?" She sounded anxious, fearing the answer.

"I will kill them all."

"That will have to be enough," she didn't like it, but she accepted it.

There was another long moment of silence, which Lucia broke first, "Roland?"

"Yeah?"

"When this is over, I'm taking you shopping." Her tone had finality to it. This was not a negotiation.

"Shopping?" the giant asked, bewildered. "For what?"

"Clothes," she replied. "You simply cannot keep walking around looking like you robbed an Army surplus store and then slept in whatever crap you stole. You look ridiculous."

"Really?" Roland couldn't understand what was happening, "this is when you want to discuss my wardrobe?"

He heard that musical chuckle again, and she wiggled against him in a manner not altogether innocent. "It's the perfect time. You can't avoid me in here." Roland understood quite well that she was just being playful, probably to mask her own terror. "You're a captive audience!"

… but it was obvious to Roland the woman did not understand how uncomfortable his reaction to it was proving to be.

Lucia, being a mature adult, knew precisely how uncomfortable she was making the big 'borg. Roland may have been the more seasoned fighter, but Lucia had already ascertained that he had the emotional sophistication of bedrock and the social awareness of a topiary. She (correctly) guessed that no woman had offered Roland anything more than a terrified glance in a very long time. Nor could she blame them; the man's physicality was challenging and his whole demeanor was a deliberate ploy to put people off. It may have been an understandable defensive mechanism, but it was also transparent and immature. Lucia had no trouble seeing right through it, and she was acutely aware of how conflicted Roland was with how he looked at her.

She could feel his discomfort in his voice when he replied, "It's not my fault. Nothing fits me."

The attention of men was something Lucia had become accustomed to. She was pretty, moderately rich, and not at all snooty. Except for an awkward phase in her early teens where she developed the worst case of klutziness mankind had ever recorded, she had never struggled in securing affection from the males of her species.

It wasn't until her anxiety attack in his storage unit that she decided that she couldn't help but like the big guy, as well. He wasn't really her type, and now was a strange time to be considering it, but the giant oaf was charming in his own simple way. Sure, he lacked social graces, basic table manners, and had all the romantic allure of a sasquatch. He was neither rich nor handsome, and she was still working through the whole 'thousand-pound cyborg' thing. But he had also been solid, dependable, fearless and kind all the same. He was a man utterly incapable of deception or subterfuge. If she was being honest, Lucia had to admit that she really liked that in a friend. She patted him on the leg, enjoying his discomfiture, "Don't be stupid. You need a tailor, that's all. Anyone can be fitted if you make a little effort."

"Never saw the point. I try not to attract too much attention, anyway." As a rebuttal it was unconvincing, and she sensed his fear. Her body pressing against his, and the flirtatious turn the conversation had taken was overriding his already strained verbal skills.

"Do you even own a mirror?" She giggled, "You are going to attract attention no matter what you wear. It might as well look decent." She teased him without mercy, "Imagine all the girls you'd get with those muscles and a nice tailored suit!"

Lucia wasn't sure, but she was pretty sure she actually felt him flush. "That's not really my… uh… thing."

"You don't like girls?" It was couched as an innocent question, but her wicked grin belied the fun she was having.

"No! I mean, yeah, I like girls, ah, women, that is." He growled, "Arrrghhh, you're fucking with me, aren't you?"

People like Roland or her father were rare, and the looming presence of the big man behind her seemed like a tangible rebuttal against all the horrible things happening outside. He made her own fear manageable, so she would do the same for him. It was only fair.

Lucia had walked into his life out of nowhere, told him that a man he hadn't spoken to in twenty years needed his help, and twenty-seven hours later he was holding her shoulder as they rode off to wage war on the entire criminal underground. To think a little light banter from an attractive woman could put him in this state was simply too much, and she decided in that moment to let him off the hook.

"A little, yes," she conceded. "Am I making you uncomfortable?"

"Very!" It was two syllables delivered with finality and conviction.

She squeezed his hand a final time, and nestled in against him, resting her head against his bulk and closing her eyes.

"Good. I like you uncomfortable. If we live through this, maybe I'll make you even more uncomfortable."

Roland had absolutely no idea how to feel about that remark, but he made a mental note to kill everyone within a mile of Umas anyway.

Just to make sure they all lived through this.

There was a loud banging on the outside of their crate, indicating that they were getting close to Umas. Roland felt the tension spike in Lucia's one small shoulder, and her spine stiffened. Banter and flirting were age-old ways to avoid the terror of an impending battle, but there was no way around it now.

"I won't let you down!" she said, her voice shrill through gritted teeth.

"I know," he said, and he meant it. "Let's go get your Dad back."

Chapter Twenty

Roger clawed his way to consciousness with tortuous effort.

He was accustomed to waking up instantly, with near-perfect awareness of his surroundings. This new lethargic awakening was unsettling. This time, perception came creeping up in subtle dribs and drabs of sensory input funneled at random intervals to various sections of his brain. Vision was the slowest to arrive, which left him in a half-blind, half-awake stupor for what seemed like interminable minutes.

It started as clips of sounds, at first, and he could hear Doctor Johnson, talking with clear academic detachment to someone else in the room. The voices were faded, and tinny, but he could understand them just fine.

"I've never seen anyone with that much intra-muscular weave before. I don't know how he can even move. Look here."

There was a dim, distant impression of pressure on his leg, "Look at the scarring, most of this is synthetic. It's not even Myofiber, either. It's something industrial that I suspect he got off-world."

"Will that be a problem?" Another voice was heard. Familiar, but not very. Is that Fox? Roger wasn't sure. It was too hard to focus.

"Probably not. If anything, it means we can likely bring the tolerances in the armature up to more than spec. Look, his joints are nearly fused there is so much reinforcement!" Johnson sounded either amazed or disgusted. Roger couldn't tell.

Johnson continued, "His skeletal mass and density are excellent, but his marrow is shot to hell because he took it too far. We'll go full transplant on that to avoid rejection."

Roger listened in bemused torpor while Johnson critiqued his extensive body work.

"His other internals are all garbage, because he spent all his money on becoming a super-man instead of taking care of them. He would have been dead in a couple of years at this rate. Five at most. We will have to regrow most of his internals just to get twenty years out of him."

That didn't sound good. Roger lived life at full speed and then some, so some excess wear and tear was to be expected. But a mere five years to live? That couldn't be right. Either way, it looked like his new employers would be fixing him up, so no big deal. Being in a semi-conscious fugue state was making Roger very zen about many things.

The other voice grunted, "We knew that might be the case. What about the rest?"

"His neurologicals are a bit of a 'good-news-bad-news, scenario."

"What's the good?" the mystery man asked.

Johnson's answer was quick and practiced, "Successive treatments over many years appear to have layered without antagonistic effects. I haven't seen anyone with this kind of speed and perception since Golem. With these neuro numbers and his better-than-expected musculoskeletal system, we can expect the armature to outperform our projections easily."

"I very much like the sound of that, Doctor. What's the bad?"

Johnson cleared his throat, "The neurological activity is too high for effective cognition and proprioception. His brain is still faster than his body, and just too damn fast overall. The subject has been using illicit pharmaceuticals to subdue brain activity when not in combat. It was the best he could do it seems, otherwise his life would probably be a perpetual series of psychotic breaks. There is serious damage to the organic template."

It can't be that serious, Roger thought, *I haven't had an episode in months.*

"Shit. Is it recoverable?" Roger had decided that this was Mr. Fox. His vision was sharpening, and the amorphous blobs of color seemed to match his model for Johnson and Fox well enough, and he didn't have the energy for further speculation.

There was a loud, heavy sigh, "I can work with it, but it will bear very close watching after integration. I can't promise he will ever be stable."

"That's what the fail-safe is for."

"… What… fail… safe…?" Roger forced his mouth to speak, and the Johnson blob flinched in startled reflex.

Fox's voice came in with a nervous edge, "He's awake?"

"Kind… of…" Roger's voice was a weak croak.

Johnson recovered his nerve, "Nurse! Increase Thorazine drip and get me another 5ml Haloperidol! Let's do another round of Piperidine as well."

The blob moved over to the bed and shined a small light directly into Roger's left eye, "Mr. Dawkins, I apologize for this, but we need to sedate you again. You are experiencing withdrawal from… er… I forget, but it's several different illegal drugs. We'll get you sorted out in the next few days, though."

"Feel… like… shit…"

Johnson stuck something into Roger's arm, "Good night Mr. Dawkins."

Chapter Twenty-One

Lucia and Roland were being as quiet as they could. The truck had stopped, but from inside the shipping container neither one of them could tell how it was going outside.

At the gatehouse, McGinty's men were making casual conversation with the guards. That much Roland could make out, but there seemed to be some confusion. It sounded like the van was being redirected from its usual route. Roland frowned, that wasn't unexpected, but he had been holding onto a wan hope that they would pass through the gates unmolested and with no change in the routine. Changed routines meant preparation. Preparation meant coordinated opposition. Like any respectable infiltrator, Roland preferred 'disorganized resistance' over 'coordinated opposition.'

But the truck pulled through the gate without being searched, and that was enough of a blessing. Fixed defenses would point outward, and those were the guns with the highest chance of stopping Roland. Getting inside the walls reduced the chances of getting pummeled with things like 50mm HE rounds and other more forceful munitions. Anything smaller than that should be manageable.

The truck lurched to a halt about five minutes after clearing the gate. Roland heard a noise he figured was a bay door opening, and the van pulled ahead with agonizing slowness. They were moving indoors somewhere. He heard footsteps and barked commands from outside.

Roland forced his mind to relax. One of three things was about to happen, each with its own corresponding plan.

If the van was unloaded without a search, they would continue to lie low in the crate until they could sneak out and find Marko. Roland dismissed this scenario as highly unlikely.

If the van was subject to only a cursory search, then they would lie low and wait for an opportune moment to sneak out as well.

If the search was thorough, then they would burst out guns blazing and fight their way to Marko the old-fashioned way. Roland felt that the second scenario was at least a bit likely, and that the third was probable. Just getting this far had been a miracle, and he could not hope for more than what they already had accomplished with stealth.

"Get ready," the big man whispered to the trembling woman in front of him.

He felt her nod, and her hand went back to her pistol butt.

There was the sound of a bay door being closed by mechanical apparatus. And then more voices speaking in commanding tones. The rear door of the truck was thrown open with a rough clatter, and the sounds of crates being dragged to sleds was obvious.

Then there was the telltale hiss and clang of a crate being opened, and voices calling out inventory.

They were searching the crates. So much for stealth. Roland preferred the rough stuff, anyway. He squeezed Lucia's shoulder once, twice, and on the third squeeze he shoved the crate open and the two burst forth. The cargo space was narrow and cramped, so they had to get clear of it with as much speed as possible.

This part was actually quite easy, considering how fast the pair could move when properly motivated. Motivation they had in spades, and Roland was probably the most effective battering ram in human history. The giant drove forward with complete abandon, hurtling cargo containers and surprised workers before him with indiscriminate violence. He and Lucia exploded from the back of the van in a rain of hurtling bodies, broken cargo containers, and an impressive cloud of narcotic debris.

Lucia was like a streak of black mercury, darting between flying shards of detritus and sailing with a raptor's grace through the space between adversaries. In a heartbeat, she found herself out of the truck and moving among at least a dozen of Marko's goons. Roland had a very uncomfortable thought as he paid passing attention to her movements. *Too fast! She's moving too fast!* She would break an ankle or tear her shoulder out of its socket if she didn't slow down.

What Roland lacked in easy, fluid grace, he made up for with pure kinetic energy. His barrage of improvised projectiles had scattered men and materiel and pushed them away from the truck in a wide semicircle, and they scrambled for cover like startled insects. He could currently assess at least twelve men in the opposing force, and two of them had just gone down hard from contact with high-velocity shipping containers. With staccato popping like tiny lightning strikes, Lucia's gauntlets accounted for two more in short order. It bode well for their chances to see a third of their enemies' total strength gone in less than one long second, and Roland allowed himself an instant of approval. Dropping all their opposition without gunfire would be very nice as it meant that some level of stealth may yet be preserved.

Roland did not bother to pull his weapon, he just tore into the scrambling enemies like a gorilla after pigmies. First, he grabbed a screaming thug by the head, and whipped him in a violent arc towards two others. The force of the throw separated some of the unfortunate man's cervical vertebrae and shredded the spinal cord of the man-cum-projectile. With terminal velocity the flopping corpse hit one of the intended targets with enough force to drive him down and bounce the live man's forehead off the concrete floor. The impact was marked by an audible crunch and neither man moved after that.

A quick backhand killed another thug that failed to get clear of Roland, and a seventh went down in a fountain of blood when the van driver drove a seven-inch blade through the back of his neck with the practiced stroke of a professional killer.

Roland turned to go after the remaining five, but he needn't have bothered, Lucia had them well in hand.

The lithe woman sped like a hunting cat through the group of bewildered men. She kept her center of gravity low, and her movements were short, precise, and too fast to follow. In one motion, she slid low and to the left of a goon, driving her right fist into his groin. What was soon to be the familiar sound of the gloves discharging and the capacitors squealing signaled that this man was never likely to sire any children after this day. Without hesitation, she spun off of this emasculating blow to wheel a savage spinning heel kick to the chin of another, which she followed with a straight left to the throat. The kick and ensuing punch were so fast that there was almost no delay between their respective impacts. With a pop and a whine of charging capacitors, the armored glove shut his lights off instantly, and he went down in a choking, gasping mess. A third man received a vicious Thai kick to the inside of his left knee, which buckled and caused him to stagger. Lucia finished him with an uppercut. Pop! Whine! Three down.

Lucia stomped a push kick into the chest of a fourth attacking man, which stopped his momentum cold and widened his eyes. This gave her enough time to score two direct hits with her reinforced fists on his jaw. The gloves left bloody streaks and scorch marks across his cheeks, but the unconscious man wouldn't know that until he woke up much later.

The final man, still not understanding what was going on, had just started to raise his pistol at the speeding woman. Lucia streaked over and grabbed his gun arm at the wrist, extending it away from his body. Then she drove her gauntleted fist into his exposed armpit, sending tendrils of electric agony directly to the poor fool's heart.

All five men hit the ground within one second of each other and Roland's internal clock said the whole exchange took just two-point-eight seconds. Roland did not think that sort of thing was possible without physical augmentations, but he didn't get the chance to ponder it for long.

There was a scream behind him, and Roland turned to see McGinty's driver yanked into the air and slammed down into the floor with a sickening splat. As life and blood oozed out of the poor man, Roland got a good look at his attacker.

It looked like a robot or a piece of heavy equipment. In a way, it was both. It was close to ten feet tall, and at first glance could have passed for any other piece of large industrial apparatus. It was nominally bipedal and had it had two arms after a fashion. Both the legs and arms were just a mass of large, articulated and reinforced hydraulic joints and actuators, though. The legs seemed too short, or perhaps the arms were too long, but either way, it looked like a huge, mechanical simian. Each arm terminated in a three-fingered claw, similar to the Dwarf's arm, but much larger. Where the machine's 'chest' would have been sat a spherical canopied cockpit framed by a heavy reinforced chassis. Through that screen, Roland could see the head and upper torso of a scrawny bald man connected to various panels by tubes and wires and lit by the blue-green glow of screens and dials.

Roland had seen similar things off-world; on mining colonies, especially. When a miner was hurt or injured on the job, the big corporations would sometimes offer to augment the aggrieved party with cybernetic enhancements that benefited the company. They would give the biggest raises and benefits to the employees willing to be turned into heavy machinery, simply because it was cheaper and more efficient that buying the heavy machinery and hiring new employees. These volunteers were not given new limbs, but instead attached to a piece of equipment called an 'armature' designed for an industrial purpose. The pilot's quality of life did not factor strongly into these designs, but they got to live and work and make a bunch of money. Most people took the deal when offered.

Roland was looking at an industrial-class heavy cyborg, with an armature probably rated for the harshest environments the galaxy could offer.

Roland's tactical assessment was unnerving. That thing was heavier and almost certainly stronger than he was. Its builders looked to have been rather liberal with structural reinforcement and durability modifications, as well. A closer look revealed that at some point ballistic armor had also been added to the chassis. It wasn't unheard of for licensed industrial 'borgs to turn to the far-more-lucrative world of freelance mercenary work, so Roland was unsurprised by this. It didn't make him happy though.

The torso in the fishbowl cockpit grinned, "Roland goddamn Tankowicz! I've heard a' you, man! You just went and got all the bigwigs pissed off, didn't ya!"

The three-fingered clamps spun like propellers, whirring in a high-pitched squeal.

"You got a hell of a rep, man!" The face was young-looking, too young to have a complete armature like this. Whatever accident had taken most of his body had to have been horrific.

Roland squared off, and tried to stall for a little time to assess the massive machine in front of him, "Do I know you?"

The man in the machine looked disappointed, "I'm fucking Tom Miner, man! I'm famous."

Roland chuckled, "Not here you're not. Enceladus?"

That made the man smile, "Hell yeah! At first, but I've been all over the galaxy, now." He beamed. The idiot seemed to think this was all a big game.

"You want to die here on Earth?" Roland growled, shifting his weight to his rear leg, "Because if you get in my way, that's what happens."

"Big, bad, Tank man!" Miner laughed, "You definitely got some slick shit under the hood, man. I've seen some of the video feeds of you in action. But you ain't never met anything like me." The enormous arms and whirring claws waved in vague menace, "This is totally gonna seal my rep!"

Contrary to his opponent's claims, Roland had seen things like Miner before. He had spent a hellish twenty days on Enceladus dealing with a rogue AI that had turned the mining robots into killing machines. It had been a brutal campaign. Mining equipment had to be some of the toughest hardware in the galaxy. If this really was an Enceladus mining 'borg, then Roland would have some serious work ahead of him.

Being indoors meant that HE from Durendal was a bad call. It would probably kill Lucia and there was no guarantee it would break anything useful on Miner. Flechette would punch holes, but tiny holes wouldn't stop a mining bot, the damn things had so many redundant systems that he'd run out of ammo before slowing it down. Anti-personnel beads were a joke. Against a machine designed to mine asteroids in deep space, beads would be about as effective as a light drizzle. That really only left blunt-force trauma, and based on the size of the opposition, it would take a lot of blunt force to cause any real trauma. Roland stifled a sigh. This would definitely burn a percentage point or two off the ol' power cell.

"Walk or talk. The only thing talking will give you a rep for is noise, son."

The face behind the glass grinned, "Let's go for a walk, then!"

Both cyborgs moved at the same instant, and Roland was disappointed to note that Miner's arms moved with blinding speed. He doubted that Miner had any neurological enhancements, they were too expensive and didn't really enhance mining tasks. But, the brain in question wasn't controlling a human body, either. If Miner's brain coded a strike for maximum speed, then the armature would throw at its maximum speed, even if that was faster than the brain of the pilot could think. There was no organic nervous system in the mechanical pieces, so there was no reason to slow them down or use human nerve conduction.

The right arm of the mechanical monster thrust straight forward in a furious attempt to snatch Roland by the head or to strike the upper body. Roland's speed was just sufficient to juke inside the path of the attacking limb, and he sent a right fist streaking toward the canopy.

But Miner's left arm, travelling a millisecond behind the right, grazed his shoulder and sent the blow off course. Roland's fist clanged off a reinforced section of Miner's torso in a shower of sparks and a screech of strained metal.

Miner's right arm had already begun a third blow, and even with his reflexes dialed as fast as they could go, Roland was caught by an arcing backhanded strike that lifted him off the ground and sent him flying.

Roland skidded to a halt forty feet from his opponent and looked up. Miner was re-orienting on Roland and the big chassis turned and lumbered toward the downed man.

Despite the setback, Roland had some valuable intel, now. His opponent had needed a second to re-acquire his target and to re-orient the chassis before continuing. If Roland wasn't already running at his maximum temporal dilation, he may not have noticed the delay, but he caught it. Roland had brawled with enough cyborgs to know what that implied.

Tom Miner wasn't controlling the chassis directly in the sense that Roland controlled his own body. Miner was sending pre-coded instructions to the frame with his brain. It was a cheap and efficient way to achieve superhuman levels of speed without having to jack up the entire nervous system.

Numerous military drones and armatures employed the exact same system, and skilled operators could string multiple attacks and complicated maneuvers together the way a composer assembled a symphony out of different instruments and different notes.

Roland was confident that Tom probably had thousands of pre-coded attack patterns and reactions that he simply queued up and sent out as needed. Against ninety-nine percent of opponents, this would be more than adequate. Pretending that his lack of enhanced reflexes was going to make Miner an easy opponent was not the sort of tactical blunder Roland was known for.

He resolved himself to not be in that ninety-nine percent and sprang to his feet. Miner was far too big and heavy to locomote with any real speed, and Roland intended to exploit his advantage there.

He immediately ruled out a direct frontal assault, which irritated the man because that was his favorite approach with most things. Miner was just too strong to stand toe-to-toe with, so with some reluctance Roland elected to play a more strategic game. A game that took advantage of Miner's pattern-based tactics.

At a run, Roland made his way to the truck that they had arrived in. It weighed somewhere in the vicinity of eight thousand pounds, so Roland took an extra quarter second to secure a good grip on the frame before flipping it as hard as he could towards the oncoming metal monster.

Eight thousand pounds was not terribly heavy by Roland's standards, and the vehicle tumbled and rolled like a kicked beer can at Tom Miner. It shed parts like water droplets as it tumbled, but Roland didn't notice that. He was already moving.

Inside the clear bubble, Miner keyed a standard defensive maneuver followed by a series of blows. The armature folded the arms over the canopy and braced the legs so the truck crashed into a two-ton armored wall. The truck did not fare well in the collision, and two subsequent swipes from gigantic metal arms tore the offending vehicle away and cast it to the side with contemptuous ease.

Miner's cockpit lit up as sensors tracked and scanned for the target as soon as the dome was clear, but the target was moving. And man, could he move!

The chassis' servos automatically reoriented to place Roland squarely in the center of the HUD. This was good because Tom was too busy queuing attack macros and building scenario trees to follow his opponent manually.

This Tank fucker is running some serious shit! Miner observed to himself, as strength, speed, armor, and reaction data popped up on the HUD. *High-end military tech. It's gotta be...*

BANG! CRRRKSHHT!

A circular, spider-webbed crack formed in the canopy right in front of Tom's face. At the center of the crack, lodged and suspended in the thick, transparent armor of the dome was a single flechette. Miner gulped in shock and scurried backwards to avoid follow-up shots.

Despite its size, Tom's chassis was not 'slow,' per se. It had needed less than one full second to reorient on the darting black cyborg, but Tom Miner the man was saddled with reflexes that were only slightly better than average. This meant that while his body was oriented to the threat, Tom's brain was too slow to code a response to Roland's attack. Roland had exploited this delay to sneak an armor-piercing round past the arms and into the softest target available. The flechette failed to penetrate the bubble, but Tom Miner was rattled just the same.

Miner coded a defensive posture on instinct, using the arms to cover the canopy, while advancing towards Roland. He lined up four separate patterns and added them to the scenario tree based upon the new tactical information. Now a single arm would track Roland's weapon hand automatically and protect the cockpit. It meant one less arm for attack, but it effectively shut down that particular strategy for Roland.

Roland observed the behavioral shift from his opponent and watched the left arm create a barrier between the barrel of his weapon and the canopy.

Clever, he conceded, *but still playing into my hands*. Roland was beginning to enjoy himself. He so rarely got to stretch his legs in a fight, and this scrap was feeling like the good old days. It wasn't often he fought someone bigger and stronger than he was.

He held his ground and pumped rounds into the defending arm until Durendal's flechette slot ran dry. The projectiles lodged and tore holes in the limb, but the damage would never be enough to shut that arm down. Sparks flew and coolant hissed in white gouts of vapor, but the arm stayed up and the monster kept advancing.

At twelve feet away, Roland holstered his weapon and charged. In that languid, underwater fashion he was accustomed to, Roland saw the big claw clench into a misshapen fist and accelerate towards his head. That is when he planted a right foot hard into the ground and pivoted as hard and fast as he could.

Waiting until Miner committed to a strike was a calculated risk. Once Miner's armature started a pattern, things would happen faster than the pilot's reflexes could follow. Miner relied on the speed of the armature and the cleverness of the selected attack to do the job because his brain couldn't act fast enough to change in the middle. Roland was betting that he could switch tactics with enough alacrity to get some free hits in while Tom reacquired his target and keyed the next maneuver.

The armature, however, was every bit as fast as Roland was, so there was a very real element of risk involved. If Roland guessed incorrectly which direction to move, he was likely to receive the kind of hit that could crush a tank.

He just barely made it.

There was the impression of moving air as the giant metal arm cruised past Roland's head with less than an inch to spare. Roland was past the first strike, and even though the second was already on its way, he wasn't anywhere near where it would be in eight one-hundredths of a second.

As far as Roland was concerned, Tom Miner was swatting at empty air until he could reorient. In real time that was about three-quarters of a second later.

Or an eternity if you are Roland Tankowicz.

Chapter Twenty-Two

Lucia had kept herself busy during the frantic opening moments of Roland's battle with the giant machine. She first went to McGinty's driver to see if she could help, but the oozing mass of bloody bone shards and gray matter where the man's head had once sat precluded the administration of the limited first aid at her disposal.

The horrified woman refused to retch or even acknowledge her disgust with the display, because that was what let the fear in, and the fear would accumulate until it shut her down. She could feel that terror. It was ever-present and hungry, waiting for her focus to slip if only for an instant. Lucia beat back her fear and poured her focus into the simple tasks of the moment. This kept her hyperactive brain from running all the potential horrors of the situation through her head at ten times the speed of anyone else's. She was learning that if she filled the frantic traffic jam of her thoughts with productive scenarios, the non-productive versions stayed in the background.

It was how she had handled the five men outside of the van. She had observed them, evaluated them, and formulated at least five different plans for taking them out in the first instant.

And then she had moved. It was so different when she moved now. Her body knew where to step, how much pressure to apply, when to turn, and exactly where to put a strike so far ahead of the moment she actually had to do it, that the whole thing felt leisurely. Like she was cheating. Fighting five regular men had felt like fighting five people trapped in gelatin.

Lucia reveled in the fact that she was unlocking the secret power of her brain and body. If she put all the thoughts into the solving a problem, all her enhanced cognitive speed and bandwidth went into finding solutions for that problem. The trick, she had found, was to focus on the solutions themselves, not the problems. Her imagination and training did the rest.

So, when four more men in black armor and harnesses came skidding in through the man door next to the bay door, Lucia was on them instantly. She struck four times in half of a second, and the gauntlets put two of the men down before they even saw her. Lucia was confused for a moment by the two remaining men *not* going down, but then she realized what had happened. She had struck too fast, and the gloves hadn't had enough time to recharge. With casual ease she dodged a counter punch from one man and grabbed the gun hand of the other, long before he could bring the muzzle to bear on her.

Her leg snaked out and her heel dug deep into the ensnared man's guts, folding him in half and leaving the gun in her hand as he fell. With a twist of the hips and a pivot on the balls of her feet, she turned and slapped the pistol from the other man's hand before serving him with an elbow to the cheek.

Her gauntlets were back up, and each man got a blow to the skull, blasting them into unconsciousness with terrible efficiency.

Blood was roaring in her ears when she looked back on Roland to see the big man locked in a terrifying ballet of nuclear-powered cyborg war machines.

The colossal mechanism's arms windmilled in giant circles, smashing chunks from the concrete floor and hurling debris like shrapnel. Clawed fists smashed crates and dug furrows with every floor-shaking impact. Meanwhile Roland, looking small and thin in comparison, darted between them to slide behind the giant. It seemed to Lucia that Roland had endless seconds to react from there, as the misshapen metal monster appeared helpless to stop its own frenzied smashing. It looked like Tom Miner had forgotten about Roland and declared war on the floor of the warehouse instead.

Tankowicz hurled himself into the back of the armature and rained furious blows against the metal giant. Fists like black cudgels struck with staccato clangs so fast it sounded like the frantic ringing of an alarm bell. Though outweighed by several thousand pounds, Roland's strikes were delivered with the flawless technique of a trained boxer and the full force of his synthetic musculature. Having spent many hours in the ring herself, Lucia could appreciate the sharp precision of those strikes. His monstrous opponent was caught off-guard and off-balance by the fury of the assault. A freight-train punch found the weakness of an exposed hip linkage, and the sound of wailing hydraulics was added to the din of combat as the huge machine lurched off balance. With an ataxic stagger, Miner pitched forward so hard he had to catch himself with his arms to keep himself from being hurled to the floor. This bought Roland time for another flurry of punches, which Lucia noticed now targeted those exposed hip joints. Sparks flew, and the strikes resounded like the crash of a triphammer in the warehouse.

Lucia had no idea how much punishment Tom's armature could take, but it looked like Roland was trying to find out.

But it was not long before Roland's moment of advantage passed. With the arms splayed outward, the top half of Miner's chassis rotated 180 degrees and a whirling backhand connected with Roland's hastily erected defensive block.

When that giant hand contacted Roland's defending forearm, Lucia felt the impact from her molars to the soles of her feet even though she was forty feet away. The furious strength of the horizontal strike tore Roland from the ground and spun him away from the enemy in a disconcertingly flat trajectory. Lucia realized to her terror that her companion would hit the wall hard, and she could only hope he'd survive it.

Roland Tankowicz shared that hope as well.

Being aware of his flight speed and the inevitable result, he oriented himself such that he struck the wall with his feet first. He was nominally successful in avoiding a broken neck, but the impact drove him into the reinforced concrete of the wall with enough vigor to buckle it. His vision flashed white for an instant and he didn't need the diagnostic readouts his helmet would have given him to know that real structural damage had been done to his legs. Roland could feel pain, albeit in a muted, abstract sort of way, and he acknowledged that while not severe enough to affect his combat efficacy by more than a point or two, he would definitely feel this hit tomorrow.

He could not afford himself the luxury of injury assessment though. As soon as the unforgiving wall finished arresting his flight and he had settled in a graceless tangle of limbs on the floor, Roland clawed himself to his feet. With exasperated determination, the black cyborg began a sprint directly towards Miner.

That, Roland knew, was going to be the key to winning this fight. Miner could act every bit as fast as Roland, but he could not *react* with the same speed. When Roland gave Miner the opportunity to act, Miner's superior strength and size came into play and Roland went flying. When Roland forced Miner to *re*act, he had lots of time to score hits; not to mention avoid the likely fatal situation of getting grabbed and held by those terrifying clamps.

Roland sped upon Miner from across the room, and Miner quickly coded a defensive macro that began with blocking Roland's charge. When Roland saw the armature's limbs cross in front to cover the canopy, he used his split-second reaction advantage to alter his angle of attack by just a few degrees, and transition to a low wrestler's tackle. Instead of an earth-shattering collision with the canopy (which would have certainly resulted in Roland getting grabbed and pummeled), there was an oblique slide towards Miner's right leg, which Roland scooped up in both arms like a wrestler.

Roland seized the enormous column-like right leg with both arms and yanked it from the floor. The machine tilted precariously, but the mining armature had sophisticated balancing gear. Though it wobbled, the hips and arms adjusted the center of gravity so it did not go down. Since no subsequent attack seemed forthcoming, Roland arched his back and yanked the leg to the side, dragging the machine sideways and splaying the entrapped leg like a wishbone. With a kick that sounded like a car accident, Roland knocked the base leg out from underneath the cockpit and the armature plummeted to the floor hard in a face-down tangle of ropy limbs and grasping claws.

The immense arms reeled around and the terrifying three-fingered clamps made frantic grasps at Roland like metal snakes. Unfortunately for the mercenary, Tom Miner did not have a defensive macro for this situation, so there was no coordination to the attack. Roland, still holding the leg, stepped hard on the hip joint of the armature and twisted the trapped leg with all his prodigious might. Miner instantly realized what Roland was attempting, and braced the arms against the floor, digging the claws deep into the concrete. He rotated the torso as hard as he could, trying to wrench the leg away from Roland's vice-like grip. Roland planted his other foot on the floor hard enough to crack the cement, and twisted back.

For a moment, everything stopped moving. It was eerie and still if not exactly quiet. But there was only the sound of Roland growling through gritted teeth and clenched jaw, mixed with the whine of hydraulic actuators straining against some unfathomable force.

At peak output, Roland could press twenty tons over his head, and lift three times that from the floor. Tom Miner's armature was made to survive multiple gravities, destructive accidents, and the unmerciful physical torture that is heavy mining off-world. For an instant, they were frozen in place as the two mighty machines opposed each other in a tense stalemate. It was unclear for several seconds which would prove the victor: Would it be the irresistible force, or the immovable object? Lucia held her breath.

But with slow, inexorable, tortuous finality, that leg began to twist backward. The thick column of metal began to groan in morose protest of its own unavoidable fate. It was a fruitless protest. With agonizing slowness, the captured limb continued to bend further and further until, with a shriek of capitulation and a shower of sparks, the hip joint surrendered and the leg came free of the armature. Coolant and hydraulic fluid sprayed in dramatic gouts not unlike blood from a severed artery.

Roland could not stop a feral, predator's grin from stretching across his face.

I have you now, motherfucker!

Chapter Twenty-Three

Tom Miner was in a very bad position, and he knew it. The unit had no contingency for fighting with a missing leg, and his screens were lit up with a host of structural emergencies and diagnostic bad news. He quickly switched his focus to escaping, because Tom Miner knew when a fight was lost, and he damn sure wanted to live.

But Roland was having too much fun, now. The cockpit thundered and the screens flashed static as something struck from behind. Tom had to check the rear camera to see that Roland was wielding the severed leg with both arms like a massive club, and then another blow drove the mining 'borg's cockpit back into the concrete.

Miner keyed a series of flails and kicks to move Roland far enough away to stop the battering. It was an ungainly and undignified spasm, but he got the armature into a three-limbed crawl that started him scrambling towards the door. He wasn't sure what his plan was, but he knew he had to get away from that guy and fast. He keyed the radio for backup and hoped it could buy him enough time to eject the cockpit. Losing the armature would be a financial blow he may never recover from, but it sure as hell beat dying.

Then the left arm stopped working and Miner couldn't figure out why until he saw the eight-foot hulk smashing at the shoulder with fists like obsidian wrecking balls. He must have severed the control lines! Miner fumed and attempted to reroute the controls to get the arm moving again. His rig had multiple redundant systems, but Tankowicz was breaking things faster than he could fix them.

Roland took advantage of the appendage's apparent shutdown to target several more vicious blows to its mechanical actuators before Tom swatted his antagonist away with the other arm. Miner took great satisfaction in how far the muscle-bound bastard flew before crashing into the wall with another impact that shook the ceiling.

His relief was short-lived. His onboard diagnostics indicated that even though the controls circuit was back up, the left arm would not be operable any time soon. Most of the mechanical apparatus was too damaged at this point. His left arm was now limp dead weight.

"Shit shit shit!" Miner shrieked at his machine. With far too much haste, he keyed up several improvised movement macros to continue his flopping escape, but the increasing futility of the attempt was not lost on him. His frustration evolved into panic when he saw the big man leap up nonplussed from the rubble of his landing, and sprint right back at him.

What the fuck is this guy made of? Tom lamented to himself. He searched in desperation for an escape route that his crippled armature might survive, but he never got the chance because Roland was on him in a fraction of a second.

Down an arm and a leg, it was all Tom Miner could do to throw an arm between himself and Roland. He was far too slow, and Roland sped around the sloppy, off-balance defensive swat and rocked the armature back to the floor with a stomping boot to the chassis. As soon as Miner braced his good arm to lift the cockpit again, Roland clamped onto it with both hands around the elbow joint. Tom could only watch in fresh horror as the grim cyborg braced his right boot against the cockpit. He knew where this was going.

Fear and crushing despair took residence in the pit of his stomach as the ruthless mercenary gazed at the tread of Roland's size 21 boot, pressed against the canopy so hard that thin cracks were radiating outward from the compression. A quiet whimper snuck past his lips as the onyx titan torqued his remaining arm further and further until the shoulder joint shrieked, snapped, and died. But there was nothing Tom Miner could have done to stop it. This wasn't a man, it was an inexorable engine of destruction; and Tom Miner had plopped himself right in front of it. There was a grim finality to that final twist; then the useless limb tore free of its moorings and crashed flaccidly to the floor.

Miner didn't even bother to thrash his remaining limb. The big son of a bitch would just tear that off, too. He was going to be in debt for millions getting the armature fixed if he lived through this. He considered ejecting the cockpit from the frame, but that would mean abandoning the entire armature, with no guarantee that the limited mobility of the escape pod would get him to safety.

So, he resorted to negotiation, "Shit! You win, man! You don't gotta kill me!"

"Convince me not to," Roland growled.

"I got reinforcements coming. I can call them off," was the weak opening gambit.

Roland raised his pistol, and a woman Tom had barely noticed earlier chimed in. She was dressed in black tactical gear and perched over the downed bodies of five of Marko's best men.

"Do they look like these guys?" She kicked the limp form of a man she had obviously dropped personally, "because that's not much of issue for us, actually."

Miner's face fell and Roland growled again, "Call 'em off, anyway. I don't want to have to kill everyone here." He placed the barrel of that huge pistol against the canopy, directly in front of the terrified pilot's face, "Then we are going to talk about the best way to get to Marko."

Miner keyed a stand down order to the rest of the compound, but no one was convinced that would work for more than a minute or two. For the moment at least, none of the reinforcements outside were displaying excessive eagerness to step inside the war zone that the warehouse had become. Miner could only imagine what his battle with Roland must have sounded like to anyone outside.

Scared or not though, if Tom Miner didn't walk out of there soon, somebody was going to come in looking.

"Good," Roland grunted. "Now where is Marko hiding?"

Miner really didn't want to answer. Marko was the lowest ranking guy on the Combine board, but he was still a Board member. If anyone found out he had snitched on a board member, he was dead. But the barrel of Roland's gun, pressed against the canopy less than twelve inches from his own face, was a much more pressing concern. Miner spilled his guts after only a few seconds' musing, "He's usually in his office, top floor of the main building." He shook his head, "But he will have bailed out by now."

"Just tell me where!" Tom Miner was learning quickly about Roland's lack of patience. The black cyborg grabbed the armature roughly by a piece of twisted shoulder mechanism and smacked the cockpit against the floor with a jumbled crash.

"Gahh!" Miner sputtered, as screens flashed and the harness holding his torso in place bit into his shoulders. "Cut the shit, man! Jeezis!" He sounded whiny, and Tom felt a moment of shame as his tone reminded everyone of the mercenary's apparent youth.

"In two goddamn seconds I'm going to crack that thing like an egg, boy." Roland's irritation was not feigned.

The woman's voice offered advice, "Just tell him, kid. Otherwise I'll end up having to hose most of you off my boots later. He's a real bitch when he gets like this."

Miner gave up, "He'll be in his panic room. It's under the cafeteria in the admin building. It's the big gray one near the main entrance. Now let me go, man!"

"What do you think, boss?" Roland looked to the woman in black armor. He never loosened his grip on the broken mechanical monster.

The terrifying woman sniffed and affected an air of benevolent nonchalance, "Good enough. Let him go, Tank." Tom did not understand who this chick was, but he made a mental note to steer clear of her in the future. If she could pull this bastard's reins, Tom wanted no part of what she could do to him.

"You're lucky," Roland growled in a deep, guttural snarl as he dropped his defeated opponent. Tom didn't feel lucky, but there was relief at not being dead and a small hope for salvaging his body.

"Oh!" he heard her call abruptly, "but make sure to pry him out of that thing, first. I don't want him flopping around and getting bright ideas about calling Marko…"

Roland's normally impassive visage split from ear to ear, "Yes ma'am!"

Tom Miner screamed…

Chapter Twenty-Four

Marko was pissed off. He was pissed off because he was nervous, which was as close to being scared as made no difference. Being scared was the one thing Marko hated above all others, and he was starting to think he might, in fact, be scared after all. But for now, he was going with 'nervous.'

When the call came in that the truck was a Trojan Horse, he had scrambled two teams of enforcers and that idiot kid, Miner to action. Marko, citing strategic insight, had retired to the panic room to watch it play out in safety through the monitors. He was now questioning the wisdom of this decision.

Miner had radioed for back-up seven minutes ago and then sent the 'all-clear' three minutes later. That should have made him happy, but fifteen of his boys had gone into Building Nine, and not a damn one had come out yet. No one was on the comms, either.

The four guys with body cameras that he sent in to see what was going on had been taken out so fast that no information could be gleaned from the less than three seconds of video they had captured. Marko trusted his gut, and his gut said shit was going horribly wrong in there. He had a pessimistic gut.

Fatir was piping the live feed from outside the warehouse to his DataPad and everything looked very quiet right now. Way too quiet for the war that had to have gone on inside those walls.

The mob boss cursed himself for not putting a video feed inside Building Nine, but the damn thing got so little use it just seemed like a waste of money. Now he cursed himself for his legendary frugality.

Not that he had been all that cheap when it came to this bounty. Bringing Miner in had been something of a lark. The cyborg mercenary was already planetside for a refit, so his price had been less usurious than normal. Marko supposed that with the current bounty on that Ribiero bitch, he might need Miner's horsepower to push other squads off the hunt. Now he was wondering if he shouldn't have brought in even more heavy hitters.

Had Miner taken Tank down? Or was his expensive mercenary scrapped and all his boys dead? What was the story, here? He considered sending some of the guys guarding the admin building to check it out. He had twenty good, solid, goons on his personal detail, and maybe another thirty standing by to back up Miner if necessary. But discounted pricing aside, hiring the Mercenary 'borg had still cost a fortune. Marko was loathe to spend any more of his boys on a job he was paying someone else to do.

He stayed glued to his screen, batting potential scenarios around his imagination in a vain attempt to construct a believable reason for the deafening silence. Long seconds stretched into longer minutes. Marko's anxiety continued to intensify.

Fatir's voice over the comm was too loud, jarring Marko from his reverie and startling the big man far too much for his liking.

"Sir!" There was a very disheartening intensity in Fatir's voice, a jagged edge of fear that that made each word rasp, "One of the men inside has reported in. Miner is down and unresponsive!"

Motherfucking shit! Marko thought to himself, well beyond 'nervous' now, "Where the fuck is Tank!"

Fatir was not calming down, either, "He left through the back of the building sir!" A pause, "He is heading for the admin building, sir!"

"I thought you were watching all the doors! How'd he get by you?" Marko knew he would not like the answer. Fatir was smart and competent, and Marko was not some comic book villain who punished underlings for things outside of their control. If Tank had gotten by Fatir, then there was a good reason.

"He broke through the wall, sir."

"How the fuck did he..." Marko stopped himself. If Tank had dropped an industrial mining armature like Tom Miner's, then it followed that a regular concrete wall would not be an obstacle.

"Get on him! Intercept that fucker!" Marko knew his men needed more specific guidance than this, but it was all he had right now, "Use the truck-mounted shit and bring him down!"

Marko heard Fatir's voice, tinny and distant, as the young man echoed his leader's commands to the rest of the men, then he came back to the mic, "Done sir, we'll be on him in—"

The admin building shook to its very foundations. It felt like someone had crashed a bus directly into the lobby, which was not far from the truth. Marko dropped the comm in startled fright and scrambled for the safety of the corner.

It didn't feel safe at all to the big gangster. The sounds of total war resonated above him, and he could tell his bodyguards were fighting in the lobby area. His was an experienced ear, and the panicked shouts and enormous quantity of unrestrained gunfire indicated with depressing clarity that his boys were losing this battle. Marko's heart sank. In just the span of a few minutes, the thick steel walls and impregnable vault doors of his panic room had become far less reassuring than he wanted them to be.

The cacophony felt like it went on for hours, and yet the trembling man perceived its end with painful abruptness: There were the muffled reports of weapons above him, and the screams of hardened underworld enforcers as they were maimed and killed. Then nothing but empty stillness. An auditory void containing no more sound than the terrifying silence of a grave. Less than one minute, in all, and the madness upstairs was over.

Then, with horrible slowness, came the heavy rhythmic thuds of giant footsteps overhead. Marko looked at his shaking hands and heard the roar of his blood in his ears. He wasn't nervous anymore; he was truly and inescapably afraid.

"Fatir! Get those men over here now! He's in the building!" Marko tried not to sound like a terrified child, but he may not have been entirely successful. Fingers numb with adrenaline fumbled with the locked cabinet in the steel-encased panic room, and he dropped the keys twice before he got the cursed thing open. From inside, he grabbed a plasma caster so illegal just owning it could get him a life sentence. Its heft and awesome destructive power reassured him, and the big gangster slammed a charging cell home in the butt of the stock. His panic retreated slightly when the controls lit up and the weapon came to life with a keening whine.

Marko gathered his courage. *Fine, I'll do this myself.*

He shouldered the glossy black weapon and set the reservoir to a full-power blast. It would burn out the cell in three shots, but he'd be damned if they wouldn't be good ones. He almost forgot to slip on the light-blocking glasses, but remembered as soon as the brightness of the holographic targeting reticle burned dancing green spots into his vision. Surviving this was his top priority, but not going blind was also high on the list.

Marko's preparations were interrupted by a thundering impact on the door to the panic room. The crash was so loud that Marko's ears rang like a fire alarm for several seconds after. There was a sigh of deep relief when he saw that the door held, but closer examination brought his reprieve to an abrupt halt.

It had moved.

There was a clear line of light ringing the edges, showing that the air-tight closure had been warped off its seals by whatever horrible thing had struck it. A thin rectangle of blue-white luminescence was all it took for Marko to realize that his men were not going to get there in time.

Then the bashing began in earnest, and Marko had to drop his weapon to cover his ears as the universe's loudest battering ram struck the six-inch thick steel vault door five times per second.

It was a good door. It lasted four seconds before heaving inward with a horrible tearing screech and crashing to the floor with a heavy thud. Bright light flooded the panic room and Marko's hands went back down to the plasma caster. He tried to bring the weapon up, tried to make his stand; but a black shadow stretched out from behind the massive silhouette in the door and snaked across the room to strike his arm like an obsidian dagger.

There was a pop and a keening wail accompanied searing electric pain that blossomed in his arm. His fingers, now dead and numb, could not grasp the gun before two more needle-like fists sent their poisonous stings to his shoulder and then the back of his thigh.

Both weapon and man collapsed to the floor, one inanimate the other disoriented. A dozen more fiery bites from the black monster struck him with horrible rapidity and casual ease. The demon never let up, never paused. Every other contact would kill the nerves and muscles around the point of impact, and the popping and crackling noise played like castanets in his burning ears.

Soon, the most feared man in Big Woo was a wheezing, drooling, sobbing mess on the floor of his own fortress.

"Lucia! Enough!"

Marko barely heard the booming voice through the haze of pain and fading consciousness. He was grateful for the respite that came with it, for only then did the interminable stinging cease.

The next voice was smaller, but all the more terrifying for the pure feral rage that was evident, "Make him talk, Roland. I don't care how."

"Count on it. You go watch for his reinforcements. You don't need to see this part." The big shadow, which Marko now could see was Tank (as if it could have been anyone else, he conceded), spoke with a quiet compassion that conferred a horrible finality to the implications it contained. Whatever it was he was going to do, he wanted to protect the angry woman from seeing it. That did not bode well.

"Fine," the woman spat, "How long do you need?"

Marko's eyes found Tank's, and the two men locked gazes for a long second. Roland's response rang with professional confidence, "two minutes."

Marko's senses were returning, and the burning numbness that marked every part of him the woman had struck was already fading. Mark Anthony Johnstone was many things: A slaver, a drug peddler, a thief, a murderer. But he was not stupid, and he had made a long and illustrious career out of escaping situations like this.

No, Marko wasn't done, yet. Down? Yes. Out? Never.

He thought about the plasma caster, laying on the floor three feet away. He needed time and a distraction, that was all. Then he could put a megawatt of pure energy through this fucker's face and be on his way.

Tank was a Dockside fixer, Marko remembered. This was a professional negotiator. He could work with that.

The lumbering capo was slow to sit up, feigning more hurt than he felt. It wasn't hard to be convincing; he was in enough real pain that it was easy to make the act convincing. He raised his hands in surrender and coughed, "You win, Tank. I'll deal. What's your price?"

Roland's body relaxed, and the lantern jaw stopped flexing and bulging with agitation. This was now an ordinary interaction between businessmen. Marko understood this part and so did Roland.

"That's easy, Marko," Roland's smile was cold, yet polite, "Where is Don Ribiero?"

Marko smiled back, "So she hired you to find her old man, huh? Figures." He shifted on the floor to get more comfortable, only incidentally moving an inch closer to the plasma caster, "The board will kill me if I tell you, you know."

Roland started to talk but Marko interrupted, "I know, I know... You'll kill me if I don't. I wrote that playbook, pal. So let's figure out how to get you want you want without me getting killed, shall we?"

"All ears." Roland was a poor conversationalist. He also knew that the less you talked, the more the other guy would.

Marko smiled, all business, "I can't tell you where he is, because that would embarrass the Board. But if you were to steal my DataPad, you might find a lot of correspondence about Corpus Mundi, and a list of their research facilities that are doing the kind of work Dr. Ribiero is good at. You might even notice that one of those facilities is owned by a Combine Shell Corporation and is completely... uh... off the books."

Marko waited for Roland's reaction. He was playing a tight game here. He was telling the truth about his DataPad because lie detection technology was not difficult to obtain and this whole gambit centered on Roland believing him. The discarded DataPad was a pale rectangle of plastic across the room where it had been dropped earlier. If Tank went to get it, Marko would have a chance to go for the caster. If Tank made Marko retrieve it, he'd get to walk right by the damn thing.

It had been a while since Marko had gotten his own hands dirty, but he remembered how to win a fight. Sure, he avoided fights, because fights were risky and risk was for suckers. But since there was no way out of this battle, he prepared himself to win it.

Tank strolled over to the discarded Pad with confident, relaxed strides. Marko's heart quickened, and we waited for Roland to lean over to collect the device. Marko timed his lunge for the moment the towering fixer's eyes went to the DataPad, and then exploded like a coiled snake toward the waiting weapon just three short feet away.

His fingers closed around the grip and he rolled to his back, bringing the muzzle to bear on his unsuspecting foe.

To his dismay, Marko discovered far too late that he did not have an unsuspecting foe. It was immediately clear to the doomed man that his foe was very much of the suspecting variety. A black fist closed over the front of the plasma caster and squeezed with inhuman strength. With a depressing crunch, the muzzle of the expensive weapon disappeared into a crumbling mess of bleeding-edge materials and shattered crystal focusing arrays.

Marko stroked the trigger in a futile effort to make the gun do something, but the effort was wasted. His caster had gone from luxurious military hardware to useless lump of parts in a fraction of a second.

The other massive hand clamped around Marko's throat and hoisted him choking and gurgling into the air, "They're designed to go inert when damaged, dumbass. Otherwise they'd blow up." Roland's admonishment was a cruel taunt, his face twisted in a contemptuous sneer.

Their eyes met, and the fury and loathing Marko saw there made him wince. Roland's hatred for his enemy was a palpable thing in that painful and extended moment. It confused and terrified Marko. The gangster lacked any capacity to comprehend what was going on behind the soulless black gaze of his tormentor. His life as a remorseless criminal had gifted him with neither the ability nor the perspective to understand hate on the level Roland Tankowicz was experiencing.

Roland had never hated anyone the way he hated Marko right now.

Mark Anthony Johnstone was responsible for ruining the lives of thousands, and to the seasoned gang lord, this was no more heinous than selling produce. Roland hated that the greed and selfishness of one man could do so much harm. This, however, was not the confusing part. As a hateful person himself, Marko could understand the kind of antipathy one man might have for another quite easily. That was not what was so terrifying to the choking, dangling man.

Marko saw something very different from naked malice in the twisted mien of his enemy. The furious tension in Roland's massive jaw and the deep, pained furrows of that heavy brow told Marko that this went well beyond one man's hate for another. The fat crime lord hung in the air, terrified and perplexed.

As he considered his fleeting mortality, Marko completely overlooked a basic reality that had been gnawing at Roland since he first set down in the Woo: People like Marko existed, because people like Roland had done nothing to stop them. The fact that Roland had done nothing to stop Marko over the years made perfect sense to the criminal; it was none of Roland's business. Why should Roland concern himself with what Marko was doing over in Big Woo? A person would have to care for the feelings of others to know that the apathy and inaction of the last twenty years were eating Roland Tankowicz alive from the inside out. Marko was just not that kind of guy.

The egomaniacal mobster would never comprehend that at this moment, and in this place, the only thing Roland Tankowicz hated more than the quivering, sniveling piece of human garbage in his hand, was himself.

Roland hated himself for having done nothing. He hated his weakness and his apathy. He hated the coward he had become.

Marko would die blissfully ignorant of the silent promise an angry old soldier would make in that terrible, gravid instant. It was the worst kind of promise. The kind of promise you make to yourself, deep within the part of you that you don't tell people about. It was the kind of promise that would be easy to break because nobody would know it existed unless you kept it.

No more.

The grim cyborg had willed it to himself.

No more dead innocents. No more slaves. No more kidnappings. No more petty dictators.

The horrible, merciless grip tightened, and Marko's eyes bulged.

No more looking the other way. No more 'that's just the way it is.'

In the grim darkness of the panic room, an empty black hand curled into a fist so tight it could have turned coal into diamonds.

No more cowardice, soldier.

The last thing Marko saw was Roland's clenched fist rushing toward his face. The blow was so fast, he did not even have time for his pupils to dilate in terror before the techno-organic bludgeon drove his maxillary bones straight though his brain.

Then Roland's gore-spattered hand opened, and the most feared man in Big Woo spilled to the floor of his panic room like jelly from a broken jar. There, Mark Anthony Johnstone died with no more dignity than any of his victims. The mutilated dictator leaked brains, blood, and urine onto the concrete while his body twitched in futile spasms.

It was an undignified, inglorious, and pathetic death. He died never comprehending the motivations of his killer, or the unspoken oath his own blood had sealed. It was a fitting end for Mark Anthony Johnstone, and the remorseless black giant nodded to himself in grave satisfaction before leaving the room without a backward glance.

Chapter Twenty-Five

Roger Dawkins was in a great mood. In less than two days, Dr. Johnson had replaced most of his failing organs with synthetic ones, and had rebuilt his joints with the latest Corpus Mundi prosthetics. Roger had not known how much pain he had been in until the doctor fixed him up and it was gone. He felt lighter, younger, stronger. There hadn't been time to regrow his organs from his own DNA, so the doctors had installed cybernetic versions. This was not ideal as it meant that there would be anti-rejection issues for the present. But the doctors assured him the current hardware would get him by until DNA-compliant versions could be grown.

They had reconnected his spinal cord and rebuilt his spine from Osteoplast™, and then reinforced it with something Roger had never heard of that wasn't even available on the black market yet. Like his organs, a brand-new spine would be grown for him eventually, but the program needed Dawkins in the field in seventy-two hours and not eight months.

The surgeons had been working in shifts, non-stop for two days straight. Roger faded in and out of consciousness while the teams worked in hushed fervor. The beeps and whooshes of unidentifiable medical devices kept time like ominous antiseptic-smelling metronomes while the operations commenced. Roger had neither the education nor the aptitude to discern what the various fluids in the IV bags were. It was all lost on him. But he had been a very hard drug user by necessity for a long time, and he hadn't had a fix of any of his usual barbiturates or downers in a while. One did not need to be a pharmacist to figure that something was keeping the DTs away. He was eternally grateful for whatever it was, and that was all the thought power he could spare for the subject. He felt a very detached warmth in the scant moments he was awake and otherwise existed entirely behind the solid black curtain of chemical coma. The doctors would drag him through the veil to ask him a question or test his cognition from time to time, and then with cursory nods send the man back under.

Roger didn't mind. He had been in this situation more than once, and he appreciated the free overhaul.

The last time Doctor Johnson woke him, he was kept awake. Fox was in the room, looking pleased in that oily, weaselly way corporate types effect when they believe that they are about to advance themselves.

Doctor Johnson, adjusted a device plugged into Roger's various new parts and asked, "Good Evening, Mr. Dawson. How do you feel?"

Roger thought about his answer, actually assessing his situation before replying.

"I should be hurting like hell, but something's blocking my pain receptors. Other than that, I feel better than I have in years."

Which was the truth. His mind was clear and sharp, his joints felt good for the first time in a decade, and as reported, he was in absolutely no pain.

"Yes," Johnson replied, "We had to block that part of your brain to have this conversation. Otherwise you'd be unable to speak."

Fox smiled even wider, "You look great, Roger. The Doc says that you are flying through all the operations and doing far better than we could have hoped. You are through the worst of it, and it should be smooth sailing from here. We are all very pleased!"

"Yes, that is true"— Johnson's fingers tapped across his DataPad— "You are no longer in any danger of terminal rejection, and the extent of your augmentations has allowed you to survive the various implants and cybernetic additions we have fitted you with. The next stage is to get you fitted for the armature."

Roger, like most people who opted for biological augmentations over cybernetics, was not fond of armatures. Despite his extreme level of enhancement, Roger had at least *looked* entirely human. He could sit at a restaurant, walk into a bar, or drive a normal car without issue. As long as he avoided places that had the technological capability of scanning for augmentations, he could live a completely normal existence. Well, at least an existence that appeared completely normal. His dependency on drugs to get his brain and body to move at the same speed when he wasn't fighting was just the price he paid for his professional success.

Roger had met and known a few armature pilots, and he respected them. Armatures made the best, most powerful cyborgs in the galaxy; they were always far stronger and more versatile than prosthetics. If a man lost his legs in an accident, he might get a quality set of prosthetic legs to replace them (if he could afford them). That man may go on to have a somewhat normal life after that. But contrary to the conventional understanding, those legs could not be made much stronger than the originals. Legs that could lift a thousand pounds were useless if the arms could not hold onto the weight and got torn from their sockets. If the spine could not support that mass, then you just crippled the poor jerk you were trying to augment. Because they were attached to normal bodies, a new prosthetic would always be limited by the strength and durability of whatever they were anchored to. It was the same story for any body part: Replacement was easy, but unless the whole body got upgraded, there was not much of a marketplace for super-powerful prosthetics.

If a skilled deep-space construction foreman suffered a crippling accident, however, the company may be very excited to equip him with a fully upgraded system purpose-built for his role. Instead of having to hire a man and replace a piece of equipment, they simply turned the man into a piece of equipment. It was a good system: The worker gets to keep making money (and likely much more of it) and the company doesn't lose hard-to-find expertise.

Prosthetics were about vanity and quality of life, and an armature was a tool assembled for a task, plain and simple. No one had made a full prosthesis reliable yet; and until they did, a guy with a bunch of missing limbs and a mechanical respirator could still enjoy life a little if he had an armature. It was easier to think of them as a large, semi-permanent wheelchair rather than an actual mechanical body.

Roger had been briefed on all of this, and was excited and scared in equal proportions. He looked down at his arms.

He saw the nine one-inch round plugs that had been surgically implanted along his humerus and radius bones. Little round caps sat on top of his skin, looking like silver buttons poking just through the surface. There were more of them on his legs and along his spine. One had been installed on each temple, as well. Getting dates was going to be a little tricky after this gig, but thanks to the 'net, there was a kink for everything. It would all be worth it if he got to avenge himself on that big bastard from Dockside, at least.

But Roger was still not entirely cheerful about getting an armature. Armatures were what you got when you lost large chunks of your body, or ended up needing permanent life-support. If you were obscenely rich, you might get an armature that at the very least could fit under your clothes. If you weren't, you got whatever the company was willing to give you.

So, when Fox told Roger that they were developing a new type of armature, he had balked a little. Then they showed it to him, and he was sold on it right away.

Johnson had explained it best, "You have enhanced your body far beyond what any reasonable person should have. Your augmentations are going to kill you, and soon. You have the brain of an eighty-year-old drug addict and your organs will need replacement every three to five years. Your joints have no organic material left in them, and your muscles are atrophying at six times the normal rate because they have been laced with inferior materials and are constantly fighting infection and rejection."

"You are lucky we hired you, Mr. Dawkins, because you are fast approaching the point where the maintenance on your body will cost more than you can ever hope to earn. You will die slowly, in agony, while simultaneously going mad, Mr. Dawkins."

"Well, gee, Doc. Don't sugar-coat it or nothin!" Roger had not realized that he had damaged himself that much. He supposed that's what he got for only using underworld biotech.

"What we propose is to fit you with an advanced armature that…"

"Whoa, there, Doc!" Roger remembered well that moment of brief panic, "I've seen those things. That's not what I signed up for!"

"Oh relax, Mr. Dawkins," Johnson admonished, "this is something altogether different from what you think it is."

And it had been. First of all, they were rebuilding his body anyway, so he would not have to depend on the armature for survival. That was the most important thing as far as Roger Dawkins was concerned. Second, this was no bastardized worker 'bot they were talking about. Granted, the military versions he had seen were good-looking in their own functional way, but Roger still had no desire to be welded to a twelve-foot 'mech that looked like the bastard love child of a tank and a hoversled.

He needn't have worried. The apparatus in question was something else entirely. It did not look like an unwieldy machine at all. To the contrary, it was sleek and clean and bright white. It bore a superficial resemblance to power armor or a heavy space suit, but with a smooth, unmarked exterior. Joints and overlapping armor plates created a pattern of lines and facets across articulated joints like shoulders, waist, hips and elbows. But otherwise it was smooth and humanoid, even to the extent that the designers had obviously duplicated human anatomy on purpose. The chassis was very clearly meant to evoke human features and even proportioned in such a manner as to not appear too ridiculous. If Roger squinted, the shape was vaguely reminiscent of a very athletic man. The shoulders were wide, the waist narrow, and its legs were long and powerful-looking. It had two arms, two legs, five fingers per hand and an otherwise normal-looking head with square, black eyes and a blank faceplate. It looked more or less like a nine-foot tall service android; except bigger, stronger, and with obvious armor plating.

Johnson gave the briefing, "The armature is entirely anthropomorphic" —he studied Roger's face for comprehension— "that means it mimics the human body, Roger."

"I know what 'anthropomorphic' means, Doc," Roger lied. He had always hated school.

"Of course," the Doctor acknowledged with dry sarcasm. "The armature is designed to move exactly like you do. Underneath those external plates, is an authentic human muscle analog created for a top-secret military program. It connects directly to your nervous system and is equipped with an analogous and entirely sympathetic nervous system of its own. If it works the way we hope, it will feel exactly like your own body."

Fox jumped in and rescued Dawkins from having to pretend he understood any of that, "You will feel what it feels, and it will move like you move."

"Don't they all do that?" Roger asked. He had seen enough cyborg armatures to know that most of them moved in a smooth, precise manner. Good pilots could drive a giant excavation 'mech through a crowded street without stepping on any toes.

He had also seen enough prostheses to know that they did a good job of mimicking the original body parts as well. The big white caricature in front of him, creepy as it was, didn't look all that high-tech to his uneducated eye.

"Not like this!" Fox grinned.

Johnson interjected, "Most cybernetic systems simply read the electrical activity in the brain or nerves and map an action to the signal. There is no direct feedback from prosthesis itself; there are no nerves there to carry a signal. The user simply learns to accommodate for the signal delay and to manage the prosthetic such that its limitations do not impact their day-to-day life."

"A soldier with a prosthetic arm does not feel the rifle with the fingers, but the prosthetic mimics the force feedback signal that has been mapped to the brain. He can avoid breaking things and get a sense of weight and resistance, but he's not feeling it. Not really."

Roger nodded slowly, "So this thing"—he gestured to the imposing metal man—"will feel stuff?"

Johnson returned the nod, "Eventually, yes. If we do our job right, this armature will feel like the body you've already been walking around in your whole life. No feedback delays, no dyskinesia, perfect balance and proprioception. When coupled with your already impressive enhancements, you will be the most lethal and effective fighting system ever developed."

Roger liked the sound of most of that, "Eventually? What do you mean 'eventually?' "

Johnson's face contorted in a pensive frown, as if he was searching for the right words to make Roger understand, "we have not… uhm… perfected… the symbiosis between the armature's virtual nervous system and yours… yet."

Fox interrupted again, "Don't worry Roger, just the usual R & D hassles. We have the best man in the field working on it right now…"

Roger was not the most learned man in the world, but he had squeezed enough intelligence out of enough informants to know when the whole truth had not been spoken. His face must have betrayed his suspicion because Dr. Johnson rushed to reassure him.

"It's not a big deal for now, Roger. The armature has already been seeded with your neurological parameters and our best bio-technicians have written an AI to bridge the gaps between your nervous system and the virtual one in the armature. You will be 100% safely operational with or without that last bit."

"So why do it all?" Roger wasn't too proud to acknowledge he was getting nervous about this deal.

Johnson again: "Because when we have it fully operational, you will be faster, more comfortable, and more effective. You will be able to pick a flower and smell it while mounted to the armature. The armature will be your body when you are in it."

"With the current system, you will still be most of the way there. It will feel more like a cross between a good prosthetic and a high-end suit of power armor than a true symbiosis; but thanks to the bridging AI, you should be nothing short of devastating. No currently available biotech will be up to your specs."

Roger relaxed a little. He didn't trust Fox as far as he could throw the doughy bastard, but Johnson was the same kind of tech-nerd Roger had been stealing lunch money from since he was nine. Johnson was incapable of deception when he talked about his toys because his exuberance over his own brilliance prevented him from being a convincing liar.

"And I can un-mount at any time, right?" Roger had nightmares about being permanently attached to that machine, trapped forever in a robot body.

"Of course! That is the real genius of the system!" Even Fox was gibbering at this point, "It's just a big suit of armor, except we built it to the exact specifications of its pilot…you! When you are done with a job, pop right out and go about your business."

"Since your reflexes are already superhuman, and your body is so physically durable, you will be able to run the system at its maximum capacity," Johnson was still sputtering, "far faster and at higher G-forces than any regular pilot could!"

Johnson's grin was ebullient, "You don't even comprehend how perfect you are for this machine, Roger. It has been built for you, and you have been re-built for it. Basically, the machine will multiply the abilities of the pilot. The tougher the pilot, the tougher the machine. This is why we wanted you, specifically, to be that pilot." That rang as mostly true, but something was missing, and Roger knew it.

"And this will mean I can take out the big fucker who damn near killed me?"

Fox's grin was more reserved than his excitable partner's, but no less cheerful, "We are counting on it. Eliminating him and bringing in that woman are essential for completing the symbiotic nervous system."

"Really?" Roger, was not brilliant, but he was sly. He knew a con when he saw it and this stank like a con job. The trick was in piecing it all together.

"Yes, Mr. Dawkins. She is turning out to be a critical factor in completing that phase of the project." Roger wondered if Fox ever turned that fake smile off, "I believe you knew of that when you took the original job?"

Fox's question was a revealing slip. Roger had not known exactly what his client had needed the girl for when he took the work, but he was sorting it out. He had known the gist of the job when he took it, but he hadn't realized it was biotech development that the girl's family was caught up in.

Roger hated kidnap and ransom work, it was always so messy and relied on too many separate things going right for a chance to be successful. Corpus Mundi had to be very anxious to resort to such a ham-fisted strategy. It reeked of desperation.

But what could make a large, well-funded corporation so desperate?

In that instant Roger's felonious mind slapped another puzzle piece into place, and he grinned like a monkey, "You need me to run the suit because the nervous system bullshit doesn't work yet, don't you?" Fox's smile wobbled for the briefest of seconds and Johnson frowned, "Hah! That's it, isn't it? I'm so hopped up that when I drive the thing… it's going to look like you've got it all worked out… but you don't!"

Based on what Fox and Johnson had just revealed, Roger would have bet that whole bounty whatever tech they needed to get the suit to work was locked in either that pink-haired bitch's head or her father's. It was the only logical conclusion.

Johnson's face went red and his eyes blazed indignation. Roger continued his assault on the man's dignity, "And you need that girl because she or her dad know how to fix it."

Roger further surmised there must be big money on the line, and that promises had been made about the new armature. Promises that Mr. Fox was having trouble keeping, it seemed.

He beamed, caught up in his own cleverness, "Tell me if I'm wrong, boys: This thing is probably for the military, right? Did you pitch it as armor for regular soldiers?" A barking laugh, "Of course you did! Oh man, you two made a shit-ton of promises about it and got a big military research grant, didn't you? How am I doing?"

Fox could not maintain his smile, "True or not, Roger, nothing like that would be any concern of yours."

Roger snorted a derisive laugh, "That's rich. I figure you've gotta make that 'bot run like the next greatest thing in biotech, or you're gonna lose a big fat contract, aren't you?"

Roger plowed on as the whole picture finally came into stark focus. It was comforting for him to see that the contortions of liars and thieves were the same no matter the scale of the crime. Fox was running a hustle, just like any other con man. Roger didn't let up. He wanted to make sure that Fox knew that Roger Dawkins was no fool.

"This hunk of shit is just a fancy exo-suit without that mumbo-jumbo, right? Can a regular guy even drive it without that weird brain shit working?"

Fox's face twitched. Not quite a wince, but it was a microscopic tell that encouraged Roger to run with this thread.

He paused, still smiling, "But me?" he smirked with smug satisfaction, "… a guy like me can already move faster and take more hits than anyone else. My brain doesn't need any fancy hardware, and my other shit is so jacked up I'd make any tech run like a champ. Yeah. That's definitely it."

He gave the two company men a hard, triumphant stare, "The only way your toy robot there will perform like you've promised, is if I run him."

Johnson could not contain his agitation over the insinuation, "It's not like that at all! The system is beyond anything else ever made. We just need more time to get everything perfected," he mewled.

"Oh, shut up, Doctor." Fox ladled sarcasm onto the title, then turned to Roger. His stern tone was incongruous with that implacable fake smile, "Roger, you have been hired to drive that armature, and you are being paid handsomely to do it… both in cash and in new body parts. You are a goddamned investment, Dawkins, so don't get any ideas."

Fox straightened his tie and continued, "Why we are paying you to do this is entirely irrelevant, because you are not part of that equation. Our agreement is predicated upon your discretion. Am I understood?"

Roger was content with his victory and relaxed, chuckling quietly. He couldn't care less about their corporate screw-ups, he was simply filing the information away for when it came time to renegotiate his contract. Fox's reaction and Johnson's whining had him convinced of his correctness.

It would never be Roger's problem either way. If these chumps wanted to rebuild his fucked-up body and brain to fool some other chumps, and pay him to kidnap some uptown lady, that was their issue.

"As long as I get paid, man."

"Naturally, Mr. Dawkins," greased Fox, "We're not savages, after all."

Chapter Twenty-Six

The smoke from Umas climbed hundreds of feet into the yellow-orange expanse that was the night sky over Big Woo.

Billy McGinty took in a deep breath, inhaling the jumbled mélange of competing aromas: smoke, ozone, squalor, burning flesh, and blood.

Smells like revolution, was his silent comment.

His eyes sparkled darkly in the firelight, and he exhaled in another long slow breath. Standing in bleak silence atop the 10th floor roof of an old office building gave him the perfect vantage point to observe his minor little mutiny grow into a full-blown coup. He could see for many blocks in all directions, like a general fielding units from a hilltop vantage point. To his left, he watched small teams of rag-clad shadows snake in and out of Marko's supply houses. Like rats, they scurried to and from the nondescript buildings and hauled boxes and crates to waiting hoversleds and old cargo vehicles. In six short hours, every supply house in town would be emptied of drugs and contraband.

Behind him, he heard sporadic gunfire as his Teamsters assaulted the dormitories of the sex slaves that Marko had made so much money from. The faint, yet satisfying screams of overseers and pimps played like the calls of terrified night birds as throats were slit, or bodies riddled with projectiles. Every time a slave was freed, his army grew by one.

The radio on his hip chirped and chattered with updates. The Z-Streeters had just secured the Front Street landing platforms and the mass transit station. Mickey Targa's squad just locked down the labs in the chemical quarter.

Everything was going well. For now.

He had planned this day for years. In one way or another, he had been imagining this for his whole adult life. But he had never truly allowed himself to believe it would come to this. Now, he watched his enemy's citadel burn; while his men and women fought in the streets and alleys below to seize control of the entire Big Woo criminal apparatus. They were off to a solid start and he had Roland Tankowicz to thank for that.

Marko's army had been decimated by Roland's assault. The Boss of Big Woo had held control over his territory with a scant hundred and fifty men. They were of course backed up by whatever army the Combine wanted to throw at them, and fear of that eventuality had kept the gangs in line. Even with minimal manpower, Marko's men were well-equipped, well-trained, and well-paid. Their advantage had been modern guns, body armor, and a fortress to hide in. As a whole this had been more than sufficient to hold the territory for a very long time. At least until a certain massive cyborg and a small woman from Uptown had wandered into Billy's parking lot marketplace.

Roland and Lucia had crushed Marko's best men and killed the man himself, right on time and according to plan. The snake was now headless, and a headless snake is no snake at all. The united support of all the Big Woo gangs swiftly followed Marko's demise, and the now Teamsters had grit and numbers on their side. That intimidating fortress was currently a smoking wreck packed with cowering disorganized bullies. There was little enough to fear about terrified bullies who fought for money. Less when those bullies had lost a third of their strength and all of their courage in just under an hour. When he compared the remnants of Marko's enforcers to the thousand or so highly motivated gang members on his side, Billy McGinty liked his chances just fine.

From his vantage point, it was easy to see the frenzied activity inside the compound. Black-clad men ran in uncoordinated furor from walls to buildings and back to walls again. Terrified thugs fired weapons at shadows and shouted meaningless instructions to other men, who weren't listening, anyway. Every few seconds, one of Billy's people would toss a grenade over the wall or take a random potshot at one of the scurrying figures inside the walls. That was all it took for the few well-placed troops to keep a small army confused and hiding. The manpower expense was a small price to pay for keeping those fools occupied while the real battle was fought elsewhere.

Marko's men had fallen back behind the safety of the walls when Roland had started smashing things, and this left the streets almost entirely undefended. That had always been the plan because there was nothing in Umas that Billy wanted. It would make a great base of operations later, but had absolutely no strategic value for the time being.

The panicked men inside did not understand that while they scampered about in terrified impotence, billions of credits in criminal infrastructure was changing hands just outside the walls. The dregs of Marko's troops flailed about, blissfully unaware that the balance of power in Big Woo was undergoing a tectonic shift while they waited in huddled terror for reinforcements. Billy figured it probably take three or four days for the Combine to finally grasp what had happened this night.

Billy McGinty and his Teamsters were playing the long game. What they needed to do was to lock down the labs, the warehouses, the brothels, the garages filled with vehicles, and the tons upon tons of product. If all went well, every bit of contraband, every smuggled weapon, and every gram of illegal narcotics would be under his control by morning.

The chatter from his radio was all good news on that front: his people kept checking in, one by one, to report that they had achieved their objectives.

The radio on his hip relayed the news in clipped, practiced shorthand: The brothels and dorms were secure. Another supply cache had been liberated. Sixteen more trucks were under gang control. Billy could taste victory, but he knew better than to start celebrating just yet.

Billy allowed himself a small, private, surreptitious smile. Marko's men could run and hide in Umas all they wanted, the war was being won out in the streets of Big Woo. Billy's streets.

Our streets, he corrected himself.

They were winning, and it made Billy happy and scared at the same time. This was a big thing to undertake, and he hoped he was ready for it. Secretly, he feared he may not be. Then his reverie was interrupted by the crunch of gravel under giant feet on the rooftop behind him.

Billy didn't turn, he knew who it was from the heavy footfalls alone. Then the big man spoke.

"Hell of thing you've started here, Billy."

"Yeah," Billy was uncharacteristically taciturn tonight. There were no jokes at Roland's expense and no sardonic wit.

"Lucia and I destroyed the servers and records in there on the way out. It will take the Combine weeks to sort out what happened and where the assets are." Roland moved up and stood next to gang leader, "I estimate that we killed twenty-one of his men and seriously injured another thirty or so. They won't counter-attack until they get reinforced from some other territory."

"I know," Billy's voice was small and pensive, "I have eyes inside."

Roland nodded. This was not surprising. A military man to his core, Roland finished his debriefing anyway, "It will be Flint's crew from the Sprawl, most likely," Roland felt a strong desire to help Billy as much as possible. Marko's rule of Big Woo had been a litany of petty tyranny and a bitter testimony to what evils could be accomplished by greedy men with no morals. Roland's own complicity in allowing it tasted like bile in his throat, and his guilt drove him to make amends the only way he knew how.

The next few weeks would be very hard on the residents of Big Woo, and Roland could not be there to help them through it. It would be their fight to win or lose, but Roland was sure he knew who he was rooting for; and he had never been above cheating. "Flint's boys won't be any tougher than these guys. You can handle them if you play it smart. When the Board realizes that you're holding the supply chain? Well, then it will be mercs from the Uptown crews. Maybe frontier guys if they get desperate."

Roland paused to watch Billy's face, looking for signs of fear or hesitation. He saw none, "Be smart when that happens, Billy. They will have cyborgs, armatures, heavy weapons. Get the supplies and get underground before then."

"I know," McGinty said, the quip soft and small. A lot of his friends would die, and he knew it, "We will wait them out. When the money stops flowing, the Board will negotiate. We aren't trying to commit suicide, here."

Roland looked back over the burning compound below him, "No one ever is, McGinty."

"I know," he repeated a third time, still softly.

They watched in silence for a moment, listening to the sounds of revolution and mayhem as they built to a heady crescendo around them.

Then it was Billy's turn, "How's Lucia?"

"Exhausted," that was the least of it, "she burned the candle hard in there, really pulled her weight like a pro."

"She's something else, isn't she?" Billy chuckled.

"You ain't shitting me, McGinty." Roland shook his head, a wry smile cracking his stoic veneer, "She is something else entirely."

"Is that why she's in trouble? Why they grabbed her dad?"

Roland thought about his answer, there was still so much he did not know, "I can't really say. There's a connection, but I'm not convinced it's about her specifically. The smart money says it's about what her father knows."

"And what does he know?" McGinty was prying now, but he was a man who had learned to look for angles, even in places there might not be any.

Roland wasn't ready to tell Billy the whole story, but he felt he owed the red-headed gangster something, "Her father is probably the smartest man in biotech right now. The problem is that he has an acute case of the 'moral fiber' disease. He wants to help people, so he has refused to do weapons or military shit for a long time. I suspect someone is trying to make him change his mind."

Billy's head shook in wry acknowledgement, "It's always something like that, isn't it? Try to do the right thing, be a good person, and then bad people shit all over you."

McGinty barreled ahead with that thought, suddenly vehement, "You try to build something good, you know? Try to do right, try to make good in a shitty world, and what happens? Some fucker with money, or guns, or lawyers swoops in and shuts you down or takes what's yours. What the fuck does a guy have to do, man?"

Billy was mad, now, "So fuckin' Lucia's dad doesn't want to make shit that kills and they fucking kidnap him and go after his kid?"

"Yeah. That's about the size of it, I figure."

"Shit. We get one good genius who doesn't want to produce murder-machines, and this is what happens to him?" Billy shook his head, not noticing Roland's jaw clench at how close to home the diatribe was hitting, "Fuck all those fuckers. We need to hit back."

Roland gestured to the chaos all around them, "I think we just did."

"Fuck yeah we just did," Billy snarled, then shifted gears, "Did you get what you needed in there?"

Roland nodded, "Yeah. We know where our guy is, now."

"How bad?"

"Bad. Uptown office park. Right on the edge of the Sprawl. Tactical fucking nightmare."

"Can we help?" Billy also felt like he owed something. This was the most ridiculous collaboration in the history of insurgency, but it was working so far. He had already fulfilled his part of the bargain, but sneaking two people into Umas felt like poor coin indeed against what Roland and Lucia had done for his people.

"I don't think so," Roland sighed. "It's a goddamn Corpus Mundi black site for biotech research." He shook his head, "Didn't even know they had those."

Billy felt his first genuine smile of the night coming on, "Those places sure do use a lot of pharmaceuticals, don't they?"

Roland scowled, "I honestly have no fucking clue what they use. Why?"

Billy turned back to the city, "I dunno. If I had a secret biotech research facility that I had put lots of creds into keeping a secret, I can't imagine how I might come across all the drugs and shit I'd need without blowing the secrecy."

Comprehension took root in Roland's brain, "Oh. Shit. Don't tell me you can get in?"

Billy's answer was slow and measured, "Not directly. We really only run recreational drugs out of here. But when it comes to smuggling, all the good talent is from Big Woo." He slapped Roland on the arm, wincing when the unforgiving armored appendage stung his fingers, "I'll call some guys who could get into a nun's panties without her ever knowing they were there."

"That's amazing. Thank you." It was all Roland could think to say.

Billy shrugged, "Shit's going to be very hard around here for a few weeks. If I am going to make this shit work, I'll need friends. Friends who can punch through walls and take down entire gangs when they have to. Friends who aren't so afraid of the Combine that they shit their pants at the very mention of the Board."

Roland nodded assent, "Friends like me."

"Yup," Billy was pensive again, "Are we friends, Roland?"

"I'm warming up to you." Roland couldn't hide the smile in his voice though. Friends like Billy were good for a guy like Roland to have, and friends like Roland were good for people like Billy to have, "But take care of these people, Billy. Do right. Build something here, and you can count on me for anything."

"Of course, man. That's what this is all about."

"Good, because if you fuck these people over I'll kill you twice. Don't ask how. It's a top-secret cyborg thing. We know shit." Roland's tone was jovial, but Billy suspected that he wasn't really joking, "Weird cyborg shit, McGinty."

Billy's radio squawked again, excited voices reporting that the overland route checkpoints to the Sprawl had just been secured. Big Woo was shut off from New Boston now. There was no way for anyone to get in.

And no way for Billy McGinty and his ragtag group of revolutionaries to get out.

Chapter Twenty-Seven

"Let's tally it up, shall we? Marko is dead. Big Woo is burning. An entire division of my organization has been crippled. Do you mind explaining and feel free to use tiny words so I can fully comprehend, exactly how your little bounty hunt has suddenly resulted in a loss to my organization of... how much, Laura?"

The stern brunette in the slate-grey suit consulted a DataPad for the briefest instant and responded, "We estimate 130 million credits, sir. Plus or minus twenty-five."

"Thank you, Laura," the silver-haired man in slacks and a white silk dress shirt replied warmly."So Mr. Fox, please, do explain this to me."

Fox, for all his greasy corporate charm, was more than a little uneasy. Pops Winter was a tall, spare, regal specimen. Piercing blue eyes sat deep under craggy white brows, and his gaunt features and sharp cheekbones lent an air of the diabolic to his face. His casual appraisal of a 130 million cred loss was all the more chilling for the quiet acceptance that accompanied it. Pops always spoke in a cool, calm, baritone. Never agitated, never angry, but always reserved and poised. Why be otherwise? The fortunes of great and small men rose and fell upon his words, so there was never a reason to be excitable. Lions, Pops had always told people, did not get distraught over the actions of the sheep. The old gangster had always made certain that there was never any question as to who was the lion, and who was the sheep. It was a flawless facade of effortless arrogance.

Fox envied it.

Leland Fox was feeling all kinds of sheepish. He had made three very serious errors already in dealing with the Ribiero family, and it looked like the third had finally gotten the attention of the most powerful crime lord in the Solar System. This was not a man you wanted doing your quarterly evaluations.

Fox catalogued his screw-ups. First, he had failed to secure the daughter when he picked up Dr. Ribiero. Both he and Johnson had underestimated the good Doctor's reticence to revive the Golem program's work on symbiotic nervous systems. The good doctor, optimistic fool that he was, had been convinced that the armature approach would have circumvented Ribiero's moral objections. Johnson, of course, had been dead wrong.

Second, he had sent Dawkins in to grab the girl without involving the Combine. *How the hell was I supposed to know to do that?* Fox whined to himself, *I don't deal with kidnapping on regular basis!* At least he got the windfall of Dawkins' injuries out of that blunder. Now at least he had a pilot that could make the armature live up to the lofty promises he had made getting the whole project approved in the first place.

Adding off-world mercenaries to the mix before consulting the board had further cemented this screw up.

And now, making things infinitely more complicated, Lucia Ribiero had found the last goddamn Golem to hide behind, and the two of them had just declared war on the entire Combine. Fox was not even sure if he wanted to tell Pops about Lance Corporal Roland "Breach" Tankowicz. This deceased Marko character had been entirely unaware of Roland's capabilities, which meant they all probably were. There was nothing to be done about that now. If Fox told them everything he knew about the Golems, the Board would only get even more pissed at him for not telling them before. Knowing that Breach's involvement was possible is why he had called for all this expensive help in the first place.

Why couldn't they just let me handle it? Fox griped to himself.

There was no point in going down that road though, and Fox accepted that unfortunate reality with frustrated resignation. The pudgy manager had been at this game for close to thirty years, and at this point he counted himself an accomplished executive. Though confused by the Combine at first, he felt he was figuring them out now.

Criminals are territorial and egotistical pricks, Fox mused while contemplating Pops' words. The ambitious company man had run afoul of that by not bringing the Board in early enough for them to make some money and preserve their petty domains. Operating a criminal enterprise like kidnapping and extortion without the approval of the board had been a huge mistake, Fox understood that now, but he had deadlines and he needed to move forward with or without the crusty objections of these bronze-age plutocrats.

Personal feelings notwithstanding, Fox appreciated the care with which he needed to tread here. Pops could have Fox killed with a nod of his head, and the old demon would never see the inside of jail cell over it. Internalizing that had been the hard part, but there was a silver lining to that particular cloud: if these idiots wanted to break their teeth trying to bring down a monster like Breach, then that wouldn't ruin his day one bit.

"Respectfully, Mr. Chairman, I must point out that Corpus Mundi was and still is bringing in their own assets to handle this issue. While I apologize for our inadvertent breach of protocol in doing so, we never wanted any of your assets to be at risk."

It was gamble, taking this tack, but he figured that Pops would respond better as long as Fox was negotiating from a position of strength, "We are, of course, mortified that you have suffered this inconvenience, but Corpus Mundi cannot be responsible for losses your organization suffers when attempting to collect a bounty."

The old man's eyebrow rose to such a lofty height that Fox wondered if it would pull away from his head. The measured baritone was flawless, even a little incredulous, "Mr. Fox, do not insult me by assuming I am blind or stupid. You have a very serious, very dangerous game afoot and you have been keeping us in the dark about it."

Fox doubled down, "It is not the policy of Corpus Mundi to comment on or disseminate information pertaining to our research projects until they—"

"Oh, shut up, Mr. Fox," Pops had a sardonic smirk on his face, Fox stopped talking, but forgot to close his mouth.

"You think this is some sort of negotiation? Or perhaps a parlay of some kind? It's not."

The satanic old man was grinning with a relaxed grace. It was the grin of a man who has already won a battle that the other side did not realize had started. "Mr. Fox, I have as much stock in your company as your CEO. Corpus Mundi runs twenty-five million credits through my organization a year. I bought and sold ten executives more important than you before I ate lunch today, so please spare me the corporate obfuscation."

This was not a development Fox wanted to hear. He felt the first trickles of cold sweat under his nice suit. Pops didn't let the squirming man of the hook, "I made some enquiries about you and your current project, Fox. I suppose, since you and I are now so closely acquainted that I can tell you that those are not the sort of enquiries you are accustomed to."

That satanic smile never even twitched, "Your people are neither as loyal nor as smart as you think they are, young man. Neither, it seems, are you."

Fox ground his teeth at the insult. If Pops noticed this or cared, he did not show it.

"So, let me tell you, Mr. Fox, that when I found out how badly this 'Better Man' thing was going for you, I had two competing thoughts. Can you guess what they were?"

Fox was startled to realize Pops had asked a question, but he tried to keep his voice even and salvage his position of strength, "I couldn't speculate, Mr. Chairman, but I don't think you — "

"It was a rhetorical question, Mr. Fox," the older man interrupted, and then sighed like a teacher with a particularly stupid student. "My first thought was to expose you to your board of directors and then have you tortured and killed as an example to any other emerging executives with more ambition than sense. The Combine will not be bullied by anyone, even Corpus Mundi." He shook his head slowly, "Your company may have more money, but my people will do things that yours won't. Money is a powerful motivator, but fear is always better. I seriously considered using you to make that point Mr. Fox."

Fox was sweating profusely now. The point about fear was well taken, and the old bastard knew it.

"But then I thought about what would be the best outcome for my people, and that led me to this conclusion," a pause to go to a cabinet and refill a brandy snifter from an ornate crystal decanter turned into a tortuous interlude. Pops was delighting in dragging out his point to maximize Fox's discomfort. That Fox was aware of this ploy did nothing to ease the tension he ultimately felt. A sip and a sigh of satisfaction before Pops continued, "I concluded, Mr. Fox, that if I did that, I'd never get my 130 million credits back, nor any of the interest owed on it."

A goddamned shakedown? Fox almost smiled at the puerile simplicity of it. No matter how fancy Pops Winters wanted to act, he was a street thug at heart, and some things just came naturally to him. This was an exploitable weakness as far as Fox was concerned, but this was obviously not the time to go after it. His immediate goals were far less ambitious: first and foremost on that list was getting out of the building in one piece. Winter smiled, but it was feral and merciless, "When you get this Dr.—uhm—" — he looked over at the stone-faced woman—"… Laura?"

"Ribiero, sir."

"Thank you," he turned back to Fox, "When you get Dr. Ribiero to incorporate his designs into your armature, the latest estimates and forecasts indicate that the resulting contracts will be worth hundreds of billions. Be advised, Mr. Fox, that you now have a very enthusiastic new booster for your little program. About 130 million credits worth of enthusiasm, I'd estimate. Laura has assembled the appropriate shell corporations that will appear to supply your project with parts and expertise. She will send over our schedule of invoices. Please pay promptly, our Accounts Receivable office is legendarily… thorough."

Fox wasn't sure how to consider this development, but it appeared likely he was going to live, "And what sort of services are you going to provide?"

Pops laughed so explosively he almost lost his brandy, "I promise not to have you killed provided you keep paying, first of all." He wiped his mouth with a wry chuckle, "But far be it from me to not deliver value to a paying client. You may consider all further efforts to secure Ms. Ribiero authorized and draw from our current talent pool and intelligence network as necessary."

Fox sighed. This had not gone well. But he wasn't dead and the project could continue. It wasn't a victory by any stretch, but at his point, Fox considered any meeting he didn't get tortured and killed at to be a successful one.

"Obviously, Mr. Chairman, your terms are acceptable," he tried to sound respectful, but failed.

Winter sighed again, "That was never in question, Mr. Fox. Laura will show you out."

He contemplated his next move as he and the severe assistant rode the lift back to the ground floor. Upon exiting, he attempted a polite "Have a nice evening," to the taciturn brunette, but he found himself talking to her back before the first word could be spoken. Thus, it was in grouchy, petulant silence that he walked to his waiting car.

The Better Man Project could not support another 130 million credits in expenses, so he was going to have to trim some fat from the budget. He could only hope that the invoice schedule was not too aggressive. The Combine Accounts Receivable department did in fact have something of a reputation, even among those not normally associated with that sort of business. Fox was very much invested in not having to deal with them.

He really needed that girl. Don Ribiero would not budge or break; that much was obvious. Fox had already figured out that it was no coincidence that Lucia had found Tankowicz, so the old bastard was self-assured and smug in his daughter's safety. Fox could find no flaw in that logic. He had been a minor project manager for Project: Golem, but he had seen everything. He knew what just one Golem could accomplish, and Ribiero was right to be confident.

Fox wasn't stupid either, and that's why he had been sent out to Galapagos and Thorgrimm Station. These mobsters were just not going to cut it. At least they recognized that now and would let him handle it.

Too bad it cost me 130 million plus interest to get them to realize that.

Fox went straight home and then straight to the liquor cabinet. He had two squads of mercenaries arriving in the morning, and there was little hope for him getting any sleep tonight, now. Tomorrow was going to be a very long day.

At least it's probably not going to be any worse than today though, the pudgy man reassured himself.

Chapter Twenty-Eight

Lucia's eyes fluttered open, and she was greeted by overwhelming brightness that blinded her at first. Confusion followed as she tried to reconcile the bright light, scratchy blanket, lumpy mattress and bizarre clothes that she was experiencing.

Then, with plodding slowness, comprehension and orientation reasserted themselves. She was on a cot in one of McGinty's safehouses. She was wearing weird clothing because she had strapped on body armor and raided a mobster's compound. There was the dim recollection of murdering a major crime boss as well.

That, she admitted to herself, *was one hell of a Saturday night.*

Once again, her mental agility and the speed with which she was acclimating to the new paradigm of her existence was just a bit frightening. It was like her brain was reorienting to the increased levels of stress and gaining new skills as fast as it needed to. She had always been a quick learner, but this bordered on the ridiculous. It was enough to make her suspect there was far more to her neurological upgrades than just speed, balance, and coordination.

But then why couldn't she shake that sense of imminent panic though? It was always there, waiting for her concentration and focus to slip, ready to flood her with the hundreds and thousands of tiny niggling anxieties that her souped-up brain could now process at many times the speed of a normal person. *Why didn't Dad fix that part?* She lamented, *Why is that still there?*

It was a question that would have to wait until they got him back. She spared herself a moment of fear and sadness for her father, trapped and held prisoner by the largest corporation in the world. She hoped they weren't torturing him. Would they torture him? Would he break? Why didn't he just give them what they wanted? Is he still alive, even?

STOP that!

She caught herself before it was too late, but only just. She focused on the combat breathing Roland had showed her:

four second inhale, four second exhale. Ten cycles. No cheating. She took three tries, but she got her heart rate down and eventually pushed the panic back to its normal resting place as a bunch of buzzing alarms at the edge of consciousness. It was the best she could do.

That was when the hunger hit her. She was starving. Roland had not exaggerated how many calories she would burn up in a prolonged fight, and it felt like her stomach was trying to digest itself. She stood up from the bed and prepared to go in search of one of McGinty's terrible burritos.

Before she could get that particular mission started, however, there was a knock at the door.

"Yeah, come in," she called absently, mind still fuzzy with sleep and hunger.

The door opened and Roland hunched through it with uncomfortable grunts. Nothing was built to his size, here.

He started to talk and stopped. Lucia threw him a quizzical look, and then followed his eyes. She could not contain a laugh of pure malicious glee when she realized what had happened.

"Eyes up, soldier!" she barked in her best drill sergeant's voice, and Roland snapped his head up and stared with military intensity at the center of her forehead.

"You didn't expect me to sleep in the body armor, did you?" she teased him. Lucia was wearing only the tiny cotton shorts and thin tank top that she had worn under her clothing for the raid. Both were simple and practical, but also very form-fitting by necessity. The ensemble was adequate for preserving her modesty, but even Lucia had to admit, there was really very little left for the big man's imagination to fill in. Lucia was not entirely unaware of how physically fit she was, and as a woman she was quite pleased to see that she could still drop a man's jaw from time to time. She was neither insecure nor immature; and men had ogled her often enough in the past for this situation to be far more humorous than anything else.

For her, anyway.

Roland was uncomfortable in a charming way though. She appreciated that he was polite enough to want to avoid being rude and delighted that he was confident enough to want to look, anyway. It was also nice to see he was sensitive to the reality that she may not want to be looked at.

Lucia, in an instant of playful cruelty, decided she wanted to be looked at. Mostly for the humor value of making a half-ton war machine squirm like a teenage boy, and partly because, she liked it when he looked at her that way. It was one of the more human things he did, and it reminded her that there was a scared, angry, and very real person under all that hardware. She had also noticed that he only seemed to look at *her* that way. That too, was very appealing.

Oh god, she thought to herself, *I really do kind of like this one, don't I?*

At first, this had made very little sense to Lucia. Roland was absolutely nothing like the men she preferred to date. She had always liked handsome, witty, urbane men. She liked artists, and thinkers, and men of letters. Roland wasn't any of these things. At least, not like the others were, anyway.

Roland wasn't stupid, that much was obvious. But he was neither witty nor urbane under even the most generous definitions for either. Neither was he particularly handsome in any way she could articulate. He wasn't ugly, per se, but he was just too big, too blocky, and too bald to make a girl's head spin.

She pondered her bizarre attraction to this man while he stood there vibrating with tension. It wasn't his looks, and it wasn't his style. There was the whole tough-guy thing, but that didn't really account for her fascination, either. Lucia had many male martial arts and weapons instructors over the years, and every one of them had been tough as nails. But while she respected it; that was never what had impressed her much in a man.

No, it was something about the inevitable sincerity and implacable reliability of the man. Roland did what he said he would and didn't lie about what that was going to be. When something needed to be done, Roland simply did it. If he had something to say, he said it. It was a different kind of interaction than the usual, and it felt nice.

Being around a man who was attracted to her usually meant navigating a whole series of steps and maneuvers designed to convince her that the man was worthy of her attentions. Lucia was positive that Roland had never once done that sort of dance. Roland didn't seem like the type to court a lady in the traditional sense under any conditions. Even when Lucia teased and flirted with him, he simply said what he needed to say and told the truth.

It was obvious to Lucia that Roland was interested. Just watching him struggle with where to look made that painfully, hilariously clear to her. The big goon had demonstrated absolutely no ability to mask his attraction, even when he tried. Somehow, he had combined the confidence of a bullet-proof cyborg with the obtuseness of a man who obviously had no clue how to interact with people outside of his preferred environment. When the fear and apprehension caused by his physicality was added to that formula, the result was a strained respectful discomfiture plagued by moments of lustful yearning. It was all very noble, in its own maddening robotic way.

It's working on me, she acknowledged wryly. There was good news at least; he was terrible at this and so she got to torture him. Lucia could be a little mean that way.

Roland attempted to escape the trap he suddenly found himself in, "I can come back in a few minutes," he mumbled and turned to leave.

"Don't be silly, just give me a second, you prude." This was going to be fun, "Served in wars all over the damn galaxy but gets all flustered over a girl in her underwear, sheesh."

"Most girls aren't very comfortable around me. Didn't get a lot of chances to practice my military comportment at sorority pillow fights." Lucia suspected he may have been trying to be funny, but there was real pain there. She realized that Roland's body probably meant that most women were more terrified of him than anything else.

That's a shame, she thought, *he doesn't deserve that.*

"But," he went on, turning his head a respectful ninety degrees, "I do try to be gentleman." That was the worst thing he could have said. Lucia had a competitive streak a mile wide, and this was now officially a contest: her sex appeal versus his composure. She intended to win it.

"Fine. I'll get dressed. Hold on."

She turned away from Roland and went over to the bed to retrieve her clothes. She knew it was immature, and she knew it was mean, but she made sure to bend at the waist and linger just a few seconds longer than necessary to pick up the discarded items. The tiny shorts, only barely adequate for proper coverage under normal conditions, crept up her thighs even further, exposing the curve of her buttocks below the hemline.

She swore she could hear the muscles in his jaw clench when she did it and stifled the urge to celebrate the small victory. Military discipline be damned; the big bastard had looked.

She straightened and stepped into the fatigues, then made no small a show of shimmying them up over her muscular thighs and the graceful sweep of her hips. The pants were more than loose enough to not require any wiggle at all. But now that she had him where she wanted him, mercy was not going to be part of the equation.

Now for the shirt, and another, long slow bend to retrieve it, followed by an exaggerated arch of the back to slide her arms though the sleeve holes. The tank top stretched and strained in all the appropriate places, and with a final toss of her hair, she knew she had won. She didn't even bother to button the shirt. This had been way too easy.

"You know," the low voice grumbled, "I can dilate time, too."

Lucia smirked at him, face beaming with coy innocence, "Yes?"

"That little show lasted about twenty minutes in my head." She was surprised and a little pleased to find him rising to the bait.

"Worth it?"

"Absolutely," it was a statement of pure fact.

"Some gentleman." She shot him a sarcastic eye roll.

Fuck it, she thought.

She hooked a finger into the neckline of her tank top and tugged it diagonally downward, exposing the top half of her right breast. Roland's eyes betrayed the loss of his ironclad discipline at the unexpected sight of soft flesh. At his height, Lucia was confident Roland could see just about everything she wanted him to. "Want to see it in reverse?" Her look was no longer playful.

His reaction was not what she expected. She saw panic in his eyes. Not discomfort, not embarrassment, not fear of rejection. Panic.

She had never seen him look that way before. It looked so wrong on his face that it frightened her. It was the purest, most heart-wrenching thing she had ever seen. When he spoke, all she heard was his fear.

"I… I can't…" he stammered, but Lucia came at him like a thunderbolt. She had to step on his knee to get the height she needed, but she leapt up and wrapped her legs around his torso. She grabbed him by both sides of his head stared directly into his eyes.

"Yes, you can, you colossal idiot." She couldn't believe how frightened he looked, "You are allowed to be human, and this is what humans do when they like each other!"

She kissed him. Hard. She was surprised to find that his lips were warm if a little on the stiff side. One hundred and thirty pounds of woman felt all nine-hundred and forty pounds of killing machine stiffen with fear. She could tell he wanted to run, but was also afraid to hurt her. Lucia held on tighter and didn't stop for a long time.

Eventually, she felt him relax, and then his hands were on her back, soft yet strong. He lifted her away with a gentleness she did not think could be possible with hands so large. She disengaged the kiss but didn't release his head.

She was surprised and saddened to see a single tear suspended in the corner of his left eye. It hung there in resolute defiance, as if he was too stubborn to even allow himself to shed it. He spoke, and there was so much pain in his voice it nearly broke her heart, "Please," he said quietly, "don't… don't do this…"

Her tone was gentle, but incredulous, "I do whatever I want to. I always have. I know what I'm doing now."

"I'm not like other guys…" Roland winced at the stupid cliché of that, "It's not… good? I'm not a good choice… I can't make babies, I don't have skin, I… I'm just not good for you is all…" It was a mumbling, stream-of-consciousness attempt to explain a well-maintained suit of emotional armor.

"Good for me?" She laughed in his face, "News flash, Roland: raiding mob fortresses isn't good for me. You, on the other hand, have kept me alive and un-abducted. I could easily argue that you are the BEST thing for me!" Still hanging in the air, she gave his chest a playful kick, "I don't give a fuck about your… chassis, is it? I like you, dumbass. Even if you can be an enormous twit much of the time."

He put her down, but she didn't back away or let him past her. Lucia asked him the hard question, "What are you so afraid of, Roland? I know you like me. I can tell. I like you, I hope you can tell. I'm not afraid of you; or of being with you. So, if it's not me, then what exactly is the big strong man afraid of?"

Roland shrugged the shrug of rebuked teenager, "I'll hurt you, eventually. I'll disappoint you. I'm trying my best to be a good man, but I will always be a weapon, too. I'm just…" Roland couldn't make the words work, he knew how it felt, but the sounds coming from his mouth weren't conveying it correctly. They sounded hollow, inadequate. But they were all he had, "… I'm wrong, inside, Lucia. Broken. Ugly."

Lucia could tell that Roland was trying to make a point, so she let him continue.

"You're special, Lucia. You deserve an amazing guy who can give you the life you want, not an old piece of Army surplus *ordnance*." He spat the last word with more venom than he intended. The wound, twenty-five years old now, remained fresh and raw as ever.

But it didn't ring true. Not to Lucia, anyway.

"That's not it at all, Roland. Oh, I get it." She rolled her eyes, "that's the story you tell yourself, and maybe you even believe it, but I don't buy it." Her face softened into a gentle smile, "Roland, you are a magnificent idiot. But I like you, so I'll spell this out." She put her hands over his and looked him in the eyes, daring him to flinch. "This has nothing to do with me deserving better, it's about you assuming that you deserve worse. As if somehow you are cursed to walk the earth like a goddamn action movie trope, alone and miserable, just because you got caught up in some bad stuff when you were younger. Seriously, you can be such a child sometimes."

She gave him a stiff poke in the gut for emphasis, "That's not how life works, dumbass. Now, I already know why you are being obstinate here, and it's not healthy. So, just get it over with and tell me the truth, Roland. Tell me now."

Roland could not know how transparent he was to this woman, but he was figuring it out. He hung his head, speaking honestly of his secret fear for the first time to anyone, "I'm afraid that this"— he knocked on his chest with a fist and the sharp, muffled thump emphasized the density and mass of his armored body —"is all I have to offer. I'm afraid the best part of me really is still out there"— he gestured to the sky— "soaking into the dirt of some forgotten battlefield." The big man spared a thought for that bright-eyed twenty-year-old, still pounding the ground on Venus. That boy was full of the righteous pride of a soldier who loved his planet and loved his Army. He couldn't see himself in that person anymore. Now he saw only the weapon. He saw Breach.

His eyes pleaded with the woman in front of him. Pleaded for her to back away, to let him go. "I'm not built for love, Lucia, I'm built for war." It was a hollow lie and a cliché attempt to dissuade her.

"That's why I can't let you do this. I want to. Dear god do I want to!" He set his face in a grim mask of resolution, "But it wouldn't be right, and doing what's right is all I have left."

The small woman did not react the way Roland expected. In hindsight, it was exactly the reaction he should have expected, but he had only known her for a couple of days at this point.

"Let me? Let me?" Lucia, Roland noticed, was beautiful when she was angry.

"You patronizing self-righteous metal-domed son of a bitch," she began, shaking her head in furious denial, "you do not 'let me' do anything! And you do not get to tell me who I should and should not be with."

She gave him another hard poke in the belly, "Do you think I'm stupid?"

"No!" Roland was not sure where exactly this had gone awry for him, but he knew he had again screwed up.

"Good. Because I'm not. I know exactly the kind of man you are, Tankowicz, and when you are not wallowing in self-pity, I like it. When I like something, I go get it. When I like a man, I go get him."

She arched an eyebrow and struck a saucy pose. Every curve of her body found a seam on the tank top to stretch, and Roland inhaled reflexively, "Do you doubt that, soldier?" Hers was the look of a woman who got exactly what she wanted, and who wise men had learned not to test.

"No, ma'am," he croaked, acutely uncomfortable.

"Good." She put her hands to her hips and leaned forward to emphasize her next point, "It would be in your best interests to recognize that I am a grown woman who doesn't fucking ask permission to like a man. You do not 'let' me think or feel anything." She cocked an eyebrow, "Are we communicating yet, Corporal?"

Roland was again trapped, "Yes. Of course. You know I meant no disrespect, right? I'm just… bad at talking sometimes…"

She took his hand in both of hers, "You have been an amazing person for the last few days, Roland. You've done many things that were sweet and charming and admirable. Because of that, I have decided that I may want to be more than just friends with you."

She clapped her hands, startling the big man, "And that's it! That's the whole stupid process. Boy meets girl, and so on…"

Roland feared what she was trying to do more than any opponent or battle he had ever faced. He wanted to push her away, and he knew why. If Lucia couldn't hate or fear him, how could he go on hating and fearing himself? He wasn't sure he deserved happiness; not when he still had so much to atone for.

"Not when the boy is a living weapon," Roland admonished.

She rolled her eyes, "You are not a weapon. You're just a man. A stupid, stubborn, deeply flawed, flesh-and-blood person who deserves happiness just like I do."

She gave him a stern look, "Stop being such a victim. You're a real boy, Pinocchio. You always have been."

Lucia prevented any further introspection when in an iron voice she declared, "This is happening, Roland." Her smile hardened, "So please, for both of our sake's, stop making this harder than it needs to be, OK?"

Roland wanted to believe that. It certainly sounded like Lucia believed it. Maybe that was good enough? It was going to have to be because he was losing this argument. For some reason that made him happy.

The big man still looked confused and a little scared, but she could tell that she had won when the corner of one side of his mouth curled into a smile. He nodded slowly, "Ok, lady. But don't say I didn't warn you."

"You just worry about your own ass, buddy. I'll be fine." She shrugged out of the shirt, "Now, lay down."

At that point, Billy McGinty wandered down the hall towards Lucia's door. They were supposed to be getting set up with the smugglers, but Roland had not come back from going to fetch Lucia. When he got to the door, something made him pause, and for many years afterwards he thanked whatever powers that be that he did.

The sounds coming from that room were unmistakable if somewhat bizarre. Billy had no idea whatsoever as to how it happened, or how it was going to work, but he was absolutely sure that those two would miss the meeting with the smugglers.

Good for them, he chuckled to himself, and headed back upstairs.

Chapter Twenty-Nine

The late afternoon Monday meeting found Roland and Lucia once again pondering the imminent assault of a fortress.

McGinty, his smugglers, and the two fugitives had finally gotten together to discuss a plan for retrieving Dr. Ribiero. But Billy could not help himself, and made a big, dramatic show of teasing the two about their tardiness.

"Weeeeeellllllllll, just lookie here at who managed to get out of bed and join us?" His goofy smirk and laconic drawl betrayed his obvious mirth, "Y'all well rested?"

Roland was relieved that he could not blush. Lucia for her part never blushed. She fired back at McGinty without missing a beat, "I don't know that I've ever rested that well, Billy, thanks for asking."

"Must be the bed. We have nice mattresses here, that's for sure," Billy snickered.

"I wouldn't now, Billy, the damn thing couldn't handle the weight of both of us," the woman deadpanned.

Billy frowned, "If you aren't even going to have the common decency to be embarrassed, then how do you expect me to have any fun with this?"

"I don't," Roland growled with a menace so pure and intense that Billy feared he might have gone too far with the ribbing for his own safety.

"Besides, I think I've had enough fun for the both of us already," the giant cyborg finished with what could only be described as a shit-eating grin.

Billy looked at Lucia aghast, "Did he just smile?" He looked back at Roland, concern on his face, "Are you gonna be OK? I hear it hurts the first time."

"At least now we know how get him into a good mood," Lucia added.

"Yeah, yeah, yeah." Roland grumbled, "Everybody have a good laugh at the happy cyborg. Get it out of your systems because there is work to do."

"Well that didn't last long," Lucia chuckled, as Roland's grey demeanor reasserted itself.

"Do it harder next time, see if that buys us more time," was Billy's helpful suggestion.

"Your building wouldn't survive it," was her arch response.

Billy whistled, "Damn, girl. My condolences. Want an ice pack or something?"

"Enough!" Roland almost shouted, exasperated.

"There he is," Billy said, "back in form, now."

The two smugglers, whose names were not offered, looked on in equal parts confusion and bemused indifference, and Billy decided he had antagonized Roland enough for one day.

"Let's talk about your building, shall we?" Billy invited.

"Thank you. Yes. Let's do that," Roland replied with exaggerated formality and no small relief.

"First things first," Billy started, "here are the reports from my people at Enterprise."

Billy's people had confirmed that two teams of private security contractors had accessed the Enterprise Anson Gate late the previous night. Roland was not foolish enough to believe they were for anything else but him.

Billy's intel on the groups was impressive for a bunch of Big Woo stool pigeons, but Roland had learned that Billy ran a very different type of street gang than he was used to. He was taking the unexpected as rote when it came to McGinty's Teamsters.

The grunts from Galapagos matched no one Roland had heard of, but those crews changed all the time, anyway.

Billy had only ever heard stories about the Galapagos system and its colorful denizens, "How big a problem are they gonna be, you think?"

Roland considered that for a protracted moment. The teams from Galapagos weren't so much a cohesive unit of like-minded tradesman as they were a loose association of sociopaths with better-than-average people skills. McGinty's spies had counted one re-purposed construction armature and enough weaponry to subdue a small country in that group.

Other than the 'mech, these guys didn't bother Roland too much as opposition. They amounted to untrained, uncoordinated animals with a common goal and stacks of augmentations. While physically tough as individuals, they would be easy pickings for a guy like Tankowicz if he kept his head on straight.

"These guys are high-tier muscle, but low-tier talent. If it comes to slugfest I like my chances, but the specs on that armature would be nice."

One smuggler shrugged, "We don't really have the expertise for that. It was big. It was obviously an old construction 'bot. That's all I can tell you about it."

Roland shrugged, "I'll figure it out. Can't really deploy that in an office building, anyway."

The Thorgrimm crew, based upon descriptions, had to be a detachment from Pike's Privateers.

Roland winced and shook his head, "That's both good and bad, folks." He explained further, "Good because they are an actual professional paramilitary group. Real soldiers."

"That's good?" Lucia asked.

"Yeah, they won't be prone to fits of ultra-violence or cruelty. These are real, honest, specialists with ethics, at least," he explained, "They will be reasonable and predictable."

"So, what's the bad part?" McGinty inquired.

Roland grimaced, "Unless a lot has changed in twenty years, those are absolutely A-list quality hardcore badasses."

There was small consolation in that the manifest showed no sign of heavy cyborgs, but the weapons list was impressive enough to give Roland pause.

"I really don't want to tangle with the whole squad. No guarantees on success if that's how it goes down." Roland did not have to elaborate on what he meant by 'success.' If any single group could bring Roland down, it would be a group like Pike's.

But Corpus Mundi could not afford to have an off-the-books biotech facility exposed in Uptown, so the mercenaries were almost certainly going to be deployed to search for them in Big Woo or Dockside. Two squads of exotic muscle walking aground what was supposed to be a regular old office park would raise red flags everywhere, including the local constabulary. That was the hope, at least.

And the constabulary was a complication that would be factored in as well. Uptown was not like Dockside or the Woo. Uptown had a modern, well-equipped, professional police force that was largely competent and reasonably free of corruption. When the situation got energetic enough, they would descend upon the building with overwhelming numbers and force.

Nobody from Corpus Mundi would call the police on their own illegal operation, but one could only make so much noise in Uptown before the police would assert themselves. Thus, they factored that into the plan.

The reluctance to call the cops could buy them the time they needed to seize the initiative at the outset. When things got bad, or if Roland made enough noise, the police would come anyway. The hope was that a robust police presence meant Roland and the Ribieros could play their respective victim cards and secure a clean getaway while the crooks all went to jail.

Roland did not expect everything to go according to plan because they never did. But the framework had enough flexibility built in that he liked their chances well enough, with a few caveats.

Most importantly, dealing with the mercenaries.

The mercenaries were another reason that law enforcement would have to play a role. The permits and charters for operating Earthside required that all operators be subordinate to local law enforcement. Nobody was sure if the Galapagos crew would lose any sleep over the rules, but it was a foregone conclusion that Pike's Privateers wouldn't risk losing their charter over any single job.

If they got their timing right, there was a solid chance they could avoid fighting the mercs completely. Which, Roland conceded, would be a nice thing.

The building itself was unremarkable. It was a twenty-story office building that had been re-purposed for laboratory space and some light manufacturing. The need to keep its purpose secret had precluded Corpus Mundi from using heavy fortifications or employing excessive security. That was helpful, but no one seriously expected the place to be undefended.

McGinty had not been exaggerating when he bragged about the skills of his smugglers. In just six hours they gained a ridiculous quantity of intelligence on the facility and its occupants. The sheer bulk and detail of what they had assimilated made Roland want to go update all his own security procedures immediately.

The smugglers were confident that the fifth floor was where Donald Ribiero was being held. By hook or by crook, the two had gotten their hands on some security camera footage that showed the Doctor being led to and from a room on that level regularly. Lucia had gasped when she saw it; Donald was looking old and frail in the video, a far cry from the vital man she had seen only three days prior. Roland couldn't think of anything else to say other than, "We'll get him out." Her look of icy resolve indicated that she would do her part, which is a thing Roland had never doubted in the first place.

The building was part of a larger office park, which had a perimeter wall that was more decorative than defensive, and four gates for access and egress. Corpus Mundi had purchased the whole office park, and the combination of privacy and access to the less-well-patrolled suburb of The Sprawl meant that illicit supplies could be brought in from many different places with little to no risk of detection. The smugglers, it seemed, knew of the more common methods for achieving this. The most viable of those was accessing the maintenance tunnels that began at the North gatehouse and ran to every building. Trucks and transports bearing office supplies and mundane sundry items could pull in and appear to unload at the North Gate's receiving docks. Normal-looking dock crews would offload regular supplies and contraband at the same time, right under everyone's noses. The normal supplies would go to receiving, and the illicit goods got whisked underground to find their way to the black site building.

This was the obvious infiltration point; but there were several problems with that. First of all, Roland was too big to hide as office supplies. Stuffing him in crate worked for major cargo movement, but no one was going to believe that the office park needed so many styluses or trash bags that a container the size Roland would require would go unnoticed. Never mind how they would explain the weight.

Second, Roland was impossible to shield from scans. His mass and density alone meant that unless he was especially shielded, the lowest-ranking security guard in the world would spot him in seconds with a cheap handheld scanner. This facility had layers of scanning and security checkpoints that Roland was simply never going to get past.

The smugglers had been very disappointed when they saw Roland for this reason. One look at the size and mass of the man had dashed their hopes of slipping him in under the radar, making the whole job a lot more complicated.

"Infiltration has never been in my wheelhouse," he apologized. "I was designed for a different role."

Roland spared a wistful thought for Alicia Walker, or "Sneak" as she had been designated in his old team. She'd have been in and out in seconds, he mused to himself, and they'd never even know she was there. But Walker was dead, and could not help them.

Now, Lucia, on the other hand, was a different story.

"Can you climb?" they had asked her.

"Like a squirrel," she said. "Only faster." It was a brag, but based upon what she had done at Umas, Lucia was confident she could out-climb anyone in that room.

Three hours, four pots of coffee, and two spirited arguments later, the plan came together with three major elements:

Roland breaching the gates because that was the only thing he could do. Smuggling Lucia inside during the chaos because she could move through the building faster than anyone. Finally, the timely arrival of law enforcement so they did not have to fight the two teams of mercenaries that would almost certainly show up if this took too long.

That last bit was going to be the trickiest element, but a crucial one. There was a 'right' amount of speed and noise for getting this job done without taking casualties, and they would need to walk that tightrope with all the care of a circus acrobat. If they made too much noise too early, Donald Ribiero would get moved to another location, and they would have to start all over. If they didn't make enough noise, Roland would have to face down at least one elite squad of heavily armed mercenaries. In a pinch, they could call the police themselves at any time and bug out, but that defeated the purpose of the operation if it happened before securing Donald.

The smugglers would get Lucia to the basement of the building undetected, employing a complicated dance of bribes, forged documents, and intimate knowledge of Corpus Mundi security procedures and codes. She would await Roland's signal from a storage locker adjacent to a lift tube. When the time came, she was to slip up the tube's maintenance shaft and get to the fifth floor.

Once Lucia had secured her father, Roland would either exfiltrate or arrange for the police to arrive, one way or the other.

They decided on a nighttime raid, to keep the numbers of civilians and non-combatants in the area to a minimum. The security force would be the same, but at least this way Roland would not have to pull his punches on this run. Roland would rather fight powerful opposition with no risk of collateral damage than a weak opponent in a crowd of innocents. For Roland, pulling his punches was much more complicated than maximum output.

Thus, it was that same evening, after a quick rest and some food, that Roland stood in the back of a shielded delivery truck used by the smugglers to block scanners. He prepared himself mentally for what was about to happen, an old routine from his days in the Army. His mind played the script in his head as distinct individual moments in the overall procedural.

As soon as he stepped outside of that truck, every scanner on the street was going to light him up as both an augmented human and a cyborg. Since all his enhancements were licensed and legal, this would not cause an alarm or call for the police.

But every building in Uptown had their own scanners, too. When spying devices could be built into an eyeball, or superhuman cat burglars were walking about; smart businessmen and women scanned everyone who came through their doors. There wasn't a building in Uptown that was going to let Roland Tankowicz through their lobby without a serious security check if at all. If anyone familiar with Project: Golem was looking, there would be no doubt as to who it was that had come knocking.

Roland's job was simply to charge the gate, smile for the cameras and smash his way in. His goal was to get as much security response pointed at him as possible so Lucia could get to her father unmolested. Since Roland blasting his way through the front door is exactly what people expected him to do, it wouldn't raise any suspicion at all about their ace in the hole. The trick was going to be looking convincing without wrecking the whole place outright.

The plan hinged upon this, because no one should be looking for anything else at that point. Corpus Mundi did not know that Lucia was there, or that she was augmented. That gave them an edge.

When Lucia signaled for exfil, Roland would start really cutting loose, which in short order would bring the police into the equation. When the police arrived, Roland and the Ribieros would exfiltrate, or Roland would extract himself and let the Police take custody of Lucia and Donald Ribiero.

He took a breath out of habit and picked up his helmet. The protective head covering was a simple affair; a black and form-fitted skull cover, with a blank silver-white faceplate that slid down and locked into the chin bar and gorget. His eyes would see through two small, lensed slits shaped like upside-down acute triangles set deep behind the contoured nasal bridge and under the heavy brow plate. When it was on and secure, the helmet covered his entire face and neck, leaving no part of him unarmored.

It settled on his head like an old friend. It smelled of plastic, and the displays lit up as soon as he pulled the faceplate down and locked it into place. A menu of diagnostics popped up, indicating the status of his various onboard systems.

His ShipCell was at 98.9%. He liked to keep it above 99%, but too much activity over the last few days and not enough recharge time was showing. Armor integrity was 100%; no surprise, there. Nothing he had been hit with over the last few days had been too intimidating. Musculature and skeletals were showing very minor damage. The nanobots could not fix all the leg strain from his fight with Tom Miner yet, but it was nothing that was going to affect his performance in combat. Much.

It had been a long time since he had worn the helmet. Strapping it on made him feel like a soldier again. He had liked being a soldier, before the Golem program had made that a living hell, and watching the menus scroll and the scanners relay information back made him feel good.

He shrugged yet another of his army-surplus jackets on to cover Durendal in its holster. Not that concealment mattered. With the helmet on, he was an inhuman looking behemoth; skull-faced and towering. Nobody was going to let him in anywhere, armed or otherwise. But old habits die hard, and he felt weird walking around Uptown with an exposed weapon.

With a last mental check of his gear and person, he sighed and grasped the release handle of the smuggler's truck. It was time to go.

Chapter Thirty

When his comm chirped just after midnight, Fox was still awake. Morose and agitated, he was sitting crumpled in an overstuffed chair in his living room and trying his damndest to finish a bottle of brandy all by himself. He took a perfunctory look at who was calling and swore in vehement exasperation when he saw it was Johnson.

He was too drunk and too stressed to deal with whatever banal inconvenience Johnson would claim was a catastrophe right now, so he kicked the call over to his auto-answer and returned to his Armagnac.

Sweet heat warmed his throat and settled in his belly like the comforting warmth of a mother's love; and the florid, flustered man closed his eyes. He was a third of the way through the DeLord Recolte, and the dull, numbing detachment caused by expensive liquor was the only balm that soothed his frayed nerves. He was not a man prone to excess in any behavior as it was unbecoming someone who looked to lead a financial empire; but he'd be damned if he wasn't going to put a solid drunk on tonight.

He would deal with whatever-it-was that was bothering Johnson in the morning. Which is when he would also try to figure out how to pay 130 million credits to crime boss who wanted to kill him. Tomorrow, it appeared, was going to be a hell of a day. He refilled his glass and took another long sip.

Fox was not destined to continue with his brandy and his brooding in earnest, however. Fate granted him only a few precious few minutes to enjoy either before the comm chirped again. It seemed that Dr. Johnson would not be so easily rebuffed tonight.

What the fuck is he so worried about, now?

Fox considered sending this call to auto-answer as well, but gave up on that thought. If Johnson was in a mood to whine, then he would not stop until he got his chance. Best to get it over with.

"What?" he answered in his most irritated voice. He might as well set the tone for this conversation early. If

Johnson was going to be whiny, then Fox would be cranky. It was only fair.

Johnson's voice was not whiny at all. It was shrill and terrified. It was the voice of a man on the ragged edge of pure panic, and the tone of it sobered Fox in seconds.

"Breach is hitting the facility! Right now!" Johnson's terror was a palpable thing, "He crashed the gate and is tearing his way through security right now!"

An icy knot formed in the pit of Fox's gut. He and Johnson were the only two people at Better Man who had the background to comprehend all that meant, so they were the only two people who grasped the magnitude of the threat. Fox remembered vividly the progress data from Project: Golem, and he had seen some of the demonstrations. As a man who prided himself on objectivity and detachment, Fox wasted no time on best-case thinking. Breach was easily the most powerful member of a squad of already powerful cyborgs. An assault from any member of that team would have been a tactical challenge, but Breach was a force of nature. Everyone who had ever worked on Golem knew it as uncontested fact: If Roland Tankowicz wanted into your building, there was no practical way to stop him.

"How the fuck did he find us?" was Fox's first question, and he immediately realized it was a stupid one, and disregarded it. "Fuck that. Is Ribiero secure?"

While inarguably brilliant, Johnson was not a clutch asset in a crisis, and his stammered response was almost unintelligible.

"Y-yeah... yes. Still in his cell."

That was a relief, at least. They were still in this game, for now. Losing Ribiero meant the end of the whole program. It was the only scenario that concluded with a total loss, and Fox was invested in avoiding that outcome. He could handle the gangsters, the Company, and even the looming threat of a mob execution as long as they got the armature working in time to secure those contracts. Ribiero was the key to turning a bunch of regular grunts into super-soldiers, and in time they would get that recalcitrant pacifist to cooperate. Hundreds of billions of credits were on the line, and Fox was not going to let them slip away.

The pudgy man's mind raced, "Johnson! You need to slow him down until we can get those psychos from off-world over there! Can you manage that?"

"I don't think so! He's halfway through the first floor already and we are losing security androids really fast!" The good doctor was attempting to sound like he wasn't about to defecate himself, but the act was not convincing.

Shit! Fuck!

Fox knew that Johnson's assessment was likely accurate. Breach used to train on security androids, and Fox had never noticed the big 'borg exerting himself too much in the process. Staffing the black site with a huge security contingent had been too much risk, so it was unlikely that anything Johnson had would do much more than irritate and delay Breach.

But that was exactly why he wasn't sure if redeploying the talent was such a good idea, either. The mercenaries were at least an hour if not more from the compound, and introducing them to the fray would only get the site compromised. Better that then losing the whole project; but a firefight between Breach and a whole squad of elite mercenaries was not really a "winning" option either. It was a very unfortunate scenario indeed: All of Fox's current options existed on a spectrum that ranged from 'bad' to 'apocalyptic.'

He was desperate, and so he made a desperate play.

"Bring Dawkins online."

"What?" Johnson sounded incredulous, then more confident, "Yeah. Yes. Yes, of course!"

Dawkins was not all the way up to spec yet, and he was still inexperienced with the armature. Even so, after a mere eight full hours of drive time the pair was already a powerful engine of destruction. The testing had gone far better than anticipated, and the man and his machine were operating at a level far surpassing any competitor's numbers.

It was not his favorite idea. Using it now would reveal the project's results before he was ready to present them to the board which was a sub-optimal outcome considering the state of the pilot. But using the Better Man Armature to stop Roland could also be the best press possible if spun with the right angle.

The state of the art model retiring the old and obsolete? It's a good hook, Fox conceded, *I can make this work if I have to.*

There was the inevitable issue of the armature not being able to perform without augmented pilots. It was unfortunate, but Fox could always stall deployment any number of ways and buy time to sort out the good Dr. Ribiero's objections.

This could work.

It was not the best solution, and not the way he wanted this to unfold, but that was how it went sometimes. A good executive needed to be a flexible and bold problem-solver, and Fox considered himself a good executive.

"Get him up and running and have him secure Ribiero." He paused and decided to add some insurance, "I'll move the mercenaries into overwatch, but tell them not to engage without my order. If things inside go so badly that they need to jump in, getting the site burned will be the least of our problems."

"Ok," Johnson sounded calmer, which was good. Fox had lot of confidence in the armature, and Project: Golem tech was two and a half decades old at this point. Even with Roger's relative inexperience, the machine was likely up to the task.

Fox closed the connection and sat up. He was going to have to deal with Johnson soon. He was brilliant, to be sure, but his other issues were beginning to become a liability. Once Ribiero was cooperating, Johnson could be phased out.

At least Ribiero has some goddamn balls, he mused.

Much of the confusion and fear Johnson was experiencing was borne of the fact that he was a small and petty man. Fox considered the issue: Genius? Yes. Essential? For now. Stable? Not so much these days.

Johnson, deep down inside, was a fearful egghead who still hated the jocks and the punks. He had always been jealous of Roland's athleticism and prowess, and now he was afraid of Dawkins because Dawkins was a bully and a sociopath. The scientist feared and resented both men because they each represented all the things he couldn't be and were emblematic of the abuses the inconsequential scientist had endured as an egomaniacal nerd throughout his life. It was affecting the quality of his work, and Fox had noticed. If Fox could get the good Doctor to keep it together for the next few months that would be enough.

Then he is out, Fox concluded with finality and emptied the glass of brandy in one gulp, *better make those calls.*

Across town, sealed inside the command center of the black site, Warren Johnson wasn't so sanguine about how things were going.

He had been a senior design lead back in the Golem days and knew the specs better than anyone other than Ribiero himself. Against any other member of Golem, Johnson was confident that the Better Man system would prevail in a straight fight. Even without full nervous system symbiosis the armature was simply too well-built. It was stronger, faster and more durable. But Roland had always been a different animal. His chassis was almost as strong as the Better Man, and the man inside Breach was, Johnson had to admit, a 'better man' than his.

Roger Dawkins was a fierce and competent fighter. That part was not in question. Johnson had seen him in action and knew with absolute certainty that Dawkins was a ruthless and relentless warrior. In the armature, he was a thousand times more so. The numbers spoke for themselves on that front. But Dawkins was also a bully and thug at heart. While physically the perfect candidate to pilot the armature, psychologically, he'd never have passed the first round of screening in Project Golem, and Johnson knew it.

Roland, on the other hand, was a soldier's soldier: determined, focused, unflinching. Johnson still had all the records from those years. Roland was a master of most weapons, a highly trained hand-to-hand fighter, and gifted with a good head for tactics. Improvements in the technology had been made in the intervening years, but that didn't mean Roland was obsolete. Pretending that Roland was too old to challenge modern tech was a species of stupidity Fox might accept, but Johnson had been in weapons development his whole career. He knew better than to fall for that trap. He had seen enough weapons systems come and go in his time to learn a few things about war and warriors. When things got hard on the battlefield, a sharpened stick was still a dangerous weapon in the right hands.

Johnson considered himself a very experienced stick-sharpener, and he was nervous all the same.

Could Dawkins stop Roland? Johnson wasn't so sure. Not with scientific certainty anyway. The armature was faster, stronger, and piloted by a man who was no slouch as fighter himself. As much as he admired Roland as a successful project, Dawkins was a terrifying thing when he was mounted to the Better Man. His academic curiosity would have been highly piqued by the matchup if his own life wasn't riding so precipitously on the outcome.

As it was, he was just plain scared. With trembling fingers he initiated the pre-deployment procedures for the armature and started the process of waking Dawkins up. The stupid thug's brain was so damaged from years of drug abuse and back-alley augmentations that they kept him in a chemical coma most of the time, just for safety. Waking him up took about fifteen minutes and getting him into the armature took another fifteen.

He hoped he had that long.

Chapter Thirty-One

Roland was a little disappointed in how easily he was breaching the facility. He had hit the doors at what was close to his full speed, and the reinforced transparent screens had exploded like so much sugared glass. His kinetic energy had been sufficient to carry him through the vestibule and into the security checkpoint with minimal loss of speed, and his landing had sent the kiosk and both security androids hurtling across the lobby like humanoid tumbleweeds.

Alarms blared with the predictable intensity, and red flashing lights directed people to emergency exits. It was after midnight however, so there were no people in the lobby to be evacuated. Which was all to the good, Roland felt, considering how much damage he and the security forces were about to do.

A brisk tumble across the lobby was not going to put down a good security android. These were proper security 'droids, not disguised man-hunters like the last time. Roland anticipated a spirited interaction with them.

They were humanoid, but very little care had been taken to make them appear human. They were painted bright yellow and red, as the law said they had to be, and their faces were blank, expressionless analogs. Meant to be evocative of human features, it was apparent that making the faces expressive and friendly had not been a priority in the design.

Roland was familiar with this model. It was one of the better ones; strong, tough, and fast. But nowhere near capable of challenging something like a Golem. The two 'droids charged him immediately after regaining their feet, and the first to meet him exploded in a shower of sparks and polymer fragments when a black fist the size of a melon tore through its torso.

Arms, legs, and a smoking head flew past the towering cyborg as their momentum kept them moving despite the complete and utter destruction of the core. The pieces were still clattering to the floor when the second android got snared by the throat and hoisted high overhead. Limbs flailing, it was brought to the floor with all the force and weight at Roland's disposal.

The floor collapsed under the strain and the 'droid disappeared into the indentation it had made. Its head sheared off in a shower of blue sparks and the body jerked up to a sitting position, where it lurched like a decapitated chicken. Roland twisted his hips and kicked it like a soccer ball back out through the gap he had created upon entering. It struck the ceiling on its way and pinwheeled to the floor, shedding body parts as it skidded to a smoking, squealing stop in the vestibule.

As he stepped further into the lobby proper, he spotted the lift doors on the far side. A security barrier had dropped, barring him from accessing these. Or they might have if they had been built to stop a thousand-pound military cyborg. They had not, and he swept the steel bars aside like so much tall grass.

He wasn't stupid, and Roland knew that destroying the gate would power down the lifts, but he wasn't interested in using them, anyway. Shutting the lifts down would also mean that security reinforcements could not use them, either. There almost certainly were dedicated lifts for security somewhere in the building, but he had slowed any incoming guards, nonetheless. Which was the point; he was just buying time and making noise as per the plan.

More security bots arrived from the far side of the lobby, armed with shock sticks. These baton-like devices were sized and set up to incapacitate regular folk. They'd even work on augmented threats, since there was no way to augment a biological against electrocution. But Roland was only 10% biological, and his chassis was rather non-conductive. The weapons were little more than sticks that tickled as far as he was concerned, and four 'droids with shock sticks would not tax his systems. Maybe if he wasn't wearing the helmet he might have to work a little. Getting a shock directly to his head would probably have been very disorienting.

With the helmet though, all he saw were targets. The HUD lit up with make, model, capacities and weaknesses of his opponents; and superimposed helpful targeting reticles over his adversaries' weakest points.

Roland drew Durendal and keyed up the targeting data, then activated the Press Point option. Holding the trigger down, he simply swept all four droids with the muzzle. The targeting software touched off flechette rounds automatically when the muzzle aligned with the area of each android's torso that the helmet had designated as the power cell housing. Roland didn't even have to squint; the helmet told the weapon when to discharge, so missing was impossible.

In three quarters of a second, four armor-piercing flechettes drilled four neat little holes through four separate androids. Each hole was precisely five and a half inches left of dead-center on the torso.

All four droids hit the floor at the same time, limp and lifeless.

This is too goddamn easy, Roland griped, *I don't like it.*

They had never assumed that the building would be heavily guarded, but Roland had expected more than this. The big 'borg considered the possibility that it was just the first floor that was poorly defended. He decided to make his way up a flight to see if there was more mayhem he could cause up one level. Going too high would be counterproductive, since his job was to pull opposition away from the fifth floor, but this meager response could not represent the full commitment of the facility's security forces. He needed to draw more fire if Lucia was going to have a chance to do her part.

The lifts were out, but there were always stairs. He spotted the sign indicating the stairwell and moved over to it with brisk purposeful strides. Despite the staggering durability of his armored body, Roland always moved with care through a stairwell. They were tactical nightmares where enemies had the advantage of a choke point, lots of corners, and a height advantage. His habits were old and deeply ingrained, and he had never lost his respect for an enemy with the high ground.

Roland kicked the door open and angled his view across the aperture. Never extending himself into the opening, he swept the entire doorway with his eyes, scanners, and muzzle from left to right. This gave him a wedge-shaped view of what was beyond without exposing him to fire, and that was why this technique had been called 'slicing the pie' for centuries.

He was met by a sustained hail of incoming projectiles that shredded the doorway and ripped jagged holes in the surrounding walls. Plaster, metal, and plastic flew in all directions as something large and fully automatic pushed him back and away from the stairwell.

Roland grinned a wan, feral grin, *Thaaaat's more like it*, he thought, *the first floor was just for show. The real shit is upstairs.*

It made sense. It would have been hard to keep up the façade of regular office building if too much security was visible. Sacrificing the lobby had always been part of their security plan, it seemed. Roland approved of the practicality of that strategy.

Approval notwithstanding, Roland needed to get up those stairs. He contemplated just walking into the fire. Whatever was holding the stairwell didn't look too nasty, but it was never solid policy to just tank incoming when you weren't sure what it was. You only had to guess wrong once playing that game before you lost forever. Losing meant dying, and even worse, mission failure. Both were unacceptable outcomes as far as Roland was concerned.

He keyed up infrared and magnetic overlays to the HUD and scanned the stairwell. There was good news and bad news in the readout. There were no biologicals in the stairwell which was good. But it looked like his obstacle was a Vogt Mobile Turret stationed on the landing.

The Vogt company made fantastic hardware, and their Mobile Turret series of drones were extremely popular remotely operated area denial systems. With three radially mounted and individually driven wheels attached to a central axle on each side, and a low center-of-gravity, these devices could climb stairs and navigate both indoors and outdoors. Depending on the specific model, it could come equipped with 30-caliber auto cannons, 10mm HV bead, 20-mm anti-materiel, anti-armor flechette, or even beam weapons.

It wasn't 20mm at least, which was a relief. 20mm probably couldn't pierce his hide right away, but constant bombardment from it would wear the armor out and smash his internals over any appreciable period of time. It wasn't a beam weapon obviously, so he could relax on that front.

Beads would bounce off him like pebbles, but flechette could be a problem. The holes would be small, but a lot of them would take time and energy to repair, and if by chance one nicked his biological components, he could bleed to death.

All of this he analyzed in a quarter of a second, and the helmet's AI determined with high confidence that it was armed with HV bead.

This was good news, but Roland still wasn't sanguine about charging into a hail of bullets. The cyclic rate on that turret was 900 rounds-per minute, and even though they wouldn't kill him, they would wreck his clothes and probably break Durendal.

It seemed likely his belt of grenades would not appreciate getting shot to pieces, either. He burned another full second to run some scenarios through the combat AI and picked one he liked.

He selected a grenade from his bandolier and had the AI mark the aim point on his HUD. With a sidearm throw, he bounced a chaff grenade off of the floor directly across from the stairwell door. It bounced hard from the floor and struck the back wall at a steep angle. From there it caromed up the stairs and popped directly in front of the turret; a perfect two-bounce bank shot.

The grenade cast a misty sparkling cloud of tiny particles in a blossoming sphere that filled the stairway with charged metallic chaff. It would only hang in the air for a few seconds, but for that time, the drone was completely blind.

Roland was only a fraction of a second behind the detonation. His own sensors were useless as well, but his advantage lay in the fact that he could simply use his old-fashioned biological eyes for this part. Thus, he suffered little for the handicap.

With a single leap he cleared the first staircase and hit the landing with a crash. His touchdown put him within striking distance of the turret and he forbore any high-tech responses and simply punched the drone as hard as he could. He could not recall exactly how heavily Vogt built this model, so he erred on the side of caution and put everything he had into the blow.

Vogt made a quality product, so Roland's caution was well-placed. The punch connected with one of the bead cannons and tore it clear of the mount. Despite the glancing blow, sufficient force was conveyed to drive the drone over sideways, and send it to the floor.

Before it could right itself, Roland began a series of kicks and stomps that were not coordinated in any strategic pattern. The big man simply wanted to stomp it to death before it started shooting and thus spared no thoughts for finesse.

In short order, the expensive drone was a tangle of twisted metal and twitching, whirring shrapnel. When he was satisfied that it was finished, Roland moved up the second flight to the second-floor landing.

The big man paused for a few seconds to let his sensors clear the chaff, then he scanned the door to the second floor before opening it.

There appeared to be, for all intents and purposes, an army of security droids and several Vogt turrets on the other side. His HUD fed him the numbers and specs, and Roland took a moment to absorb it all.

The tally was suitably impressive: Twenty-four security androids, nine Vogt turrets, and at least eight biologicals in power armor.

Well shit. At least it's all going according to plan. He shook his head in grim acknowledgement, *I wonder how Lucia is getting on?*

He shrugged, grabbed another chaff grenade from his belt with his off hand and hefted Durendal in his right.

"Time to punch the clock," he said out loud, and kicked the door in.

Chapter Thirty-Two

Even if the alarms had not gone off, Lucia would have known when it was time to move from the sheer racket Roland made when he crashed the lobby.

He's not a subtle man, she acknowledged, *but I guess he's my man now.*

It was the most bizarre aspect of a most bizarre few days. Finding herself in bed with an eight-foot cyborg had never really entered her realm of imagination, but nevertheless, it had happened. She didn't know if she was in love with him or not. She was too canny to go down that rabbit hole just yet. But now that everything she had ever thought she knew about the world had been a revealed as a lie, she was extremely enamored of the fact that Roland always told the truth. No man she had ever been with had done as much for her in any time period as Roland had in just three days. The obtuse goon hadn't even been trying to get into her pants, either.

She had grown up in a world where everything was a transaction and heroes only existed in her father's stories. Then, out of the blue, she had met that hero from Dad's stories and it turns out her old man wasn't exaggerating. There may have been an element of schoolgirl infatuation with meeting the subject of her father's tales, but she was far too old to have let that push her as far as she had gone. For good or ill, she liked the big man, warts and all.

But now it was time to go get her father, and she set her accelerated brain to the task of getting up the shaft to the fifth floor and freeing him. Lucia was really getting the hang of that part. She could completely preclude the ever-present panic if she crammed the myriad information channels of her mind full of productive scenarios. If she curated her thoughts with care, the anxieties and fears could not force their way in. Plans and strategies got examined and rejected six or seven at a time while another part of her brain ran her arms and legs with perfect precision. Her fear remained a small but persistent buzzing behind the scenes; but it stayed there at least.

Lucia yanked the access door from roof of the maintenance closet and leapt up to grab the opening. She hauled herself up with athletic grace and scrambled into the dark narrow maintenance shaft. When she looked up, she could see all twenty stories of narrow tube overhead, and the single slender ladder secured to the side of it. It was lit to a dim iridescence for the entire length by emergency lights that pulsed faintly to indicate the alarm status. She grit her teeth in resolution, grabbed the first rungs, and started climbing.

Fortunately, this part of the task required no special tactical skills so her brain continued to run search and rescue scenarios while her arms and legs cycled in absent rhythm through the repetitive actions of scaling the ladder. Lucia was always in good shape, but a sixty-foot ladder climb at speed proved to be somewhat challenging, and her forearms burned by the time she got to the alcove where waited the fifth-floor access hatch. The nondescript square door sat on the floor of the dark niche expectantly; awaiting her decision.

McGinty's smugglers had a decent set of schematics for the building, but they were a few years old and may have been out of date. They knew that Corpus Mundi had probably changed the layouts of the secure floors; but there was nothing they could do about that. They just had to hope that this hatch didn't open into a guard station or worse.

She tried listening at the door to see if she could make out voices or footsteps, but all she heard was the screeching of the building alarm. Nothing left to wait for, she twisted the latch and let the hatch drop open. She looked down into a maintenance closet identical to the one she had used to access the ladder five floors below. She breathed a sigh of relief and dropped silently to the floor of the closet. Another gift from her father, it seemed, was the ability to land as softly as she wanted to.

At the closet door, she stopped to listen again, and once more heard nothing but the wailing of the alarms. She knew from the plans that she was on the far side of the building from her father's cell, and the pilfered security camera images seemed to indicate that the path would be more or less clear of obstructions. All she had to do was get from here to her father's cell, get the door open, and get back here undetected.

That sounded far easier than it was likely to be. Roland had lectured her at length about all the things that could go wrong, and how she should handle each one. The moron did not understand that every new wrinkle he presented her with sparked a spiderweb of branching anxieties in her frantic mind. He was just trying to help, and she had appreciated the effort if not the execution.

But at least she had an idea what to do if things went sideways, and she took as much comfort in that as she could before bursting through the door.

If the hallway was empty, her flurry of activity would go unnoticed, anyway. If it wasn't empty, her speed and violence of action would almost certainly give her the drop on whoever was there.

The hallway was not empty.

Even though she had hurled herself through the opening as fast as she could, it felt painfully slow to her accelerated perceptions. There was a moment of panic as she immediately registered the man in full body armor who had just turned down the hallway to face her. Lucia hesitated as she tried to remember what she should do in this case, but shook herself free of the indecision when she remembered Roland's advice: Any decision is better than no decision.

So, she sprinted. Roland had warned her about her brain driving her body beyond its physical limitations. It was a common problem with neurological augmentations, and Roland had told her more than one story about snapped leg bones and torn joints to make the point.

But Lucia had been doing some of her own experimenting, and suspected she could move as fast as she wanted to if she was careful. With this in mind, she pushed off the carpeted hallway floor as hard as she could, bunching and tearing sections of it away as her feet drove her forward. The decorative floor covering capitulated in the face of the immeasurable forces. With each stride, she willed her legs to cycle as fast as they could. It felt like she was flying and the guard suddenly loomed large in her view. She watched in detached satisfaction as his face evolved from blank, to confused, to angry, to terrified as she closed the distance.

To her everlasting chagrin, Lucia hadn't thought about slowing down and realized too late that she wasn't able to control her braking well enough to avoid a collision. She cocked her right fist and drove it ahead of her as she came upon the hapless man. If she had not been wearing armored gauntlets, she would have shattered the bones of her hand.

As it was, she killed the guard outright. She did not know which was the more fatal aspect of her attack: the staggering amount of kinetic energy her hurtling body must have had or the prodigious electric discharge from the glove. But she knew right away and with complete certainty that he was dead. She didn't know if you could actually see the life leave a person's body, but that was exactly how it felt. She got to watch it in slow motion as she sped by the man at thirty-five miles an hour. His eyes spread open as wide as possible before rolling back in their sockets as his head snapped back so far the back of his skull seemed to touch his spine. Every muscle in his body strained and flexed for an excruciating moment before all tone and tension evaporated and the soulless husk crumpled to the floor in a limp pile of flesh and bone.

Lucia could not stop her forward motion for several more long strides. Though it took only the space of two or three heartbeats, she was already sobbing by the time she came to a halt. She wanted to look back, to say something, to explain it all away.

But she didn't. She didn't turn back because there was no turning back now. It didn't make her feel better to know that the man had been a criminal who helped keep her father prisoner, it made her feel worse. She felt the guilt of taking a life, but she also felt the guilt of her own judgement of Roland.

It was easy to think of him as a weapon sometimes, and a person at other times; as if he could simply switch between the two roles as needed. In retrospect, this had been a stupid thing to believe. Roland was always a person, and always a weapon.

In one brief second, it became clear that she had been deluding herself into thinking that convenient labels somehow made what Roland did different or easier than what she had just done. Soldiers killed, but Roland was still a person like any other underneath it all. Sure, Roland was a soldier, but a soldier is a just a person who kills for a cause. It took the death of that guard for her to finally comprehend that the distinctions were purely academic.

Is this what it's like to be him? She wondered, guilt and pain blossoming in her mind.

Does Roland feel every kill like this?

She couldn't bear the thought of that. She sobbed again, a great big gasping cry of shame and pain and fear. The man was dead because she had killed him. She was a killer now. A line had been crossed. But then an ember ignited in the core of her pain, and she was smart enough to feed that fire.

So what if I am a killer? I have a cause, don't I? Maybe I'm not a soldier like Roland, but I'm no murderer.

She caught her breath and started combat breathing. Four in, four out. Four in, four out.

Don't you dare turn around.

She was angry now. But she could understand that. War was an angry place and in war people did angry things. Watching Roland had taught her it was OK to be angry in battle. So she welcomed the rage and surrendered to it.

Her focus returned, her thoughts became ordered again, and she let her fury wrestle all her fear and pain down and force it all into the back of her tortured psyche. She spared a single thought for the dead man behind her, *you don't have to apologize to him. He made his choice and so did you.*

Then came resolve. Merciful, righteous resolve:

Get up, soldier. You've got a job to do!

She got up.

The corridor was plain, unadorned white passageway with silver metal doors and endless brown carpeting along it. The security footage indicated that her father was the only person kept on this level, so she could presume that most of the doors were to empty rooms. Her eyes closed as she tried to remember what the corridor around her father's door looked like, and she seemed to recall that it was on a corner. She decided to look at all the rooms on corners near a security camera first, and circle back around if that didn't work.

Lucia set off at a dead run, relying on her accelerated perceptions to pick out the details she needed to make a call on whether or not a door warranted inspection. The process felt slow and inefficient to Lucia, but an objective observer would be flabbergasted at exactly how fast she was actually moving. The fifth floor was a labyrinth of twists and turns, and there were many doors near many corners to check. She pounded on each and called loudly for her father, uncaring as to whether or not there were guards in the area.

After the fourth door, she stumbled upon another guard and she brought him down with ease. He would live, but he would limp for the rest of his life unless he could afford a new knee.

At door eight, she met her first drone. Roland had briefed her on this possibility, and despite a moment of panicked hesitation, she dispatched it with several well-placed flechettes from her CZ-105.

She made a mental note to thank Roland with appropriate enthusiasm for telling her the best places to shoot a drone because it didn't look like the type of thing one wanted to take on with just a handgun. She had managed to dump the whole magazine in the process of landing those few good shots, but that is exactly why she carried all those extra mags in the first place.

"Nobody ever left a firefight complaining about having too much ammo," Roland had said, and she had believed him.

She slapped a fresh magazine into the grip and charged the weapon with a fresh cell. Then Lucia resumed her search.

Two more disabled guards and another dead drone later, and Lucia found her father's cell.

Door sixteen responded to her frantic pounding with the muffled and incredulous voice of her father.

"Hello? Who is that?" The voice was weak and thin, a far cry from the strong baritone of the Dr. Donald Ribiero, she had grown up with.

"Dad!" She cried, "It's me, Lucia! I'm getting you out!"

Then she swore loudly as realization struck.

She needed a key to get the door open.

"Hang on, Dad! I have to find the key!"

"Lucia?"

"I'll be right back!" She tore off at a gallop, trying to memorize the twists and turns of the corridors until she found one of the unconscious guards. Twenty seconds of panicked rifling later, she emerged with a keycard that she hoped would open the door. Then she ripped off like a greyhound back to her father's cell.

She jammed the card into the slot with far more vigor than was strictly prudent, but she was so amped up her nascent control over her augmentations was slipping. The card slid home without snapping, and the panel blinked green. Relief washed over Lucia like a tsunami and she felt her adrenaline ebb as she keyed the latch.

On the other side of the door was a weak, tired, old man. Donald Ribiero's eyes were sunken and hollow, his face drooped, and his shoulders slouched. He was a mere shade of his normal vibrant self, despite a mere four days in captivity.

"Oh, Dad!" Lucia cried and hugged him tightly, "What did they do to you?"

"Lucia!" he cried, tears forming. "I can't believe… why, er… what are you doing here?" His face went frantic, "It's not safe at all, you have to go! If they get you I… I…"

"Dad!" Lucia barked with stern authority, holding her father by the shoulders, "They won't get me. We have a plan!"

"We?" His tired, bloodshot eyes gazed in confusion at the black-clad and armored apparition of his daughter.

"I brought Roland!" Her face twitched in a flash of bestial glee.

"Oh," the old man breathed, "I see."

He gave his daughter another quick hug, "We should hurry then. We don't want to be anywhere near him when he's working."

Chapter Thirty-Three

Roger Dawkins came online with a rush of sensations at an intensity that still made him acutely uncomfortable. The armature made everything feel vibrant, but in a detached distant sort of way. It was like getting a finger smashed with a hammer while high on morphine: You were intensely aware of what was going on, but you were not getting the full experience.

But it was also the only time Roger felt one hundred percent awake. The bridging AI and the artificial nerves of the Better Man Armature were more than capable of feeding his brain information as fast as he could process it, and the armature itself could handle as much as Roger could give it. For the first time in years, Roger felt at home in his own skin. The sad irony being that 'his own skin' in this case meant a giant plastic and metal superstructure.

The Doc wasn't lying when he said that it would be his body while he was in it. Roger actually preferred being in the armature more than out of it at this point.

With his nervous system directly connected to the suit via the surgically implanted plugs, Roger's body was paralyzed. His entire nervous system had been hijacked by the Better Man AI and duplicated in the artificial nerves of the nine-foot mannequin. With his physical body cocooned in the torso of the armature, limp limbs were folded to take up as little space as possible while his too-human head nestled inside the hollow dome of the armature's expressionless skull.

Roger didn't care, because his other body was much better than the three-hundred pounds of flesh locked inside it, anyway.

The startup sequence took four minutes, which felt like hours to Roger. But, soon enough, it was complete and the Better Man rose from its docking chair. Cables and hoses fell away, and the blank-faced beast strode out through the bay doors and into the main area of the penthouse.

At the speed of thought, Roger keyed up the security cameras and alarm stations all over the building, and with superhuman alacrity he cycled through all the feeds.

Johnson had told him to secure the prisoner on level five, but Dawkins was not interested in babysitting an old man while his nemesis was trashing the building. He found his quarry on level two, waging a pitched battle against the security team outside the stairwell. A quick check of the alarm panel told him the main lifts were down, but the freight lift and the security lift were operational if you had the correct code.

Roger strode over to the freight lift and keyed the door open. He could stand up straight in this one and fit though the door without too much trouble. This made it the obvious choice.

He checked his internal systems and power levels. Everything was nominal as he knew it would be. He spared a whimsical moment to lament the lack of weapons systems, but the suit had only been operational for three weeks, and no weapons systems had even been designed for it yet. He would have to do this with his 'bare' hands, as it were. Roger was OK with that. It felt poetic. They had started this fight bare-handed, and that was how they would finish it. Roger was not the dramatic sort, and he never sneered at an unfair advantage if one was available, but there was certain visceral pleasure in the thought of beating that Dockside trash to death with just his fists.

With a lurch and a chime, the lift stopped at level two. The doors whooshed open and Roger strode out into the warehouse section. In five long strides, he crossed the crowded storage space and made his way towards the sounds of battle.

He keyed into the security cameras again and overlayed their data with his own infrared and EM scans. The big bastard was well on his way to mopping the floor with the security team and had pushed them back to just outside the warehouse.

He considered for a moment pushing his way through the wall to take his enemy by surprise, but the decision was taken away from him when the wall between the shipping offices and the warehouse buckled inward and collapsed, leaving a gaping aperture large enough to drive a truck through.

Chunks of ceiling and other debris rained down on the armored figure that had been the instrument of the destruction, burying the unfortunate security guard and his sophisticated battle suit in dust and rubble. Roger was impressed. That was close to eight-hundred pounds of powered combat armor, and something had hurled it hard enough to bring down a wall. Well, someone had, and Roger was unsurprised to see a Vogt Mobile Turret bounce off the rising security guard with enough force to send both skittering into the warehouse proper and tumble past Dawkins and his towering armature.

Both man and machine crashed into a shelf of boxes and assorted parts, then came to a still, quiet halt under the resulting pile of detritus.

Roger nodded in satisfaction. As a professional, he respected the work of a peer. It cost him nothing to acknowledge that was a hell of a throw.

Roger hung back to observe his foe, taking a rare and measured tactical approach that was not his usual style. Getting off the drugs and having his neurological augmentations modulated by the AI allowed him a clarity and calm that was new and refreshing for the leg-breaker. His telemetry fed data to the AI in real time as he watched the big black cyborg in the next room finish off the security force with workmanlike efficiency.

The men in powered armor were doing better than the drones, at least. Skilled fighters and ex-military guys were all the more lethal when strapped into a suit of power-armor. Each suit was equipped with forearm-mounted HV Bead cannons, and a 40mm grenade launcher was secured over the right shoulder. The problem, Roger identified it immediately, was that 40mm HE grenades were too dangerous to use indoors, and bead didn't seem to even scratch the finish on the muscle-bound 'borg.

With perfunctory detachment Roger noticed that the grenade launchers were loaded with non-lethal stingball and CS gas rounds, which did exactly nothing to the enemy. That left hand-to-hand combat for the armored guards, and they simply were not up to the task. Readings from his sensors were conclusive on this. The power armor was rated for what appeared to be about half what the opposition cyborg was putting out, and Roger could not even be sure if the big bastard was even exerting himself yet.

The last guard in armor tried to take advantage of the distraction created by a concerted assault from three security 'bots. He charged low from behind, trying to bring the black monster down while it smashed the androids to smoking scrap with quick, confident blows. When the guard hit, driving a reinforced shoulder into the back of his enemy's thigh, he nearly succeeded in toppling the black giant.

But the cyborg's speed and poise were too fantastic for so clumsy a maneuver. The hips immediately dropped and turned, and a club-like right hand, still holding the thrashing top half of a security android, brought a blow down on the guard that shook the floor and pancaked the man face-first into the deck.

Two more hammer fists twisted the exo-suit in irreparable contortions, and Roger spared a wince for the poor operator inside. For he too, was now also likely irreparably twisted and broken as well. Roger remembered all too well how that felt.

The security 'droids used this brief interlude to pile on four or five at a time. It was like watching a colony of ants try to bring down a goliath beetle; the more they swarmed, the faster they died.

'Droids designed to absorb small arms fire and muscle flesh-and-blood people around were hopelessly outclassed by the big cyborg, and no quantity of frenzied punching and kicking from the red and yellow mechanical men was going to bring the monster down.

The androids flew off the dog pile one at a time, at what looked to Roger like escape velocity. The brawl rained sparks and metal body parts in noisy disconnected double-time. A brutal, industrial tattoo that would deafen anyone who did not have the forethought to wear hearing protection filled the open spaces and caused anything not firmly secured to rattle and vibrate.

It was nothing short of a war zone, condensed into the tiny footprint of a warehouse and some offices. At one point, Roger's scans indicated as many as nine androids in the fray simultaneously, with Vogts raining sustained fire into the mix whenever a target presented itself. The stupid turrets were doing more damage than anything else, Roger noted, as the ricochets were bringing down androids almost as fast as the cyborg was. Bad planning and poor situational awareness from the operators, but that was to be expected. This situation was very far outside of what anyone here knew how to handle.

Well, except maybe for Roger, of course. For all the high-tech, superhuman bombast of the battle he faced, they were just two men about to have a fight, and Roger knew how to handle that situation better than most. Adding a few tons of bleeding edge cybernetics didn't change the fundamentals of that equation.

That's why Roger was content to watch millions of credits' worth of security technology get smashed like children's toys by the snarling monster in the next room. His turn to play would come soon enough, and he'd rather not have the distractions of weak AI and panicked fire from clueless drone pilots when that time came.

The last of the security androids met their ends as projectiles employed to eliminate the few remaining Vogt drones. The withering fire from their bead cannons had not even warranted a response from the big man until the powered armor and androids were under control. As it was, the broken bodies of the security force served as clubs and hurled missiles to shut down the remote-controlled turrets.

Roger's sensors, having observed and cataloged all the action, pinged an identification on his foe: Lance Corporal Roland Tankowicz, Planetary Army, retired. The list of registered augmentations associated with him was long enough to fill two screens, but most were simply listed as "classified." As a matter of fact, virtually all information on Tankowicz came back as "restricted," "classified," or "redacted."

A slow smirk spread across the face of Roger Dawkins.

A goddamn top-secret military fucking cyborg, he mused, *well fuck me sideways, folks. Welcome to the big-time, Roger!*

He was going to be so fucking rich when this was over; Roger just knew it. Reputations and careers were made on opportunities like this, and his was a reputation for taking all comers.

Johnson's voice crackled over the secure comm, "Dawkins! What are you doing! Ribiero is not in his cell and the detention level has been compromised!"

Roger did not want to deal with that whining nerd right at this moment. He had man's work to do and whatever the sniveling prick of a doctor needed was a distant second to the career-defining battle ahead of him. His response was curt and authoritative, "I'm dealing with the fucking problem, Doc. I'll call you back in a couple of minutes." He closed the channel without waiting to hear Johnson's reply.

"Boring conversation anyway," he grumbled to no one in particular.

He went ahead and pumped the armature up to full output. That much at least, he knew was going to be necessary. Then he keyed the PA system and broadcast at full volume.

"Hey Mungo! Remember me?"

It was time to go make some money.

Chapter Thirty-Four

When the last Vogt had gone down under a relentless barrage of clubbing strikes, Roland cast aside the remains of his improvised bludgeon. The top third of the now-defunct security android crashed to the floor with a sad, impotent clunk. As it clunked to the floor, the space became eerily quiet for a moment, if one disregarded the hissing, whining, and clicking of the assorted twitching bits of android and drone that littered the offices where the brunt of the fighting had taken place.

The battle had been a strange throwback to his Army days; reminiscent of some of the tight spots the squad had fought in on far-away worlds. He had never really felt fear as his own tech had all but guaranteed his success against the security forces arrayed against him. Although he had to admit, the power armor had been nerve-wracking, as skilled soldiers in good armor were one of the few things that could bring him down under the right circumstances. Roland's memory of the Armored Corps was replete with concrete examples of how brutally effective a platoon of Heinlein's' Harriers could be. This bunch had (fortunately for Roland) been beneath the standards of an Army Off-World Expeditionary unit by a significant margin.

A quick diagnostic check revealed that he was none the worse for wear, considering the scale of the scrap he had just finished. Surface armor would need at least seven hours to get back to 100%, but all armor was still well above safe operating levels. Structurally he was as close to nominal as he was going to get, considering the last few days' activities. His shirt was completely gone, of course. They weren't even lasting long enough to get dirty these days so he was saving money on laundry at least.

Durendal had taken a few direct bead hits in the fray and was well and truly broken. That was disheartening. The weapon was as close to a trusted friend as he had ever known. He was reasonably sure he could repair it given enough time and tools. But for now, it was out of commission. At least it looked like the fight was pretty much over; time to check in and see where Lucia was at.

As a precaution, Roland re-keyed and focused on the scanners that he had been forced to ignore during the frenetic skirmish. Before he could lock in Lucia's position and status, IFF immediately registered a bogey in the next room.

"Hey, Mungo!" He heard the thing say, "Remember me?"

Roland remembered.

"So, you survived, huh?" Roland's growl was not overflowing with congeniality, considering the nature of this reunion.

"I did." Roger's voice dripped smug amusement, "You won't."

"That's what you said last time," was Roland's rejoinder.

That was all the effort the two spared for pre-fight repartee. These two were not big on talking; action suited them much better. With the requisite banter complete, the two titans charged each other without further ceremony.

They collided with a wall-shaking crash, trading blows like steel prizefighters. Roland immediately noted that the taller armature was faster and stronger, but not by the kind of margin that granted significant advantage. Roland, being more machine than anything else, assumed that he was marginally more resilient. Either way, it looked to be a battle for the ages.

Roland snapped jabs like jackhammers, probing for weaknesses in Roger's defense. Roger blocked with practiced ease, his years as a fighter evident in the methodical footwork and evasive head movement. Roland pressed forward with hooks to the body and was rewarded when one slipped through and his fist drove into the armored carapace with enough force to make the big armature slide six feet to the side.

Roland tried to capitalize on this with a lashing Thai round kick to the knee on that now-undefended side, but Roger's speed was too much. With lightning speed and casual ease the thug caught his kick in both hands. Snarling, Roger whipped his arms to the side and threw Roland across the warehouse. Roland careered through shelves and racks, scattering parts and supplies in all directions.

"Too slow!" Roger crowed. Then charged his fallen foe.

Roland rose to meet him. The men collided for a second time in the center of the warehouse space, and for a second time a furious exchange of strikes and parries ensued.

Roger got the upper hand again when he snapped a back kick that Roland blocked, but got upended by the force of it, anyway. Roger fell on top of his downed opponent and with a fusillade of furious punches tried to pound that helmeted cranium through the floor.

But Roland was too skilled a wrestler, and Roger could not hold onto his perch atop Roland for more than a few seconds. With a lurch and a heave, Roger was swept off to the side and onto his own back. Soon he was fending off Roland's methodical attempts at returning the favor.

The armature was sturdy enough to buy the time Roger needed to scramble away, but not before taking more than one savage fist to the faceplate. Both men tried to tackle the other as they rose, and a scramble of entangled limbs followed. Roland's skill as a wrestler again prevailed, and Roger was again slammed to the deck. The floor of the warehouse, having done all it could to contain the carnage, capitulated under the onslaught. With crackling acquiescence, it collapsed under the two fighters, and both fell through to the lobby below in a tangled and thrashing mess of bionic appendages and blank-yet-snarling faces.

While the brawl was going on, Roland had set the entire suite of sensors at the helmet's disposal to gather as much data as possible on the thing he was fighting. The data was trickling in slowly as there was nothing in the database to compare it against. When his combat AI compiled the information, the results were strange and more than a little disconcerting.

It had looked like an oversized android, painted white, but the structure was wrong. His helmet AI had pieced together the probable reason for this, and cross-referenced the performance data with all known cyborg configurations. One terrifying configuration had an 89% correlation to the available data set.

Oh no. Oh no no! Roland could not decide if he felt fear or rage in greater proportion, *They couldn't have!*

Underneath the dermal plating of that machine was synthetic musculature almost identical to his own. EM scans showed a complex neural network that had all the hallmarks of his as well, but with several key alterations.

Those bastards! The final insult was yet to come. Inside the machine was the telltale warmth and mass of a person.

They had built a Golem.

Roland could not believe that after all the political and physical fallout from the end of that program, anyone would be stupid enough to revive it. Only a madman would have tried. The realization of what he was facing hit him as he rose again to battle with this twisted vision of what he had once been. Or maybe what he still was. He wasn't sure anymore.

Fear, sadness, and rage drove Roland into the giant white avatar of his own insecurity with an intensity that startled Dawkins. The armature was driven backwards by a furious barrage of punches and kicks delivered at the full speed and strength at Roland's disposal.

Roger's counter attack was instantaneous and vicious. He sent three streaking punches followed by a ferocious round kick to the head. The punches landed unopposed, Roland's head hardly moved as he tanked the hits deliberately. His rage had him well past subtlety and he ate the punches with stoic indifference because it bought him the sixteenth of a second he needed to step inside the arc of that kick and sweep Roger's base leg.

Roland followed him down and rained punches on the helmeted skull of his foe. Roger again scrambled, and the big armature's advantages in speed and power made Roland's perch atop the machine precarious. With the practiced ease of long experience Roland secured a good grip on Roger's elbow and transitioned to a side headlock. From here he had a tremendous advantage in leverage, so he held the enormous armature down and immobile long enough to deliver a spitting inquiry:

"Do you even know what they did to you?" Roland had to ask this. His own tortured soul required him to give this poor fool a chance to understand. The chance no one had offered him. No matter how disreputable the thug was, he had the right to know what had likely been done to him.

"Yes," the faceless head snarled, "they made me a better man."

"They made you a slave." Roland's tone was flat and brimmed with certainty. A certainty that Roger Dawkins recognized.

"What the fuck do you know about it, Roland?" Roger tried to throw his opponent off by showing how much he knew, as if using the man's given name would convey some sort of advantage. His struggles against Roland's hold intensified, and the mass of entangled machines skittered along the floor as Roger tried to escape the hold.

"Do a scan, tough guy," Roland growled through gritted teeth.

Roger frowned inside the helmet, but targeted his scanners directly to Roland's body. There was nothing there that he had not already determined during the fight. Then Roland continued, still firmly restraining Roger, "Now overlay your own specs, smart guy."

Curious now, Roger did what Roland said, and the results were a little shocking. Roger, not being the overly intellectual type, needed a moment to sort out what he was seeing. But in a few seconds' time realization set in. Roger knew it was bad, but the ramifications were not immediately clear to him.

"Well look at that. Seems we're related! So, what?" Another attempt to shrug Roland off of him got stuffed by the other's merciless grip.

Roland shook his head, and a devious idea entered his mind. "Here," he said, and he beamed an encrypted data packet to Roger. Roland waited patiently, maintaining his vice-like grip on Roger's armored skull and allowing no chance of escape.

Roger scowled when the data packet arrived, afraid to open it, "What the fuck is this?"

"No tricks," Roland assured. "Just some family history is all."

Roger's curiosity got the best of him and he opened the files. It didn't look like he was going anywhere soon, anyway.

Fucking jujitsu faggots, he thought uncharitably, *can't even manage a proper stand-up fight.*

He speed-read the small portion of Roland's personal history with detached bemusement until he got to the part where the Golem program had turned Roland's brain off. Roger did not fully understand it, but what he saw made him afraid.

"What the fuck is this?" He repeated. He had no better words for what he saw. It was all he could think to say.

"Your future, pal." Roland was determined to make the man understand the magnitude of his folly, "If you ever decide to disobey your new masters, slave, they will shut your brain off and drive your body around like cheap drone. If you try any independent action they don't like? They will stop you." He gave Roger's head a bounce off the floor, "You let them into your brain, pal. Now they won't leave."

"Bullshit!" Roger cried and finally dislodged the iron grip of his captor. He rose to his feet in triumph but did not press his attack. He wanted, no, needed to deny it all but he couldn't even believe his own words.

Roland stood slowly, "How much money do you think they spent getting you set up in that rig?" Roland didn't wait for an answer, "Do you really think Corpus Mundi will ever let you walk away? Do you think they would ever risk a multi-billion-dollar project on a crook like you without a fail-safe?"

The term 'fail-safe' stuck in Roger's mind like a ten-penny nail. Johnson and Fox had used that word when discussing the instability of his mind.

Roger Dawkins had an instant of perfect clarity, and swore out loud, "Shit!"

Roland kept rolling, "There is a piece of software, hidden somewhere in one of your implants, that gives them total control of your body. If you try to have it removed, it will shut your organs off. I watched it happen to two of my friends. Believe that."

Roger did believe it, there was no lie in Roland's words and Roger could spot a lie at three hundred yards.

With the hook set, Roland reeled his prey in, "Check my records. The only man who knows how to remove that program is being held prisoner on the fifth floor."

Despite his lack of intellectual talents, Roger was again putting the pieces of Fox's machinations together. There was no way Roland had faked the data in that packet; it was too complete and had too much insider information. Not to mention the sheer logic of his argument. Roger was a self-aware guy. He would not have trusted himself with a multi-billion-credit project either. He cursed his lack of foresight on that front.

But what could he do? If Corpus Mundi could kill him with a flick of a switch, he was screwed either way. Unless…

There was no delay between decision and action. Roger keyed into the security loop and accessed the fifth floor. He located the old man and a woman on the cameras and leapt into action with all the speed his new body could muster.

Roland followed.

Chapter Thirty-Five

Leland Fox didn't know where he should be. Reflex and instinct had driven him to head directly to the black site building, but as soon as he landed on the roof it occurred to him that his being there brought absolutely no measurable improvement to the situation, and exposed him to the threat of arrest should they need to burn the site. He could have coordinated and administered the various moving parts to this problem just as well from home.

He was considering climbing back into his car and retreating to a safer locale when his comm chirped again, and the stock photo of Johnson that popped on screen told him that at the very least he should secure that twit of a scientist before scrambling away.

"I'm on the roof, Johnson, what is it?" he barked into the comm.

"Dawkins went to take on Breach!" Johnson was screaming.

"Settle down!" Fox barked back, "Isn't that what we wanted?"

"I told him to secure Ribiero, first, he ignored me and went right to Breach!" To Fox's mind, Johnson was not making a lot of sense.

"What's the problem, then?" Fox really wanted to know.

"Ribiero has escaped! Someone let him out of his cell when security went to fight Breach! He's out and we can't find him!"

"So, have Dawkins track him down and... Oh."

That stupid, egomaniacal, pig-headed piece of criminal trash had gone off to have his big macho punch-up with his nemesis, when he was supposed to be on-mission. Fox was no military man, but he had been around them long enough to understand how important it was to stay on-mission.

"What's the situation, then? How long before Dawkins puts Breach down?" Fox was walking and talking with brisk efficiency now. He needed to get to the command center in the penthouse fast. Johnson was not going to salvage this clusterfuck without his direct assistance. That much was painfully obvious.

"I don't know... it's not... I just don't know!"

Fox slammed the comm closed and pushed through the command center doors to find Johnson still shouting into his comm. The scientist dropped it when he saw Fox and gibbered, "They just crashed through the floor of level two, and are smashing each other to pieces in the lobby now!"

Fox wasn't listening to Johnson any more. He had the screens and readouts arrayed around him and was absorbing all they had to say as quickly as he could. This was a shit show coming and going and he knew it. But the exterior was still quiet and Donald Ribiero did not appear to have gotten outside yet. This was bad, but salvageable. The feed from the lobby showed the two armored giants smashing the hell out of each other and destroying everything around them. Fox caught sight of Roland taking Dawkins to the ground and watched their struggles as Roger tried to escape Roland's pin.

He opened the channel to Roger just as Breach let him up from the ground. Part of Fox's brain told him that was a strange thing for Roland to have done, but he was already talking. Roger had closed all the channels though, and Fox was talking to dead circuits.

"That arrogant piece of shit," he mumbled and tabbed through the menus in front of him until he was in the command tree for the Better Man communications suite. He entered his PIN and initiated a command-level override. He turned Roger's comms on remotely just in time to hear Roland say words that made Fox swear like a sailor with a stubbed toe:

"The only man who knows how to remove that program is being held prisoner on the fifth floor."

He saw his prized armature turn and bolt for the freight lift and knew in the pit of his stomach that he was losing control of the situation faster than he could re-establish it. "Dawkins!" Fox shouted into the mic, "You get on-mission right now and secure that prisoner!"

The shouted response was so loud it made the speakers crackle, "WHAT THE FUCK DID YOU PUT IN MY HEAD!?!"

"Calm down, Dawkins!" Fox didn't know what to do. He did not understand these criminal types well enough to feel confident in his standard responses, "you need to focus on doing your job!" Fox tried an appeal to professionalism. Roger had demonstrated a proclivity towards protecting his professional reputation in the past. Fox hoped that the proclivity still existed.

The armature was at the lift and heading to the fifth floor. According to the telemetry, Dawkins was not calming down. His verbal responses supported that conclusion as well, "You fucking corporate pieces of shit! Did you put that thing in my fucking head?"

"Put what in your head, Roger?" Fox tried to play the innocent, but he knew with cold certainty exactly what Roger was talking about.

"THE GODDAMN FAIL-SAFE!"

Fox didn't respond. This was a waste of time. He turned to Johnson. "Shut him down."

Dr. Johnson nodded, it was the first sign of confidence the squirming academic had demonstrated all night. Johnson was always confident in his toys.

Now they would see what the Fail-Safe could do.

With a few deft keystrokes, Johnson switched Roger Dawkins off, and turned the Better Man on.

The Better Man had been Dr. Warren Johnson's crowning achievement. Fox remembered the day Johnson had brought the seed of this idea to his attention and implored him to rekindle Project: Golem so he could try it out. Fox had rejected that idea as a non-starter; but he had pitched it as a new, unrelated project and gotten the funding and clearance he needed to raid the Golem archives. It had taken seven years of setbacks, meetings, and two extra rounds of fundraising to get to this point. As he watched the armature stiffen on the screen, he could imagine exactly what was happening inside. Johnson had explained it to him a thousand times.

A swarm of nanomachines quietly disconnected Roger's brain from the armature and swapped its priority decision-making apparatus with the custom-built artificial intelligence that ran the body.

The AI needed Roger's nervous system to run the machine, but the catch was that it didn't need Roger's will to make that happen. Roger Dawkins' brain was simply a framework upon which the larger OS was built. The whims and desires of Roger Dawkins were carefully compartmentalized to a non-operative section of the neural architecture and the AI moved its own priority matrix into the body's command role.

Johnson had designed the system, so that there was no hierarchy between Roger's brain and the armature's brain. They existed symbiotically in parallel decision trees. While Roger may have thought that his brain was filling a gap in the armature's control system, it was not. The neural network was a separate, symbiotic entity that mirrored his own. The AI that lived there simply existed to make sure that the armature reacted in the same way Roger's body would have.

Roger Dawkins' brain was essential to building that network and controlling the armature because coding an entire lifetime of reflexes and reactions into the OS would have taken centuries. Without a live, augmented, and functioning human brain the AI was going to be no better than any other robot's. But with a pre-built, highly trained, and fully evolved neural framework like the brain of a professional fighting man to work off of the AI became a sublime combat tool. It was so much better than the Golem had ever been. Instead of a becoming a remote drone like the Golems, the Better Man AI retained the skills of the man inside, even if that man wasn't exerting conscious control over it anymore.

That meant that the AI was more than sophisticated enough to handle most missions without input from anyone. Even better, the more time it spent linked to Roger's brain, the more like Roger it would become. As it recorded and duplicated the pilot's neurological activity, the Better Man would gain more skills and more sophisticated subroutines. Over time, there was hope that a soldier's entire lifetime of instincts and experiences could eventually be duplicated in a Better Man AI.

An army of symbiotic armatures that multiplied and acquired the talents and abilities of the best soldiers, and could preserve those even beyond the death of an operator was what Fox had been selling. The response from potential buyers had been beyond positive: every military in the galaxy was watching this project very closely.

Currently, Fox had to admit that the project was suffering some setbacks. Without Ribiero's expertise in creating synthetic nervous systems, Johnson was stuck trying to duplicate the system from Project Golem notes. This was not Johnson's area of expertise, and the resulting product was very much inferior to the original.

The AI was only as good as the connection between the organic and the synthetic nerves, Fox had learned. If the symbiosis was poor, the signals each system shared would lose fidelity in transit, and the AI would be highly inefficient at acquiring and duplicating the skills of the pilot. As it stood now, the signal latency was so high in the AI that a regular brain suffered dyskinesia and ataxia executing anything but the simplest of tasks. It wasn't as simple as the armature performing no better than power armor, but that it actually fared far worse. Fox couldn't show that sort of data to the board.

Fox didn't understand a quarter of it, but his impression was that there was just too much 'ghost in the machine' still. So they cheated. They couldn't build a better machine, so they went and found a faster brain. Using heavily augmented individuals as a template took what would have been catastrophic signal delays and made them manageable. Finding someone like Roger, who had acquired multiple neurological upgrades without irrevocably damaging his mind had been a godsend. Those signal delays had been all but eliminated by his hyper-fast brain. Fox remembered highly qualified candidates who could barely make the suit walk without stumbling. With Roger? It could dance.

Fox and Johnson had never accepted this as a viable solution though. There was only one Roger Dawkins, and they were trying to sell an army of Better Man armatures. But it was enough for now. Showing the board just a few hours of the trials with Dawkins in the machine had saved the program from cancellation.

There were other unsavory limitations as well. The pilot had to be awake the whole time the Better Man AI was operating. The sleeping brain was far too chaotic for any sort of reliable symbiosis. In the event of loss of consciousness, the link would be severed, and the armature became as stiff and limited as any other robot. So, until full symbiosis became possible, the pilot needed to be awake and aware while the AI was in charge.

Fox shuddered at the thought of that, and the telemetry monitoring Roger's biologicals indicated that this was exactly as hellish as Fox could have imagined it to be. Norepinephrine, cortisol, adrenaline all spiked, and alpha wave activity in his brain nearly broke the gauges. If Roger stroked out, the suit would end up little more than an ambulatory and expensive coffin. But the Better Man would never allow that to happen, and the appropriate drugs were automatically introduced to the paralyzed man sealed inside the towering white goliath.

Roger could only manage a silent, wordless scream as he realized what had just happened. He felt his own body betray him as arms and legs stopped responding to his mental commands and a leaden, numb weightlessness came over him.

His eyes, however, stayed open, and he was forced to watch as his new masters twitched the strings of the hapless marionette that had once been Roger Dawkins.

Chapter Thirty-Six

Roland had opted for the stairs, figuring that the lift would be shut down as soon as the company realized that their man was off the reservation. He took a moment to ping Lucia for her status.

"Where are you?" His voice was terse with exertion when she acknowledged his call.

"Maintenance shaft, heading for the basement"— a pause— "Dad isn't... uh... he just can't move very fast."

Roland had to admit he had been expecting to hear something like that. His captors were trying to coerce and break him. He couldn't imagine that they had been feeding him steak and lobster while giving him massages for the last four days.

"I'm headed to level five. There is something that I have to settle here. Don't wait for me. Get clear of the building as fast as you can. It's about to get kinetic."

'Kinetic' was the code word for the 'Roland loses his shit and blows everything to hell' part of the plan.

"How much security is between us and the gate?" Lucia asked with professional demeanor impressive for someone only three days into her combat career.

I really dig this chick, was all he could think, *she really has her shit together.*

"Honestly?" He gave it some thought, "None. I'm pretty sure I've taken out the whole force." He scowled, "With one exception. I'm handling that now."

"Roger that." Her voice changed tone, and the fear that always plagued her was a little more noticeable, "No stupid shit, Corporal. If you get yourself killed, I swear I will kick your metal ass."

"Understood, boss." He tried to sound nonchalant, "Just some old business I need to handle."

"Roland..." there was an admonition coming, he could hear it, so he cut her off.

"Just get you and your father clear. The police will be here shortly. Tank, out." He killed the connection and sprinted up the stairs.

With his customary subtlety, Roland crashed through the stairwell doors into the fifth-floor lobby. He tried to orient himself to where the freight lift would be, but ended up not needing to.

All he had to do was follow the sounds of crashing and stomping to locate his quarry. It didn't take long.

Roland wasn't sure if it was a suit of armor, a cyborg, or something else entirely, but the big white humanoid made plenty of racket as it stomped through the corridors of the detention level.

He found it after a barely minute or two of searching. He turned a corner to find the alabaster giant tearing one of the metal doors out of its frame. It paused, and Roland realized it was scanning for something.

"He's not in there, pal.," Roland interrupted the search, "We've already gotten him out."

Roland tried to sound reasonable, "It's over. Give it up. We can help you."

The machine stiffened and pulled its head out of the doorway to turn and look at Roland.

The voice that came out of the metal man differed greatly from the one Roland remembered from mere minutes before.

"Corporal Tankowicz. You are looking well."

The voice, amplified and altered by the speakers in the machine, was still vaguely familiar. Roland strained his too-human memory for a clue before he wised up and ran it through the helmet's recognition routines.

"Fox." It was one word. One tiny syllable with decades of fear, rage, shame, and hatred layered over the three letters.

"I see you remember me? How flattering."

Roland didn't really remember Fox that well. Fox had been a project manager for the Golem program, but Roland had only interacted with him occasionally. What Roland did remember of the man was not, in fact, flattering. The mechanical voice continued, "Dr. Johnson is pleased to see you running up to spec as well."

Johnson, Roland did remember. Johnson had written the fail-safe and had been the one to make them all slaves. Roland suddenly felt the urge to shout, rage, and spit a blistering diatribe to the both of them. He wanted to make them understand what they had done to him, and to the rest of his team. He needed them to grasp the horrific toll their avarice and arrogance had exacted on hundreds, maybe even thousands, of innocent people. Roland wanted his catharsis, he wanted his closure, he wanted his big dramatic moment of truth.

Then he looked at the nine-foot thing in front of him; and Roland Tankowicz realized he wasn't going to get what he wanted. Johnson and Fox would never lose a moment's sleep over any of it. Roland thought of Marko, and the Combine, and even Rodney the goddamn Dwarf and he knew that this thing he wanted was a childish pipe dream. It would amount to little more than a tantrum.

These were the kinds of people who would never change. Marko had a dozen slave pens, and the Combine happily paid for them. Corpus Mundi would be positively thrilled to sell mindless slave-drones to a slew of militaries; who in turn would be thrilled to have soldiers that could have their morality switched off when it became inconvenient.

The glittering white insult that stood before him was living proof that no amount of suffering by others was going to spontaneously make either of those two bastards realize anything of value. The problem, Roland realized, was that they already understood.

They just didn't care.

The regular folks would suffer, and the companies would make billions. That was all they needed to know to make something like Project: Golem and whatever that towering pale machine was seem like a good idea.

Roland was at a loss for words. But he had to say something.

"Shut this thing down," Roland whispered, but with a voice like steel on stone. "This is your only warning."

Fox laughed through his machine, incredulous, "Oh no. I don't think so, Corporal. What you don't seem to understa-"

Roland charged the armature, covering the intervening thirty feet in two strides. A giant white fist tried to intercept his head as he closed, but Roland slipped it and put an answering blow directly into the gut of his opponent.

That seemed to shut Fox up.

The machine staggered back two steps, but recovered easily and met Roland's subsequent blows with Roger's practiced ease and skill. A counter-right hand and following left hook rattled Roland's head to the side and caused his HUD to flicker and reboot.

Roland was certain that whoever was inside that rig had been disconnected, so he had expected the machine to be stiff and slow like a robot would have been. But the machine was moving exactly like it had been. This was a new wrinkle, but not one Roland had time to contemplate right now. The big metal creature was stringing combinations of strikes together like a man born to the ring, and the endless barrage was connecting as often as not. Roland had enough experience to keep from getting smashed to pieces, but despite his best efforts he was getting knocked around in a most disheartening manner.

Roland's previous rounds with Dawkins had made it clear Roger had been the superior stand-up fighter. It did not appear that this had changed simply because Roger was no longer in control of the armature. Roland was having to slip and dodge to avoid the worst of the hits, and because his foe was faster than he was, he had to accept a blow every time he wanted to land one of his own.

Fighting a human and fighting a robot were very different things. Roland could count on a human to want to preserve its own life and avoid pain. It was how he could get the better of Roger downstairs. When Roland wanted to make a man move a certain direction, he simply gave the man a reason to do it via existential threat. If Roland wanted his opponent to move to the left, he would attack from the right, because good fighters move away from threats and attack weaknesses.

Robots did not fight that way. Robots just attacked, sparing only the tiniest quantity of processor power on danger avoidance. Their ability to assess a threat meant that they could decide in real-time whether an attack warranted a defensive response. If it didn't, the robot was likely to ignore it. This propensity for straightforward offense when coupled with a general lack of creativity and imagination usually made robots difficult but predictable opponents.

Roland was detecting no such weakness in this 'bot, though.

It has robotic fearlessness and human skills, Roland lamented to himself, *So, that's what the next-gen looks like?*

Roland tried to avoid another blistering combination from the armature. He heard Fox's voice, taunting him the whole time, "You are obsolete, Breach! You should have just stayed in your dark little corner and kept out of this!"

Then an aside, "Are you getting all this, Johnson? This is exactly what they'll want to see." Fox didn't realize the mic was still on. A thought occurred to Roland; if they were recording all this, there was a solid chance the two were in the building right now. Johnson he knew almost for certain would be. The man's ego virtually guaranteed it.

Roland bought himself a breather by letting the armature land a strike to his chest, where the armor was thickest. He grasped the offending arm in a firm, two-handed grip and smashed the 'bot into the hallway walls, crushing both of them into the metal and buckling a twenty-foot section of ceiling. A quick mental command and his musculoskeletal system's safeties were overridden, driving the techno-organic chassis well past its original tolerances. With alarms blaring in his HUD, Roland pressed and held the giant white humanoid in place.

"You guys in the penthouse?" He asked with a nonchalance he did not feel.

He could hear Fox's confusion at the bizarre non sequitur, "What does that have to do..." The voice trailed off.

"Be seeing you shortly, then."

The armature, not content to with being restrained, rained punches into Roland's ribs with its other hand at a speed that left nothing for the eyes to follow but a white blur. Eight impacts per second, each with enough force to crush a car sent shock waves through Roland's entire torso. His HUD again lit up with alarms and damage readouts while his combat AI routed potential responses to the threat directly to the screens.

Roland ignored all of it.

The way to beat a robot that fights like a man, he pontificated with wry bemusement, *is to be a man that fights like a robot!*

The plan was imperfect. But it was a plan. While the armature applied its full attention to smashing Roland's internal structures to a paste of polymer and human remains, Roland routed more and more power to his arms and shoulders. He continued to keep one of his foe's arms pinned, while his other hand went to the armature's neck.

Then, with all the strength he could access, Roland squeezed that neck and pulled on that arm. Like Orion drawing his bow, Roland slowly stretched the limb while simultaneously collapsing the column of that neck. For six tedious, horrible, pain-filled seconds Roland endured the jackhammer blows of his antagonist while he tried gamely to rip its arm off. He had to silence the damage alarms from his helmet just to concentrate, and he did not need the prioritized list of structural damages and other failures to know that he was getting pummeled to death.

Mercifully, as the joints in its shoulder creaked audible protest, Roger's AI finally decided that this threat warranted a response. The strikes to Roland's ribs ceased and the explosions of pain retreated to a dull ache. The 'bot's remaining arm snaked up to push on Roland's face, trying to dislodge the crushing grip before the organic host brain was damaged or the arm failed completely.

That worked for Roland. He abandoned his grasp on the neck and looped his arm over the pressing limb of the white giant. He pulled them together and pressed his chest tightly against his opponent's. Their faceplates were inches apart, and Roland sent a perfunctory head-butt over just to keep the AI on its toes. That was enough of distraction to allow Roland to secure a grip that no machine could dislodge. Now Roland had both arms trapped, and he sat his hips low and under the armature's hips.

Roger Dawkins had never been much of a grappler, so the AI had no response for Roland's vice-like over-under grip. When Roland dropped his hips, the AI could not calculate what that meant until after its feet had already left the floor.

His HUD screamed alarms at Roland when he hoisted the armature over his hip. Much of the internal structure of Roland's left side had sustained severe damage, and the lifting and twisting action of koshi guruma was not exactly advisable under the circumstances. But it worked.

With a floor-shaking crash, a full ton of cyborg war machines struck the deck and their flailing limbs smashed great dents and rent long tears in the metal walls of the hallway. Roland landed on top and secured his opponent in a head and arm triangle hold while he took a moment to assess his damage.

The results were not good. The ribs on his left side were displaced and fractured, and several of the support systems were backed up by structural failures as well. It would take days for full recovery, and he was down to barely enough integrity for movement. More damage to that area carried a high risk of harming his internal organics. Roland needed to shut this fight down fast.

The 'bot beneath him never stopped thrashing. But with no tactical understanding of how to escape a good wrestler's pin, it was like a landed fish flopping on the deck of a boat. It was a fish that could throw cars around like beach balls though, so there was a real element of danger to it nonetheless.

Roland elected for the simplest response and started jack hammering short punches directly to the head of the flopping 'bot underneath him. He was not in an ideal position to apply a lot of power or leverage to the strikes, but transitioning to a more advantageous position felt risky. He contented himself by making up for the poor quality of his punches with quantity instead.

Short punches clanged off the armored white skull like an alarm bell, the sounds of the impacts blurring together in a monotonous ringing toll. Individually, they were not impressive by the standards of advanced military cyborgs. Collectively, they rattled the beleaguered skull of Roger Dawkins like a never-ending car accident.

The movements of the trapped armature became slower and more robotic as the repeated impacts gradually concussed Roger's brain into blissful unconsciousness.

Roland felt the change in the machine's reactions, but didn't understand it. He knew better than to let an opportunity pass, however, and he quickly leapt up to mount the fallen 'bot properly and deliver full-power, full-force strikes en masse. Like a bull gorilla drubbing a challenger, Roland's thick obsidian arms rained up and down in a furious drumbeat. The old soldier's fists cycled like twin pistons; alternating thunderclaps of rage into, and ultimately through the expressionless faceplate of his implacable foe.

In twelve frenzied seconds, Roland's onslaught completely collapsed the head of the Better Man armature, and the skull of Roger Dawkins inside it. Where the stark white skull had sat was now home to a twisted and flattened pile of chunky pink sludge flaked with jagged white armor fragments. One lone eyeball peeked out from the mess to stare at Roland in blank accusation, but its indictments washed off black armored skin like so much spring rain.

Roland didn't waste a single thought for the dead man in the suit. The world was better off without his kind. But he did pause to get his bearings and run some more diagnostics. He knew he was in bad shape, and the readouts confirmed that his body had no more pitched battles in it right now. Situational awareness just got moved to the top of his priority list, because in his current condition, bumping into an armature or some other heavy weapon could be terrible indeed.

At that very moment, his comm pinged. It was Lucia's voice.

"Roland, you need to see this."

He heard the urgency in her voice and keyed her comm's location to his HUD.

"On my way."

Chapter Thirty-Seven

Fox and Johnson stared at the screens in blank awe and terror.

Johnson was a blubbering mess of panic and incoherent sobbing as Fox could have predicted. Fox was just numb. He did not know how to recover from this, but the ramifications of not recovering were too horrible to think about. First, he had to get out of here without getting murdered by a pissed off cyborg. Then he had to burn the site in a manner that kept the company unexposed to liability.

Both required that he get moving, so he shook himself from his awestruck paralysis and grabbed Johnson's coat by the lapel, "We have to leave. NOW!"

He shoved the sniveling scientist towards the hallway, "Get to the roof and wait for me there!" He ordered, "Don't fucking leave without me!" He added that afterthought when he considered the mental state of his accomplice. Courage had never been Johnson's bailiwick.

He pulled out his DataPad and checked on his mercenaries. The Galapagos crew was only a few minutes away. He ordered them to assault the facility and then blow it. It was better to use those animals for this work anyway, he assumed. Pike's crew was likely to have scruples about dropping civilians or arson. Thank goodness those Galapagos freaks didn't have scruples.

He also set the building's main reactor to override, guaranteeing an acceptable level of destruction and plenty of plausible deniability with respect to any collateral damage scrubbing the site would cause. If those merc's got caught in the blast, so much the better. As it was, he would be buying off investigators and prosecutors for years, more than likely.

The setback to the Better Man program was going to be huge either way. There was no way around that. Fox just hoped that he could somehow get it back on track before the Combine had him killed over the 130 million they had decided he owed them. This whole thing was going to shit in front of him, all because of one thirty-year-old loose end. Fox hated no one more than he hated Roland Tankowicz right now. Except for maybe Donald Ribiero, that is.

With his preparations complete, he locked down all the exterior doors to the building and headed towards the lift that would take him to the rooftop landing pad and his waiting car.

The roof was quiet and Fox sprinted across it to the shadowed bulk of his luxury AeroClast. The door slid open, and he sidled into the seat next to Johnson. He called to the driver, "Get us out of here!" and sat back on the plush seat, taking a moment to let out a big expressive sigh.

When he opened his eyes, he realized that the car hadn't moved yet. He prepared a snarl for his driver but stopped when saw the look on Johnson's face. Johnson, Fox realized, wasn't saying anything. He was just sitting, looking very, very, nervous.

Fox inspected the front of the car where the driver would be if the driver was not missing.

Sitting in the driver's seat was Donald Ribiero.

"Oh, shit!" Fox's hand went for the small bead pistol he kept in his pocket, but an inky black shadow snaked from the other front seat to strike his forearm like lightning. His whole arm went numb, and the pistol fell from nerve-dead fingers. Then a heavy-soled boot shoved him roughly back into the seat, next to the trembling Dr. Johnson. The quiet whine of charging electronics serenaded the eerie black calm of the car's interior.

Dr. Ribiero's voice was thin and raspy, but still radiated the calm intelligence of a man in complete control, "Oh no, Mr. Fox. That will never do."

After four days of sleep deprivation, mind-breaking pharmaceuticals, and the omnipresent fear for his daughter's safety all they had done was give him a sore throat, it seemed. Fox cursed the iron will of the old biotechnologist. None of this would have happened if he had just accepted the ludicrously large cash offer they had made him. He tried to play this strong, "I have two teams of mercenaries on their way. If I don't call them off, we are all dead."

"Then your mercenaries should arrive right about the time the police do." Donald smiled, "That should be exciting."

Shit! Fox swore internally, *They called the police!* That could be disastrous. If any cops got killed by mercenaries or if the building's destruction was at all suspicious, Fox was as good as dead.

No amount of bribery is going to un-fuck that cluster. The florid little man began to panic.

"I can be reasonable, Ribiero!" Fox hated negotiating from a position of weakness, but there was no other choice right now, "We need to get out of here now, then you and I can discuss how to move forward from this. In fifteen minutes this whole place is going up, cops, mercenaries, and all of us. No matter what. There is no point in all of us dying."

The voice from the other seat was a woman's and Fox couldn't place it. It was too dark in the car for him to make out a face, either, "Plenty of time, then. Our last passenger has arrived."

A gauntleted hand gestured to the lift door across the landing pad. Fox didn't have to look to know who was coming through those doors. But he looked anyway.

Roland Tankowicz looked like hell, but he strode across the rooftop with fixed, determined strides. The silver of his faceplate was marred by deep gouges and scorch marks and his clothes were in tatters. The armored black skin of his torso was scored in a dozen places, leaving the silver-white fibers of his internal musculature exposed. He walked with a pronounced lean, and he was obviously favoring the ribs on his left side. Durendal, his mighty weapon, hung from the tatters of the holster dangling from the big man's clenched fist.

The broken twisted helmet, with the eerie silver face and black, hollow eyes gave the illusion of skull-faced death itself walking across that rooftop. Spotty, directed lighting from the landing pad turned the endless inky blackness of the giant's body into a writhing mass of light and shadow as he walked; and this only confirmed the aspect of a grim reaper come to collect.

Only this was no illusion, no trick of the light. Leland Fox was quite certain he was about to die. Johnson sobbed like a lost child in the seat next to him, but Fox refused to break. Oh, but he wanted to. This fear was a real, tangible thing, and despair followed it. He prayed desperately for the mercenaries to show up. For the police to show up. For anyone to show up and take this cup from his lips.

But no one came.

Johnson's terror got the better of him and he bolted from his seat. Exactly where the pudgy scientist thought he was going to go, Fox couldn't say.

It didn't matter. The woman in the front seat turned, and a booted foot tripped him on his way out of the door. He fell sprawling and mewling at the feet of the man called Breach. One black mitt closed over Johnson's twitching form and slammed him against the side of the car. There was a hollow thump as the back of the doctor's skull bounced off the metal skin of the limousine. Johnson collapsed in a sodden heap and rolled to his side. Then he vomited groggily on the expensive car's landing foot.

Fox never took his eyes off Roland.

"Do you even know how many?" The voice was deep and metallic, filtered through the helmet's speakers.

"How many what?" Fox answered, playing dumb.

"Dead," the grim reaper replied, "how many they made me kill when I couldn't say no?"

Fox was neither sentimental nor stupid. He had known exactly what the Army was going to do with the Golems when they built them. He had seen every after-action report, and while the numbers were always couched in military jargon, he understood well enough how loosely one could define 'enemy combatant' when there were no witnesses alive to debate your definition.

"More or less," he answered truthfully. "You were a soldier. It was your job." The justification sounded stupid. Even as he heard the words escape his lips, he felt them ring hollow.

"Oh dear," he heard the woman say, but did not get time to wonder why because he was hauled out of the car and hoisted aloft by the man he had spent the last several days and many millions of credits trying to kill. His legs kicked in futile desperation at empty air while the sounds of the wind and distant sirens roared in his ears.

It'll all be over soon, he thought, *there's that at least.* But he didn't want it to be over. He wanted to live.

Fox tried to speak, to talk his way out of the inevitable, but got dropped to the ground before he could form the words. The breath left his lungs as a massive booted foot shoved him roughly into the side of his car. He lost his footing and fell into the puddle of puke next to Johnson's semiconscious form.

"It was a rhetorical question, asshole. You don't get to talk anymore. You've said enough." The giant loomed over the quivering executive, "You don't even care how many, do you? Of course you don't. I don't expect you to understand, because you are an erudite, self-absorbed piece of shit, but when you took my free will away, I couldn't be a soldier anymore. You made me a slave."

"I am not a slave anymore."

Fox found himself face to face with the blank, unflinching faceplate of the monster he helped build, and realized too late how poor his choice of words had been. The voice on the other side of the metal barrier was not angry though. It was heavy with depressed resignation.

"Years ago, I promised that if this ever happened to anyone else again, I would kill you all, do you remember that?"

Fox could recall that day with photographic clarity. Roland could be very dramatic when he wanted to be, and he had been sure to illustrate his conviction on that matter with several grisly demonstrations.

Fox nodded, "I remember."

"Well, I've changed my mind. You get to live."

Now Fox was both confused and scared. It must have showed on his face, because Roland laughed, "I have it on good authority that you owe Pops Winter a lot of money. I also suspect that you will be unemployed very soon."

Fox was starting to grasp the gravity of what he was hearing, and his terror was wearing at the edges of his composure. Roland twisted the knife harder, "The police will be here shortly, and they will catch your little death squad of mercenaries in the act of clearing out this building."

Fox tried to calm himself; at least there was the reactor overload to cover his tracks.

"And I have already pulled the reactor core so the building won't burn down and hide all the evidence."

Fox cried, "That's impossible!"

Roland laughed a hearty laugh, "I'm radiation-proof, you moron. I pulled it out with my bare hands. It was just good luck that Lucia and her father were leaving by the basement and noticed the overload alarm."

That had been the call from Lucia earlier. Roland sent her up to commandeer the car while he went and fixed the reactor. It was a straightforward task for someone who could ignore the high temperatures and ionizing radiation.

Fox began to cry, which made Roland chuckle, "You are going to go to jail, Fox. But that's not how your story ends. One day, a couple of Combine men looking to curry favor with the bosses will catch you in a quiet corner of the prison. The guards will be conspicuously absent when it happens."

The deep voce betrayed sadistic glee, "We both know what happens next, Leland. These guys are going to murder you in ways that can only be described as deeply disturbing and probably pornographic."

Roland crossed his arms and stared down at the crying executive, "That is how the rest of your short life will go, Fox." The malice in his voice was tinged with approval, "I'm choosing not to kill you. Because as a man that is my choice to make. You and that prick"—he kicked Johnson's bedraggled body—"tried to take that choice away from me. People died because of that. The only solace I get to take from that is how you are going end up as one of those dead."

The grim cyborg grabbed the squirming executive and dragged him to his feet, "Most importantly, asshole, the last one!" Roland brought his hand down across Fox's thigh, and a crack signaled the breaking of his femur. It sounded like dry kindling being snapped for the fire and Fox collapsed, screaming in agony. Lucia winced.

"That one was for the Ribieros, dick." Roland turned to Johnson, still a blubbering mess. He squatted down and peeled his helmet off to get a good look at the man who had the temerity to bring back one of the most horrific programs in military history. The architect of his own slavery.

What he saw was pathetic. "You aren't even really a man, are you?" He growled. "I wasted years wondering if I was truly a human being anymore, when all the while it was you who was the monster."

Johnson sobbed like a baby, he couldn't even form words, and tears and snot ran unchecked down his face. Roland's voiced cracked, heavy with rage and sorrow, "I was a goddamn soldier, you sackless invertebrate! I've put bullets in bodies in nineteen systems. My footprints are on twenty-one planets. I have seen the length and breadth of this galaxy, been to places I'll never have the words to describe. But that doesn't amount to a pile of shit to you, does it?"

A black fist stood the doctor up with ungentle haste and held the trembling mess at arm's length.

"What do you think of me now, Geppetto? Are you proud of your great creation?" No one could tell if Roland actually wanted an answer to that. He was somewhere else, eyes distant and voice shaking. Even through his pain, Fox knew to keep quiet. There was something very dangerous and terrifying going on inside of Roland Tankowicz.

The doctor, oblivious to everything but his own terror, just sobbed all the louder.

Roland released the man, who collapsed in a blubbering heap. With a weariness borne of abject despondence, the looming warrior's head sagged and his voice broke, "I've hated you so much for so long that I forgot how pitiful you really are. You don't deserve the death I'd give you."

It was all so stupid and meaningless. Roland had so much more to say, so much he wanted to get out. He wanted to put all the weight of his own guilt and rage on these two where it belonged. But they wouldn't care about any of it. Trying to make them understand what they had done to him was wasting his breath and wasting his time. His pain, his guilt, his fear: it was all meaningless. It always had been.

"Fuck you both," was all he could manage, his voice choked with grief and fury. The only regret they would ever feel was for the consequences they had to endure themselves. There was no catharsis here, no closure. There never had been. The desolation of that realization overwhelmed Roland. He would never be free of what these two had done. He could only live with it.

"... just... fuck you..." He couldn't stop his tears. He didn't want them to come. Soldiers didn't cry. These pricks didn't deserve to see him cry. But the tears would not be denied. He cried for a twenty-year-old, head to toe in army green, trying to save the world and do right by his people.

He blinked, and he cried for the broken twenty-two-year-old with no arms or legs being told he could still be a hero and save the world.

Roland sank to his knees. He cried for the armored soldier who watched his friends murder women and children while his masters congratulated each other on their cleverness.

Finally, he cried for that perfect weapon. He cried for the machine locked in an empty cell under a mountain.

He cried for a young man trapped in a shell, being told that the world he was trying to save didn't want him, just the machine he had become. It was made very clear in that cold and dark place that all he could do was kill, and that was all anyone had ever wanted him for. Without an enemy to fight, Roland Tankowicz was just aging military ordnance, and that was all he could ever be.

His despondence was not fated to linger, however. The melancholy internal monologue was abruptly interrupted by small, strong arms around his neck. Distantly, he heard the only thing that had made him feel human in decades: Lucia's voice. Hearing it made all his creator's words ring hollow, and a flame flickered to life at the bottom of his soul.

"Roland! It's OK. We've won. We can go. Let's go, big guy." She was gentle, and pleading, and full of sympathy. When Roland turned to look at her, there was neither fear nor confusion in her eyes. She wasn't looking at a killing machine. She couldn't even see the weapon anymore; just a hurt, desperate old soldier who wanted to know that what he had fought for was still there. He felt something in that moment, and the part of him that was still a man latched onto that feeling, if only to save itself.

I can be OK, he realized, *as long as she says I'm OK.* The giant shoulders slumped as he surrendered to her embrace, if only for a moment.

Buttressed by Lucia, the iron resolve that had defined him as a soldier began to assert itself. Roland didn't understand what it meant or what the consequences would be, but he wasn't ready to give up yet. Not when that tiny woman refused to let the spark of humanity at his core die out. If she thought he was worth saving, then maybe he was.

The thought came unbidden, but he welcomed it. *I don't have to be what they made me. Maybe I can't be who I was before, but I can still be what she wants me to be.*

His broken body shifted, and Roland prepared himself to do the last thing he needed to. A duty to himself and his dead friends remained, and he was the only one left to see it done.

"It can't… It can't ever happen… again" he breathed through his tears.

"It won't," Lucia said. "We'll make sure of it."

Roland shook his head and tried to rise, but Lucia held him tightly. He pleaded, knowing that he had this one terrible task left to complete. It was a task he didn't want her to see, "You don't understand, they won't stop, they'll try again and again and again…" He was a soldier still. He had to be. If not a soldier, then what was he? He wasn't ready to answer that question.

The mission wasn't over yet.

But he never got the chance to execute on his resolve. He was interrupted again, this time by a gunshot, and he looked in stark disbelief at the 5mm hole in the center of Dr. Johnson's forehead as it lightly wafted thin grey smoke. Behind the scientist's frozen visage, blood and viscous grey brain matter ran in chunky pink streaks down the side of the car. Johnson's body pitched forward and crumpled face-down onto the landing pad. His eyes gaped in blank emptiness and his left leg twitched as the last of his living nerves fired in stubborn defiance of reality. Warren Johnson died in a puddle of his own vomit, taking all his secrets and knowledge with him.

"They'll have to do it without him, then," Lucia said with enough iron in her voice to build a skyscraper. She holstered her pistol, "Now let's go, Corporal. Cops'll be here any minute."

Roland took one last look at Fox, moaning in agony and glassy-eyed with shock, and gave the broken executive a sarcastic salute.

"Have a nice life, asshole." It wasn't much of a send-off, but it was all he had.

Roland and Lucia piled into the car, and she took the controls from her exhausted father. Donald looked into the back seat and smiled, "It is good to see you again, my friend," then he scowled slightly, "but I'm not sure I am thrilled with the influence you appear to have had on my sweet little Lucia!"

Roland's moment of sadness evaporated at the sheer, bleak, ridiculousness of that statement. He laughed a deep, guttural laugh that made his broken ribs sting, "Oh, you are just gonna love the rest of the story then!"

Lucia snorted from the driver's seat, "Not the time, Corporal!"

Chapter Thirty-Eight

Donald Ribiero needed a full week to recover from his ordeal. Roland needed about the same. During this time, Lucia doted on them both as only a daughter could, much to the old man's chagrin and Roland's consternation.

Having the Doctor Ribiero available for Roland's recovery had been helpful, as he was the foremost living expert on the cyborg, and could ensure that all his systems returned to optimal ranges. Once he had felt his own mind clearing from the drugs they had used to make him pliable, and after a few hot meals and some sleep, Donald had been raring to get out of bed and get caught up.

Of course, at the age of eighty-one his body had been somewhat slower in recovering than he would have preferred. Lucia's iron will and newfound ferocity were well-taxed with the task of keeping her father in bed.

There was much to get caught up on as well. Corpus Mundi was in the throes of a full-on press blitz trying to spin the debacle near the Sprawl in as positive a light as they could. It seemed that a certain mid-level executive had hired a rogue group of Galapagos mercenaries to raid the building on behalf of a nefarious competitor. The sobering truth was that not even the mighty Corpus Mundi was safe from the threat of corporate espionage. Only the timely intervention of the brave men and women of the New Boston PD, with assistance from the legendary Pike's Privateers had contained the carnage.

Since that fanciful story kept all of them out jail as well, the team decided to let it ride. Roland hoped that enough of a message had been sent to the brass at Corpus Mundi to keep them out of their hair, and their own silence should help seal that unspoken deal. The Combine was likely to be pretty pissed at him, but he could handle them if it came to that. They were going to be busy dealing with Big Woo for a while yet, and Roland knew he could count on McGinty if he needed to.

Though tastefully avoided, eventually they all wanted to hear an answer for the big question: Why had Donald

Ribiero augmented his own daughter knowing what that would mean for her life?

The answer, it turned out, was both simple and complicated at the same time. It came over breakfast, eight days after their flight from the Corpus Mundi building. The three of them were in Donald's spacious apartment, seated at his dining room table and chowing down on stacks of French toast and mountains of scrambled eggs. Lucia's appetite had not waned, and Roland had always been a big eater.

"I did it to save your life, Lucy," he finally said, when his strength had returned.

"When you were in your early teens, you developed a rare neurological condition." He explained, "Due to a bizarre form of seizure activity, you were losing the ability to make new neurons, and some other types of brain cells as well. We had to assume it was a neurological mutation of some kind, because we didn't really have an analogue for it to compare to."

Lucia nodded. Mutations were not uncommon, and it was a rare mutation that generated an entirely positive effect.

"We could stabilize the condition by controlling the seizures, but we could not reverse its effects. You would have always struggled to learn new things after that point, and there was a very high probability that you would continue to suffer cognitive losses in the future."

The old man turned misty-eyed, "I couldn't bear the thought of that, so I took a lucrative offer from Corpus Mundi. I already held several patents on synthetic neurons, and I knew that they would assign me to something that would give me access to better equipment and an unlimited budget. Which is exactly what happened: They assigned me to the program that was developing Roland's team."

Roland was confused, "Wait a minute, you said she was in her early teens, but that was more than twenty-five years ago!"

"Closer to thirty, actually," Donald agreed.

Lucia looked at Roland like he was a moron, "Yeah? So? I'm forty-four years old."

Roland's jaw dropped and his eyes bugged slightly. Lucia just had to have some fun with it, "What? You thought you were dating a younger woman? Sorry to disappoint you!"

Now Donald looked shocked, "Dating?"

Lucia's face betrayed instant regret and more than a little panic, "Never mind, Dad. Go on with the story." Lucia attempted to put the conversation back on track. Donald gave Roland a long look through narrowed eyes. Roland pretended to be fascinated with the contours of the table top.

"Well," the old man continued. "Well, with the help of Dr. Johnson"—he sneered at the name—"I figured out how to build functional nerves and signals from nanomachines that worked with the synthetic neurons, and we used those to make Roland's chassis work. That's when I knew it could help Lucia."

"Now, I had also figured out how to use those machines to enhance the parallel processing power of a host brain." He looked at their blank faces, "I could grow fake neurons that were better than regular ones." They nodded, and he shook his head in frustration, "The problem was that the host brain was always attached to a regular body, and then the signal latency the brain perceived from the host body would create horrible feedback loops."

Donald realized that he had completely lost both his listeners, so he paraphrased, "I had made a prosthetic nervous system out of little robots, but unless they were carefully matched to the right kind of body, they caused seizures and paralysis."

Lucia looked at her giant companion and said with exaggerated slowness, "Those are bad." He nodded sagely in return.

Lucia and Roland then looked back to the doctor and nodded in unison, and Donald went on, "It was easy in Roland's case, we built the body from scratch specifically to house this new tech. No latency, no problem. They are a matched set."

"With Lucia it was much harder. I did the best I could, dear, but I couldn't perfect it before I had to leave the program."

They all knew what he meant by that, and no one begrudged him his choice.

"I had to flood your body with the nanobots, and then monitor and adjust them on the fly as new feedback loops developed. Remember your clumsy phase, dear?"

Lucia did remember it, and had chalked it up to pubescent awkwardness. "Well that makes more sense now!" she chuckled.

"Yes," the old man smirked. "That was when I realized that I'd have to do the same thing for your body as I had for your mind. Fortunately, I had done the hard part already. Brain and spinal tissue is so much more difficult to work with than bone and muscle. I simply created nanobots that would gently enhance your body to better bring it in line with your mind."

He shook his head, "It was very difficult to get the systems calibrated, though. You had fourteen years of proprioception and reflexes that had to be relearned and readjusted to your new nervous system. It took a ton of feedback and testing, over many years." He smiled, "All the martial arts and other such training was to help with that calibration, dear."

He grunted, "You always hated ballet. At least it looks like all that Muay Thai silliness was more useful in the long run, anyway."

Lucia had to agree with that, but a mouth full of syrupy French toast prevented her from giving more than a nod of agreement.

"So, dear Lucy, you can do all those wonderful things because your body is host to millions of machines that are replacing a sizeable portion of your regular cells."

He frowned, "There are incredible ramifications of this technology, I imagine. But I could never make the machines entirely stable in a normal brain. I was always working to cure Lucia, you see, so my template was not specifically, er... normal. But Lucia's mutation seemed to prevent minor feedback problems and blunt the impact of the major ones. I still don't know exactly how, but the chaotic electrical activity caused by your condition seems to help regulate the signal transfer, dear. I'm not sure if it would be a good idea to try these on a regular brain. Not without a lot more research anyway…"

Roland nudged Lucia, who was shoveling food into her mouth, "Told ya your brain wasn't right." She scowled at him and tossed an elbow into his healing ribs; then grunted in pain when it bounced off his armored skin.

Lucia took a moment to contemplate her father's words, and then swallowed her food to speak, "What does that mean for me?" She asked, realizing too late how open-ended the question was.

Donald smiled, "Right now, based upon what we've seen already?"

He shrugged, and gestured to her, "You are going to continue to age very… uhm… gracefully?" He looked over at Roland, "Which is probably good if you are going to… *date…* that one over there…" No one was exactly sure how much of the growl in the doctor's voice was real and how much was for humor's sake. Roland didn't dare guess, "… since he won't age much at all, either," the doctor finished.

"You will continue to get stronger and faster, and you will gain new skills more quickly and more easily. Even your anxiety attacks should improve, as the machines learn to better regulate your brain chemistry under stress."

"I did notice that the more action I saw, the better I got with it," the small woman opined, "I could feel myself getting better and being less scared with each fight. By the time we got to you, it all felt kind of… I don't know, normal? Is that right?"

The doctor scowled, "That is not how I would have preferred to calibrate those parameters, but yes. The machines will correct abnormal brain chemistry outside of a predetermined range. I was working on dialing them in manually, as I did not want to expose you to that sort of stimulus." He sighed heavily and scowled at Roland, "But yes, the more you challenge the machines the more they will try to adapt, within certain limits."

Lucia frowned, "Limits? That sounds ominous."

Her father bobbed his head in thought, "Nothing serious, dear. You have a finite number of the 'bots, and they will need periodic replacement unless we can get them to self-replicate somehow. That was another item I was working on when those bastards grabbed me."

He continued, "They also can't enhance anything beyond the genetic potential of the host itself. You will eventually reach the limit of muscle mass you can grow and the speed at which your brain can operate without latency issues." He took a gulp of black coffee, "That's why you were getting those migraines, by the way. Too much signal loss. I was working on calibrating them during our treatment sessions these last few weeks."

He shrugged, and looked into his daughter's eyes, "Please don't be angry with me for not telling you all of this. I honestly did not know how well it would work or for how long, or if it would terrify you to know. I just couldn't bear the thought of losing you like I did your mother…"

Lucia reached over and gave her father a hug, "It's all right, Dad. I never doubted you had your reasons. I just needed to know what they were is all. As long as we are all OK, we can figure the rest out as we go. I've actually rather enjoyed being a bionic super commando or whatever these last few days."

The old man leaned back in his chair, and took in the scope of the two people across the table from him, "And how, pray tell, does the rest of this go?" His thin gray eyebrows rose like the twin arches of a suspension bridge, "I presume you will want to return to your hovel on the docks, Roland? And what of you, Lucia? Will you return to your old life or are you going to be a… ah… 'bionic super commando' professionally now?"

The old man's face was a study in paternal disapproval, which Roland correctly discerned was aimed squarely at a certain giant black-skinned cyborg. Roland didn't have sweat glands, for which he was eternally grateful at this moment. Lucia rescued him. "However the hell I want it to go, Dad."

"Donald pointed to Roland, "Does he know that?"

Roland finally spoke, "He is figuring that out. The hard way, mostly."

Donald nodded sagely, "That is the only way anyone ever does, my friend."

Roland was feeling good. It was not a feeling he was accustomed to, and it was taking some getting used to. He could not deny, however, that sitting here with a pretty girl who seemed rather fond of him and the man who had saved his life, eating breakfast and laughing, felt very nice.

But he also knew that Uptown was not his world, and he could not stay here. Both Lucia and Donald had made it clear he was welcome to stay, but Roland had no taste for the clean, antiseptic, and sterile world of glistening glass and steel towers populated by the wealthy and the banal.

Lucia knew that she couldn't keep him here either, but she didn't feel like she wanted to. Roland was a soldier, and he needed a fight every now and then. She was beginning to understand that herself, as a little fire was smoldering in her belly, too.

Donald resumed the conversation, "So what are you two going to do today? Since this frail old codger won't require your immediate care and attention?"

Roland didn't know what to say, and as usual, Lucia rescued him, "Oh, I don't know. I was thinking we might want to go see Billy McGinty and check on his latest project. What do you think, Big Guy?"

A grin took shape on Roland's face.

Yup. Pretty sure I'm in love, he thought.

"That, my dear, sounds like a great idea!"

"Who's Billy McGinty?" Donald asked.

CPSIA information can be obtained
at www.ICGtesting.com
Printed in the USA
FFHW01n1307300718
47598541-51106FF